THE SE   R

The Secret Sex Life
of
Polly Garter

Tom Davies

Copyright © by Gwasg Carreg Gwalch 2001
All rights reserved. No part of this publication
may be reproduced or transmitted, in any form
or by any means, without permission.

ISBN: 0-86381-888-9

Cover design: Dylan Williams

Published with the financial support
of the Welsh Books Council.

First published in 2004 by
Gwasg Carreg Gwalch, 12 Iard yr Orsaf, Llanrwst, Wales LL26 0EH
℡ 01492 642031   📠 01492 641502
📧 books@carreg-gwalch.co.uk   Internet: www.carreg-gwalch.co.uk

Tom Davies is the author of sixteen books including three novels set in Wales: *One Winter of the Holy Spirit, Fire in the Bay* and the best-selling *Black Sunlight.*

His *Merlyn and the Pacific Coast Highway* was short-listed for the Thomas Cook Travel Book Award and named by U2's frontman Bono as the one book that changed his life. *Stained Glass Hours* won the Winifred Mary Stanford prize for the best book with a religious theme.

Married with three sons Tom lives in a coastguard tower overlooking the Bristol Channel in Penarth, South Wales.

*This is a work of fiction based on the time
when Dylan Thomas went to stay at New Quay
in West Wales during World War II
and the way Under Milk Wood may have
come together in his mind.*

*But it is not recommended that anyone
should take any part of it as true,
because it isn't. None of it.*

*This novel is dedicated to my
three beautiful Celtic grand-daughters,
Ellie, Megan and Siân*

Chapter One

THE SMALL Welsh fishing town of New Quay was basking in an Indian summer gorgeousness that afternoon as its terraces, chapels and shops clung to a high headland overlooking a shellfish factory and a pocket harbour where yellow-eyed gulls hung around hoping to pick up fishy scraps off the moored fishing boats. Many of the townsfolk were out taking the sea air, either strolling along the curving beach and squinting into the unreal brightness of lots of sun surfing on lazy waves or standing in huddled groups on the stone quay as if waiting for some French master to come along and capture their gossiping rapture in oils.

Dai Thomas, the ice cream man, complete with his trolley, hand bell and fake French boater, was having an exceptionally busy time next to the lifeboat station, unusual for his irregular business in which, they said, he even watered down his water, in this deeply strange part of Wales.

Just after two o'clock a furniture lorry came clattering down the Cardigan Road with its exhaust emitting minor explosions mingled with equally worrying bangs coming out of its big end which made passers-by jump and think of the bombs of the Luftwaffe.

Three people were sitting in the front seats as the lorry braked outside the Black Lion pub and the brawny driver, with a broken nose and a wall eye, jumped out shouting, 'Right. That's it. This far and no further. The Black Lion, you said Mrs Thomas, and *that* there is the Black Lion.'

'Well, we haven't got there yet. The house is on the other side of the Bay. Over there. You can't just dump us here.'

'You've heard the engine for yourself Mrs Thomas. It's as knackered as poor old Mr Thomas in there. It just will not get along that cliff path. It simply is not enginely possible. But this is where you said you wanted to go. Now give me my fifteen shillings because I need to get home to my house.'

'Well, go home to your fucking house but you can't just dump all our fucking belongings here. How are we going to get that lot over there? There's cupboards, deck-chairs and Christ alone knows what else in there.'

Caitlin Thomas had a strong senatorial nose, fierce blue eyes and corn-coloured hair while her vivid personality was rendered even more vivid by an upper class English accent which became the true voice of the Irish bog particularly when, as now, she was angry and wanted to frighten the shit out of the working class.

But the lorry driver remained unmoved, both in stance and bowel, so, after a bit more glaring she screamed at the man inside the cab who was holding a sleeping baby in his arms and whose head seemed to have disappeared deep within a massive turban of a wound-up scarf as if telling everyone, including his beloved wife, that he did not want to get involved in this – or indeed any other – argument.

'Dylan, get out here and say something will you? At least tell this oaf that he can't dump all our fucking belongings out here in the street.'

Three old women and five children had now gathered in the square outside the Black Lion, all watching this exchange with a lively, if slightly horrified, interest, along with five male faces through the windows of the bar itself, all waiting to hear what the turban had to say except, when the turban finally got out of the cab, the sleeping baby still in his arms, the turban didn't seem inclined to say anything at all, merely looking at his irate wife and then at the wall-eyed lorry driver and then at the towering edifice of the Black Lion.

'I don't suppose that bar would actually be open would it because I've got a thirst on me I wouldn't sell for a fiver,' the turban said after a while.

'Dylan, tell this man he just can't dump our fucking belongings out here in the street.'

Dylan Thomas lowered his turban to reveal a pair of eyes which bulged slightly as if he was being strangled, a chin which was a good deal flatter than a frog's and a nose which looked as if it had been bashed out of true in a boxing booth. His clothes were also not that much more prepossessing what with a crumpled, dirty white shirt, a green polka dot dickey bow and a thick worsted jacket which you might well have worn in the middle of winter but certainly not on a hot Indian summer afternoon such as this.

If he was at all concerned that the driver was going to dump their belongings out here in the street he did not show it although his mouth did open and close a few times as if he was about to launch into a speech and, when it did finally start coming out, the words came slowly and ponderously in a querulous mock-Oxford accent, almost as if he had become a Hamlet trying to explain something very difficult to a particularly dim Ophelia.

'What I say, Mrs Thomas, what I say is that this is clearly a pub here with a bar where they serve strong drink and a man – *any man* – can always find what he wants in a bar where they serve strong drink. This is one of the immutable laws of life and indeed the whole universe. So we will burst open the bar door, imbibe some Buckleys and doubtless bag a bearer to bundle up our belongings and convey them over to our new home over the Bay.'

At the conclusion of the speech Dylan handed the baby to his wife and exited towards the bar door of the Black Lion, *pursued by a thirst*, leaving Mrs Thomas to pay off the lorry driver with his fifteen shillings, *but no bloody tip for you, mate*, while also nursing the hope that the bombastic bastard, who otherwise masqueraded as her husband, would indeed find a bearer to bundle up their belongings and take them home over the Bay.

Why she had thrown away her life and career by marrying a fucking poet, she had never once understood and neither had anyone else. There was no work inside him, as one X-ray had once proved, just a load of bastard hot air.

AROUND TWO hours later Caitlin was sitting on a garden wall outside the pub, feeding the baby with her left tit and guarding their little mountain of belongings, while her other, rather older, baby was inside the bar, three pints in and running smoothly in second gear while entertaining the locals with a stream of stories about how he had managed to avoid the call-up into the Army.

'I convinced them I wasn't worth having after I drank Empire sherry and boot polish the night before the medical. I turned up covered in red blotches and shaking like a leaf. My big problem was all this tuberculosis in the lungs, I said, banging my chest. You wouldn't believe what I cough up in the morning. Blood, soot, snot, pus, bus tickets. Bits of this and bits of that. They made me C3 in the end. "We don't really want you in the army, Mr Thomas," the doctor said. "We've got the slight feeling that we might be able to win this war without you. I suggest you go straight home to bed."'

As the poet's story unfolded, pegged out on such anecdotes, Caitlin was sent the occasional bottle of something brown or a bag of crisps as she waited for Dic Morgan, one of the bar regulars, who had returned to his farm on Llanina Point to pick up his horse and cart in order to transport the Thomases and their treasures to their new home at Majoda, a small asbestos house about half a mile away across the glittering waters of Cardigan Bay. She was extremely morose at being told to stay outside the pub since she also liked to drink, but the landlord, Percy Hoskins, took a dim view of babies in the bar – as did all the boys in the bar – and anyway she had to stay outside to keep an eye on her things because you never knew with these Welsh.

The watching townsfolk had now swelled to twenty three – eleven adults and twelve children – and the children, particularly the boys, were more than interested in Caitlin's left tit which she had casually flopped out to feed her baby over the top of her flowing gypsy-style dress, tied around the waist with a silk scarf in the Chelsea Arts Club manner. Everything, even her dirty, hammered toes and nicotine-stained fingers with badly bitten fingernails, told sordid tales of wild times in Bohemia and, whatever else New Quay might have been, it had never been Bohemian. This was Welsh Wales where everything was done the way it had been done the year before.

Why she had ever got herself mixed up with these chapel-haunted Welsh she had never once understood. When they weren't down on their knees in come chapel with a leaking roof they were throwing up into some hedgerow after drinking too much in the pub. She had always hated the Welsh and here she was, banished to a real Welsh hole by the sea where Dylan said he hoped to write a few poems in peace and quiet. Peace and quiet! He had always loathed peace and quiet and so had she. She liked loud parties and bloody fights. The louder and bloodier the better.

The crowd began to build if only because a furniture removal was about the only chance you ever had to inspect what people owned while an even rarer sight, in a place ruled by the pulpit which saw unbridled lust in a dirty pair of ankles, was any woman's naked left tit, particularly one as full as the one now on public view outside the Black Lion. The Rev Enoch would certainly have had something to say about that naked left tit, had he been around. Except he wasn't, thank God.

The Thomas treasures formed a bizarre hillock on the pavement: three bulging suitcases tied with odd bits of string, it was duly noted and reported back in the gossip, an old leather armchair with the horse hair stuffing exploding out of the arms, a large sepia photograph of Walt Whitman, a few reproductions of Picasso and Rousseau, a deck chair, "Property of Barry Island Council" burned into it, a lop-sided dining table with matching chairs, a senile bed with many broken springs, some flea-bitten and stained rolls of bedclothes, three orange boxes of books, a cracked pitcher, an extremely suspicious looking piss-pot, a couple of rackety bicycles and a child's scooter with but one wheel.

Dic Morgan returned finally, together with his younger brother Gareth, driving a horse and cart which looked to Caitlin to have last seen service in the Middle Ages. The axles squealed and rattled in prolonged pain and the horse's every joint was stiff with advanced arthritis and rheumatism – the kind of horse Dylan always backed in the 3.30 at Cheltenham.

'I'm afraid I can't help you to load up, Mrs Thomas. I've got to stay up here and hold the reins in case the horse bolts,' Dic told her, keeping a careful eye on that left tit.

'Bolt! That horse couldn't bolt anywhere. There's more life in a fucking Beecham's Powder than there is in that horse.'

'Well, wrong in a way and right in a way, Mrs Thomas. He never likes going faster than dead slow it is true. You are right on that. And most of the day he spends lying somewhere between a coma and death. But, if he thinks there might be a bit of heavy work around, he's liable to bolt faster than diarrhoea with daps on. Young Gareth here will help you load up.' He looked over at Gareth before adding mysteriously, 'He's good at loading up is this boy.'

But young Gareth Morgan didn't look to be about loading up anything either, just sitting there with the blood drained out of his face and belly and transfixed by Caitlin's left tit; a nippled vision which he had never expected to experience in the next life let alone this.

'I've got a husband here somewhere. I'll see if he can be of any use but don't go putting any bets on it,' Caitlin said, standing up with the baby's mouth still opening and closing and trying to get a gummy hold back in the divine nipple. 'But I'll tell you now there's even less work in him than in that horse of yours.'

All faces in the bar turned as she poked her head in and asked Dylan to come out and help load their furniture.

'But Catey, darling, you know I get a bad back if I lift anything heavy.'

'That's the first I've heard about you having a bad back. You keep telling me you've got T.B. You don't get T.B. in your back do you?'

'Catey, I've told you often enough the doctor said I can never lift anything heavier than a pint or a cigarette. I must not lift heavy weights, the doctor said. I might get a hernia or something.'

'*Might*? What do you mean *might*? You *might* get anything at all. You *might* get falling arches or something wrong with your drinking arm. Your hair might fall out, you might get crabs in your pubics. And what *might* I get? Or doesn't that matter? Why do I always have to do all the fucking hard work?'

'You *know* I've got to be careful, my darling Catwoman. You know how it is with lungs. These timorous balloons in our clamorous chests. They're very delicate are our lungs.'

'Tell me exactly what we're talking about will you? Your impending hernia, your hypothetical T.B. or your fits or what? And, come to think of it, tell me how many pints you've had. Are we heading towards the stupid or the incoherent yet?'

'Oh, you're mocking me now, Catey. But you do know my lungs aren't the full shilling don't you? You do know that. They're not a bit of good, my lungs. My pair of conscientious objectors, if you like. And that's why we're here isn't it? To rest my lungs in all the therapeutic arms of all this lovely sea air. Anyway I'm sure all these gentlemen will help you load the cart.'

NO SOONER said than done since, with the clatter and scrape

of wooden chairs on the flagstones, Stephen Stephens, Joshua of the Bluebell, Dai Fred, Norman Lewis and Terry Hughes left the bar and began hoisting the Thomases' belongings aboard Dic Morgan's cart until they had built a new Leaning Tower of New Quay with the two bicycles perched perilously on top of the lot.

'Dylan, those things are *not* going to stay up there. Can't you see? One move from that horse – always assuming he can move, he looks due for the knacker's yard to me – one move and the whole fucking lot is going to collapse into the road.'

'I tell you what, Cat. Why don't we just try it for now and see how it goes?'

'Try *what* for now?'

'Moving the horse and cart down the road. Moving it all down to the house. If the stuff falls off, we'll have another think about it.'

'Oh, that's typical of you, that is. Absolutely fucking typical, you stupid bastard. Of course it's going to fall off. I should have thought that even an idiot like you would see that. This stuff may not be valuable but, in case you haven't noticed, it's all we've got.'

Caitlin glared at Dylan hard and the mystery of why she had married this oaf thickened considerably since he clearly wasn't listening to a word she'd said and had got locked inside some daydream as he stuffed his right hand down inside his trouser pocket and leaned forward slightly while he fiddled with his bollocks. He was forever fiddling with his bollocks but she was slightly horrified to see that he had clearly now got his forefinger down inside the hole in his pocket and was busily scratching his scrotum. It was appalling. Here they were newcomers to this dump and there was her crapulous old man scratching his scrotal sack in front of everyone. He had told her once that he liked fiddling with his bollocks when young and had never quite grown out of it.

'Dylan, are you listening to me or your fucking bollocks? This stuff may not be valuable but, in case you haven't noticed, it's all we've got.'

The poet snapped out of his daydream momentarily and studied his wife carefully only relaxing when he saw she wasn't about to hit him with a left hook. He knew all about these things and anyway her left tit was still hanging out and what with the baby in her arms, yes, he was pretty safe. He stopped fiddling with his bollocks and moved around to the other side of the cart, his eyes squinting up at the perilous pile of furniture and bicycles as he poked and pulled parts of it with all the authority of a house surveyor looking for possible movement in the foundations.

'Seems pretty safe to me, you know,' he announced finally. 'There's nothing going to fall off there. Stable as Snowdon that is. Go on, Mr Morgan. See if you can get that horse moving down the road.'

Dic clicked his tongue and, after a bit more clicking, followed by a hefty kick in the rump and a few encouraging obscenities, the horse did move off, albeit hesitantly, while Caitlin kept circling the cart worriedly.

Dylan and the others stayed put outside the pub, watching the furniture cortege make about ten yards of progress when Caitlin began berating Dic for going too bloody fast.

'Too bloody fast! That horse has never gone fast in its whole life. I've known dray horses with polio move faster than that horse,' Dylan muttered to his new drinking mates.

'A good runner once, that same horse. When he was young and wild Dic Morgan was always being picked up for speeding and being drunk and disorderly on it. A regular little Spartacus he was, when he was young. Always thought he was on a chariot going down Beach Hill.'

'I was a good runner when I was young,' Dylan mused as his hand tried to get hold of his bollocks again. 'There were wings on these feet when I was chased by policemen. I was a Pegasus of Cwmdonkin Drive breaking free from all the forces of law and order. But the only time I run now is when I'm worried the pub is going to lock its doors. Talking of which. This pub here.

It will be staying open won't it?'

'The Black Lion? Well, aye – as long as there's someone buying a drink. It's always open to anyone buying a drink. They say Percy lost the keys to the place years ago and never found them again. It did close once when his Mam died. For half an hour.'

'Well that's as nice a bit of news as I've heard since they turned me down for the Army. I've already got this feeling in my water I'm going to like living in this town.'

At that moment several loud crashes were followed by distant banshee shrieks. A smashing of what sounded like glass followed together with a few more shrieks.

'The bloody furniture must have fallen off. Come on. Let's get back in the pub out of the way. It's always smart to be out of the way when my darling Cat woman starts wailing like that. Survival it's called. Staying alive.'

DYLAN – now five pints on – had moved into top gear, attracting a big and appreciative crowd who, many were to say later, can never remember laughing so much as Dylan dug deep into his extravagant arsenal of disgusting stories like how to rape a dog – 'First you catch it by the ears and jam its head in a drawer . . . ' or the one about the naked woman with a daffodil up her bum who pursued him even through his dreams begging him – no, *pleading* with him – to pull it out.

But then he would slip into wild monologues which had a sort of sense about them but not a lot. 'I always wanted to be an Ovaltiney, you know, one of the happy boys and girls, but it always slipped away from me, like a rat in the dark, leaving me not happy at all but black with the black dogs, blacker than the blackest night. I wanted to be happy – ah yes – there was nothing I wanted more and it came to me sometimes, often after a few drinks I do admit, but it slipped away again, back into the dark and I always felt as it I had been crushed like a fly on a window ledge, a dark smudge of dead legs, gone, done for, as sad as an eternity of rain.'

Yet the strange thing about this strange man was that even when he was telling shaggy dog stories and even when he was plunging into dippy monologues there was still a part of his consciousness which always knew what was going on. He missed nothing around him and had already noticed that none of them seemed to be quite sane what with the draper who went to the bar, ordered a pint, sat down with it and then proceeded to take his shoes and socks off before putting them back on again, and the blind sea captain who kept telling long and ever more elaborate stories about his days at sea, brawling in bars and lying with *grateful* whores – except that no one ever seemed to be listening to him – and the postman who allegedly read all his mail out loud to his wife in bed in the morning before actually delivering it and was even now telling a few people that Stephen Stephens had been summonsed before the beak in Cardigan that morning for letting his dog out after sunset when, as Dracula will tell you, dogs should be kept in at night since that's when he goes out.

As Dracula will tell you . . . Jesus! . . . What sort of people were these? It was all like wandering around inside some strange cartoon where everything was slightly more cartoonish than usual.

Their every utterance had a sort of mad illogicality about it and not only that but some of them spoke like speak-your-weight machines or laughed like whinnying horses; they had dirty teeth and ill-fitting clothes; the caps were too big or too small; they scratched themselves as if suffering from terminal scabies and gave fog-horn belches but, more than any of all this, they all drank as if they had several hollow legs, just sloshing it down as they stood around Dylan's table, listening to yet another of his mad monologues as people might gather around a particularly amusing chimp in a seaside zoo.

And he looked up at them all as they looked down at him – a motley gang of cobbler, farmer, undertaker, drunkard and blind sea captain – all doubtless due to get a big pension for bad or dodgy behaviour, all gazing down at him and sort of all laughing and speaking their wild lines at the same time and, even then, and as drunk as he was getting, he could see them all packing their bags and climbing into the bed and breakfasts of his mind and memory, where they would one day break into his work and busily spread themselves all over his unsuspecting phrases.

Oh yes, one day, my strange new friends, one day I will immortalise you with my immortal words and you will all live forever. I can see it all now. You don't know it yet but you lot are going to live forever.

But something else rather strange was going on in that bar too since, as word went around about this very famous poet who had come to live among them, they started bringing him gifts, not huge gifts exactly but, a box of tomatoes, several cabbages and a freshly poached salmon from the River Teifi which, now and in a time of war, made them very expensive gifts indeed.

These gifts were moving Dylan almost to tears, although the amount of beer he had sunk may also have had a lot to do with that welling lachrymose state, when a thin scarecrow of a man, who seemed to be wearing half a dozen overcoats, loomed up over him; a fisherman by the name of Verney Matthews, who had a blob of snot dangling off the end of his nose which sat squarely in between his dark, weasel eyes and bristled, famine-haunted cheeks.

'I've got you another present here, Mr Thomas. I fished it up out of the Bay so you can put it on your desk when you're making your poetry. A gift from the seas, Mr Thomas. This is a gift from Neptune himself.'

Dylan's drunken eyebrows soared up into his forehead as Verney pulled a human skull out of one of his many pockets and everyone applauded as he put it down on Dylan's table to take its place along with the salmon, tomatoes and cabbages.

Just what were they going to give him next? He'd only need some flowers and a few bibles and he could open his own shop. And if this

18

THE POET was incoherent with drink and human skulls when he was finally put on the back of Dic Morgan's cart and transported to his new home of Majoda on the other side of the Bay. Indeed he babbled nonsense to himself for almost all the journey, Dic was to report to the boys in the bar the next day and, as long as he lived and died, Dic never, ever expected to see a sight so funny as Dylan swaying up to the front door of Majoda bearing an armsful of cabbages, tomatoes and salmon with a human skull plonked on top of the lot.

'My darling Catey you just look at what all the good people in the Black Lion have sent over to you. And let me introduce you to my new friend. Meet Yorick.'

Caitlin, who had been standing in the middle of the doorway with arms folded, showing she was unimpressed, stood to one side to let him in and, when he was half way through the door, her fist hit him on the side of his head, just above his ear, which, in turn, banged the door frame, making the asbestos house shake and sending a small wave, of tomatoes, cabbages, salmon and skull spilling out into the living room in a most unlikely tidal wave.

She might be small but that woman packed an even better punch than the great Jack Petersen, Dic told the awed boys in the bar. 'It was a real brahma it was, boys, but I didn't hang around in case she decided to stick one on me.'

Chapter Two

DAWN BROKE across the Irish Sea and Ernst's eyes fastened on to an albatross as it wheeled across the grey and dark rivers of light, rising up towards the ragged clouds as it caught a ride on another rogue gust of wind or else dipping down towards the riffling waters, a complete master of the skies since it hardly ever moved its wings and glided effortlessly like the perfect flying machine it was.

More light kept sweeping up the breaking crumbling darkness as he stood on the conning tower, surrounded by endless vistas of space and wind as his gunners remained at ease on the deck around the gun with their hands clasped behind their backs. Another four of his crew were standing around him scouring the sky, sea and horizon inch by inch with their heavy Zeiss binoculars, searching their own section minutely, lowering their binoculars for a quick visual search of the whole area and then picking up their glasses for another careful search.

The winds were north-easterly, 15 knots, astern.

Ernst always found such moments perfect as he, a humble kapitanleutnant from the Bavarian Hills, stood at the altar rail of his own private cathedral, a lone pilgrim in a world which God had long abandoned, nursing the fact of his own humanity and sufficient unto himself as he travelled through a time broken by the pain and trauma of war. At such moments he could meet himself even though he never actually liked sitting on the surface in the daylight like this, which always seemed to be asking for trouble, but, thanks to a malfunctioning electricity supply, the air below decks had become almost toxic so they could just sit here for as long as they dared and actually breathe.

But should they be attacked the facts were almost brutal in their simplicity and they were that this boat, the U-258, was a type V11C, built by Germania Wehrt in Kiel, which could be easily spotted from 18,000 ft – or picked up by enemy radar or hydrophones – and needed at least thirty clear seconds to crash-dive and a further thirty seconds to get clear of any bombs. There was no way out or around these simple empirical facts which, in many ways, limited and defined their U-boat world with a neat and almost attractive precision.

There were other, allied, facts, of course, like a shortage of food and fresh water and a crew all dangerously at the end of their tether, particularly after the death of their engineer. They simply had to get home soon to La Rochelle – or at least somewhere safe – or he was going to have a lot more trouble on his hands. He could almost see the mutiny in the air; he could almost reach out his hands and shape it. His men had become like trapped rats and, in this state, they would become capable of almost any disorder and disorder was about the last thing he wanted to deal with, particularly on a U-boat.

The dawn grew fuller and he was almost surprised to discover how much noise his ears could find in it from the gentle wash of the waves up against the hull to the crying of the sea birds and the whispering chatter of the winds. But then another sound began splitting up and dominating the others: a high-pitched whine which could almost be the sound of a giant tuning fork or even a monster drill. He frowned as he tried to identify it when a gloved hand slapped down on a red button and a klaxon began whooping hysterically throughout the boat.

'A Tommy aeroplane, kapitan.'

The look-out pointed at a small black blob flying low and fast through the shifting light of the morning, at around 5,000 ft, and all faces turned towards the kapitan who lifted his binoculars to his eyes and saw it was a blue-grey Mariner bearing down on them and already bobbling from side to side to present a more difficult target for his gunners.

'No time to dive. Fire at will.'

In a fury of barked orders his wheelsman began turning the U-boat so they only presented their stern to attacking aircraft while the deck gun began exploding with ferocious bangs of yellow fire, sending up a furious flak of 20mm shells which burst all around the Mariner in eerily silent brown puffs of smoke. In just a few seconds a gentle, albatross dawn at sea had been transformed into a screaming chapter of explosion and flame straight out of *The Inferno* with the Mariner spitting with red and gold fire and still bobbling from side to side as it flew directly over them, dropping sticks of depth charges spaced at a 100ft and across their bows, scorching their eyes and ears and making the sea *whoosh* into foaming mountains which broke over the U-boat and swamped the men working the gun.

One gunner flew directly up off the emplacement, rising a good fifteen feet into the air, atop a bank of furious spray, before turning slowly like an expert high diver and coming straight down again, arms akimbo and legs spreadeagled when he disappeared into the angry waves.

Almost miraculously in the circumstances the other gunners managed to stick to their task and, as the Mariner passed over, Ernst noticed a bright fork of flame spurting out of her port side just near the galley door. They had managed to hit her and, as she bled with guttering black smoke and began banking up again to mount another attack Ernst realised they still didn't have time to crash-dive but guessed they might now have a chance to fight it out to a proper finish, ordering one of his lookouts to replace the gunner washed over the side.

But noisy battle then turned to farcical pantomime because the gunners started shouting they needed more ammunition – more *proper* ammuntion – since the bungling bilge rats hired to maintain Donitz's navy had struck again. The gunners could not dislodge the fuse caps from the shells to prime them which meant they were useless.

The Mariner had now banked up high and was about to start attacking them again so, even though Ernst knew the plane would probably get them on its second pass, he also knew that he now had little real alternative but to order a crash-dive, shouting *Zeum, tefel, gehen* – Let's get the hell out of here.

The U-boat's foreplanes were digging deep into the sea, with waves washing over the deck, but they were still far from safe when the Mariner came screaming down on top of them again but, unaccountably, the expected deadly rain of depth charges never fell, possibly because the plane's hydraulics had been jammed by the shell they had managed to lump into her side.

We could all be playing silly games out here not fighting a war. We cannot get our ammunition ready and they can't even drop their bombs. I am not looking forward to writing a report on this mess.

IT WAS unusually quiet with nothing coming up on the sonar so, about twenty minutes later, Ernst decided to risk taking a look around with the periscope and it was with no satisfaction that he saw the Mariner was suffering from a lot more than faulty hydraulics since she had ditched about five hundred yards away with her rear rising up into the air and the crew all frantically trying to clamber into one dinghy. On another day he might have surfaced to finish them off but the lack of usable ammunition meant that he had least had a good excuse to leave them alone and anyway other Tommy planes would soon be buzzing around frantically looking for revenge with depth charges which would almost certainly work next time around.

So yes – *zeum, tefel gehen* – let's get the hell out of here, but where exactly?

He was reasonably sure the Tommies wouldn't now allow them to make their way home back to La Rochelle, even if they could in this wounded state, so, in the circumstances, they might as well slink back to the coast of Wales and hope their luck would change.

Well one thing was very sure. It couldn't possibly get any worse.

Chapter Three

YOUNG GARETH Morgan crouched down behind a dry-stone wall where, through a strategic hole he had made in the loose stones, he was monitoring the movements on the Morgan farm – those of his brothers Dic and Trefor, his father, Tada, and, most crucially, those of his Mam, Mrs Rachel Morgan. He caught his breath and his nose gave a sharp, frightened sniff when he spotted his Mam, dressed, as usual, in a filthy pinafore with black, serge stockings and wooden clogs, walking across the farmyard, carrying her three-legged milking stool and bucket-full of milk and into an outbuilding where she would start making cheese in the separator.

This was one of the first of her morning chores which would include carrying water into the stables from a well in the yard, black-leading the grates and making the beds, washing the kitchen flagstones and not forgetting peeling the potatoes and preparing the vegetables to feed her men who always ate as if a famine was about to break out at any second.

The Morgan farm spread out across the full width of Llanina Point, a wide promontory which stretched away from New Quay and right into the riffling, glittering waters of Cardigan Bay where, just now, Dic was leading a horse across the yard and Trefor was hammering some planks together out in one of the stables. Beyond the farmhouse were fields of corn, which feathered and whispered in erratic sea breezes, and green fields where sheep munched as Tada examined them each, in their turn, closely looking for whatever it is that anxious farmers look for.

Tada knew everything about animals, he often said, like when a horse had a dropped elbow or how a dog needed rabbit skins if he was going to be wormed properly. But he was a sheep man really and his speciality was flipping ewes on their backsides and forecasting when they were going to lamb or else smoothing them all over with his hands and spotting any ailments, often well before they had even arrived.

Gareth, still on his school summer holidays, spied on his Mam obsessively because he was convinced she was about to abandon them all at any day and run away to America as she had often jokingly threatened. One day she cracked that joke once too often and he burst into tears like an old water-pipe and didn't stop bursting until she took him in her arms and declared, again and again, that she was just having a bit of fun; that she was going to stay with him forever and she certainly had no intention whatsoever of running away to smelly old America. Her words calmed him down for a while but he still kept an almost permanent watch on her just in case and wanted to know exactly where she was and what she was doing at practically every hour of every day. What he feared the most was being left with the other three members of his family – his surly Tada, the humourless Trefor and the satirical Dic who he hated with a real and unflinching passion.

He remained kneeling there for a while, savaging the flesh around his fingernails and with his cheeks twitching, until he was satisfied that no removal van marked AMERICA was about to turn up at the farm. He decided to take a break from his watchman duties and run down to the end of the headland to take a look at the sea.

He ran in short spurts, almost as if his sails were filling up with a terror from which he was hoping to escape, down along the twisting shale path, past blackberry bushes trodden in parts by people anxious to get to the fruit and through clouds of midges swarming incandescently in the passing sunlight and over a kissing gate on the verge of collapse until he came to the edge of the cliff where he stood panting and looking out over the Bay.

It was a strange, moody day with fat clouds cruising fast overhead and big columns of sunshine breaking through them from time to time, flashing and moving around like giant pillars of light trying to find some sort of stable position so that they could hold up these shifting skies in some kind of order.

All at once he saw something mysteriously beautiful taking shape around the bases of all these pillars of light standing in the sea except that it had no real shape but was clearly something that kept shifting from a long sliver of darkness to a shoal of shadows and then into something altogether huger and fatter, like nothing he had ever seen before, in fact, and, in his mounting excitement, he had to stop himself getting too near the edge of the cliff in case he fell over it. Indistinct shadow moved to shoal and to long sliver again. He kept shading his eyes with his hands and stopping himself moving forward, now becoming really confused since the rear of the black shape started to rise up before it slowly sank beneath the silvered waves, sending up white torrents of foam.

He began clapping this spectacle in a sustained burst of applause, his eyes watery with marvel.

That's a whale that is. A big whale in Cardigan Bay. They always said you could never get a whale in Cardigan Bay 'cos it was so shallow it would scrape its belly button. But that's a whale. With or without its belly button. Mrs Dylan Thomas' bare tit was a very great sight and this was another. A whale without a belly button and one huge naked tit. What was he going to see tomorrow?

He was off running again, back over that collapsing kissing gate, through those clouds of swarming midges, past the trodden blackberry bushes and down along the twisting shale path until he got back to the farm and, completely out of breath, blurted out, 'There's a whale in the Bay. I seen it with my own eyes. Massive it was.'

Dic and Trefor looked up from their tasks but, apart from a

quick glance at one another, said nothing. Gareth could see clearly what that glance said which was that the boy had long been suffering from something extremely serious in the mental department and here was yet another sign of whatever it was.

'I seen it with my own eyes. It was a whale. There's a whale in Cardigan Bay.'

Dic moved towards Gareth, dropping his voice and giving a small cough before asking: 'Have you been pulling your wire again boy? I always said your eyesight would go funny one day if you kept pulling your wire.'

Gareth turned and turned again before running into the kitchen and blurting out his hot news to his Mam who was sitting at the table shelling peas.

'Really, *cariad*? Those whales do get everywhere don't they? Here, come and sit and help me with all these peas.'

The trouble with his family was that they never showed any curiosity about anything at all outside the farm, the boy thought bitterly. They all just lived in their own little worlds and, much deflated and even a little angry, he walked back to the headland on his own to have another look at that whale except that the whale had gone now, probably vanished forever beneath the shifting waters of that huge and unfathomable Bay and off somewhere where whales lived and had no trouble in actually getting people to believe in them.

ALL THIS was yet another worry to add to his rapidly growing arsenal of worries and so he continued creeping around his farmyard home distilling them into even newer worries. This was a boy who was born to worry and who even worried about being born. Best of all he liked to sit in the outside lavatory for hours on end, surrounded by smells and swarming bluebottles as he worried about something he had eaten or why all the other children in the class were bigger than him; worried about why he wasn't as brainy as anyone else or that, when he grew up, he would have to wear leg irons. He worried that he might one day have to have false teeth which would affect the way he ate his food or that one leg was longer than the other and he would have to wear a surgical boot and worried that everything Dic said was true and that, if he kept bashing the bishop, he would indeed go blind if he wasn't getting that way already. He even worried about the way the weather was turning but, most of all, he worried that his Mam was going to get on that ship to America without him and what, oh what, was he going to do then?

But the worry of the hour was undoubtedly if that was a real whale in the Bay and, if so, was it now too dangerous to go swimming off the beach and, if he did, might he get swallowed up by that whale.

Better to stay out of the sea really. Better to stay near his Mam who would never allow him to be swallowed up by a whale. Better to give up swimming altogether and go climbing mountains or hang around Majoda again hoping to listen to more delicious foul language or catch a glimpse of Mrs Dylan Thomas' bare tit. That was some tit that was too. How he longed to touch it or squeeze it or even slice it up in a sandwich and eat it. That little baby of theirs had to be the luckiest little baby in the whole of Wales.

So there was indeed much to worry about in that outside lavatory until he was flung out by another member of the family who wanted to sit among the smells and swarming bluebottles for less cerebral matters.

BUT ALL such worries quickly became redundant since the road men arrived that afternoon, coming from wherever it was that road men came from, striding down the dung-littered lanes towards the Morgan farm with bags on their shoulders, all stinking of cider and tobacco, their ripped hands the size of shovels, their baggy trousers yorked at the knees with bits of rope and unshaven cheeks belching with haphazard thunder. These lumbering, dishevelled giants were from another time and place; another species of humanity altogether who just appeared mysteriously once a year rather like the swallows and announced the start of the harvest before disappearing just as mysteriously to yet another time and place presumably to announce the start of another.

Everything about the road men was shrouded in mystery and Gareth simply did not worry about anything as he stood watching them, from a safe distance, all quickly getting to work out in the fields where they attacked the corn with their scythes, felling it with strong, rhythmic strokes, sweat and snot flying out in all directions, stopping only to sharpen their blades or knead their sore backs with stumpy fingers. Other road men followed the first wave of scythers, building up sheaves and setting them out in stooks until the bundled corn seemed to be marching down to the sea in long, orderly lines of tiny, gold wigwams.

For tea in the fields they all had slices of bread with onions and hanks of cheese but, for supper in the barn, Mrs Rachel Morgan brought out enormous pots of stew or boiled potatoes, followed by equally generous helpings of Spotted Dick, which they all ate with a grateful, if savage, relish.

Gareth always liked to help serving up this meal, later rising the cider for them after they had finished eating and again watching them carefully, from another safe distance, as they drank their cider and smacked their lips theatrically, their eyes going bloodshot as they roared with unreal comic laughter at jokes he could never understand.

When they had drunk their fill the road men slept in their clothes in the hay lofts, carrying their own buckets up with them and taking ages to climb the ladder, often falling off it but never seeming to get hurt since, no matter from what height they had fallen, they just seemed to lie there on the barn floor, still clutching their buckets and laughing some more.

Gareth's bedroom was right next to the main hay loft and his slumbers were often disturbed by the strangest symphony of noises ranging from fat snores rasping through the darkness to the continual chomping and spluttering of lips and through to the moments when, barely awake and mumbling to themselves, they pissed into their buckets, the sound slowly changing from a bright pinging to a full, throaty roar.

The boy did manage to nod off at one stage, finding himself standing in a field of cabbages and watching a dark and menacing shape drifting through the blue sky towards him like one of those barrage balloons over London which he kept seeing in the newspapers. This shape drifted ever closer to him and, for a moment, he thought he might make a quick escape only to see that it wasn't a barrage balloon at all but something far greater and lovelier in the form of the fat, fleshy shape of Mrs Dylan Thomas' bare left tit, a flying saucer of throbbing passion, just flying towards him radiating mysterious promises of ceaseless pleasure.

With a loud shout of triumphant excitement Gareth ran towards the flying tit with his trembling, sweaty hands outstretched but, unfortunately, just before he could take a firm hold of it and cup it in his palms and eat big chunks out of it – which was roughly his plan – he woke up.

THE WAR did finally arrive in New Quay three days later but not with a Balfour declaration on the wireless nor with a shower of Luftwaffe bombs nor even with a few houses going up in flames but rather with a lorry from the War Office which had been specifically sent there to fit an air raid siren to the roof of Megan Evans' chicken shed.

Now quite why New Quay, a town which few had ever heard of in Whitehall and even fewer in Berlin, a town which furthermore had carefully maintained a careful neutrality in all matters, especially this war, quite why this forlorn and fish-smelling hole needed its own air raid siren and why it should be placed on the top of Megan Evans' chicken shed, which was not even in the town, no one anywhere – not even the philosophers in the bar of the Black Lion, who knew everything – could work out.

But there it was.

Dylan and Caitlin shared a Rizla roll-up as they stood in their own garden and watched the erection of this air raid siren which took four men almost two hours, including many breaks for tea and fags, to manhandle it off the lorry and on to the roof of the chicken shed when everyone in sight was told to clamp their hands on their ears as the air raid siren was tested. Unfortunately Megan Evans' chickens did not have the wherewithal to clamp their hands over their ears and began fluttering around in the most fearful panic, not even calming down when the tests had finished with the main cockerel whimpering almost tearfully and another managing to burst through the wire mesh and make an escape, never to be seen again.

Dylan's joy was unconfined, however, when it was later learned that not only had the traumatised chickens stopped laying eggs but the rooster had lost his will to sing too.

Megan Evans, however, was absolutely incandescent with rage and some high-up in the War Office was called back to New Quay to meet with Megan Evans personally and explain to her how important it was that the town maintained an air raid siren on the roof of her chicken shed.

We hear what you are saying Mrs Evans but the War Office simply cannot stop fighting this war because your chickens have stopped laying their eggs. It is not of any real importance – and particularly of any national importance – that your chickens are crying so much and you rooster has lost his enthusiasm for waking everyone up long before the crack of dawn. All that matters is that there is a war on and you, Mrs Evans, fully understand the difference between a Full Alert and an All Clear.

But, with the best will in the world, Megan Evans simply could not understand the difference between a Full Alert and an All Clear and so they tried putting her extremely dim son Albert in charge of the siren but he couldn't grasp it either so, after a few more practise wails, which continued to play havoc with the mental stability of her chickens, Megan Evans made so many threatening phone calls to the War Office that, in the end, the same four men returned in the same lorry and took a quarter of an hour, with no break for tea or fags, to take the siren away and her chickens never had to put up with that fearful, blood-curdling wailing ever again.

Chapter Four

IT WAS a Thursday morning, time for his weekly soak, so Dylan was stretched out in the suds in the zinc bath, sucking a boiled sweet and murmuring with a quiet contentment as he read an especially trashy American detective story, 'sugared with stiffs and stiff with cigars'. He had already settled well into their new 'wood and asbestos pagoda' on the headland overlooking Cardigan Bay and what he especially liked were the constant changes of light on the sea, particularly early in the morning when everything could move from a bright crispness to a foggy grey within seconds. On some mornings, when the rain had washed the dust out of the sky, he could see a school of bottle-nosed dolphins jumping out in the Bay and even pick out the thin, dark coast of Ireland but, on others, the visibility was so bad he could barely make out the curve of the beach about a hundred yards away from their house.

His poetry was going well here too – possibly the best and most creative period of his career – and he had managed to chip out such small gems as his *Poem to October* (marking his thirtieth year to heaven); *Vision and Prayer, A Winter's Tale, A Refusal to Mourn the Death by Fire of a Child in London* as well as marshalling the first bouncing syllables of *Fern Hill*.

Caitlin had not understood much of *Fern Hill* but she could see that it sure did bounce.

Indeed the only real thorn in his tender bits was neighbour Megan Evans' cockerel who, unlike other normal cockerels, actually began crowing with some stilted warm-up crowings just before midnight and then get ever more louder and shriller throughout the night in descant until, come the dawn, it got down to the bone of its horrible song, really belting out its wretched phrases again and again down the long, cold corridors of Dylan's early morning hangovers. That cockerel drove Dylan quite barmy and he begged Caitlin again and again to go over there and remonstrate with Megan Evans but Caitlin never did, probably because she didn't want him to get too comfortable here. She had her eye on that lovely cockerel as a sort of future lever to prise him out of this hole when she was ready, which would be very soon now.

The other slight threat to the poet's fragile sanity came in the form of the characters in the town who were taking over his thoughts, forever talking to him in the insomniac night, telling him about the twisted truths of their insanity or else engaging him in long conversations about their priorities, their humanity and extremely weird way of looking at things. Almost all of them had taken up lodgings in his mind and dreams and although he managed to snuff them out when he was good and drunk they had already become something of a torture to him in his sober hours so, he was concluding, he would simply have to write about them if only to fully and finally evict these noisy, mad bastards once and for all.

He selected another boiled sweet out of the soap dish and popped it into his mouth before turning the page of his book when Caitlin came in with another pitcher of water, pouring it carefully around his feet, which he kept lifting up and down, until the temperature was to Milord's satisfaction. She picked up a flannel, motioning him to budge up and proceeded to wash his flabby, pimpled back.

'Dylan, I know you love it here but I'm afraid I'm going to have to tell you again we have a really terrible problem with money and there's no food at all in the pantry. We've got some stale bread and scrape and that's it. At least we always had a chance of picking up a stray cheque when we were in London but, in this cabbage patch, there's none at all.'

He lowered his book and put his head to one side where the light from the window revealed the extent and deep texture of his very newest black eye and, in between a few speculative sucks on his boiled sweet, said, 'I've been thinking a lot about that Captain Port Talbot, that old blind sea captain in the Black Lion. He's been coming to me in my dreams, you know, with all that fag ash and stale bits of food in his beard, but it's that strange, tremulous voice of his that always gets to me. It's got a sort of drowned quality to it and sometimes I hear other drowned voices in his voice, if that makes any sense. All very curious, Cat, all very curious indeed.'

'Dylan, you're not listening to me again. We need to find some money somewhere and fast or it's going to be the big chop for the lot of us.'

'I've been wondering if I could capture that drowned voice in a poem. That watery, distant ghostliness has got such poetic and even mystical echoes about it.'

'Money, Dylan. Fucking money to pay for food in the General Stores.'

He stood up sharply, the bath water and suds dripping off his fat curves as she picked up a towel and began drying him off, paying special attention to his bollocks because he always liked having his bollocks rubbed and she could usually get her way with him when she was rubbing them.

'Your problem Caitlin, if I may say so, is that you yearn to earn. Money is something the Thomases have always been bad at. All this is true but, if money is all you want, then money is all you will get. Dreams are important too. And love. Never forget love.'

'But dreams and love don't buy the fucking food, Dylan. They don't feed the baby or pay the rent. I've already sent the rent man away twice. We can't keep doing that indefinitely.'

'But, Cat, we can keep loving one another indefinitely. And we can dream for all time. Come on, be purely positive and the nasty negatives will look after themselves.'

'Why did I marry you?' she sighed, flinging down the towel to let him dry his own bollocks. 'Prospects have never come any dimmer than you.'

BUT THEY did later agree to try and get a slate at the General Stores and, after depositing baby Aeronwy with Mrs Rhys next door, they ambled along the headland towards the town, Caitlin striding ahead purposively and Dylan dawdling along behind like some aged dog who had long grown out of walks and far preferred to spend its days snoozing in a warm basket.

He understood the absolute need to get a slate in the General Stores but didn't quite understand why *he* had to get involved in this distasteful business, particularly as Caitlin could always talk the Robin off that packet of starch while he often suffered from a crippling shyness, particularly with strangers and especially demanding trades people. He needed at least two pints before his tongue loosened up sufficiently to converse with anyone at all except his Caitlin, of course, and little Aeronwy who, at least, never punched him in the eye or answered back except with a smiling dribble. He even tried to play with the baby for five minutes a day, pulling her toes around perhaps until he got bored and wandered off looking for something else to pull. He had never been in the running for the Father of the Month award, he was the first to admit.

He actually stopped at the outskirts of the sea town, much to Caitlin's obvious annoyance, to marvel at the picturesque orderliness of all those prim rooftops and twisting terraces as they sat there scattered around Manchester House and Cloth Hall, all rising up to the grim-faced chapel in Margaret Street, which seemed to be sitting there scolding the sun and then down to the sea-facing windows and potted ferns of the Bed and Breakfasts in Sea View where, even now, a pair of bare feet were sticking out of one window with the bunioned toes waggling in the cooling ozone breezes. Everywhere he peered there were exciting details of activity from the women out scrubbing their slate doorsteps to the cats basking on the corrugated roofs of the garden sheds; from the woman sweeping up the pavement in front of The Ritz cinema to the milkman making his way from door to door in a quietly applauding chorus of chinking milk bottles.

There really was a strange spiritual atmosphere about New Quay and, just being in those rising streets, he often felt as if he had somehow just emerged from the depths of the ocean, casting off seaweed and dripping with sea water, as his mind shuffled with files and his memory made deposits and phrases were created – all for future reference in the work for which his imagination was already putting up the scaffolding.

The Black Lion was open – when was it otherwise? – with the bar busy slaking the eternal thirst of the lifeboat crew but Caitlin spotted that danger a hundred yards away and speedily managed to catch Dylan by the elbow and propel him forwards lest he slipped his leash and disappeared into the bar, never to come out again until he was in a legless heap. She had already got a firm eye on those drunken bastards in the lifeboat crew who, one extremely disgraceful afternoon, which had escaped being reported in the Press, launched the lifeboat for no good reason and then managed to lose the skipper over the side and were forced to turn around *to save him*.

Caitlin did manage to sheepdog Dylan inside the General Stores but he moved away when she approached the store owner Mrs Pauline Pryce, and actually hid himself behind several bags of potatoes near the door.

But even as they spoke together in a quiet, business-like way, the writer in him was at work again, checking out and splitting up the shop's main smells which, lemme see now, included the sharp clean smell from the block of salt, the acid tartiness in the barrels of vinegar, the mothy mustiness of the ha'penny candles, the fat, full smell of the sacks of flour and broken biscuits, the earthy smell of the farm in the bacon slicing machine and not forgetting the straw brooms, the paraffin lamps, the rat-killer, the blocks of carbolic and the hundred and one other necessities for maintaining life as we know it in a small Welsh sea town.

Caitlin emerged finally from her discussions with Mrs Pauline Pryce, announcing to her unconcerned husband that the bitch had agreed to a slate of three pounds only, which was hardly much even if they didn't want to know about ration books which was just as well since Dylan had lost them all ages ago on some drunken trawl around the pubs of Soho. Indeed she was quite enraged by the smallness of the slate but Dylan was as cheerful as a lark with a bag full of fresh worms as they walked back to Majoda, pointing out that a credit limit of three pounds could easily last for three months at least and such was the real success of his work these days, he was anxious to get straight back to it and not have to worry about such things.

BUT IN spite of all the neurotic accusations and bouts of violence, even Caitlin knew when to step down which was for the two or three sacred hours each afternoon, which Dylan put aside for his work and she felt a flicker of almost religious awe – although she never openly admitted to it – when he picked up the tools of his trade, namely some paper and pencils, and went to work on the kitchen table on his 'craft and sullen art'. She knew he was one useless sod, as lazy as buggery, but also accepted that he had The Gift, often feeling soppy and even girlish as she hung around outside the closed kitchen door hoping he might call out for her to make him a cup of tea perhaps or complain that he was feeling cold so that she could rush in there – yes, *rush* – and put a pullover on him to make him feel warm again.

She never tired of listening to him work either, just sitting outside and often smiling, his greatest and most devoted fan, as he tackled his poems, often shouting out the words again and again, testing them for their strength and sonority or else crumbling up his sheets of paper into many balls and scattering them around the floor as he moaned and groaned and sighed or else wrote the complete poem out all over again as he tried to meld all the dislocated words with an infusion of King James magic which brought majestic order to raucous disharmony.

Be it sonnet or villanelle, no craftsman was ever more dedicated or scrupulous and sometimes he took two weeks to write a single line or else he would write out a poem as many as a hundred times, taking the most simple words and stringing them together in the most complex and unexpected ways, searching, always searching, for that elusive condition of music as he played with repetitions and phrases until, by sheer hard work and not forgetting a good ear, he tried to uncover the dark secrets of life itself.

Not that he wanted any tea or warm pullovers that afternoon, just muttering quietly to that bastard skull of his – which seemed to be getting even more attention than her these days – and so finally, almost in despair and certainly in rejection, Caitlin put Aeronwy in the pram and took her out for a walk. It was so unfair she had become so obsessed by that frog-faced little twot, she thought as she walked next to the sparkling sea, and it wouldn't have been quite so bad if he'd been any good in bed except he wasn't – too drunk late at night and too hungover first thing in the morning.

They did sometimes manage a bit of the *oh be joyful* on the kitchen floor during the day, if he was in the mood and had been relaxed by a few Black Lion pints. She would get him down on the flag-stones flat on his back and mount him to do all the work, banging away like Stephenson's Rocket as he just lay there, his eyes wide open, sucking on a boiled sweet and his mind doubtless thinking up mighty metaphors and storming similes.

It wasn't at all bad like this – not good but not bad – as long as he stayed erect, which he usually did unless he had thought of a terrible mighty metaphor or a really storming simile, which he was anxious not to forget, and then came a big droop in the big valley and everything plummeted downwards like a shot bird. But as long as it stayed up she could take her fill until he managed to squeeze a reasonably decent surrender up between her legs. Then there was a peace of sorts in Majoda.

War broke out when she got drunk in the night – often on whisky – and became wretchedly horny and wanted a bit more than a few press-ups on the kitchen flagstones. But, if she was drunk, he was almost certainly drunk too and, although the spirit was willing, the flesh wasn't and he never got reasonably close to a hard on. Then hostilities began, often in the form of warring words and a few left hooks, which could also spill over into the next morning – particularly if it was raining – and it was Murder in Majoda.

She got more and more vengeful on such days, torturing him to the limits of his endurance. If it was Thursday morning she wouldn't wash his back in his weekly soak, coldly informing him to wash his own bloody back and then she poured cold water into his bath or hid his detective stories and boiled sweets, all to make his life ever more miserable. Then he did his few hours of work and escaped to the Black Lion from where he did not want to return, nor could he return, unless he was brought home in Stephen Stephens' wheelbarrow or on Dic Morgan's cart and dumped at the front door like an unwanted delivery of coal.

Caitlin thought long and hard about the vexed question of love and had long concluded that Dylan was just a little boy she had once picked up in a Soho pub after he had lain his head on her lap and had kept gabbling non-stop. She loved and looked after him like a little boy but he had never really come close to filling the yawning gap inside her: never once came close to the sacred status of a real lover.

The great white horse, when he did arrive, was always riderless or had some dribbling oaf sitting on it. Sometimes the oaf got lucky briefly but he always rode away again empty-handed and leaving her grappling with her inherent loneliness.

The only life-replenishing climaxes she had ever experienced had been through her two children: their births had given her a real contentment and her only real happiness had come when cuddling her babies even if there wasn't too much of that any more particularly as Llewelyn had been left with her mother in Blashford. Yes, all happiness had long been squeezed out of Caitlin, like the juice out of a lemon, leaving her careful, embittered and looking forward with no optimism about anything.

So no, she wasn't remotely in love with Dylan even if she was absolutely adamant on one point: if she wasn't in love with him then no one else could love him either. Her little boy was *hers and hers alone* and she would pick up a knife or mallet and kill for him if she had to. Except she wouldn't really know what she was fighting for: this heap of contradictions who used his charm to plunder every relationship for whatever he could get out of it; this rogue who weighed everyone up in the light of whether he could possibly get money or a bed out of them; this feckless tramp who often stole his host's clothes and was once caught by a woman in a London street as he was on his way to pawn her sewing machine.

HER LIPS gave a short putter of exasperation. What she really needed, of course, was some kind of adventure which would stop her thinking so much about him or, more to the point, herself; something to take herself out of herself; a return to the flesh-pots of London preferably where she could have a little fun and laugh and drink and dance again since there was little hope of that in this cabbage patch by the sea.

Aeronwy began grizzling so Caitlin sat among the lobster pots on the quay and breast-fed her, seeing from the general glares and frowns of the townsfolk that they still didn't much approve of this continuing public display of her bare tits which had already entered into the folk lore of the town. But she couldn't care less. Fuck 'em all and the chapel. She was with that great Welsh writer Caradoc Evans on the subject of the chapel; that every last one of them should be burned down and a decent pub built on the ashes thereof.

Verney Matthews, who had just finished working the tide, was loading his flapping boxes onto the quay and she *forced* herself to smile at him because he wasn't the loveliest man she had ever come across what with that dangling blob of snot on his nose, his oily ratting cap and his eight overcoats which the boys in the bar always swore you'd need a can opener to get off him – or at least a major hospital operation. God alone knew what else he kept in all those pockets of his and she hadn't quite forgiven him for giving that bastard skull to Dylan but he seemed amiable enough, nodding and even scurrying over to her for a few words like some extremely smelly, overdressed Uriah Heap.

'What's it like out there then?' she asked, pleasantly. 'Out at sea.'

'Fine, some mornings, Mrs Thomas, but sometimes it can freeze your balls off . . . '

'Really cold, is it?'

'Colder than the Aaanatanaarctic, Mrs Thomas. That's why I've got to wear all these overcoats. The boys are always taking the piss out of me but I need every one of them. Has Mr Thomas still got his skull has he?'

'He has. You wouldn't be looking for any help, would you, Mr Matthews?'

'What kind of help are you thinking about Mrs Thomas?'

'You know, with your fishing,' she said, lowering Aeronwy and exposing her right tit to Verney's hot and bothered gaze before moving her body around so he could have an even longer look at her lovely, greyhound legs.

Mrs Thomas had worked out long ago that she could get men to do almost anything at all if she gave them a flash of flesh. She had ways with men that Verney Matthews had never dreamed about and she was desperate for a job of some kind since there were mouths to be fed *and* she really did long for something to do except mooning around after her husband.

'You mean you'd like to go out fishing with me, Mrs Thomas?'

'Yes. I do. I've always loved the sea and I'm the only woman I know who likes getting up early.'

'Couldn't pay you much. Couldn't pay you much at all in fact.'

'I'm sure we could work something out. Perhaps you could pay me in fish?'

'Oh sure. I've always got plenty of dog-fish you could have. Make a nice stew, dog-fish do. But I can't have babies on board. Babies is bad luck on boats.'

'There won't be any babies. I've got someone who'll look after little Aeronwy here. Oh that's settled then, Mr Matthews. What time do we sail?'

Chapter Five

ALMOST UNBELIEVABLY the somnolent tempo of the war began quickening again in New Quay the very next day when two wooden crates containing twelve rifles and a small cardboard box with twelve bullets were delivered to the police station and Police Constable Ianto Jones was ordered to set up a group of Local Defence Volunteers. So he duly and dutifully got on his bicycle and went from pub to pub looking for recruits although, perhaps predictably, the response from the boys in the bar of the Black Lion was deeply disappointing.

'There's something of a problem with my lungs in particular and my health in general which is why they wouldn't have me in the Army in the first place,' Dylan intoned in his usual organ voice with a confidence, which suggested he'd had about three pints, before adding, 'if you gave me one of those blunderbusses of yours there's simply no telling where the bullets might bounce. Hitler would be in clover if Dylan Thomas got his mitts on a matchlock. My little Cat-anchor probably wouldn't mind one though. She's good at shooting things is my wife. I'll ask her when I get home.'

'We don't have women in the LDV, Mr Thomas. I didn't make the rules. We just don't have them.'

'Well I couldn't handle a rifle and that's a fact. Everyone knows I'm as blind as a bat,' Captain Port Talbot pointed out.

'I've had trouble with my nerves ever since I was little. Couldn't hit a haystack, I couldn't,' Norman Lewis chipped in.

'Ianto, my nerves are terrible too. Couldn't hit anything

unless I had at least four pints inside me and then it would be by accident,' was Dic Morgan's considered stance on the subject.

'Why don't you have women? What's the matter with women? My tender-as-shrapnel Caitlin is a one-woman massacre in her own right. Give her enough guns and bullets and she'd bring down the whole of the bloody Luftwaffe in five minutes flat.'

'No women. The defence of the realm is no place for women. Women are not built for fighting. Rules.'

'Well we're hardly fighting on the war front in New Quay are we? It's probably just as well you've only got twelve bullets.'

'No volunteers then? Well, I am disappointed. But remember, tonight I'm asking. Tomorrow night I might be telling. There's a war on, in case no one has heard. Everyone has to play his part. Rules.'

'Don't take it personal, Ianto. We're all too old and drunk to go shooting any rifles. Why don't you stay and have a pint of something?'

But Police Constable Ianto Jones did not want a pint of anything and all they could hear was the dejected ticking of the ball bearings of his bike as he wheeled it uphill to try the next pub. Not that he had any luck in there either, they heard later and, as it turned out, still less with his own wife who wouldn't even let him store the rifles and ammunition in his own house, insisting he stuck them out in the garden shed.

'You are *not* bringing those things into this house. What if the children got hold of them?'

CHANGES WERE were being threatened on the Morgan farm too since The Ministry of Food had decided that Welsh farms were not efficient and almost every morning farmers were getting new orders in long, brown envelopes from the County War Ags and Tada would get more and more worked up reading them, continually muttering his strongest Welsh oath which was '*Arglwydd*' or 'God'.

'*Arglwydd!*' he would cry as he read that, in future, he should use Methoxene on the weeds and DDT on the rats.

'*Arglwydd!*' he would go as he read that, in future, any spare rubber should be saved and he should always be on the look-out for scrap metal or he could even have a woman conscript from the Land Army.

The War Ags also offered him a loan for a new tractor, instructions on how to plough and manure fields properly and diagrams explaining how fertilisers worked on crop growth and the best way to pull mangolds or spread lime.

'*Arglwydd!*'

Everything he had ever done as a farmer was now subject to a new directive from the War Ags and, Tada Morgan being Tada Morgan, he didn't like it one bit because Mother Nature, he always said, was a supreme machine, sufficient unto herself so he never felt the need for these 'poisonous' fertilisers and nor did he want a loan for a new tractor since he had perfectly good horses and already knew the best way to pull mangolds and spread lime.

'What use is a woman out in the fields? Can she dig ditches or control a mad bull? Can she pitch hay or lay drains? When did you ever see a woman pulling potatoes or spreading muck? They haven't got the muscles for that kind of work, they'd all be far better off in the kitchen. I'll never have a Land Girl here. You just see if I do.'

Tada didn't want to learn anything because he knew everything already so he ignored all those directives from the War Ags – even the questionnaires about acreage and stock – until late that morning, a man wearing a shiny black bowler arrived on a bicycle with a clipboard in the basket on his handlebars. His fat features made him look like a rather angry bulldog whose jaw was continually moving around as if he was trying to eat half a dozen, foul-tasting and lively wasps. He took an age to lock up his bike before picking up the clipboard and marching up to the farmhouse to find the whole of the Morgan

47

family, including young Gareth, sitting around the kitchen table and gawping at him as he stood framed in the doorway.

'Good morning. I am William Brown of the Cardigan War Agricultural Committee and one of you here, a Mr Thomas Morgan, would be the owner of this farm.'

'That's me.'

'Good, right, fine. We don't like answering questionnaires do we Mr Morgan? We don't like it one little bit.'

Tada shrugged and glared at Gareth as if, somehow, the boy had been responsible for not filling them in.

'Good, right, fine. I am here to take a full inventory of your farm stock, Mr Morgan. We need to list these things so that your farm can be put into a category. When you are put into a certain category you will then be expected to meet certain quotas.'

'I've never been one for categories or quotas, Mr Brown. Just carry on the way I've always carried on.'

'Yes, I don't doubt that for one minute, Mr Morgan. Not for one minute. But all this has got to stop. It is my job to see that all farmers in the county become more efficient. If you do not become more efficient your farm will be requisitioned and sold over your head to someone who will make it efficient. I am making myself clear, I hope.'

'This farm is efficient. There's no one more efficient than us.'

'We are going to make you *more* efficient. You are going to get a new tractor and become part-owner of a new thresher. There are going to be no more fields lying fallow and it's going to be fertiliser and manure on everything that grows. I am going to draw up a new schedule of working for this farm which I want you to follow to the letter. For a start all pasture must be ploughed up and all rabbits gassed.'

'Rabbits gassed?' was Gareth's only squeaking contribution to this exchange.

'All gassed. And the rats and the voles and everything else that's getting free food around here.'

In the face of this new menace in a black bowler not one of

48

the Morgan family – not even chopsy Dic – said so much as one word.

VERNEY ROWED out to his fishing boat, moored with a dozen others just inside the harbour breakwater as Caitlin sat on the aft seat and spoke to him about what she hoped they would catch that day which Dylan liked; what she hoped they wouldn't catch because Dylan didn't like it and anything else that just happened to wander into her mind, usually connected with Dylan.

Not that Verney ever took the slightest bit of notice of anything she ever said about anything at all, with his eyes only occasionally glancing up at her worriedly as she dropped another obscenity into the virgin dawn but, otherwise, managing to almost completely ignore her with even the blobs of snot hanging off the end of his nose just hanging there serenely, not in the slightest bit disturbed by his new shipmate's wandering, off-colour monologues.

Caitlin always liked to talk and didn't even much mind that Verney didn't seem to want to listen, embracing her new job with a real and even suspicious fervor, later telling Dylan how wonderful it was to be out so early in the Bay, watching the sun rub its eyes and get out of bed and glorying in all that ozone silence as they pulled up the lines, pots and nets and marvelling – yes, *marvelling* – at the sheer variety of stuff that went flapping and fighting around the deck. 'All those waves. You never know where you are with waves. They're all a bit like living with you.'

Dylan took her word for it: he hated the sheer, alcoholic unreliability of the sea and had no intention of ever setting foot in that little boat, which looked as though it was going to spring a leak at any moment, and he was anyway pleased that Caitlin had something to occupy herself, particularly as it took the pressure off him and placed it squarely on Verney whom Dylan had long dubbed The Ancient Mariner.

'Dylan has always had this thing about cockles, you know

Verney. They are very odd things are cockles often running around under the sand like burglars being chased by the police and you can never catch up with them. They also always eat their baby young which is why Dylan likes to eat them. Revenge on the cannibals, Dylan says, but he's very odd himself you know. He just looks like a human.'

Once aboard the fishing boat itself Caitlin began tidying up the boxes and ropes, still talking, now about Dylan again. Verney coaxed his engine into uncertain, bronchial life and headed out to sea.

The herring shoals had once been so numerous over the past two hundred years they had given rise to almost all the fishing villages along this part of the Welsh coast but now they had gone away again the fishermen had declined correspondingly and there were now only thirteen fishing boats working out of New Quay with 21 full-time fishermen, 39 part-timers and one quarter-timer, Caitlin, who, unique among them all, was usually paid with a bucket of dog-fish, which she quite liked but Dylan didn't.

It was part of Caitlin's long-term plan to be paid with something more than dog-fish but Verney hadn't yet indicated if he put any value on her work. She was working on him to pay her in money but hadn't got anywhere on that front yet which was unusual for her.

But there were other bonuses to being out here and Caitlin sniffed and smiled to herself rather loopily, loving the completely dream-like quality of the breaking dawn, the shadowy outline of the town's terraces, shops and chapels behind them; the thin sea mists curling around their heads like emaciated, slumbering ghosts; the seals that bobbed up occasionally and looked up at them with sad, black eyes and not forgetting the ever present herring gulls – the *Guto Gyglwydd* – whose beady yellow eyes were locked on their every move.

Yet more herring gulls joined the throng above the boat, screaming at the two fishermen in a sort of crazed anger but

Verney never threw them any tit-bits – even forbade Caitlin to do so – not even when he was overloaded with fish, since he didn't believe in charity, particularly to those bastard gulls who would steal the eyes out of your head, he always said, and then come back for the sockets. If they were hungry enough, let them catch their own breakfast was about his view of things. The only good gull was a dead gull. He had tried feeding them with carbide once but, disappointingly, they failed to explode in mid-air as he had been promised. A nice, big bang and a shower of feathers, he had been told.

Those gulls were all over the place just now since they had come to follow the shoals, arriving early in August and hanging around right through to February. But the trouble was that these shoals had long gone shoaling somewhere else which was why, in the absence of their favourite food, they were hanging around Verney for some of his, with one getting so frustrated he even tried shitting on the fisherman with a huge smelly dollop which missed him but caught Caitlin with a fair bit of spray.

'That's the same little fucker with one eye that tried to shit on us the other morning, Verney. Let's get the cunt. You hold out a small fish for him and I'll lamp him one with this pole.'

'You'd never catch him, Mrs Thomas. They are faster than shit off a hot shovel if they think you are going to whack them one. I'd blow the whole lot of them up if I could.'

BUT ALL thoughts of getting revenge on that incontinent gull with one eye were soon abandoned when the pair of them settled down to their work, first pulling up the prawn pots and lifting them up out of the water and staring down at the squirming contents which skittered furiously against the fine mesh of the pots like rain on a corrugated roof. Caitlin had always thought prawns were red, just like her husband's early morning hungover eyes, but they were, in fact, a translucent browny green with small black eyes and lots of whiskers which kept waving around angrily and who only went red *after* they had been boiled.

This skittering mess was then poured into a large box which began filling up quickly and noisily with all kinds of other fish too including horrible black eels and the rather fetching butter fish which Caitlin often actually threw back into the drink if Verney wasn't looking. He had once told her that he liked to eat butter fish on toast but she wasn't having any of that because they were too pretty and delicate to have on anything, particularly toast, although she was intrigued to learn that Verney actually ate anything at all – even if it was butter fish on toast – since she had never seen him eat a morsel of anything. There was more fat on a chip and more brains in a tin of dog food.

When they had finished working the prawn pots Verney was thinking – but only thinking – of putting out some lines for mackerel, to be pulled in after they had returned from the lobster pots, but decided against it because the mackerel had gone missing lately, along with the herring, and it simply wasn't worth the time and effort.

'It's just like those bastard mackerel to go missing when you need them. Here we are, in the middle of a war, when you can sell anything for three times the price, and what do they do? They go missing. They always slacken off at this time of year but never actually go missing.'

'Perhaps you're not putting the right kind of bait?'

'There's been mussels on them hooks. Live mussels. They normally queue up for mussels or climb on one another's backs to get at them. But not any more they don't. Nothing.'

'Put other bits of mackerel on the hooks then. All fish are fucking cannibals when you get down to it.'

'All fish are cannibals? Where'd you learn that then?'

'In a book somewhere. Or maybe Dylan told me. You wouldn't believe the nonsense he comes out with, particularly after he's had a few. You always know Dylan is talking nonsense after he's had a few because his fat lips are moving.'

As they continued working the tide, next pulling up the

largely empty, lobster pots, the whole deck had become alive with creeping, wriggling things and it was difficult for either of them to step anywhere without crushing something that flapped or slipping on something that squirmed or breaking many bones of something that scuttled. A giant whelk was moving around inside a bucket trying to find a way out, an orange star fish hung off the side of one of the lobster pots, several crabs were busy trying to burrow under some nets to hide and the prawns were still hissing frantically at their sheer bad luck as they all lay crushed together on their backs in that big box.

An eel – about two feet long – was actually roaming around the deck, avoiding the others as it looked around the gunwales trying to escape this holocaust, actually managing to find a hole but finding it too small for its fat shoulders, before moving on again to find a larger hole through which it slithered and dropped into the sea with a triumphant plop of release.

They had been working the lobster pots for an hour or so and, although he could just about cope with the mackerel going missing, the fact that the lobsters had also gone awol was really beginning to get on Verney's nerves and his black anxieties were being deepened by a growing conviction that someone was poaching on his lobster beds.

They weren't his lobster beds, of course, any more than they were his lobsters but they were definitely *his* lobster pots and someone – that Tom Hunter from Aberaeron, he'd bet a pound – was probably having them away in the middle of the night.

But you'd never get those bastard crabs to go missing, would you, since they were everywhere, all day and all night, always spending their winter and summer holidays in his pots and eating all the rabbit meat he used as bait which wasn't any old rabbit meat either but meat which was exactly three days old when it went inside the pots, as he had been advised by the Fisheries people. But as they pulled up the next pot, they again had nothing by way of a squirming lobster, with a hard black shell and bright blue legs, but another crowd of crabs who were all full and happy after feasting on his three-day old rabbit.

They weren't meant for you, you bastards. Leave my bloody rabbit meat alone will you? Find your own bloody rabbit meat. Oh if only I could lay my hands on some dynamite and blow the claws off all these bloody crabs. Oh what fun that would be. Just one long laugh without end.

THAT MOMENT when the sun first became bright and hard, sweeping the dark and the grey off the tops of the waves and making the whole morning sing with the new, was Caitlin's favourite, a time when she told Verney to turn his back as, in celebration of yet another beautiful dawn, she pulled down her drawers and squatted on the aft rail and had a nice, long, joyous piss into the sea.

And you have never, Dylan, ever had a piss until you've had a piss off the back of a boat in all those fantastic changes of light in a Cardigan Bay dawn. You look around you and everything seems to mirror something else and you can't tell what's misty illusion and what's watery reality. Dolphins were actually jumping around me the other morning when I was at it and I was the queen of the world taking a piss on the very birth of time.

'I far prefer to piss into a lavatory myself, Catey. There's no sound in the world like piss hitting porcelain. That's what I call a good piss.'

Dylan, you are so fucking boring. There's more feeling in a mangle. God alone knows how you turned out to be a poet.

THE WINDS freshened in the risen sun and, abandoning the dead lobster patch, they went off in search of another which might have a bit more life in it, chugging around the far headland where guillemots and kittewakes and razorbills stood together on the cliff edges like impatient football fans on the terraces waiting for the kick-off. Two gulls sat on the forard rail to watch – and maybe laugh at – the proceedings as the waves swelled a little and they started to pull in some more lobster pots when, lo and behold, they found three lobsters sitting inside the first one, two in the second and a small red crab in the third.

But it was fuck-me-pinks all round since *four* lobsters somehow managed to pack themselves into the next one, all scrummaging down together like a gang of burly rugby forwards competing for the ball with a few of them having already lost claws in the fray. This was more like it and he snapped elastic bands on each claw to stop any more damaging brawls since people liked to eat their lobsters with claws, they always felt cheated if they had crippled lobsters put on their plates although he had never understood why because he had always hated eating lobster – it brought him out in a nasty rash whenever he ate it and the less of it on his plate – and the more crippled and clawless they were – the better.

That bed brought him an astounding twenty four lobsters and he was somewhere over the moon about them, feeling warm and happy to be an honest Welsh fisherman (albeit with a mad Irish partner) working the tide in good old Cardigan Bay. As soon as he got back to the beach he would pack them in boxes of ice and send them straight off to the market and make a shilling or two but, with his luck running like this, he swung his wheel through four or five full revolutions and decided they would have one quick trawl with the net before deciding to call it a day.

Chapter Six

WITH CAITLIN safely out of the way trawling the seven seas with The Ancient Mariner, Dylan was down to the Black Lion unusually early that lunch-time, sipping on his first pint of the day while doing the crossword in the corner before joining the rest of the boys standing at the bar for his second.

The gossip of the hour included the interesting, if speculative, news that young Norma Rees, who lived next to the Dolau Inn and had been going out with a Cunard steward from Liverpool, was now definitely up the stick and that a little Cunard steward was almost certainly on the way and would be docking any week now.

This news kept them all brightly entertained, particularly on the subject of contraception, with Dylan telling them that, yes, he had always believed in johnnies but they had never believed in him and that his greatest problem was in getting one on, especially when he was full of drink, and even if he did manage to 'bag his dick' Caitlin would often get worked up and tear the thing off. It was all down to the drink, he guessed, and his children should really have been called A Pint of Buckley's Bitter Thomas or Johnnie Walker Thomas because that's what they were conceived on and what they were mostly made of.

'The real problem was that the hole is so much bigger than anything you usually put into it like that man . . . '

But his shaggy dog story was interrupted by the arrival of Dic Morgan who had come with another bit of ripe news about a newcomer who had moved into Cliff House with a small baby that morning and who, unless he was very much mistaken, must be one of the James girls who had all gone to live with their father, a doctor in London, after her mother had been caught out having a bit of a rub with a pig breeder in Llandysul. No one had ever understood that affair, Dic recalled, because the pig breeder was not a lot better looking than the pigs under his care but the subsequent divorce had caused a terrific scandal and the mother had been left alone in Cliff House – abandoned by her husband, daughters and aforesaid pig breeder – before she died about eighteen months back.

This one must be Dolly James, one of the daughters, Dic went on, who, it was said, was something of an actress before falling for a child by an un-named man and being sent back here to New Quay to get out of the way of bombs and other un-named men. The same as her mother by the looks of it. Funny how these things run in the family. Dic hadn't even spotted a wedding ring so there was every chance she didn't even know who the father was. The Rev Enoch would almost certainly have something to say about that when *he* found out since the chapel didn't acknowledge the existence of bastards let alone approve of them.

'Ah, yes, I saw her on my way down here,' Dylan said, putting his pint down on the bar so as to use his hands the better to describe this historic encounter. 'You have never, ever seen anything like it. Enormous knockers and an arse like a clap of thunder. I'm telling you now you'd pay real money just to sink your finger-tips into that arse *and* she's got long, funny curls the colour of a new threepenny bit. There was also those big, brown eyes of a Boxer dog and, I tell you what, I simply don't know how she got into the tight skirt of hers. You could see the stocking garters right through the skirt.'

The boys all moaned with a low, collective sigh of frustrated lust.

'The other thing I noticed was she had big hands which is not good in a woman, my Uncle Joe always used to say, because big hand always makes your dick look small.'

'Tell us about those knockers again, Dylan.'

'Well, they weren't so much knockers as mammary mountains.' More collective gasps of pure disbelief. 'I am not exaggerating but you'd need oxygen and crampons to climb them. Then you couldn't ever be sure of getting down again.'

'Aw, you're pulling our pissers now Dylan. They couldn't possibly be *that* big.'

'You just take it from me they really are *that* big. Those knockers are bigger than coconuts. You really could crack walnuts with them. Anyway good luck to any man who does give her a good seeing to. That's one big woman, garters an' all. That woman really could suck you in and blow you out in bubbles.'

A full minute silence followed as all the boys – all dirty bastards to a man – stood around looking down into their beer, their minds conjuring with fantasies of stocking garters and mammary mountains and being blown out in bubbles. Ah, if only they were all thirty years younger, you could hear them thinking. If only . . . if only . . .

'Dylan, just tell us about those coconuts one more time,' Joshua the Bluebell said finally.

PUTTING OUT the trawl net was often an even more haphazard and fruitless business than pulling up the lobster pots but, almost as soon as they began winching the net up out of the sea, even Caitlin could see that they had done well.

The full net was bursting with squirming life, hissing up out of the water with any amount of fish inside it, small mouths sticking out of the holes in the mesh, some throwing up their guts in lumps of reddish jelly and others with their mouths wide open in silent screams, dead already. It was the sheer indignity of it all that always got to Caitlin, all of them jammed in there, tails and heads sticking out of the mesh, many still wriggling around furiously and others quite still, obviously accepting this was the end and giving up the ghost as fast as they could.

Verney pulled the cod end clip and, with slithering swoosh, the whole deck became alive with flapping brill, skate, plaice and dogfish, all flouncing around this way and that, some actually leaping as if they knew exactly where they were leaping to but most of them completely traumatised, staring around with wild, dead eyes at this complete outrage.

ABOUT THREE hundred yards away from the fishing boat a periscope was watching their every move intently in a calm, grey September sea and, just below the surface, three men in a U-boat were taking it in turns to watch Caitlin and Verney pack up their fish.

Even if the periscope view was clear enough the men were standing in a guttering darkness as the U-boat's lights kept failing again and again. Everyone cursed the bungling bilge rats who had been hauled in to maintain Donitz's navy, cursed their rotten, barren mothers, cursed their stinking syphilitic fathers and cursed the idle men themselves who had never once cleaned the batteries when the boat was in dry dock and had just painted over them, making their sides split and leak sulphuric acid which had corroded all the terminals.

The main diesel motor had also been tailing during the charges, leaking chlorine into the U-boat until the mere act of breathing had become even more difficult than swallowing oily balls of cotton wool, made all the worse by the constant stiff farts of the badly fed men, making them tense, edgy and full of fear.

'We could surface and ask them for food and water but it could be very dangerous,' Kapitanleutnant Ernst Gebler said finally. 'But there again it could be very dangerous to stay down here too. We cannot breathe. Without food and water we cannot live.'

The first mate, Christian, took the periscope and stared at the

59

two fishing for a while. 'Do you think they have oysters in these parts? I always liked oysters in that small restaurant in the dock at La Rochelle. Ten fine oysters and a bottle of chilled Chablis. Nothing better.'

'Well we know they have lobsters because they have lobster pots but the question is: Do we surface? Maybe we will just have to kill them?'

'No kapitan. I could not even enjoy a plate of the finest lobster if I thought I had killed for it. I would prefer to die in the darkness down here.'

'Very well. Let's just surface and talk to them. Let's see how they react when they catch the biggest fish in the sea.'

CAITLIN AND VERNEY were totally unaware their every move was being studied carefully as they flung their fish into different boxes but, there again, not even the most chronic paranoiac would have suspected he was being studied carefully, two and a half miles out at sea, with no land visible in any direction and the huge trackless surface of the sea barely moving.

They might have spotted the eavesdropping periscope had they known where to look but were so engrossed in sorting out their fish it didn't even occur to them to look up and neither did they notice anything particularly odd when their boat began rising up into the air while the sea all around them remained perfectly still. It might even have been caused by some freak conjunction of wave and current, they might have thought, had they thought about it at all, which they hadn't. Their feet merely re-arranged themselves and their balance on the deck and they continued working.

Caitlin had always enjoyed scraping the Gower sands for cockles or stabbing for dabs on the river beds but this was real fishing and what is more it was well away from that smelly little asbestos home and Dylan's incessant moans and illnesses and she still didn't notice anything was wrong when a strange, unearthly groan came up from the depth of the sea followed by the sound of hissing jets.

It was Verney who picked up on it first, sniffing the air carefully like a dog trying to decide if a bit of meat was fresh enough to eat, when the eternal globule of snot on the end of his nose fell off as did another and another.

There was another strange motion in the sea when the whole of their catch slid across the deck with quite a few fish managing to jump over the side. Caitlin managed to grab a deck rail as her feet sailed from beneath her while Verney went crashing into his lobster pots, ending up spinning around on his bum amongst all the fish. *Just what the fuck was going on?*

The sea began exploding and hissing all around them, sending them both dancing around the deck again without one good leg under either of them as a huge, black monster began roaring up out of the deep, doubtless about to open its cavernous jaws and swallow them down whole.

Caitlin, a most reluctant Jonah, began screaming as the monster continued emerging up out of the boiling water except that it was making such a fearful racket she couldn't even hear herself scream. *Oh fuck me high and low that's some monster that is. Dylan was right all along. Everyone should stick to the fucking dry land. That's why we've all got two legs and two feet, he always said and the bastard was right all along.*

Now the huge beast was spitting out huge gouts of water from its side and she was flung against Verney, clutching the smelly, over-coated wretch and screaming as they were both pitched across the fish-flapping deck again. *Oh Dylan, come and save me from this mess will you? Please come and save me and take me back to fucking London or somewhere safe will you? I can't stand any more of this. No more.*

But then, in all the screaming fear and spitting fury, a few things became clear such as a huge gun and a fucking great number painted on its side. U-258. That was some amazing whale for sure because it was now vomiting men up out of its backside and they were all still alive, scrambling along the deck to take control of that fucking gun which they were now turning and training on them.

Oh, that's not a fucking whale at all. That's a fucking submarine and a German submarine at that. A Nazi submarine with a fucking Nazi gun which was going to blow the pair of them to bits at any moment now.

Her belly had gone and got itself sucked right up into her throat while furious little stars kept bursting before her eyes and her body was completely immobilised by terror as she continued to cling to Verney whose nose was running like a waterfall in full spate. And still that fucking gun was pointing straight at them.

Then, after the fury, came the silence and all Caitlin could hear was her pounding heart as the heads of two men in the conning tower looked down at her. Her eyes also caught two gulls rafting nearby peaceably and unconcernedly as if this happened every morning about this time. There was no land in sight in any direction.

'Just stand quite still and no harm will come to you. We have no intention of hurting either of you and you are both perfectly safe.'

Caitlin let go of Verney uncertainly and raised her hands into the air, just as she'd seen prisoners-of-war do in the pictures. Verney looked at her and did the same. *There was never any soap in a Nazi prison was there? If they didn't have any soap in the stores in New Quay then as sure as eggs were eggs they certainly wouldn't have any in fucking Berlin or wherever else it was they were going to be taken and flogged to within an inch of their lives.* She thought of her two lovely babies and began crying soundlessly.

'Put you hands down. There is no need for that. I am Kapitan Ernst Gebler and this submarine is under my command. We have run into some difficulties and need fresh food and water.'

Verney's mouth opened and closed but nothing by way of words came out. *Aaaaarg, yew, yer . . .* was about all the sense

Caitlin could make of things as she lost her footing on a slippery plaice and again went stumbling sideways before banging her leg on a box and again managing to grab hold of the deck rail. The U-boat's hull knocked against their boat with a dull clank and she could feel urine, wet and warm, seeping down through her flannel long johns which she had borrowed off Dylan. *So this was what it was like being on the fucking front line. She'd read so much about the war but never expected to end up on the front line of the fucking thing. Fishermen were not supposed to get involved in wars. Fishermen were supposed to fish and stay out of trouble. They were a reserved occupation like miners or farmers. Or so she'd always been told.*

'We can also give you money if you help us. We have a lot of money – good English money – and we need fresh meat and vegetables. We also must have fresh water but we are not thieves and will pay you well if you help us.'

The mere mention of a lot of good English money made Caitlin visibly calmer. The captain was also heart-stoppingly good-looking, which was always a bonus with her, and he wasn't threatening them in any way; just asking them for their services while also offering a lot of money. You couldn't quarrel with any of that and furthermore, if these Germans were starving and short of water, they weren't going to get it by drilling holes in her. Or The Ancient Mariner here. Their bodies were going to be no use at all to them and, the more she thought about it, the more she could see that their continued well-being was assured; that she might even have the upper hand here.

'There's a stand-by pipe in the harbour and we could fill up some barrels with water for you from there,' she yelled through cupped hands as if they were a mile away. 'Vegetables would be easy and there are plenty of potatoes. We could do you some fish ourselves but meat might be a bit difficult. But money doesn't just talk in Cardigan, it roars its head off. We could probably even get you a sheep or two. If you had the money.'

'We have plenty of money *fraulein*. And we could give you

treble or even four times the market rate for anything you might supply.'

'And this money. It would be *English* money would it? You can't get much for German money around here.'

'We will buy anything you can provide and we will pay you in good English money. We have plenty of good English money.'

'Right. Fine. Well, here's what we do. Tomorrow we will be out here at the same time with vegetables, fresh water and whatever meat we can find. We'll leave you with some fish right now. If you have plenty of English money I'm sure we can do plenty of Welsh business although, in case you're at all interested, I'm Irish and we're not in this war anyway.'

'What is your name *fraulein*?'

'Never mind about my name. You just be here with the money.'

'You may rely on it. We have some urgent electrical repairs to do before we go home. This may take a week or so but there will be nothing for you to have any cares about. A week or so and we will be gone.'

Chapter Seven

AROUND EIGHT o'clock that night the strong sea winds began buffeting the walls and roof of the large manse high on the hill, whispering feverish imprecations under the ill-fitting doors, desperately trying to lift off any loose slates and blow them away or else rattling the windows in their frames like some mad man who had suddenly been seized by the desire to shatter them fast before moving off to try and find something else to destroy.

Nothing much ran in a straight line in this crumbling manse with walls which bulged as if in advanced stages of pregnancy and plaster-work which bubbled and browned with the damp. This damp ran everywhere like a river which had lost the track of its course, across the floorboards, up the legs of the furniture, into papers and even into the Rev Enoch's theological library, nourishing patches of white and purple mildew on the spines of the books which had given the minister so much inspiration over the years.

Not that the Rev Enoch ever gave the slightest damn about any of this damp since he never seemed to care about the trials and tribulations of living in the real world at all. He was just one big abstraction on two legs was the Rev Enoch: a chapel anachronism tied up in rumours of God. Tonight, sitting at his desk, serenaded by the buffeting sea winds and surrounded by all this mildew damp, he was doing what he enjoyed best in the guttering light of an oil lamp, composing yet another prayer and, in so doing, setting up a land-line to God.

His eyes and huge beak of a nose followed the course of his quill closely; the long pianist's fingers of his left hand spreading out on the sheet of paper to stabilise it while his right, which had been deformed by arthritis, scratched out the words, each one thought about with precision and care. *So we can see from this that yet again water becomes the secret essence which moves through every corner of life and it is the first food of grace on which . . .*

A moth fluttered in the light of the oil lamp which also highlighted his bushy eyebrows, dog collar and tight pursed lips. Yet his raggedy hairstyle was his most distinctive feature: an exploded hay-stack of silver which, on windy days such as this, often made him look as if he had just grabbed a wire live with a thousand volts. Even naughty boys stood to attention when they saw that silver, electrified hay-stack coming down the hill. *It is to water that our souls will one day return and become re-united with the joy of the new . . .*

Occasionally he would pause from his writing and look up and around him; at the sheep skulls he had picked up on his walks and now lined his shelves or the huge jars full of sea shells which he had found on the beaches. As he looked at his mildewed books they looked back at him while his Act of Parliament clock ticked, rumbled and periodically exploded into exuberant chimes like a child in Sunday School suddenly desperate for attention after being good for five minutes.

Over the years he had built up a great collection of prayers made even greater by the huge variety of their subjects. They had all been stored away in carefully catalogued boxes which were scattered through the manse but, these days, he had been working on a collection of prayers for a time of war and suggesting ways in which his parishioners could redeem themselves.

He read them out from his lonely pulpit to a packed congregation each Sunday and, for him, these prayers now formed a spiritual bunker into which he could invite his frail, sinful flock to come and find shelter from the storms of violence and destruction sweeping through Europe.

His quill scratched, stopped, scratched again. Tiny ink spots scattered over his paper like a small storm of black rain. He sighed and blotted them before dispensing with that sheet and starting on a new one. The Act of Parliament clock rumbled softly but didn't chime loudly. Another rogue wind rushed down the length of the corridor. A door in the town opened and slammed shut. A dog barked. The Rev Enoch sniffed when he noticed that the whole of the top of his desk was being infused with a strange white light.

He stopped writing and remained perfectly still as a flash of red fire shot through the white light. A dark church appeared in the centre of the desk and a bomb exploded inside it, blasting out all the stained glass windows soundlessly. People were moving around inside the red and gold flames and, although they were making no sound, you could see, just by the shapes of their bodies, that they were all wracked by pain.

The images of this fiery vision actually danced inside the Rev Enoch's cold blue eyes even though they didn't actually affect him physically. In fact the hotter the vision the calmer he became. He knew all about the language and grammar of such visions; he knew that this was the way God always spoke to him, not in words so much as in images like these, in the many songs of the dragon. These exploding visions were nothing less than God's dragon music and here he was, the chosen congregation of one, sitting there, listening to it and staring at it.

The flames inside the church died down and the front doors opened wide. The Rev Enoch lowered his head a little and looked down the length of the long, gutted aisle where, just above the altar, a lone dark figure was nailed up high on a singing cross of light. But this figure was not Our Saviour, it immediately became clear to him, so much as himself, The Rev Enoch, looking back at himself looking in. The drones of bombers began going around and around the room as Enoch watched himself on that singing cross of light, moving his weight around painfully from one arm to the next.

He could not see what this meant at all and his eyes filled with tears as it all became too much for him. This vision *was* affecting him personally so he put down his quill carefully and slowly before wiping his hands with the long backs of his shaking fingers. The drones of the bombers disappeared into the ticking of the Act of Parliament clock. Another wind sprinted down the length of the corridor. Someone was hammering in the town.

Yet, even if he didn't actually understand the vision, the pain in it was real and solid enough. God had reached out and told him about His own pain and this pain had broken through to Enoch too. He, nailed up to that singing cross of light, was being invited to share in God's pain and, just for now, he was the well into which God had chosen to shed his tears.

The Rev Enoch had always been happy to preach the wild word of God in a fallen world but he had never really expected to share in His personal pain too. He hadn't bargained for such a message at all and, as he continued trying to dry his tears with the backs of his trembling hands, he prayed he would have the strength to share in this pain; that he was strong enough to do whatever it was that God was asking him to do.

'DYLAN THOMAS, for one night a week and one night a week only, you are going to give your body a night off the booze,' Caitlin screamed at Dylan who was sitting slumped in his Barry Island deck chair too dejected to even lift his smoking Woodbine and take a drag on it.

'Oooooeeeeeo, Catey, ayeeeoh,' he mumbled like the great lyric poet he was. 'Ayeeeeeuuuuurgh, ayeeeeoh.'

'It's no good sitting there grunting like some old pig. For one night a week you are going to take your wife – otherwise known as me, Mrs Thomas – to the pictures where we are going to become young lovers in the one and nine pennies again.'

'Uuuuuuuuuuurgh, thurghrrrrrr, eeeeeaaarye.'

'You will buy me two packets of crisps, one for each film, and I will feed you with your favourite boiled sweets. I will pay for the tickets and you will buy the crisps. You will be entertained. *You will be happy.* And for one night a week you will actually enjoy yourself without Buckley's beer swilling out of your ears.'

'Aaaaaargh, shuss, eeeeeeaaaaaaargh,' Dylan started again, moving as if to rise up out of Barry Island's deck chair only to collapse back down into it, realising it was pointless to argue since he knew when arguments were lost with her – often well before they had begun – and this was one of them. He simply had to go with her to the Bughouse in town – or The Ritz, as it was laughingly called – if only to give his kidneys a break. He leaned forward to stub out his cigarette on a saucer between his feet before absentmindedly tapping his pockets as if trying to locate his packet of Woodbines, when he looked up at her and opened his hands wide beseechingly.

'All right, we'll go. But can't we leave at least ten minutes before the end of the film so I can just catch a couple in the Black? It's always official stop-tap when the film finishes and, that way, we'll get in just before stop-tap. You know me Catey. I need a few pints or I just won't go to sleep.'

'Oh do stop fucking whining will you?'

'I can't sleep without a few beers Catey. I need a couple or it's going to be the green dogs of insomnia all night long.'

'Green dogs of insomnia? Since when were those dogs *green*? Fucking Winston Churchill said those dogs were black. Black, Dylan.'

'Two pints, that's all. Just get out of there ten minutes before the film ends.'

'Just *what* is the fucking point of leaving a film ten minutes before the end? You might as well leave ten minutes after the start. No. You are locked into that cinema right until the very end. When it says THE END – up there on the screen – T-H-E E-N-D – you can leave then but not a moment before.'

He could feel a serious illness coming his way and began

pressing his chest with his fingertips as if feeling the air inside it. The other snag in sitting with Mrs Thomas in the one and nine pennies was that she always reeked of dogfish these days *and* he was getting mighty fed up with dogfish stew, just wishing the Ancient Mariner would pay her in mackerel or something different. Butter fish on toast would be a lot more attractive than all these dogfish they were getting.

But, as befits a poet for whom cowardly evasion was the very beat of his heart, he never complained about her smell or the food, often managing to dispose of the dogfish stew behind the bushes in the garden when she wasn't looking. The bushes seemed to enjoy this stew well enough and were practically roaring with life. Fish had sulphates which plants quite liked, someone had once told him in a pub; almost everything he knew had been told to him by someone in a pub and he had learned quite a few things while lying on the floor of a pub too.

MOONLIGHT HAD settled in huge shifting puddles on the Bay as the couple trudged down the path towards the town with Dylan, hands in pockets, lagging behind or else stopping to kick something around or even just standing still, waiting for her to sheepdog him onwards again.

He was still quite fed up with this invasion into his sacred drinking time and even the owl, perched on the branch of the dead oak near the main road, hooted with total derision as they passed under him, getting very satirical that any man who called himself a serious drinker should allow himself to be bullied out of his daily ration like this.

But what could he do? All he wanted was a quiet life of poems and pints and, if the price he had to pay for that was a Thursday night in the Bughouse, that's the price he had to pay. She hadn't been too much of a pain in the arse to be married to lately either, particularly since she had been out working the tides with the Ancient Mariner. She had always been too tired to demand any irksome sex after coming home, leaving him and Yorick to work on a few lines before he went down the pub and again attempted to drink himself into a little pickle.

Yet there was also something really strange about her lately since she seemed to be constantly slipping off with The Ancient Mariner in the afternoons and 'doing a bit of business' as she put it. He wasn't at all sure what this business was but she had even been producing pound notes from the secure safe that was her brassiere, claiming that they had been sent to her by Augustus John.

Dylan didn't believe that old skinflint artist would give Caitlin anything at all – except perhaps a dose of the crabs – but, as she occasionally gave him one of those notes, he wasn't about to start asking awkward questions. He knew the rules: you simply had to learn to duck and dive when you lived with a lusty Irish lady with great legs and a venomous tongue.

THERE WAS a long queue waiting to go into the cinema and Dylan was still practically throwing up on his own bile as they walked to the end of it; not so much at having to stand at the end of a queue, which was bad enough in itself, but having to put up with the mock stares and ironic hoots from the townsfolk in the queue who, through the gossip, all clearly knew he was first and foremost a lover of the sawdust saloon and not the silver screen.

Stories of his strange behaviour had also entered the folk-lore of the town; almost everyone had their favourite story about him, particularly about his Jekyll and Hyde character which burst through the drink; how he was a world champion boozer who bedded every woman in sight before going home, dashing off a few sonnets and then beating the living shit out of Mrs Thomas.

This was how they all saw him even if they couldn't quite relate this image with the hen-pecked husband shuffling along in Mrs Thomas's wake.

The film tonight, according to the poster in the foyer, was *When Tomorrow Comes*, starring Irene Dunne and that oil slick on two legs, Charles Boyer. Dylan was extremely disappointed since this looked to be just drivel about drivel and he had been hoping that he might at least get to see a good war film, with plenty of blood and guts being spilled everywhere, or at least a lively cowboy – with lots of bullets and slaughtered Apaches – as long as it wasn't Tom Mix whom he had always loathed even more than Charles Boyer. *When Tomorrow Comes* was probably some sort of weepy love story which always got him laughing like a drain, often leading to his physical removal from the one and nine pennies.

The usherette sat them down in the fifth row from the front and Dylan immediately lit a fag to calm him down since the film hadn't yet started but there was so much banging and crashing going on it felt like they were sitting in the middle of a Luftwaffe air raid.

Most of this noise was coming from the Gallery where boys were rushing back and for to the lavatory hoping to bump into girls. The constant thunder of the hurrying feet sounded like several cattle stampedes over many square miles of plywood mixed with the occasional excited scream of some girl who had been bumped into and, on occasion, felt up. These stampedes became even more furious in the boring bits like Pathe News and one crow from that cockerel who, Dylan thought, looked suspiciously like that noisy bastard in Megan Evans' chicken run and the whole of the Gallery seemed to rise up as one and start rushing around at a hundred miles an hour.

Then, if they were not stampeding, they were booing or hissing the villain or throwing apple stumps at the screen during some steamy clinch. They also tossed lit cigarette ends off the Gallery – which might land on a woman's hat and sizzle nicely for half an hour – or else shower pigs' trotters on the populace below. One night, half way through *Goodbye Mr Chips*, Howard Jones felt half a trotter land in the middle of his slouch hat.

Yes, it was anarchy all the way in the Gallery and Gimpey,

the projectionist, who had lost most of one leg in the Somme, was often forced to move about among them, waving a big stick and threatening the little buggers with a bump on their nappers unless they calmed down.

But it wasn't just the denizens of the Gallery who managed to annoy Dylan since there were already three people sitting around him in the one and nine pennies busy munching on something or other like a swarm of ravenous locusts. He could never work out why people wanted to eat so much when they came here, particularly as the place always stank of Jeyes fluid, and even his own wife was still rustling through her first bag of crisps and making more noise than those noisy bastards up in the Gallery as she attempted to locate that little blue packet of salt.

People had never understood his sensitive nature. *Everything* in the whole wide world gave him a pain in the arse unless he was drunk which, quite simply, was why he drank so much and he really did need one now to steady himself in this great and growing torment all around. *Hasn't she found that bloody salt yet? I mean to say who but her could turn finding a bloody blue packet into such a huge Oscar-winning performance? Why didn't she take a salt cellar in her handbag or something?*

When Tomorrow Comes, it was clear from the opening credits, had far more drips in it than the Cheddar Gorge and concerned a waitress who falls for a concert pianist with a wife as mad as a March hare. Dylan quite fancied – and even approved of – the mad wife. He had always liked his women big and mad and just couldn't understand why this concert pianist had fallen for this crummy waitress who was so emaciated she looked as if she hadn't a square meal in the restaurant where she worked – or indeed in any other restaurant – for at least sixteen years.

But then he noticed that something really miraculous had happened all around him since the story had reached out from the screen and quelled the anarchy all around. Everyone seemed to have got sucked into this doomed love story and there was no noise coming from the Gallery nor was anyone eating although noses were being blown everywhere like the sporadic eruptions of finely-tuned farts as Dylan looked around uneasily and saw that practically every woman in sight was dabbing her eyes and weeping like so many rainy days.

Then, with a genuine horror, which all but made his hair stand on end, he saw that his own wife was at it too. She often went charging around the place waving a battle-axe like the next Queen of the Visigoths but here she was weeping helplessly while also examining her handkerchief, quartering it and trying to find a dry bit. Indeed everyone had now been so completely caught up in the film he was even thinking he might be able to stand up and make a run for the pub, without anyone noticing, when the whole of the audience groaned. The concert pianist was telling the waitress that he was going back to the mad wife. *Oh no! Not the mad wife who was also as frigid as a lump of alabaster. Not the mad wife! Why didn't he just stay with the skinny waitress and live happily ever after tinkling her keys?*

Even Dylan was captured by the story at this point and lit a Woodbine so that he could better think about the romantic implications of this mess when he practically shat himself since Mrs Thomas threw an arm around his neck, dragged his face towards hers and *started to kiss him!*

He was practically screaming with anxiety, outrage and un-expelled Woodbine smoke when the heavens really farted since she began trying to work her tongue half-way down his throat. He'd heard about this French kissing but had never actually suffered it, finding it about as erotic as kissing one of those dog-fish of hers.

This was sheer bloody agony and he looked at her with wide, astonished eyes as she rubbed her wet, salty lips over his. Up on the screen the skinny waitress was walking down the road, shoulders hunched, towards a lifetime of heartbreak. This was the very last time he was ever going to go to the cinema with Mrs Thomas and that was a fact. They had given up that necking lark years ago – and he wasn't even very sure they had even begun – but here she was now trying to suck his tonsils out as he looked back up at the mad wife and wondered if he might yet be saved by the bell in the form of the end of the film.

But just then a huge scream of frustration went up because, with a loud staccato rustling, indicating that something had gone wrong with the projector, the screen went blank and the cinema was plunged into darkness.

This often happened at key moments in the plot and Caitlin gave up her amorous advances and sat back shaking her head as feet stamped thunderously and the air was full of missiles and boos. The house lights came on and the boys in the Gallery all made a mad stampede for the lavatory and you could just about make out the giant silhouettes of Gimpey's hands as he tried to sort out the rogue celluloid.

Dylan leaned forward, letting out a long puff of relieved air, when he spotted the fantastic Dolly James sitting on the other side of the aisle in their row. Now there was a woman who really did manage to stir a whole starburst of twinkles in his dangling bits; every part of her simply stank of fanny and he got such a throb on at the thought of what might be going on in the holy portal between her legs he had to keep crossing and uncrossing them to keep himself in check.

If Caitlin had noticed there was anything strange about his behaviour she didn't show it, just sitting there abstractedly and looking at the blank screen waiting for the film to start again, even taking out her second bag of crisps and beginning the eternal search for the small blue packet of salt. She had never anyway been particularly prone to sexual jealousy, especially where her Ugly Little Suckling was concerned. It was all the other wasteful jealousies she was prone to: of his talent, of his way with people and, more latterly, of his new friend and ally, Yorick the skull.

Dylan pitched forward to look at Dolly again with her wild, corn-coloured curls, lovely boney shoulders and high, tight skirts. It was her stocking garters that always drove the boys in the bar wild. Whether it was deliberate or not you could always make out the lines of those garters through her skirt and, if she was spotted out and about in the town, pushing her baby in the pram, someone, somewhere soon reported back to the Black Lion about what her garters were looking like today. They always looked the same on every day, of course, but the boys in the bar always liked to hear the news about them anyway and then discuss elaborate fantasies about which one they would like to pull down first, whether they would leave them dangling on her ankle or take them right off and all that kind of thing.

He sat back in his seat again and closed his eyes. That woman was becoming a serious mental health hazard, even beginning to crawl around in his dreams with her long gartered legs and pneumatic tits; she was a hot, Arabian desert in her own right; a place full of warm, soft patches with one great pubic oasis where he could lay down his weary head and drink his fill of joy. Oh, cut it out Dylan old boy; just cross your legs and think of Cwmdonkin Drive.

He had tried to engage Dolly in conversation in the street a few times but she had the cold reserve of the unusually glamorous. A woman like her would never put out any signs or come-ons or the men would be all over her so it was all frosty but polite; you may stand there and stare if you must but you may not come any further and you definitely cannot touch anything. So she wasn't about to tell him about any of her little mysteries even if there were a lot to be told.

Yet he was sure that Dolly was here just like most of the other women in the audience and wanting to share in the dream of the day when that great concert pianist was going to appear in New Quay and whisk her out of this cabbage patch to some plush apartment in the middle of the pubs of Soho where he would screw her brains until such time as he had to play a piano concerto in the Albert Hall.

A great woman like that would have her own great dreams

too and he would have loved to have heard about them himself but, meanwhile, they were all to remain sitting in this Bughouse, in a rain of pigs' trotters and fag ends, waiting for Gimpey to fix his projector so they could find out in whose arms *this* concert pianist was going to end up.

Chapter Eight

THE THING that made her lack of love for Dylan doubly unfair, Caitlin decided as she cooked, was that he relied and clung to her so much. She had to provide and he always took; it was never somehow the other way around which was the way she had always understood love. He had never once given her anything except a bad dose of gonorrhoea which had taken an age and several buckets of penicillin to clear up.

She even had to feed him for God's sake and it was all this cooking which she resented most of all, particularly the way that, the next day, she had to do it all over again. The shrimp didn't eat *much* it was true but she had to get something inside him once a day, if only to keep him going. So today she was preparing what he'd had yesterday and the day before that: a stew which consisted of everything that she could lay her hands on which wasn't rotten: *to wit* a head of a lamb, three onions, half a lettuce and a few dogfish, all thrown into a pot and brought to a long boil. She found a few slices of bacon too which smelled distinctly whiffy but threw them in anyway.

That was it: Macnamara Hot-Pot and if he didn't like it, sod him. She might have done a little better if she'd made more money out of that visiting U-boat but the Nazi pound notes had long been used to pay off her bills and there were none left.

Yet she had been mightily relieved when that U-boat had gone away and she could get back to her normal fishing with Verney. Even though she was Irish and – in her eyes – not part of this war she was pretty sure The War Office would have taken an entirely different view of the matter and she would have quickly been interned along with Ossie Mosley and all the other Fascist nutcases had she been caught at it.

Not that giving succour to the enemy was an entirely new practise in these parts, she had been amused to learn, since it had been the worst kept secret of the last world war that U-boats had been calling in the nearby village of Cwmtudu to pick up food, water and a bit of how's your father and no one had ever made much of a fuss about that. There had been a lot of blonde, blue-eyed babies over in Cwmtudu some nine months after the U-boats had left and no one had any sort of official explanation as to how they had all got there to this day.

And she had so enjoyed taking the stores out to the U-boat and particularly liked the way all the men used to come up on the deck and go practically crazy if she showed them a flash of flesh. They all but doubled up in lust at the sheer sight of her mighty legs and she wouldn't have been too surprised of one of them had jumped over the side to get closer to her.

She liked exercising a sexual power over men even if she had pointedly failed to exercise much sexual power over her Dylan. She still managed to get a bit of life out of him on the kitchen flagstones in the afternoon if the baby wasn't crying but, otherwise, he was usually so drunk at night or hungover in the morning she might as well have forgotten about it all together. It was so fucking unfair. The sorry truth was that she just *needed* to be fucked hard and often which made it all the more idiotic that she had teamed up with Dylan in the first place.

Matters hadn't much improved on the kitchen flagstones either since Dylan was now claiming that he had gone down with malaria. How he had caught malaria was anyone's guess since any mosquito that ever bit him would have immediately had to be treated for alcoholic poisoning but there it was. She didn't even believe it was malaria but, whatever it was, he did shake and sweat so much he got as slippery as the fish they hauled out of the sea each tide and she could barely bring herself to grapple with him on the flagstones or indeed to touch him at all.

She had fancied that U-boat captain well enough and he would have been extremely surprised had he gone ashore to find out himself. He had matinee idol looks and fierce blue eyes which suggested he might be extremely lively when he got going. But he never gave any sign of wanting to come ashore; of wanting to work off that million U-boat frustrations between her legs.

Well, they'd made about half a dozen U-boat trades and now, with the electrical system fixed, they had gone away which was good in a way but bad in another. Christmas was coming and, if nothing else, she had always wanted a good shag for Christmas. She wasn't too fussy either but with Dylan laid low by this mysterious malaria it didn't much look as if she was going to get a good shag this Christmas or indeed any other.

YOUNG GARETH was looking forward to the end of the school term and the start of the Christmas holiday since that would give him more time to scuttle around the farm and town, watching out for things. He was almost the unconscious chronicler of life in the area and you could usually spot him hanging around some corner or other, trying to overhear the gossip or spying on all the comings and goings. He was just like some bastard Peeping Tom around the place, swore Dic; didn't miss a bloody thing.

Not that there was much to spy on at the moment and Gareth was only mildly interested in listening to a civil defence meeting one night in the Welfare Hall, attended by half a dozen people and a sack of cabbages inexplicably left behind by the Allotment Society after their Annual General Meeting. A visiting civil defence warden gave a talk about gas masks, gas rattles and fire whistles – which were 'to be rattled or blown very loudly in the event of an incendiary device landing anywhere near you'. The warden also urged them to form a Local Defence Volunteer

Force but the few present were no more interested in doing that than they were when Police Constable Ianto Jones had tried it. Ianto's twelve rifles and twelve bullets were still in his garden shed.

Neither was there much more interest when the warden demonstrated the mysteries of the stirrup pump, going on about how first you had to find the fire, then some water and how you pumped the water on to aforesaid fire.

'I may be very dull but wouldn't it be better to pick up a bucket of water and just throw it on the fire?' asked Captain Port Talbot.

'That's a very good question,' said the warden but he made no attempt to answer it and adjourned the meeting.

Otherwise the only other news item of note was a fight between Dai Fred and Taffy Jones outside the Dolau Inn when Dai refused to loan Taffy his new shirt to go on an outing to Bangor. There was uproar in the street with Taffy shouting about all he had done for Dai over the years, lending him money to buy coal, helping him to pull his potatoes every autumn, painting the front of his house and God knows what else. But still Dai wouldn't part with his new shirt so the two of them got down to a wild fight in which Dai had his new shirt ripped off his back and Taffy acquired two matching black eyes. They duly ended up in their vests before Cardigan Magistrates where they were fined ten shillings each for causing an affray and sternly warned not to do it again.

Meanwhile Gareth was enjoying watching the mood of the town changing with the approach of Christmas: the way the holy patterns of the season could almost be seen taking shape over the climbing streets with the Christmas trees standing in the front parlours of the Bed and Breakfasts, most decked out with glittering stars and golden balls. The windows of the General Stores were covered in a storm of paper tinsel and cotton wool snow and the pubs were organising Turkey Shoots which brought even the most reclusive farmers in from the outlying countryside to play darts for a Christmas turkey except that they were wasting their time since no one ever beat Joshua the Bluebell who could find a treble blindfold. Every year there were strident calls to ban Joshua from the Turkey Shoots or, at the very least, to break his throwing arm and make sure it stayed in splints for the whole of Christmas. Even such seasons of goodwill had their limits but it was all no use because Joshua always managed to make off with the turkey.

Gareth never took part in the singing but, in the absence of anything else to do, he also liked to watch the small band of Christmas carollers which the Rev Enoch took out on the cold nights in the run-up to Christmas. This small band of singing warmth, lit up by their storm lanterns, always seemed to raise the temperature of the cold night air a few degrees as they sang the good news in those great, old carols, urged on by the Rev Enoch who always struck Gareth as rather mad in his fanatical devotion to the cause of a Saviour who looked suspiciously as if he had lost interest in saving anything at all in this lost and warring world of His. But Gareth did admire the old minister's steadfastness and found it all deeply mystifying; he would have liked some of that certainty for himself.

BUT THEN the furniture in Gareth's mind was rearranged rather dramatically in the final few days of school when the usual lessons were set aside as the pupils were allowed to play games among themselves or make Christmas decorations by painting egg shells or fir cones or cutting up paper to make chains. You could also make Christmas crackers from the insides of lavatory rolls and red crepe paper and put small gifts like frog clickers inside them if you had any to hand.

This morning the happy burble of a class enjoying itself began dying down and Gareth looked up to see that a new teacher was supervising them, one of those student teachers possibly because he was very young and they had never seen him before. He was smiling and holding up the palms of his hands as if waiting for everyone to be quiet but it was his smile which Gareth first noticed about him – and would always remember him by – one of the most smilingest smiles he had ever seen with a wide generous mouth and ears that actually seemed to rise up as he did so. His sparkly brown eyes joined in that smile too, glittering with life and intelligence and sitting well with his brown, unruly hair.

With a smile like that you would never know when he was being serious but, that apart, smiling teachers were rare. Most of them seemed to be in a permanent bad mood, particularly their form teacher, Maggie Brown, who may have smiled in the First World War but then clearly wished she hadn't and gave up smiling for good.

'All right, my name is Dafydd ap Iestyn and I'm a student from Trinity,' he said, smiling and rubbing his hands together as if he had just been invited to a wonderful party. 'I've got you lot for about an hour so I thought we might have a sort of general discussion about something. So what's it going to be?'

'We could talk about taking the rest of the day off, sir,' suggested Will Rees.

'What about the cold weather?' said another. 'All the ink wells froze the other day and the boiler broke down too.'

'Come on now. A good discussion about something *serious*. I want to listen to your ideas, to see how you think.'

'Why don't we talk about this war?' Gareth piped up. 'What's it all about anyway?'

'What's it all about? Don't you know what it's all about? Hasn't anyone ever explained it to you?'

'Well, we know we're fighting Germany which is trying to take over Europe. That much we know but Miss Brown says it's not good for us to know about war at our ages.'

The student teacher's smile faltered at that, as if he couldn't quite understand what he had been told, only to brighten again. 'Well, it's probably not good to know about war at any age but perhaps you've asked the wrong questions. Perhaps you should have asked what *Wales* is doing in this war. How is it that we, a proud and independent nation, have got caught up in a power struggle between Germany and the rest of the world?'

He paused, as if waiting for someone to say something, until Gareth said, 'But sir, we're with England aren't we? We're all in Britain, surely, so we're all in this together?'

'Well, in a sense you are right, but let's consider how we, the Welsh, with our own traditions, our own language and our own way of thinking have got locked into this war. The Welsh do not go to war. The Welsh have always been pacifists looking for the Christian path of love. That's the Welsh way.'

This had all become too complicated and theoretical for a class of young rural children who had been carefully protected from the dangers of thinking for themselves. A few passages of Scripture in Sunday School was about all they had ever wrestled with and they had certainly never been specifically invited to think of themselves as any different to the English.

'This war has nothing to do with Wales,' Dafydd continued smilingly while flinging his hands around as he spoke with the ringing certainty of the true believer. 'This is a fight between powerful, industrialised nations, sponsored by world Jewry. We, Wales, are not recognised as a nation so we should have no part in it. I am a Welsh nationalist and am hoping that Germany will one day recognise Wales as a sovereign nation. If we become a nation of our own we will then get out of this war as soon as possible.'

Gareth stared hard at this teacher whose words were already making powerful rumblings in his mind. *The Welsh do not go to war . . . We want Germany to recognise Wales as a nation . . . We will get out of this war as soon as possible . . .* These were all life-changing ideas he had never heard before and here was a teacher who was prepared to tell them something interesting which might also be important. Gareth took a sharp intake of air and could feel a nice headache thickening up at the top of his skull. Now here was something he could really worry about.

One thing was for sure. He was now a Welsh nationalist too. The Welsh nationalists didn't have to work very hard to enlist him.

'All Wales is going to get out of this war is her own destruction which might be another reason not to fight in it. Evil can never beat evil any more than violence can ever overcome violence. They are only ever like themselves, you see, and, when they meet, all that happens is that they get stronger.'

TWO DAYS before Christmas a familiar periscope appeared in the grey swell of sea just off the Welsh coastline and the bedraggled U-boat men took it in turns to watch Caitlin having a piss off the back of Verney's fishing boat. They said nothing as they moved away, only for another to take a look but their tight eyes and mouth told everything of what was going on in their minds and loins.

After the attack by the Mariner they had unloaded most of their men to be taken home in another U-boat and, having been refused permission to scuttle, there were only three now left on board who had somehow managed to limp back here if only because it was here that they had received help the last time. And here were their two great benefactors: one peering into a lobster pot and the other pissing off the back of the boat.

'So, kapitan, have you decided what we are going to do?'

'Well, the options are not exactly great. La Rochelle says we cannot scuttle because the sea is not deep enough here so, as the gearing in the engine has gone too, we either surface and wait to be bombed or we try and hide this boat somewhere.'

'Why can't we just open the sea cocks and scuttle. No one is going to know after all.'

'La Rochelle thinks this boat is packed with military secrets even if we know otherwise. We could easily get rid of the Enigma encryption but there are still those new splashless torpedoes they are so proud of. If we scuttled the Tommies would find them in five minutes at this depth. That new Asdic of theirs is finding everything.'

'And our other options kapitan?'

'Maybe the fisherman Matthews can find us a cave somewhere. Maybe they know a cave where we can put the boat and perhaps make a run for it overland. Our English pound notes have served us well so far and no one seems to have worked out they were made in Berlin.'

'They will, kapitan, they will.'

'It hardly matters. The men have got away home safely. That's all that matters. Now there are just us three. Three men in a boat. The Tommies would die laughing if they knew the half of it. Well let's just hope the fisherman Matthews can find us some fine food so that we can at least enjoy our Christmas.'

IT HAD begun snowing slightly when Caitlin's ears teased out something strange but familiar in the sea-girt morning. Even Verney looked up from his pots too and his nose began running, which was a sure sign of something, when the whole sea began boiling and, the next thing, the U-boat began surfacing and Caitlin realised with a fierce mixture of emotions that their old German pals had come back to see them again.

Indeed her fanny seemed to be winking with real anticipation when the U-boat captain's head appeared in the conning tower and she managed a weak smile and a wave wondering if there might be some pill which would cure her of her permanently sex-starved illness.

'I am afraid there has been a change of plan and we have been forced back here,' Ernst shouted down at them. 'We were hoping you might find a cave or somewhere safe where we could hide this boat.'

Caitlin took hold of the wheel and Verney's nose ran a little faster as everyone stared at one another. Snowflakes fluttered soundlessly around them and even the hovering seagulls seemed to have gone silent as they waited for what was going to be said next.

'We have decided we want to make fast in a cave. If you

86

know of one and can tow us in there we will pay you one hundred pounds. One hundred good English pounds.'

And still Caitlin and Verney just stood there, as if in some bobbing, snow-bound playlet in which everyone had forgotten their lines; only a lone seagull finally cried out, as if in satirical laughter at this particularly mad turn of events, in this war without end.

'WALES IS going to get out of this war soon,' Gareth announced calmly over the evening meal in the farm that night. 'The Welsh nationalists are going to do a deal with Germany and we're going to stop fighting alongside England because the Germans are going to recognise Wales as a sovereign nation. Anyway you won't be catching me fighting in any war when I grow up. I'm a Welsh pacifist who believes in the Christian path of love.'

Every member of the family stopped eating and looked at him with cold stares and comically arched eyebrows as if he'd gone soft in the head.

'Someone's been stuffing that boy with mad ideas,' said Dic. 'Who've you been talking to now?'

'Haven't been talking to anyone,' Gareth replied, indignant. 'I've just decided I don't believe in war because I'm a pacifist. Peace and love, that's what we pacifists believe in.'

'What he means by pacifist is that he's a pain in the neck,' Dic interpreted. 'Always has been. Always will be. Nothing but a pain in the neck.'

'Oh, leave the boy alone,' said Mrs Morgan. 'He's just interested in the new. His mind is feeling its way. Weren't you like that when you were a child?'

'I'd never be a pacifist who wouldn't fight for his country,' Dic snorted. 'I may have done a lot of daft things, but spouting rubbish about pacifism wasn't one of them.'

'Gareth's not spouting rubbish,' Mrs Morgan said coldly. ' I agree with him. All this killing is not the Welsh way. If we'd been a proper nation in charge of our own affairs we might have been able to stay out of this stupid war.'

'You'll change your tune soon enough when Hitler comes marching over this farm,' Trefor pointed out.

'I'll just do to Hitler what I do to everyone else who comes to this farm,' Mrs Morgan said.

'What's that then?'

'Offer him a cup of tea and something to eat. Gareth is right. No one ever causes you harm if you give them a cup of tea and something to eat. Trouble only starts when you take a gun to people. Then they take a gun *to you*.'

'You'll be saying next you've joined the nationalists,' Dic sneered.

'I might be one already. You never know do you? Perhaps Gareth and me will sign up with them in the New Year.'

'Why don't we do it now,' Gareth wanted to know.

'Just shut up and finish your food, you.' Tada had joined in the debate. 'Otherwise, pacifist or no, you're going to get a good clip around the ear.'

Gareth deeply resented the way his family – except, of course, his Mam – always treated him like a stupid child. They even made him go through the palaver of leaving out a glass of sherry and a mince pie for Father Christmas when he knew full well that Tada brought the presents into his bedroom. He also had to go through the nonsense of taking a stocking to bed and only agreed to that because he didn't want to risk losing whatever they might put in it.

IT WAS the sheer variety of the presents on the great morning that told him they hadn't a clue how old he was or even how old they wanted him to be.

The little child got lots of sweets – aniseed balls, gob-stoppers, a packet of peardrops, six chocolate medals and an Eskimo block – a chocolate as cold to the taste as a lollipop. The big boy got a Meccano No. 2 set and a toy bomb and some caps. I ask you. What was a pacifist who believed in peace and love going to do with a toy bomb and some caps? Then there was a card of plasticine, chalks, *The Universal Book of Hobbies and Handicrafts* and a flicker book with match-stick men.

Just English rubbish, really. Why didn't they at least give him something in Welsh?

ALL THE Morgans went together to the Christmas morning service in the Towyn Welsh Congregational Chapel. Corners became dangerous with wobbling bicycles, gaudy new scooters or huge wooden trains which could easily break your toe. Sunshine was busy melting the early frost on the windows and the sea looked warm enough to swim in with the whole Bay glazed by a yellow phosphorescence.

Occasionally the heads of seals bobbed up, black on yellow, as if they were wondering where their presents were. There were no ships around, not even a patrolling Corvette – everyone gone home, it seemed, to enjoy Christmas away from the war.

People came from all over for the morning service, making their way on foot up the slopes or, if they were from outlying parts, in the odd car, on horseback or even in a tractor they parked at a discreet distance away around a corner. Yet it didn't look as if they were attending a celebration of a holy birth since a lot of the women looked as solemn as if they were going to a funeral with their black handbags, lisle stockings, polished leather shoes and dark serge coats. The men were also dressed as if for a party in a cemetery, having squeezed themselves into ill-fitting suits which smelled of mothballs and now sitting on the packed chapel pews with unhappy fingers poking around inside high starched collars which had chafed many burly necks red raw. The regulars carried Bibles under their arms to follow The Reading.

The friendliness and sense of occasion were real enough with unusual fervour in the hymn-singing and the Rev Enoch mounting the pulpit and speaking with thoughtfulness and some passion about how, even on this very special day, on which we remember a mother struggling to give birth on the floor of a stable, the arrows of death are flying thick and fast across Europe. We should, in these times of darkening evil, be sure to take extra care that we hold fast to whatsoever is true, good and beautiful so that we could then live within the loving spirit of the Lord, he went on, the night is long and dark and all we can know for sure is that everything is going to get far worse yet.

He spoke with his half-moon spectacles dangling perilously off the end of his nose as his long fingers trembled over the opened pages of a huge Bible with ornate leather covers and gilt fastenings. His white hair had its usual winged shapelessness but it was the tearful supplication of his words that the congregation found the most moving. In the great Welsh pulpit tradition he spoke as a dying man speaking to dying men.

'THE WELSH became good at language by listening to preachers like old Enoch,' Mrs Morgan said as the family walked back to the farm. 'Men like him made the Welsh what they are. Our souls were hammered out on the anvil of the pulpit. Those preachers were our social engineers. John Elias, Evan Roberts, Christmas Evans. They all spoke with the tongues of dragons and we called them Eight-Inch Nails. I'd have given anything for young Gareth here to have gone into the pulpit.'

Gareth wasn't so sure about that and already saw himself worrying about his future as a preacher on the outside lavvy. There was nothing easy in life, he knew. Not even on Christmas Day.

'Did you notice that Dylan Thomas sitting just near us?' Mrs Morgan went on. 'A queer cove he is. Never seemed to be part of the service, never singing with the others. He gives me the shivers. Just looking all the time. Looking at everyone and everything.'

'He made a few notes when Enoch spoke,' said Dic. 'Jotted down some of his words on the back of a cigarette packet. The other week I saw him standing outside the chapel, listening to Enoch speaking and jotting down his words. He does it all the time. Makes notes all the time. In the streets and the General Stores. He's always at it in the Black Lion too.'

'I'm worried he's going to write us up,' Mrs Morgan said.

'Why worried?' asked Gareth.

'I don't want New Quay written up that's why. This is my home and writers never give the proper picture. They select and exaggerate. You can never find the truth in them.'

'I didn't know you were a critic,' Tada said.

'I used to read a lot before I got so worn out on this farm. I used to eat books for breakfast and one day I might start reading again.'

'I tell you who should be written up and that's that wife of his,' Dic said. 'She and Verney were around the farm the other day offering to buy any produce we had to spare. Offering really good prices too – cash on the nail.'

'Up to no good on the black market no doubt.'

'Aye. If they've started a black market out at sea – they've been spotted loading stuff in Verney's boat.'

'Where would they sell it at sea?'

'Who knows? Verney's not telling and everyone is too afraid to ask her out straight because she throws a terrific punch, often for just looking at her. Hit Dylan a real wallop the other night. They were in the bar and there he was, blood gushing out of his nose, but he still kept telling us some disgraceful story about a woman with giant breasts who tried to drown herself in Swansea Bay but kept bobbing up again.'

'That's enough of that,' said Mrs Morgan, sharp. 'Let's remember it's Christmas Day, shall we?'

THE FAMILY ate Christmas dinner on the bees-waxed refectory table in the main parlour. The only item older than the table was the oak dresser which had been patched with bits of wood from the coffins of various members of the Morgan family going back hundreds of years. This dresser was festooned with lines of old pewter, which no one liked, as well as Swansea and Nantgarw plate, which no one touched.

They worked through the soup, turkey and a black and brown Christmas pudding with silver sixpences in it as silently and carefully as the road men at the end of a working day. Then a few dry sherries loosened everyone up and the family banter began, mostly about how Dic had once again managed to get most of the sixpences and poor Gareth hadn't got one. Gareth tried to pretend he didn't care, but he was furious.

LATER IN the afternoon the men, their party hats awry, untied their belts and snoozed in front of the fire. Mrs Morgan and Peggy washed up before setting out piles of sandwiches and bowls of trifle.

When the dark fell the Penderyn family came over from the next farm and they all played charades, sang songs and acted the goat. Dic was the loudest, as usual, but Gareth left them all to it and went out into the kitchen where he sat on his own, roasting some chestnuts on a shovel.

It was his Mam who came out to look for him finally but, try as she might, she couldn't get Gareth to explain to her why he was crying on his chestnuts.

'There's things happening to me I don't understand and it's all getting too difficult,' he sobbed as she held him in her big, loving arms. 'Life's unfair, Mam. Everything about it is so unfair.'

'There, there, *cariad*. Eat a few of these chestnuts. Make you feel a lot better they will.'

Chapter Nine

IT WAS an unusually warm New Year's Eve and, as per tradition, the whole of New Quay was getting decked out in fancy dress ready to greet the New Year, flat on their faces and with hangovers which would stretch right into February.

Even so early the first of the revellers were beginning to move around the streets as elaborately dressed kings and queens, women masquerading as rugby players, witch doctors with bones through their noses and carrying cauldrons, vicars promenading with their tarts, randy doctors in search of compliant nurses and cavemen with long, black wigs and big, cardboard clubs which squeaked when they hit anything.

Dylan, who had never been much of a one for fancy dress, and had settled for his normal tattered worsted jacket and trademark dickey bow, was attempting to stay out of the way of this gathering bedlam, drinking with his cronies in the corner of the bar in the Black Lion. He was just three pints gone and telling them how he had lost his new shoes two days earlier and then gone from the General Stores to the Post Office to the Black Lion looking for them. But the real humour in his story came from the way he mimicked the various replies – he did a particularly good Percy Hoskins and Captain Port Talbot – and those listening could see that, drunk or sober, Dylan had already entered deep into the community; that he had a wonderful ear for the way people spoke and he had already got a lot of their mannerisms down to a tee.

The party outside had still not quite got going and the bar

was relatively empty when Dylan fell silent as a woman, dressed completely in black crinoline, walked in and sat at a table on her own. Unwilling to look anyone directly, her eyes were always lowered and she had the sharp, dark features of a Stone Age axehead.

A lot of eccentric people had begun flowing into New Quay since the start of the war but none quite so odd as this one whom Dylan had already dubbed The Black Widow. She remained sitting at her table with her head bowed like a professional mourner waiting for the start of a funeral when Percy Hoskins noticed her and took her a pint of cider. She counted some coins out of her purse into his hand and he returned to his position manning the pumps behind the bar. Nothing had been said throughout the transaction – not even a please or a thank you – and it was rumoured that The Black Widow didn't actually know any words since, not only did she *never* speak, but she sometimes started weeping and no amount of friendly questions from Dylan – or any of the other boys in the bar – would get her to reveal her name, where she came from or what the hell she was always weeping about.

Joshua the Bluebell reckoned she had lost her husband in the war, possibly between the legs of some beefy French tart in the Resistance. Dai Fred guessed she had got so hungry she might even have just *eaten* her husband – which is the sort of dull remark you might expect from Dai Fred – although they all then decided that might well have made her happy rather than sad. Dylan reckoned it had to be something to do with the sky-high prices that Percy always charged for his scrumpo.

All eyes remained locked on her until she took her first sip of cider but, as soon as she settled down into her famous imitation of a locked museum on a Sunday, all interest re-gathered around the story of Dylan and his missing new shoes although he hardly had time to remember where he had left off when a sugar plum fairy, complete with falsies, a tutu and wand came crashing amongst them. Dic Morgan.

'You look really, really lovely, Dic,' said Dylan with mock awe. 'You should always go around like that and you'd be picking up women all over the place.'

'I pick up women all over the place already. They're following me around already and I've been telling a couple of them that, if they want a right good seeing to, I'll meet them down at the slipway at midnight.'

'The slipway at midnight?'

'That's what I told them. I tell you what. There's more drunken shagging goes on down the slipway at New Year's Eve than there is in Rio at carnival time.'

Dylan looked straight at Dic, barely able to think of anything to say in the face of this startling revelation. *Drunken shagging down under the slipway here in chapel-bound New Quay? You'd expect it in Rio for sure and he'd done a fair bit of drunken shagging in Soho in his time but he never thought he'd come across it here. And out in the sea winds too! And on top of all those limpets. And what would happen if they wanted to launch the lifeboat over all those shagging arses? That wouldn't look very pretty would it?*

He glanced over at The Black Widow who was already warming up her nightly cabaret with a few quiet head-shakings of grief, and he fervently hoped *she* didn't go in for any drunken shagging under the slipway at midnight although, come to think of it, a bit of drunken shagging might well cheer her up no end.

'I'll tell you all one thing,' Dic went on, waving his wand around a bit. 'There are often half a dozen husbands who become proud fathers in the autumn and they've had nothing to do with it. I'd be as unhappy as toothache if my Peggy had a baby on this or any other autumn.'

'Now let's get one thing straight before we go anywhere,' said Dylan. 'If I go down to the slipway at midnight am I likely to find your Peggy down there doing a bit of drunken shagging?'

'No, you are not,' Dic exploded amidst general laughter. 'All

I was saying was it wouldn't look good if she gave birth in the autumn – *or any other woman for that matter.'*

'Right, well I'll give the place a miss then, Dic. We poets don't want to get mixed up in any of that old midnight malarkey do we?'

'No you do not. All that won't do your poetry any good at all and, if you *do* get mixed up in it, for gawd's sake take a big bag of French letters with you or you'll get buried in paternity suits come the autumn.'

CAITLIN CAME into the bar, dolled up as a Christmas tree with a star of Bethlehem in her hair, and sat next to Dylan who could see, at a glance, that she was in a foul mood so he just kept going with another story about a bat who allegedly kept chasing him down the coast road to Majoda.

'He's just like a fucking sheepdog he is, fluttering around my head and laughing at me as I scoot along the road. One night he's going to get tangled up in my hair and I'm going to have to get the barber to cut him out but . . . '

Caitlin didn't join in the general merriment and merely scowled as Dylan kept going on about how this bat was waiting in his cave for stop tap so that he could chase him. She hated the way he always made people laugh and left her on the outside yet again. They never laughed when she told any of her stories and, on the contrary, many in the group actually looked at her as if she was a monster from outer space. Well she wasn't going to take this any more and, without saying a word, stormed out of the bar, leaving Dylan getting worried as he saw her disappearing backside.

A FEW minutes later he decided he'd better go out and look for her, slipping out into the partying streets, smiling and hanging on to his cigarette for support as he made his way through this carnival throng with people occasionally calling out to him familiarly, even though he often didn't have a clue who they were, particularly in their fancy dress. They even seemed relaxed enough with him to try out a few mild insults too with the most popular being: 'I've read some of your poetry, Mr Thomas, and I didn't understand a bloody word.' But even someone as thin-skinned as him didn't mind that jibe because he very often hadn't understood a bloody word either. Fog wrapped in fog, he once described his poetry and he wasn't about to start explaining it to any of these idiots either even if he could which he couldn't.

Everywhere he wandered colourful streams of pantomime drunks were swirling from the top of the town down to the Yacht Club and chip shop on the quay and then wandering back up the slopes again to the other outlying pubs. Two of the cavemen were hitting one another on the head laughing merrily at the squeaks and the Rev Enoch strode past on the way back to the sober safety of his manse, glaring angrily at Dylan as if the poet was responsible for the growing bedlam of yet another drunken, decadent New Year's Eve.

Dylan paused among the jostling on the pavement outside The Cambria Hotel where, through the bar window, he saw Caitlin sitting next to The Ancient Mariner and talking to three strange men. He moved back a little out of the line of their sight although they just remained within his. He had noticed these three men around the town a few times before and they made him uneasy, if only because of their clear desire not to be noticed. Yet, the more they tried to shrink into the background, the more noticeable they seemed to become.

He had tried to ask Caitlin casually who they were but hadn't got too far on that front; she had said that they were three soldiers from neutral Norway who were resting here for a while before returning to the war and just needed a little help. But he hadn't believed her, was convinced she was lying, in fact, since he could always tell when she was lying because she was at it more or less all the time. He was also convinced she wasn't getting all those new pound notes from Augustus John either, as she had so often claimed, but as Dylan had accepted more than a few of them by now, it seemed churlish to complain. At least the rent on Majoda had been paid up to date and there *was* food on the table.

One of those Norwegians from Norway made him particularly nervous with his matinee idol looks and ferocious blue-eyed stare. Even despite his various and persistent infidelities Dylan could still feel the sudden cold lapping of jealousy deep in his guts; he still felt uneasy if he saw someone who might threaten his marriage and that blue-eyed bastard would certainly be capable of that. He knew Mrs Thomas all too well, unfortunately, and had long known what she was capable of even though he usually dealt with any of her sexual calamities by ignoring them. Even when Nosey Parkers told him what his wife was up to he ignored them largely because he was usually feeling so guilty at whatever it was he had been up to lately.

But, given the festive spirit of the night, he managed to shake off his unease and surrender himself to the party again, drifting back down the slopes, surfing all this chattering exuberance and stopping off at The Dolau Inn where the landlord immediately gave him not one but two pints which he had to hold in both hands. There didn't even seem to be anywhere to put one down either so he sort of managed to drink them both at the same time while also chatting to the landlord who was hoping Dylan and his pals might start coming to the Dolau more often when, who knows, he might get a few more free drinks.

Certainly everyone seemed to be taking to him and he was already feeling nicely and warmly enfolded here, known to almost everyone as a famous writer so they always liked to tell him about the local characters with the landlord of the Dolau now pointing at a farmer in the lounge who, for this one night and one night only, brought out his two women, allegedly sisters and now sitting on either side of him, both as pale and expressionless as a pair of porcelain dogs on a mantelpiece, except that *he slept in the middle of them* and it was all, apparently, a very cosy arrangement. The two 'sisters' also dressed identically and all three of them were now staring silently at the fire. A trio so dull, Dylan thought, could hardly be up to something so interesting as three in a bed but that was New Quay for you.

The night kept taking on an ever more surreal quality and Dylan, who was already getting nicely and babbly drunk, felt as though he might be walking through some fevered nightmare with high blood pressure. He was taking a piss in one lavatory when a man, dressed as an Egyptian mummy, came stumbling in next to him to have one too, only to realise the vastness of his mistake and waving his hands around uselessly since he couldn't even start working out how he was going to extricate his bursting dick from all those bandages so he just decided to stand there and piss himself.

Mad, painted faces reared up around him. The witch doctor tripped over his cauldron and had to be taken to hospital. A Viking had a fight with a Red Indian. *I've just read a few of your poems, Mr Thomas, and they were absolute rubbish.* A fat woman was sitting on a wall dressed as a fairy ballerina, her face looking like a Keep Death off the Road sign but with her fat legs open wide and something bushy up there winking deep and dark invitations to him. His hormones started jangling and he could almost feel the pet dog of his good behaviour struggling to slip its leash. *Dylan, come and have a drink with us over here.*

He had never actually known so many people who were as mad as this and they did sometimes get him down. You would never think there was a war on and the blackout was only ever imposed sporadically if at all. Even his own people in his home town of Swansea seemed quite normal compared to this lot although, when he did come to write his play about them, it would be the world outside that was mad and the people inside who would be sane. Or something.

Big Ben boomed out of various wirelesses and some sang

Auld Lang Syne as various lipsticked horrors kept kissing him. Hands were also wandering everywhere where hands weren't supposed to wander and, while he was well pissed, he wasn't nearly well pissed enough for all this and began becoming a little lost and tearful, wanting to be with his Caitlin and going back to The Cambria Hotel only to find she had left there along with The Ancient Mariner and those three Norwegians from Norway.

He had lost interest in the party, although he was drinking more and more as he went from pub to pub, now getting it into his head that his Caitlin had heard all about that drunken shagging under the slipway too and she had gone down there to join in the midnight malarkey. He actually fell off the slipway on to the sand although, miraculously, he managed to hold on to his pint of beer, now walking around the rocks and peering closely at the pumping buttocks of various couples while also trying to work out if any of them had the distinctive dimples of Mrs Thomas.

Cries and sighs slipped around the dark sands in whirlpool eddies as he continued looking around, occasionally stopping to take a thoughtful sip of beer as he spotted another pair of pumping buttocks and heard the occasional groans of deep primal passion. It was a strange, underworld moment of forbidden love games: another side of the Welsh psyche which he had barely guessed existed and he found that he was getting caught up in the excitement of it all too and, while he had first been there looking for his wife, he was now wandering around with his little man standing to attention while waiting, with some impatience, to be called up to the front line and get into some action of his own.

The dark and feckless anonymity of it all was both frightening and attractive but a squeak of real fear caught in the back of his throat when the silhouette of a woman with long corkscrew curls loomed over him. She was taller than him but he could feel the anxious warmth of her gin-soaked breath on his face. The faint starlight then revealed a few more details: a glittering Thirties flapper dress and a string of black beads coiled around her neck. She was also holding a drink in one hand and a long cigarette holder in the other. On one leg, plainly visible just above the knee, was a bold, black garter.

She dropped her cigarette holder on to the sand and took his pint off him before putting it down on a rock next to her own. Then she put her hands on his shoulders and used a slight amount of pressure to sit him down. Next she hitched up her skirt around her waist and sat down next to him taking his hand and placing it firmly between her legs as she lay back. Immediately sober he felt she had no knickers on and, moving his fingertips around in the reasonably dense forest of her short and curlies, the only words that came into the great poet's mind were: *Oh shit, just what the hell do I do now?*

But it soon became apparent he didn't have to do anything at all because she was happy to do it for him and, when she had eased down his trousers down below his knees, she sort of lifted him above her like one of those big silver claws in glass cubicles in a fairground which pick up toy teddy bears and immediately drop them. Except that this little teddy wasn't about to be dropped back on to the heap with all the other teddies but held directly above the hole into which his little man was lowered with a perfect and expert precision.

Oh bugger me black and blue with a broken bottle this is amazing. I'm into the holy melting pot with the stew all hot and bubbling and I don't even seem to have touched the sides. She's going to swallow me wholesale and I'm going to disappear for good if I don't watch it, down in the doomed darkness where I'll probably bump into that man I'm always telling them about in the pub who's been down here in a place like this for weeks looking for his horse and cart.

He began feeling the winds filling her sails so, like the champion lover he was, he took hold of the ship's wheel and began taking her on the long stormy voyage home, aware her legs were waving around in the high, sea winds all around as the swelling tides of her desperation and frustration got even higher and he had to hang on to that wheel grimly as he took her up on to an even higher roller where, as he fought to keep control of it all, she began crying out in Welsh in words he couldn't understand. By now they were sailing straight into the teeth of a tempest and she was still fervently declaiming something in Welsh when, without so much as a brief warning from a friendly lighthouse, he lost control of his ship and, with a short, hot dribble, it listed to starboard, capsized and sank without a single bubble. His erection managed to pack its bag and jump over the sides too and that, in a manner of speaking, was that.

Even as the ship of his roiling lust actually landed on the sea-bed he knew he hadn't done well by her; he had just lost control and done nothing to slake her hunger. He'd simply had too much to drink to put in a decent performance, he thought as he looked to one side wondering where she'd put his pint. He actually did quite well on three or four pints but any more and it was more miss than hit.

But he couldn't see much point in trying to explain his shortcomings to her – nor did he even have the opportunity – since she had already eased him off her, stood up, smoothed down her dress and, without so much as a polite goodbye or a boo, baa, bob's your arse, picked up her drink and wandered off unsteadily into the burbling, panting darkness, leaving the hot gun-smoke of her sexual frustration hanging in the cold night air behind her.

Dylan, with a patch of damp sand on the end of his nose and two matching ones on the knees of his trousers, was as dead and deflated as all the French letters on the beach all around him so he quickly buttoned up his trousers, located what was left of his pint and made his way back to the celebrating town.

An impromptu jug band was playing in the bar of the Black Lion and he was surprised at the fierceness of his joy, which flared in the midst of all his sexual guilt, when he spotted

Caitlin dancing with all the others. If she had worried about where he'd got to that night she was now far to drunk to care, jigging around with that fairy star still on her head but with most of the pine needles of her Christmas tree having fallen off.

He wasn't to know that the reason why Caitlin was so happy was because she had just managed to get herself a good shag on New Year's Eve although it wasn't with any of the three 'Norwegians from Norway' as she had perhaps hoped, and neither was it on the beach by the Lifeboat Station but rather unromantically with Dic Morgan on the floor of the beer cellar in the Black Lion.

Dylan called for a large whisky and sat at the bar with The Black Widow, who was looking unusually morose, as he watched his beloved dance. There she was roaring with life and laughter, the mother of his beautiful children and he had gone and betrayed her again. And on bloody New Year's Eve too. This was no way to start the New Year. This was a stupid way to start the New Year this was.

Chapter Ten

WITH THE turning of the year snow began to fall thickly and unexpectedly on the town and outlying fields, making life difficult on the farms because the sheep often got themselves stuck in snowdrifts and all hands had to turn out and prod the drifts with poles to find them and dig the 'brainless buggers' out.

But Tada Morgan never worried about the missing sheep who could last for three days buried in snow, without any apparent ill effects, he said, since they ate their own wool for grease and often came out as bald and rough as a badger's bum and had to be carried back to the barn to thaw out. The real problem with this snow was that it was lambing time and it made life difficult for the men as they stumbled around the fields, knee-deep in snow and slush, as they searched for any luckless ewes about to give birth.

This was a favourite time for Gareth, who was always allowed out for the lambing, often up late and, in the light of the hurricane lamp, kneeling down with the labouring ewe and talking to her softly as, with her warm breath pluming cloudily around her mouth, her black eyes bulged with pure fear and he tried to ease out the small fetlocks sticking out of her behind.

He pulled on the stubborn fetlocks a little more and there was a quick loosening as the baby's long body slid out, its whole length swathed in a milky blue sac as it tumbled out on to the snow, the jellied mass looking untidy and without any recognisable shape until he lifted it all up into the air and swung it around a few times like a lasso before stripping off the placenta and throwing it to the waiting dog and now putting the lamb on the freezing grass when he held his hands in worshipful acclaim as the formless mass took shape and jerked upright on bandy, wobbling legs, turning its tiny head sideways until it mouth opened with its first plaintive cry of life.

He placed it next to the mother who began licking it clean with her rough tongue, which also helped the blood flow, before feeling around up the ewe's twitching backside again, trying to find another set of fetlocks to tug on. The small body yielded almost immediately; the second birth was never as difficult as the first.

Gareth never got tired during the lambing season – no matter how late or dark it was – because it was impossible to ever tire of that miraculous moment when you slipped the jelly of that lamb's body and that which had been dead came alive before your very eyes and a tremble of warm kindness hung in the cold air. Every birth seemed like the first and everyone in the Morgan family – even dull old Trefor and cynical fat Dic – felt the same, often moved to tears, particularly if it had been a difficult one which they'd had to work on for up to an hour.

THE SNOW had a wonderfully invigorating effect on the Rev Enoch who, despite his advancing years and rumours of arthritis, continued his pastoral rounds like a ball with plenty of bounce.

'This is all absolutely marvellous isn't it?' he said to Mrs Stephen Stephens as she slipped and slid towards the General Stores. 'Snow always tells me something about the Resurrection, about the Lord is always prepared to make everything new again.'

Mrs Stephen Stephens, who hated all this snow with a real passion, looked at him as if he'd just had a bash on the head with a big brick but kept her suspicions to herself.

Yet the town *had* been given a fantastic and unexpected

redecoration, one day looking shabby and down-at-heel and the next with everything decked out in fresh colour and vibrant poise. The drab streets had been covered with smooth, white, fitted carpets. The cinema, church and chapel had acquired fluffy, white helmets and blinging icicles hung in uneven lines off the gutterings of the Lifeboat Station with even the fishing boats in the harbour looking brand, spanking new in their foaming white overalls. Only the seagulls looked unimpressed as they stood sullenly on the quay walls, their beaks turning directly into the freezing winds blowing in off the sea.

Three children were busy trying to build a snowman near the chip shop when the Rev Enoch stopped them to deliver another of his little Biblical homilies. 'Children, what I want you to do is try and stare directly into a pile of snow without blinking. Sometimes you can spot angels when you do this. Angels are usually invisible but, if you stare at the snow without blinking, you can often spot them going about their work.'

THE NEXT day the snow had thawed a bit as Gareth ran along the rough, coastal road towards Cliff House, barely pausing to look at the nodding daffodils in the snowy banks or the bright shivers of blossom in the hedgerows before letting himself in through the back door without knocking and sitting himself down at the kitchen table where he helped himself to a slice of bread and butter. Dolly was standing at the sink peeling potatoes and she didn't even turn to see who had come into the kitchen and was now stealing her bread and butter.

'You're early. Have they finished with the lambing yet?' she asked finally picking up a potato and examining it closely. 'There's worms in some of these.'

'Most of them are done but Tada says there's still about half a dozen we've got to keep an eye on. The ewes can usually manage on their own but they can get themselves into one hell of a mess if there's no one watching over them.'

'Yes, I suppose we all need someone to watch over us in

some way or another. None of us are much good on our own.'

'Did you ever let anyone look after you, Aunt Dolly, a man I mean?'

'There's been too many really – but I never got on with any of them, never found one I wanted to settle down with anyway. Yet I would like to meet the right man, to get married one day. Oh yes, marriage would be nice if Mr Right came along. But where would I find the right man now I have a baby of my own and particularly here in New Quay?'

'The Battling Thomases seem to be having a lot of trouble with their marriage. They had another big fight in the pub the other night and she even loosened a few of his teeth, Dic was saying.'

'What was it about? Did you hear?'

'Well, it seems there's some newcomers in the town who are from Norway and Mr Thomas seems to have got it fixed in his head that Mrs Thomas has taken a fancy to one of them.'

'Well, well, and there's Dylan Thomas such a good and faithful husband too.'

'There was murder in the Cambria Hotel, I heard and Mr Thomas, as drunk as a wheel as usual, went in there, found Mrs Thomas talking to these Norwegians and dragged her out by the hair. Once out in the street she managed to grab *him* by the hair and began pulling him around the pavement until the Norwegians broke it up. Then Mr Thomas began running home followed by Mrs Thomas who was throwing rocks at him until he managed to get into bed where he was safe. She never attacks him in bed, it seems. As long as gets in between the sheets he's all right.'

'And these Norwegians? Where do they live?'

'No idea. They seem to just come and go like ghosts, Dic says, although he does think that Mr Thomas might be right and Mrs Thomas is, how would you put it, lying down with one of them.'

'I just don't know how people can carry on like that. I really don't. Maybe all this fighting is their way of showing love. But it's not for me. I like tenderness in my men. I like my men to love me gently.'

'How many men have you had, Aunt Dolly?'

'Never you mind.'

'Go on. Tell me.'

'A few. But I don't want to talk about it.'

'Go on. I won't tell anyone. I'm Gareth, your new son, remember. We've no secrets between us. So. How many?'

'Well, there was the father of The Boy, of course. He's still around in London somewhere. A few others too.'

'How many?'

'Too many. Far too many. But I'm going to tell you another of my secrets now, Gareth. A top secret for your ears only. I'm always a good girl 'til I've had a few drinks and then I'm anyone's.'

Gareth swallowed hard on this bit of hot information. 'Anyone's?'

'Anyone's. That's why I almost never drink. I'll kiss any man – and do anything – after I've had a drink, and always regret it when I'm sober the next morning.'

'Why do you do it, then?'

'Well that's a good question to which I've no good answer. Something takes me over when I've had a drink. And I'll tell you another secret. When I've had a drink *and* I'm kissing a man I start spouting verses from the Bible *in Welsh*.'

'But you don't know Welsh.'

'I know. But a few drinks and a warm man, and I'm coming out with verses from Matthew and Psalms and God knows what else.'

'How can you come out with verses from the Bible when you're kissing a man? I mean, how do you talk with your mouth full?'

'Well, you know, not kissing exactly but, you know, having a bit of a rub, if you know what I mean.'

Gareth's mind and body were in a real turmoil, exploding with all kinds of dirty thoughts and images, mostly to do with Dolly's secret places, and making him quite ill. He was deeply fascinated by this new mother of his and still regarded that first moment when she had called out to him on the road to get her something from the General Stores as holy. When he had come back she had given him a glass of pop and had admitted to him – *to him!* – that she was very lonely here and had quickly befriended him to the degree that Gareth now thought of nothing else and almost all his waking thoughts were now centred on her and the way her body went in and out in all the right places. He had even long stopped worrying that his Mam was going to run away to America without him and couldn't even remember the last time Caitlin Thomas's left tit had floated across his deeply troubled mental landscapes.

'But I shouldn't tell you *all* my secrets,' she went on, clearly unaware of the deep sexual and emotional turmoil she was stirring up in her new young friend. 'A woman has to have some secrets of her own although I will tell you another thing. I have decided to learn Welsh and have got a nice student teacher, Dafydd, to start giving me lessons.'

'That wouldn't be Dafydd ap Iestyn would it? *Oh him.* He's a really great teacher, taught us about Welsh nationalism in school just before Christmas.'

'Yes, he told me about that and he got into a lot of trouble too. The parents didn't like it.'

'He won't care. He's a real man with real courage and I'm sure he'll teach you a lot of Welsh too. I'll come over and test you after he's gone.'

'You do that. I've got to crack this Welsh business somehow. Maybe I'll get a few more people talking to me if I do.'

DYLAN STOOD at the window of Majoda, wearing three pullovers and with a cigarette in his mouth as he stared out at his frozen garden and the placid waters of the Bay. All this

February cold was hurting his feet and the poetry was not going well, as could be seen by the scrunched up balls of paper all over the floor. Relations with his wife were also at an all-time low as several fresh cuts and bruises on his face vividly testified; he had never been able to make any sense of this constant war of love, the way they kept throwing missiles and pain at one another from their own senseless but deep trenches.

Such morning moments were always bad for him, his early hangover still hanging there while other concerns kept entwining around his other larger concerns – general concerns about his bills and debts, new demands from the revenue men and other sundry people, particularly impressionable young women, he had plundered yet again in search of he knew not what. He always behaved badly, he accepted, but he always felt guilt about this bad behaviour as if this somehow made it all right.

He ducked out of sight when he saw the Rev Enoch coming up his garden path trottily, rushing this way and that around his living room and almost quailing when there were three loud knocks on the front door. Ministers of the cloth always put the fear of God into him – as perhaps they were paid to do – and he badly needed Caitlin here now to protect him except she had gone shopping to the General Stores or might even be out shagging one of those Norwegians from Norway for all he knew. She had been unusually happy lately which suggested that she was getting it from somewhere and it certainly wasn't from him who had been too malarial to do anything.

The front door was pounded three more times and the beleaguered poet would have ignored them altogether except he was worried a few more such knocks might dislodge something important in the structure of his frail, asbestos house.

'Just a Christian call of love,' the Rev Enoch announced brightly as Dylan held the door a few inches ajar. 'Just want to find if everything is all right with our resident word mechanic in this age of snow.'

The door opened a few more inches.

'I make it my business to call on everyone in the parish but I can come back another time if it's not convenient now.'

Dylan opened the door wide to let the minister in, sitting down at his work table, presided over by Yorick, and indicating that the Rev Enoch should pull up a pew in the shape of one of Barry Island's missing deckchairs.

'Yes, everyone should be visited and no one escapes,' the Rev Enoch smiled as he looked behind him carefully before letting his bum make the long drop into the deckchair. 'I've noticed you a few times in the chapel trying to hide in the back row. But you've never been what we might call regular have you?'

'Not regular, no. Never regular,' Dylan said hesitantly and looking from side to side on the floor as if he had just lost something important down there while also unconsciously mimicking the Rev Enoch's quirky, interrogative speech patterns. 'Anything but regular,' he added redundantly, unwilling to even look directly at his reverend visitor.

'Was your attendance regular when you were young, Mr Thomas?'

'No, never regular. Off and on, you know, but never regular.'

The Rev Enoch had an amused twinkle in his eyes and Dylan could have seen, had he looked up, which he didn't, that the old minister was probably wondering why this man was known as a magician with words. No one had clearly ever explained to the visiting minister that Dylan suffered from a paralysing shyness when he was sober; that he only became remotely fluent after a few pints and that he needed at least six before he became the roaring boy on the runaway horse.

'Those cuts on your face look very nasty, Mr Thomas. Fallen over somewhere have you?'

Dylan just didn't know where to put himself or what to say when he was saved by the back door crashing open and the sounds of Caitlin dumping her shopping on the kitchen table. 'I don't know why they call that fucking dump the General

111

Stores,' she shouted in at him. 'They've got absolutely fuck all in there and, if they have, they're hiding it under the counter for their favourite fucking customers.'

Abject woe rippled through the Rev Enoch's holy features and he dived down between his legs to fiddle with his shoes while also humming a hymn. He didn't even look up when Caitlin walked into the living room, took one look at the wild silver haystack of his hair and muttered 'Oh shit' before quickly backing out into the kitchen where, with a polite and almost Oxford accent, she shouted, 'Would you like a cup of tea, minister?'

'Oh, if it's not too much trouble, Mrs Thomas,' the Rev Enoch replied with a similarly exaggerated politeness. 'I take milk but no sugar for me if you don't mind.'

A small uneasy silence followed with Rev Enoch still humming his hymn to himself when he said: 'Ah, I see you have a skull on your desk. False I suppose?'

'I don't think so. I've never had it looked at by an expert as such but I've always assumed it's real. Verney Mathews fished it out of the sea one day last autumn. A gift from Neptune, he called it.'

'If it's real, Mr Thomas, it should have a proper Christian burial.'

'What? Even if it's lost its body somewhere? A skull has a soul too, does it?'

'Oh yes, Mr Thomas. Most certainly yes. Even the biggest sinner there is should have a proper Christian burial and, if we've only got the skull, that's what we should bury. Remember the skull and crossbones. Before the pirates took them over the skull and crossbones were Christian symbols and seen as the minimum you needed to stage a resurrection.'

'Well, you'd better take him away and give him a proper burial, then.' Dylan picked up the skull awkwardly, carrying it over to the Rev Enoch who rose out of the deckchair to accept it formally. 'Yorick, I've always called him. He's been a good friend to me and I wouldn't want him to miss out on the resurrection on my account.'

'I don't want to take your good friend away from you, Mr Thomas,' the Rev Enoch said, holding Yorick with both hands and waving him up and down as if offering him back.

'No, please, vicar. Give him a proper burial. He deserves one, like you say. I'd never forgive myself if I'd thought I'd stopped Yorick catching the bus to the resurrection. Please. Be my guest.'

The minister tried to put the skull into his overcoat but the pocket was too small.

'I'll find a bag for you,' Dylan offered. 'I've got a paper bag somewhere. Should fit him a treat. But you'll find a nice view for him, won't you vicar?'

'A nice view, Mr Thomas?'

'When you bury him. Find a nice view for him. Myself, I've always wanted to be buried somewhere with a nice view. Somewhere where I can look at the sea.'

'Ah yes. A nice view.'

Caitlin appeared, beaming unctuously and with her hair brushed, carrying three cracked mugs of tea on a tray *and* a plate of biscuits. 'What Dylan would really like is a nice view of a pub,' she said. 'Somewhere with a big pint in his hand and a gang of oafs to laugh at all his stupid jokes. That's what he calls a nice view.'

'Catey, just shut up and find a nice big paper bag for the minister would you? Something big enough for Yorick here.'

'Oh, he's off somewhere is he? Going on his holidays? Anywhere nice?'

Chapter Eleven

DOLLY FROWNED at Dafydd before wrinkling up her nose.
'We could both do with a break, couldn't we?'

She had never thought that learning Welsh would be so
difficult. Welsh had words that weren't designed for the human
mouth or tongue. There was never a simple word for anything
and usually a choice of up to eight. Then there were all those
swinish dds and lls. You couldn't even swear properly in it.

'We'll go through that list of verbs one more time,' Dafydd
said. '*Then* we'll have that cup of tea.'

'No, we won't.' She shook her head decisively. 'I've got a
headache and what I really want is a cup of tea and an aspirin.
Is there a language anywhere in the world more difficult than
Welsh?'

'Welsh isn't difficult. One day you'll come to love it as I do
and you'll speak nothing else.'

'I very much doubt it.' She did manage to smile even though
she *did* have a bit of a headache. You weren't supposed to fancy
your teacher, she guessed, particularly when the teacher was a
student and a good five years younger than you but there was
something very appealing about him. She liked his nose and
tangle of curly hair. His smile always brought her a burst of
warmth too and the mere thought of those long fingers
caressing her backbone also made her feel strangely anxious
but, most of all, she kept trying to decide how he would feel
inside her; kept trying to imagine how those thin thighs would
feel against the insides of her plump legs.

All this sexual wondering wasn't very ladylike, she knew, and the chapel certainly wouldn't approve, but that's the way she was. Dolly James was a woman first and last. She had needs and recognised them. She crossed and uncrossed her legs, noting his eyes lift from his precious Welsh primer even if his head remained still. *Oh this is no good Dolly girl. Behave yourself. This is chapel-dominated New Quay not one of your wild drinking clubs in Soho and, if you get hounded out of this place what are you going to do then?*

She wanted to learn Welsh because she had become fed up with her isolation in this most *sospan* of communities. Almost no one spoke to her – usually people muttered to one another in Welsh behind the backs of their hands when she was around – and, although they never said as much, you could tell they weren't entirely happy about her fatherless baby. The word *bastard* always had a real sting to it in these fraught times and she wasn't exactly proud of the way it was either, telling everyone the father had gone off to fight in the war.

The sad truth of it was that she didn't actually know the identity of the father of The Boy – she had bumped into him one night in a Wapping pub with the usual consequences – and her own dear father had been so appalled by her behaviour he had packed her off back to her mother's old house, here in Welsh Wales, where she was now stuck until it was decided she could return to English civilisation.

After a long, lonely winter without the booze – even if there had been one highly regrettable lapse on New Year's Eve – she believed she had come to grips with what everyone in the family laughingly referred to as her galloping nymphomania. But it was the drink! She could just about be herself when she was off the drink. Just about. But one whiff of alcohol and . . . everything went sort of . . . well . . . *wrong*.

She let out a long wistful sigh as these thoughts crowded into her mind and Dafydd looked up from his Welsh primer. He was smiling as usual but there was a nervous tension in his smile and she could see he was waiting to be seduced – Dolly *knew* about these things – but she really couldn't seduce him yet. Could she? Her legs began crossing and uncrossing again. Oh dear, it had been such a long time . . .

It had been bad enough that she had gone out and made a fool of herself with that Dylan Thomas on New Year's Eve. She was still quite scared at how absolutely uncontrollable she had become that sorry, drunken night and how, after a few drinks, she had gone on the prowl like a battle-hardened whore looking for a customer. She had long known about what went on under the slipway on New Year's Eve – *everyone* knew what went on down there on New Year's Eve – and she supposed it was fortunate she had met the mad poet. In her state that night, she would have let the whole lifeboat crew into her. *Anyone* could have had her faster than three men could throw her on a bed. It was so depressing and now, to make matters worse, she often spotted Dylan looking at her lasciviously in the street even if she was far too embarrassed to say anything and certainly didn't want to let him in over the drawbridge again. Oh no. The pubic portcullis, as Dylan had once called it, was now well and truly down as far as he was concerned. She'd had a few lovers in her time but none quite so bad at it as him. Talk about a little sausage being waved around in the Cheddar Gorge. *Pfui!* She would have had far more fun – and fewer regrets – with a cucumber.

There was also Caitlin, of course. Young Gareth had told her all about those left hooks and flung missiles so, yes, Dylan certainly wasn't about to get under her portcullis again.

But it would be so nice to acquire a sleeping dictionary like Dafydd; she really would make great progress with this slippery Welsh language if she had him in her bed, even if she knew the chapel deacons wouldn't exactly be jumping for joy when it emerged the scarlet woman in Cliff House was enjoying 'carnal knowledge' with one of their precious students. *Resist, Dolly. Keep your knees firmly clamped together. Tight. Stay off the drink.*

And what, while we're on the subject, would her young teacher make of her spouting verses from the Bible in Welsh if they ever did get down to it? That would confuse him no end wouldn't it? He would surely conclude he had a real mad woman on his hands if she did that. And perhaps he'd be right.

'I'll make that cup of tea now, shall I?' she asked.

'No. Wait. I mean . . . '

She remained quite still, lowering her elbows and putting her hands together prayerfully.

'I mean . . . would you have any objection if I gave you a small kiss?'

'Any objection?' she echoed weakly, watching a sweet, shy blush burst up over his starched collar. A hard throb of longing throbbed between her legs and, if anything, got throbbier as she tried to take her own advice and clamp her knees firmly together. 'Exactly how small a kiss are you thinking about?' she asked, picking her words carefully and slowly. This was a novel approach. Most men just leaped on her and hoped for the best.

'Oh, small enough. Not very big at all really.'

'You could try a big one if you wanted.'

'I thought we might start with a small one and . . . and, if that worked out then . . . perhaps . . . we could go on to a bigger one.'

He stood up, let the Welsh primer fall on the floor, put one hand on her shoulder and gave her a light peck on the cheek. Oh dear, this one had no experience at all. Small kisses had never come any smaller. He was as virginal as the day he was born. She took one of his hands with both hers and placed it on the spot he'd kissed, looking up at him with her big brown eyes. And she was stone cold sober too.

She moved his hand down to her right breast, feeling the vibrations of his fingers break through in a fevered morse code to her wildly beating heart.

What was he going to do next? *She* couldn't take it any further – she knew men liked to make all the bold moves in the beginning. Also, being Welsh, they always wrote you off as a whore if you gave in straight away. Not that anything *was* happening – and neither was she exactly giving in to anything – since, apart from a lot of finger messages in morse, he didn't seem about to do anything at all, just staring at her like some goggle-eyed snake mesmerised by a mongoose.

She thought about the gossiping women in the General Stores and remembered she hadn't got any milk for the tea. The Boy would be waking soon but she had left some rusks on his pillow to keep him quiet. Give him a rusk to chomp on and he was quiet for hours. She even let Dylan's blobby face wander into her mind and still Dafydd didn't do anything so, finally, in a mixture of exasperation and desperation, she grabbed him on the inside of his leg and, ever so slowly, began inching her hand up it.

Surely they should be kissing or *something* at this stage? But there he was hanging on to her right breast for grim death as she hung on to the side of his leg. Now he was looking down at the Welsh primer on the floor. Something had gone badly wrong here and she was not at all sure how to put it right. She was about to begin fiddling with his trouser buttons, when he let go of her breast, his back arched stiff and he let out a low moan of pain – or it might even have been fear – and ran out of the room.

She remained seated, looking down at her upturned palms and deciding she was never going to understand men – not for as long as she lived she wouldn't. She heard him fiddling with the latch on the door and stood up to walk to the window, a crater of emptiness widening inside her as she watched him running up the lane. Her nose sniffed a sort of smile and her fingertips touched the window pane as he disappeared. He had gone and frightened himself with the strength of his feelings. Welsh men were always ashamed of the power of their feelings; they never quite knew what to do with them. She blamed the chapel. They were always telling people to be fearful of their feelings; nothing nice ever happened to you unless you felt deeply ashamed of it and sat around feeling deeply guilty for at least a fortnight.

118

She saw this guilt in young Gareth; he too had strong feelings which kept bringing out the same mixture of guilt and shame. Dafydd was probably another out of the same mould. All reared in the same shadow.

But Dafydd would be back; they always came back if you offered them something they really wanted and they'd had time to calm down. Yet she did hope he wouldn't turn up on her doorstep only when he was drunk like some men she had known. She'd met a lot of men who would only face her when they were drunk although, if she happened to be drunk too, their luck was really in and it was The Book of Psalms, in Welsh, from Alpha to Omega.

She looked up at the loaming dark sky and saw that it was snowing again; oh how she needed some sort of warm love in this long, cold, lonely winter but, just for now, it was all going to get far colder yet.

ERNST WAS the very picture of Teutonic contentment as he sat on the aft deck of the U-boat, his feet up on a rail, holding up Immanuel Kant's *Critique of Pure Reason* to the light in the mouth of the cave with his other arm folded peaceably around his neck.

In such an odd situation he had found it comforting to read the words of one of the most supremely rational and individual philosophers of them all; Kant taught that man should always think for himself without relying on the authority of the Church, Bible or State. This great man had also thought closely about the limitations of the human mind and showed how it could work through every problem within the limits of pure reason. All knowledge came through the senses and the only test of moral value came when it was subjected to the categorical imperative.

Within this philosophical scaffolding man could become the supreme orderer of his own life and Ernst knew that, in the real world, Kant himself was as ordered and regular as clockwork, taking half an hour walk after lunch and always at such precise times his neighbours could set their watches by his movements.

Yes, his was the ordered life of the rational mind.

Not that there was much that was ordered or rational about his situation just now, sitting here on a stricken U-boat, her deck covered with driftwood and other assorted camouflage in a cave on the Welsh coast. Fortunately the tidal movements of Cardigan Bay were quite small doing almost nothing to disturb their quiet equilibrium except lifting the submarine up occasionally on a swell and banging its hull against the wall of the cave with a doomed, graveyard clang.

The cave was such they didn't even much feel the extreme changes of weather – not even when it had been snowing heavily – although they could not now sail anywhere, even if they wanted to, because their electrical system had got so rotten and corroded they could not make the most basic communications with La Rochelle and no communications meant no more stupid orders.

He turned the page and wondered what Kant would have made of all this; how might he have found meaning or moral value in the structures these three Germans had made for themselves, particularly in the way Christian had taken out the crew's bunks to give them more living space; in the way they took water from an underground stream which came through the roof of the cave near the bow and the way Helmut had even acquired some piglets which now lived and played in a confined space around the torpedo tubes.

Yes, this was surely one situation which would actually defy all rational analysis; even Kant, the master thinker, wouldn't have been able to make much sense of three Germans living on a wrecked U-boat with six piglets in a cave on the coast of Wales *and* in a time of war.

Not that it was a bad life, as such, and certainly a great improvement on their previous existence, living in the constant terror of drowning while on the business of great waters. Life in a cave had a certain satisfying solidity about it – you didn't get the feeling you might be about to drown at any second for one

– and he had even come to know the sea-birds which occasionally went paddling by, looking in as if wondering when the U-boat was going to leave so they could reclaim their abandoned nests on the cave's many ledges. There were plenty of fish around too, only too willing to jump on their hooks when they were not swimming away in alarmed shoals with hungry seals hot on their tails.

The fisherman Matthews also called around now and then and rowed them to a cove where they could walk up the path and go into the town of New Quay for a night out. Not that they had ever really relaxed on such nights out and had never come close to becoming drunk. He had also come to know Caitlin Thomas but hadn't shown any indication of his earlier sexual desires for her, if only for the simple but mundane reason that she was married and, as an officer in the German Kriegsmarine, it had never entered his mind that you could do anything at all untoward with a married woman.

Kant continued grappling, enjoyably, with the concept of time when the corner of Ernst's eye caught something small and dark moving in the luminous waves behind him. It could have been a giant insect with long legs heading towards them and he lowered his book and turned his head fully to see the strange, dark shape articulating itself into something far larger and more substantial than a sculling insect.

He heard a familiar shout and stood up to see his two strange Welsh saviours rowing towards him – the fisherman Matthews and his even more unlikely first mate, one Caitlin Thomas.

Helmut and Christian came up in response to the shout too, eager to see what fresh provisions they were getting this time – a small urn of fresh milk – as it turned out – a sack of potatoes and several *News Chronicles* which would bring them all up to date on the progress of the war and the raids of all those 'screaming bombs' as the headlines were now calling them.

'We've also managed to get you a nice shoulder of ham,'

Caitlin announced as Verney threw a mooring line to Christian. 'Some nice ham and chips will fatten you lot up no end.'

They both climbed up the rope ladder on to the aft deck where the five of them stood around untidily, none of them quite sure what to say until Ernst handed the ham to Christian and said, 'I am sure I speak for my officers here when I thank you for the other night. We enjoyed ourselves greatly and hope that you, Fraulein Thomas, have now settled your differences with your husband.'

'I'll never settle my differences with that useless bastard,' Caitlin replied cheerfully. 'We'll even have our differences after we've died. I even look forward to fighting with him in heaven.'

'Ah,' said Ernst silently, pretending he understood when he plainly hadn't. Such relationships based on clash were well beyond his understanding and Helmut and Christian hadn't understood it either, judging by their blank looks at one another.

'Anyway we've been thinking hard about your situation here,' Caitlin continued, unwilling to discuss the state of her volatile marriage in any detail, 'and we've decided you must leave the boat here and come and live with us in the town.'

'Live with us in the town?' Christian echoed weakly. 'How do you mean Fraulein Thomas?'

'Put it another way. You've either got to stay here all the time or live in the town all the time. But you can't do both. If you stay in the town they'll soon get used to you – the poor things around here are not blessed with too many brains – but what you must not do is keep on disappearing all the time because then they start asking questions. They're asking lots of questions already and we've got to do something about it.'

'I shall need time to think about this,' said Ernst. 'But I can certainly see the thinking behind it all. Making yourself invisible by becoming totally visible. I can understand that.'

Verney looked at Caitlin worriedly and, encouraged by not receiving downright rejection of her plan, she continued. 'We might even be able to find some work for you. Most of the young men around here have gone off to work in the munitions because there's good money in that. Most of the farms are short of hands.'

'We will need to tell them *something*.'

'Just stick to the same story. You are Norwegians from Norway and you've come here to teach the British army survival techniques in Snowdonia. You're not needed at the moment and it's possible you will be sent back to join the Norwegian resistance soon.'

'And they will just accept that will they?'

'Oh no, they'll all want to know the ins and outs of a cat's arse but just keep telling them all it's top secret. Tap the side of your nose like this and keep saying: "Can't tell you anymore. It's all top secret." '

'Where are you suggesting we stay?'

'Oh bunk in with Verney in his cottage. It'll smell worse than a pig sty, I warn you, but maybe you can help clean it up. Give *him* a bit of a scrub too. Introduce him to the joys of carbolic.'

The fisherman Matthews gave one of his best, imbecilic, black-toothed smiles and the three Germans frowned at one another anxiously but, as they absorbed this new plan, nothing more was said.

THE SNOW started to fall and thaw again on the precipitous streets of the town over the next few days, leaving piled-up drifts of brownish slush in the gutters and a severe shortage of shovels in the General Stores.

Ankles were sprained and a few old bones broken due to the hazardous conditions underfoot although the most spectacular accident happened when Stan the coal man lost control of his cart and it toppled over in the slush and went crashing down the main street on its side before piling up against the main wall of the Lifeboat Station with its shafts snapped and axle broken, its coal delivery days over forever. Fortunately the horse hadn't been attached to the cart when it decided to make its headlong plunge down the hill but, unfortunately for Stan, everyone sneaked out under the cover of darkness with buckets and made off with all the loose coal before he had a chance to organise a replacement cart. 'Tis an ill wind . . .

Later that same night the Rev Enoch, a man of settled routines and regular prayer, was doing his pastoral rounds, as usual, calling on this house and that as he made his way up to the top of the hill on the highest point in the town.

Any sort of tracker could easily have worked out where he had been from the fresh footprints in the snow and slush, stopping at Mrs Pryce's next to the chip shop who had been taken down with sciatica, calling on Stan to commiserate about his runaway cart, visiting the dairy next to the Black Lion to see one of his deacons, going up the hill leading to the hairdresser's. then climbing over the kissing gate by the Butcher's Field where a twisting path took his to the top of the hill where he could stand next to the dead oak and look over the white roof-tops and the dark, cold sea.

This was his prayer point where, with Prayer Book in hand, he would read the Prayer in the Time of War out loud to the listening darkness. 'Save and deliver us, we humbly beseech thee, from the hands of our enemies, abate their pride, assuage their malice and confound their desires . . . '

Thus the lone, crystalised shepherd was erecting a canopy of prayer over the town which would also protect his wayward flock from any evil which might assail them in the night ahead. He was connecting his anxiety with the Lord while also urging Him to keep a watchful eye on every one of them, to give their beds a real safety and security, to shield them all with the transcendent grace of his own believing prayer.

'Be now and evermore our defence; grant us victory, if it be thy will; look in pity on the wounded and the prisoners; cheer the anxious; comfort the bereaved; succour the dying; have mercy on the fallen; and hasten the time when war shall cease throughout the world . . . '

He stopped muttering the prayer when he noticed his hands had become hot and slimy, both of them running profusely with blood which was also dribbling with scarlet streams down on to the reddening snow around his galoshes. Another vision was beginning to enfold him but he felt no fear, as others might who had been visited by such visionary terrors, content and even happy in the knowledge that all that was happening was that God was about to talk to him again.

He decided he might just as well continue reading from his Prayer Book but discovered that the blood from his wounds was spattering the pages too, making many of the words unintelligible in the winding, red rivulets. He would just have to be man enough for God and stand there and take whatever it was that was coming his way, he knew, as he looked up and saw a bright red mist swirling over the town.

This red mist seemed to keep turning and running in on itself, all the while swelling and hardening and obscuring the rooftops when a strange, throaty sound began whispering inside it; a sound which grew ever louder until it began transmuting into a terrible roar of prolonged agony.

At that moment even the Rev Enoch, one of God's oldest and most faithful warriors, visibly quailed when the enormous head of a beast emerged out of the roaring, red cloud with gigantic, yellow eyes, a huge tail thrashing around the rooftops and a great belly which swelled and contracted with each fresh burst of white fire which kept forking out of its mouth. The beast hung directly over him, with the heat of its fire actually scorching his face, until the old man held up one of his arms to protect himself from his own astonishment. Yet he quickly recovered his composure because, even in all this hallucinating confusion, he knew that he was not the object of the dragon's ire.

The dragon was full of pain and torn apart while suffering from internal injuries which were nothing at all to do with the Rev Enoch. The dragon was, through him, merely crying about its disappointment with the Welsh and the way they were becoming a lost and wandering tribe who had abandoned their faith and turned their back on the one true God. That's what the dragon was doing here; that's what it was trying to tell the Rev Enoch now.

The minister lowered his arm and held the town within his dragon vision for a full minute until those giant yellow eyes abruptly shattered like breaking glass, the fire in its mouth turned into a guttering dribble of black smoke and even its scales seemed to be breaking down as, with another muted roar of anguish, the whole beast seemed to just fall away back into the very night.

The Rev Enoch remained standing there, his own body full of pain and loss too; he knew all about dragon pain; he had long been listening to the siren calls of distressed dragon music. But, after the cries of pain, there was just emptiness piling up over the roofs of this old Welsh fishing town of his. A massive river of loss was flooding the weeping night and, way out in the Bay, he could just about see a late fishing boat puttering back to a snow-covered quay.

Chapter Twelve

GARETH HUNCHED down into his seat, cap in hand and gazing out of the window as the bus followed the coast road to Aberystwyth while Dafydd, next to him, was engrossed in *The Cambrian News* and its front page story that Swansea had been hit the night before with bombs falling on Danygraig Road and Kilvey Hill. He was reading every word carefully and Gareth could occasionally feel his whole body stiffen as he did so. He clearly took this war very seriously, almost personally, and had already told Gareth that he had registered as a conscientious objector who was waiting to be called up before a tribunal in Cardigan soon. As a true Welshman, he added, he was not going to bear arms against anyone, least of all Germany; he was a lover not a fighter.

Today he was taking Gareth to his first political meeting since, as he had promised Dolly, the boy had to learn everything about Wales and become a true patriot. Gareth was proud and uncertain, in almost equal parts, to be receiving such attention from the young teacher; everything he said seemed so noble, so right and it was almost unthinkable that he could be wrong about anything at all.

Gareth's only mark against him was that he seemed to have got excessively close to his Aunty Dolly and spits of dark jealousy were beginning to cloud his young, intense heart. The real problem was he couldn't see any woman resisting that gentle smile or those bright eyes or those magnificent words but he had never said anything about that to anyone and kept all such worries to himself and the outside lavvy.

The morning all around them was booming with spring sunshine as small waves were busy collapsing against the bottom of high cliffs with sheep and their young lambs scattered over the fenced fields and hawks circling the clear, blue skies looking for something for breakfast.

Gareth looked hard at the magnesium-bright surface of the sea, still wondering what had happened to that whale he had spotted before Christmas, just cruising there like some dark angel of the deep before vanishing into the watery blueness as silently and suddenly as it had appeared.

'Dafydd, do you think it's possible to see shadows that no one else can?'

Dafydd lowered his newspaper and thought about this for a while. 'Our own shadows are what make our lives different from everyone else's. So, yes, I suppose you must be able to see your own shadows just as you can see your own lights. That's what makes us unique, clothing ourselves in our own shadows and lights.'

Gareth liked the idea of clothing himself in his own shadows and lights; such an act appealed to his poetic nature even if he didn't quite understand what it was all about.

ABERYSTWYTH ALWAYS seemed the same dreary town to Gareth, the same chilly wind blowing in off the same seaweed sea, sighing along the same hilly streets past the same threadbare shops which, no matter what they were selling, all seemed to smell of the same frying chips. The only sign that Aberystwyth was taking the war slightly more seriously than New Quay came from the odd patrolling ARP warden and the fact that *all* the shop and house windows were criss-crossed with strips of black tape: otherwise there were just the usual Saturday morning shoppers and sundry rabbles of students with their green and white scarves and arms full of unread books.

The two of them took a seat in the front row as around forty people were milling around inside the small Temperance Hall in a side street off Princes Street. The three men on the stage, Dafydd explained to Gareth, were all important in the Welsh nationalist party: *Plaid Genedlaethol Cymru*. The small man in the middle was Saunders Lewis who was also editor of the nationalist magazine *Y Ddraig Goch*. Some years back this Ghandi of Wales had been imprisoned with two others for setting fire to a bombing range in Pen-y-berth on the Lleyn peninsula to protest against English imperialism. The other two were Ambrose Bebb and Gwilym Williams, both Plaid officials and among the party's most energetic workers.

Saunders Lewis was the first to address the meeting, after it had settled down, beginning by saying: 'As we gather here this morning we learn that the whole of Europe is tumbling like a house of cards. Swansea was hit last night and this is a conflict which could last ten years in which millions will die. We stand to lose everything in this war and already our best young men have been conscripted. Mother Wales has also become fully occupied by the English with their army camps everywhere. It is only left to us nationalists to do what we can to save our beloved country from this coming inferno.

'For years we have been told we are no good. We have been told we have no backbone or self-respect; that we should always speak in English because that's the best way to make money. The English have long learned how to brainwash us and undermine our confidence. We are always destined to live in the cupboard under the stairs. But we should come out and fight for Wales not England. We should remember our family loyalties, the voices of our ancestors and our roots in the past. If we do not connect with our past we are not connecting with anything. It's our glorious past that has the real value not our much-threatened future.'

In some ways Lewis reminded Gareth of the Rev Enoch with his sense of impending doom but, where the old minister took off on ranting, colourful flights, Lewis spoke with the quiet precision of a scholar. Where the Rev Enoch looked as wild and dishevelled as some prophet lost in the Sinai, Lewis was tidily dressed with a red tie and a white handkerchief folded into his top pocket. Lewis also had a high cliff of a forehead, neat hair and the wide eyes of an amazed ferret; the only eccentric thing about him was that he occasionally scratched his behind with his right hand.

Lewis continued with an analysis of the state of Wales which Gareth found difficult to follow due to a lot of big words and unfamiliar connections so he tried clothing him in his own imagination, setting him up with shadows and lights, trying to work out quite what shadows and lights might suit a Welsh nationalist leader.

The next speaker, Ambrose Bebb, said, 'The nationalist party, in conference, has declared it will not take part in England's wars. Therefore, no Welsh nationalist may take part in this war, nor agree to work in armaments factories, nor help in the war in any way.

Bebb was followed by Gwilym Williams and there was an immediate stir when he began by saying that he had brought some news which had far-reaching consequences for everyone in Wales.

'I've come to tell you today that a line of communication has been set up between Plaid Cymru and the German headquarters in Berlin. The offer is simple. If the Welsh engage in a guerilla war with the English then Herr Hitler has promised that, once the war is over and the German victory complete, Wales will become fully independent with her own parliament. There are no reservations in the Fuhrer's mind. He has always believed in the nationalist cause which, in this case, means that Wales will be handed back to the Welsh.

'His exact words were these: "Germany has long discovered her own identity and, in so doing, is anxious that other nations find theirs. We are particularly interested in encouraging nations that are the enemies of England. Help us, people of Wales, and your long-cherished dream of becoming your own nation will come true." '

Gareth didn't understand the implications of these words but he did pick up on the deep confusion and sharp intakes of breath in the audience. People started chattering with one another animatedly. Gareth kept looking up at Dafydd as if hoping the teacher would give him a lead or some clue as to what he should be thinking about this offer from Herr Hitler. But Dafydd stared directly ahead of him; the great nationalist teacher was actually dumbstruck for once.

At that point a huge crash came from the back of the hall followed by the sound of breaking glass. Gareth half-stood up to look back over the heads of the people behind him when Dafydd grabbed his arm tight. A group was standing in the rear shouting abuse. 'Bloody traitors.' A chair sailed into the air above them. 'Nazi swine.' Then it looked as if every corner of the hall was full of fighting. Gareth had never been near anything like this before and he almost began crying as yet more chairs went sailing into the air. The fat shrieks of policemen's whistles filled his mind as yet more burly men came punching their way into the hall. One Plaid man fell sideways clutching a bloodied ear. Another fought back but was also felled.

Dafydd spotted a side door opening with yet more men gathering menacingly on the pavement outside and, just then, he picked up Gareth under his arm like a rugby ball, lowered his head and charged straight out through the open door. Gareth got a nasty bang on his arm as he was propelled through the mêlée and he yelped more in fright than anything else since it hadn't actually hurt. Six men from the meeting were now running down the lane with the noises of fighting still erupting out of the hall behind them.

'There are some who don't want peace at any price,' Dafydd gasped as he put Gareth down under a lamp-post which he, in turn, leaned on with his hand to steady himself and catch his breath. 'Some really want this war and, to get it, they're prepared to start a war themselves. But this is no place for you Gareth boy. Let's get you home before any more trouble starts.'

'We can't go home yet. I've left my cap behind on the seat. Haven't got another.'

'I'll buy you another cap,' Dafydd replied sharp. 'Now we go home.'

IT WAS reasonably crowded in the Black Lion that night as Ernst and his two officers walked in with the Black Widow quietly sorrowing over her pint of cider, as usual, and Dylan sitting with Caitlin and holding court with a small gang in the corner of the bar. Terry Hughes' dog was stretched out on the flagstones, trying to warm his belly with the log fire.

Ernst nodded at the group before ordering three drinks and leading his men to the other side of the bar where they sat together around an empty table. These three Norwegians from Norway didn't communicate much with the rest of the community but, as Caitlin had promised, everyone was now getting used to seeing them around the place although any overtures for them to join in such great events as the annual Rat Hunt were always firmly, but politely, rejected.

The kapitan had long decided they could only get through this by being both mysterious and formal; that they should not get too friendly or intimate with anyone at all here or it might be their undoing. He had once bought a round of drinks for everyone with his Berlin English money but mostly the three of them kept themselves to themselves and only ever talked among themselves.

Yet, in spite of their delicate situation, Ernst's early warning radar picked up little hostility here: quite the reverse, in fact, and, when they did ask him the odd, probing questions, they seemed happy enough with his generally evasive replies and didn't push it. He was even coming to enjoy the harmless eccentricity of the people here, particularly the Black Widow, the old yarning sea captain and the boy who liked to wander around the streets in the evening yapping like a dog. None of them were exactly models of rationality but, there again, who would want to live with models of rationality? He could feel that he had changed almost daily since moving here.

But he did have to keep an eye on Dylan Thomas, who seemed to have recovered from his earlier jealous rages, possibly because Ernst and Caitlin now ignored one another totally, but always seemed unreliable and even a bit mad particularly under the weight of not a lot of alcohol. They said he was a great poet but he would have an awful lot of drying out to do had he been under Ernst's command. If there was one thing Grossadmiral Doenitz would never have tolerated in the kreigsmarine it was a man who kept making a fool of himself in drink. The poet only seemed to need three pints and he became totally pie-eyed.

So, one way and another, there was a lot of careful staring going on in that bar that night when the ashen face of Police Constable Ianto Jones came through the pub door. 'There's been some mischief. There's going to be trouble. We've had reports the Germans are about to land on the beach here in New Quay. Now. Tonight.'

It was 8.20pm, Friday, April 3, and Terry Hughes' dog opened one brown eye, looked at the fearful policeman and closed it again. Otherwise this news was greeted by total silence with the three Norwegians going rigid with shock and only a slight shake of Ernst's head indicating they should stay that way. The others continued staring at the policeman. *The Germans are about to land on the beach here!!!*

Not one of them seemed able to get their minds around the meaning of these words. He might as well have told them that the whole world was about to be painted a bright, forget-me-not blue or that the Rev Enoch had begun parading around the square in woman's clothes. It didn't make any sense and even if these Germans were about to land what were *they* supposed to do about it?

'What beach are you talking about again?' Captain Port Talbot asked finally.

'New Quay beach. Here. Now. This minute.'

The silence deepened as the gathered drinkers pondered the picture of a thousand jack-booted Nazis storming up past the moored fishing boats, not to mention the equally appalling possibility of having to show some resistance. The Norwegians became even more motionless, if that were possible, and Caitlin stared at them hard but elected for silence for once.

'How many of these Germans are there exactly?' Dic Morgan asked.

'I don't know. I just don't know. We've had a report from the coastguard in Aberaeron that some foreign ship is steaming into the Bay. So I'm going to hand out all my rifles and bullets and we're going down there to meet them face to face.'

No one budged.

'Why don't we get Dai Fred to launch the lifeboat?'

'What use would that be?'

'Well, he could take the boys out there and have a look at them.'

'To have a look at them? And where would that get us? Anyway it's gone eight and the whole crew will be down in the Dolau and drunk as monkeys by now.'

For some reason all eyes fell on Dylan who was trembling so much he couldn't lift up his drink, staring glass-eyed into space and with bright, red blotches beginning to gather all over his face.

'What's up with you, Dylan?' Stephen Stephens asked.

'Oh that's just his blotches,' said Caitlin like a mother explaining away her child's runny nose. 'He always comes out in blotches when he's scared. If it's not blotches it's boils.'

'Boils!' The bar was aghast.

'That's my husband for you. He gets blotches, boils and shakes like a castanet if there's any trouble around. He tried to fight a wet newspaper once and the newspaper won by a knock-out.'

'My one and only body I will not give,' Dylan finally announced. 'My one and only body I will not give.'

'Come on now, boys. Are we men or worms?' Dic Morgan burst into life. 'Let's get down there and show those Jerry bastards what for. Let's gather up Ianto's rifles and get anything else like pitchforks and spades and we'll muster on the beach and attack those Nazis like a swarm of bastard bees. Like bastard bees. Aye.'

This Agincourt talk had no effect on the boys and they all stared down at their beer morosely, showing no inclination to fight anyone like bastard bees. Handel Rees suggested Police Constable Ianto Jones might care to pop down the beach to count the enemy. 'I mean to say, if we know how many there are, we'll know how to play it, won't we? The first rule of rugby that is. Know your opposition. Get in your retaliation in advance.'

'Aye, aye. Go and count them, Ianto,' agreed Joshua the Bluebell. 'Then you can come back up here and tell us what we're up against. I mean to say, if there's just a few of them, we could probably manage. But, if there's lots of them, there's no point in us going down there and getting shot to bits is there? No point at all. Best we just sit tight in here and call the Army.'

The boys chorused their agreement but remained as frozen as statues, not even exercising their drinking elbows.

'Boys, boys.' Dic Morgan was back in the chair. 'Now I know we're not Army trained. We're just peaceful farmers and fishermen who do like a drink. That's all we are. So I suggest, before we get our weapons together, I suggest we do all have a large whisky each. A bit of Dutch courage like. To face the Nazis.'

'And who's going to pay for all these large whiskies?' the landlord wanted to know after yet another chorus of approving 'Aye, ayes' had died down.

'There's a war on, Percy,' Dic pointed out. 'There's a bloody war on and those bloody Nazis are going to be on our bloody beach and all you're thinking about is your own bloody pocket as usual.'

'And I'll tell you something else, Percy,' Captain Port Talbot chipped in, as if everyone had been waiting for his opinion, which they weren't. 'If those Nazis get up here you can be very sure *they* won't be paying for their drinks. They'll just be helping themselves to everything in the bar they will and they'll be busy raping your lovely daughter, Gwenny. I know all about those Nazis. We met up with a gang of them in Mombasa once and . . . '

'Not another sea story. I swear I'd rather hang myself than listen to another of this old sod's sea stories.'

With a long pantomime sigh of his own Percy took the spirit glasses from the shelf, thumping them down one after another on the bar counter before taking the whisky bottle off the optic and proceeding to fill each and every glass with the fullest and most generous measures in the history of the Black Lion. He took the first himself and knocked it back in one. At this point the three Norwegians looked at one another and dived for the door.

'I'll be having one of those too,' said Police Constable Jones, his trembling hand reaching out and grabbing the glass so clumsily he slopped most of the whisky over his wrist. 'Fill that one up again, Owen,' he added, wiping his mouth with the back of his sleeve as other trembling hands reached out for their own fortifiers. 'Didn't seem to manage most of the last one.'

'My one and only body I will not give. My one and only body I will not give.' It was Dylan again and, even with all the fierce pressures of suddenly ending up on the front line, everyone was fascinated by his blotches – bright red smudges, with suggestions of yellow pimples, spreading everywhere. *Disgusting.*

'It's just terror,' Caitlin explained as some of the boys moved in for a closer look. 'Happens all the time. If it's not blotches it's boils or he shits his pants. He heard a German bomber over Swansea once and just shat his pants. But he does get better when the danger passes.'

'Well let's hope there's no bombers over here tonight,' Percy said. 'At least he can take his blotches home with him.'

'My one and only body I will not give. My one and only body I will not give.'

The sound of a falling bicycle came from outside and the bar door burst open as fiercely as a sharp crack on the head. Every eye swivelled towards the doorway in silent terror, as if expecting a storm-trooper to come goose-stepping up to the bar toting a machine gun but it was the baker, Tony Price, carrying a Boer War rifle. 'Local Defence Volunteer Anthony Price reporting for duty,' he announced. 'Heard there was a full alert.'

'We're just having a little snort before going into battle,' Dic told him. 'Grab yourself a drink.'

'Do you know, if the worse comes to the worse, we can always gather on the beach and sing a hymn,' Percy said, now relaxed and made a bit stupid by his own free whisky.

'Oh yes, that'll do the trick for sure,' said Dic. 'The Land of Song defence. Can't you just see all those terrified Nazis sailing straight back to Germany with their hands clamped over their ears?'

A FULL MOON glowered on the still waters of the Bay as Verney came cruising back into New Quay in his boat, humming *Roses of Picardie* with happy gusto since he had pulled in a good haul of lobsters. The moonlight danced and sparkled in the foaming white V of his wake and it was one of those special moments when he could feel his spirit soaring up into the night. The lobsters had returned to his pots in force and the mackerel were showing a great and sudden enthusiasm for his baited hooks. The prawns had been fighting to get into his pots too and he'd even raised a few early herring.

Between them, he and Caitlin had also made a nice pile of money from the Norwegians and he was well on his way to raising enough for the new boat he so badly needed. He wasn't sure what Caitlin planned to do with her money – largely because she hadn't told him – but she *had* been muttering something about a New Quay Escape Fund so their partnership wasn't going to last much longer.

With a bit of luck he might catch a few pints in the Black Lion, he thought, when the *Roses of Picardie* shrivelled up in his mouth as he noticed lots of lights going on all over the town. New Quay had never taken much notice of the black-out but this seemed to be taking the piss and even the Black Lion, perched on the top left hand corner of the town, looked like a lighthouse radiating huge shafts of light. Verney could also make out the sounds of lots of running feet. A horse and cart was rattling down the slopes and that was drunken singing coming from somewhere. They're having a party, he thought bitterly; they had all waited until he had gone to work the tide and thrown a big party.

He dropped anchor next to his little rowboat, loaded his boxes down into it and began rowing to the shore. A hullabaloo of strange noises soared out of those twisting streets. After stacking up his lobster boxes on the sand he heard yet more sounds of running feet in the darkness. A cold fear began crawling around inside his many overcoats when a voice from somewhere in the middle of the moored boats began shouting: '*Achtung. Achtung.*'

That was German, Verney decided. So why was it being shouted in a Welsh accent?

'*Achtung,*' the voice shouted again. 'You just stand right where you are.'

Verney turned and spotted two lumbering shadows moving over the sand towards him. One shadow was wielding a pitchfork and the other a rifle. 'All gone off your heads have you?' Verney screamed with snot pouring from his nose. Again there was more drunken singing coming from above. 'Is this some kind of game?' Verney demanded, his eyes jerking around in alarm. 'You're all having some sort of game are you?'

One of the shadows materialised into Handel Rees carrying

a rifle and the other became Terry Hughes holding a pitchfork in one hand and a badly frightened dog on a lead with the other. 'It's only smelly old Verney,' shouted Handel Rees and others came staggering from out behind the beached boats, all bearing down on Verney with drunken menace except for Percy Hoskins who was being violently sick over the sand.

'You seen any Germans while you were out there did you Verney?' asked Norman Lewis.

'Out where?'

'Out in the bloody sea. '

Verney's cap swivelled around and looked back at the sea before turning back to confront the anxious faces gathered around him. 'No, I didn't see any Germans out there. Not unless they're coming in dressed up as lobsters I didn't.'

'Are you sure, now? They say there's some big German battleship out there. Full of Germans it is and they're all coming in here to rape the landlord's daughter, Gwenny.'

'Coming where?

'Here.'

'Well I'd better get my lobsters packed away before those Germans nick 'em. You know what those Nazi bastards are like.'

'Boys, boys.' The voice of Dic Morgan was wailing down through the night. 'There's something up in the next cove. Captain Port Talbot is saying he's got them all surrounded.' In the rush for the next cove Norman Lewis fell over Percy Hoskins who was holding on to an anchor line and still being sick over the sand. The whole of the headland was full of the screaming sounds of panic with lots of whistles blowing furiously.

An unidentified cyclist went hurtling down the slope and straight along the quay where he shouted something about his brakes before sailing straight off the end of the quay and plunged with a wailing plop into the sea. The three Norwegians were hiding themselves deep in the darkness behind the Lifeboat Station, watching every move carefully and wondering what, if anything, they might do next.

When everyone got to the next cove, near the shellfish factory, they found that somehow – and no one knew how, because he was almost blind – Captain Port Talbot had got on top of a large rock and was waving a bottle around beneath the moon and railing furiously at the advancing Germans. 'There's no welcome for you in the land of my fathers,' he was booming in slurred Celtic decibels. 'You try any of your old Nazi tricks of raping and pillaging around here and you'll be sorry. We Welsh have been stuffing the English for years and we'll soon be stuffing you Nazis. Make no mistake about that. You just see if we don't.'

Some thirty men were gathered in a semi-circle behind Captain Port Talbot's rock, rifles and pitchforks at the ready. But try as they might they could not see anything except the waves swelling against the huge rock on which the bottle-waving shape of Captain Port Talbot was framed in bright moonlight. 'You just put so much as one Nazi jack-boot on Welsh sand and the fair men of Cardigan will be feeding you to the pigs. So get on home with you . . . '

'Who exactly is the daft old bugger shouting at?' Billy Owen asked Joshua the Bluebell as they both peered at the suspiciously empty sea. 'And, more to the point, how did he get on top of that rock? He's blind as a bat, isn't he?'

'He's drunk. You never know where he's going to get to when he's drunk. I've seen him up on the roof of his cottage before now. He gets like a mountain goat when he's drunk.'

One of the waves broke into an extraordinarily bright shower of phosphorus and, right there in the middle of the luminous wave, was a little black head yelling loudly and swimming towards them frantically.

'Rifles at the ready,' Captain Port Talbot ordered and Handel Rees stepped forward, raising his. 'Rifles at the ready. Now shoot the Nazi bastard. Shoot him dead.'

'Don't shoot. Don't shoot,' a panic-stricken, drowning voice cried out from the waves. 'It's me. Tony Price. The baker. *Your* baker. My brakes failed on the quay and I fell off. Help me out, will you? I'm bloody frozen I am.'

They left their baker to help himself out and filed back up the hill, silent now after all these alarums and excursions and already clearly beginning to feel the first pinched strains of a forthcoming hangover dawn.

In the bar of the Black Lion Percy found Dylan still sitting at a table next to the fire with his wife. Both of them had clearly helped themselves to a bottle of whisky from behind the bar because Dylan, his face still covered with the blotches of pure fear, was dribbling drunk and Caitlin was not far behind. Even The Black Widow had joined them, drooping like a weed in the autumn and clearly also too far gone to speak even if she knew how.

'What I've always said is, if all is not lost, where the fuck is it?' Dylan wanted to know belligerently. 'Eh? Where the fuck is it? They're always telling me all is not lost. It's not all lost, they say. Even Churchill is always saying it's not lost. So where the fuck is it? I can't tell you. You can't tell me either so why are they saying it's not lost?'

'Oh for fuck's sake, Dylan, please shut up. Do you want another drink or not?'

Chapter Thirteen

THAT SATURDAY morning was bright with warm sunshine and speeding flies when Gareth ran straight out of the farm and followed the shale path down to the sea which he stared at for a while until he got bored.

He took off on a run again, scuttling past Majoda where he spotted Dylan in the garden, in grubby vest and baggy pants, shouting something at his wife indoors, before hurtling past Megan Evans' chicken shed and on towards Cliff House. He wasn't supposed to call there in the mornings – it was a sort of unspoken agreement – so he carried on hurrying towards the town, only to stop still and dive for cover behind a hedge because his friend and mentor, Dafydd ap Iestyn, was coming up the lane carrying a bunch of fresh flowers.

This was extremely suspicious and he remained hidden until Dafydd had passed then doubled back on the other side of the hedge, carefully monitoring the movements of his pacifist friend who walked into Cliff House *without even knocking*.

For reasons he could not understand Gareth felt a lunge of pain and even betrayal, hanging back behind the hedge for five minutes or so, struggling to find his breath before sneaking up into the garden where he felt a further painful stab of anxiety as he noticed that the kitchen curtains were drawn and it was still mid-morning. But there was a tiny gap between them so he tipped over a tea chest and climbed on its side trying to make as little noise as possible.

The sight between the edges of those curtains was certainly

the most appalling and disgusting he had ever beheld and his eyes widened with pure horror as the details seared into his brain and memory for all time. The general impression was of a formless, flailing mass of legs and arms, rather like two octopuses grappling with one another, until it became clear that his Aunty Dolly was completely naked and lying back on the kitchen table while Dafydd ap Iestyn, his so-called friend who also described himself as a pacifist, was also naked and had mounted her with his buttocks pumping up and down between her upraised knees.

Her arms were wrapped around his skinny body and what was even more disgusting about this truly disgusting performance was that she was muttering verses from the Bible out loud and in Welsh! She'd mentioned this horrible habit to him once before and he'd thought it was a joke but, far from being a joke, there she was doing it very seriously indeed and right in the middle of her kitchen. He would never, *ever*, look at that kitchen table in quite the same way again and certainly doubted he would ever eat anything while sitting at it either.

At this point he lost his footing on the tea chest and tried to steady himself only to fall sideways against the wall, grazing his leg which was already beginning to hurt like hell, as he decided he had better make a run for it or they would surely skin him alive.

He ran back up to Llanina Point with his eyes full of tears and brain full of nasty questions, stopping only to catch his breath before running again. *Why had that pacifist let him down like that? Why had she always told him she didn't know any Welsh? What was the point of shouting out verses from the Bible like that? Blasphemy wasn't it? And why were they doing this to him? He hadn't done anything to them had he?*

He collapsed into the long grass next to the cliff path overlooking the sea, rolling this way and that and still crying as his body rioted with yet more strange and unwelcome feelings.

Who wanted to be a pacifist like Dafydd ap Iestyn anyway?

Pacifists were cowards who did not want to fight for their country. Why didn't this pacifist go off and join the Army like all the other men around here? What was so special about him? The Army was the best place for him and, with any luck, his willy would be blown off by a German shell and at least not then be causing his Aunty Dolly any more pain or making her cry out to God in Welsh. But he shouldn't have run away from Cliff House. He should have run into the kitchen and attacked that pacifist with his war-like fists.

Now in an even greater turmoil he rolled over on to his front and reached down inside his serge shorts, trying to give himself a good knuckle shuffle with his eyes squeezed shut and Dolly's naked limbs all around him, when he cried out as he became aware of dark sounds and shadows moving all around him in the sunlight. He was not alone – indeed far from alone – since three men were stepping over him in single file, one giving a small warning cough but the others saying nothing as they made their way along the top of the cliff, stiff and dark as pall-bearers on their way to pick up the coffin.

He sat up, horrified by them and revolted by himself as one of the men turned and looked at him. He was sure the man was going to come back and fling him off the cliff-top – he deserved it, after all – but, in the event, the man merely gave him a little, sorrowful shake of the head and walked on after the others.

This was awful *and* he hadn't even come close to finishing himself off but he wouldn't be doing any of that now so, when he was sure they'd gone, he also took the path down into the town. They must be the three Norwegians from Norway that Dic had been telling him about. The ones with more money than sense. Staying with Verney Matthews. So what were they doing out here?

But he was going to have to give up bashing the bishop. Dic had warned him often enough about Wanker's Doom and here it was, with shame so heavy he'd soon need a wheelbarrow to cart it around. First he'd feel hair growing on his palms, according to Dic, or he'd go blind or have to spend the rest of his life in an iron lung.

HE WALKED down through the town with hands thrust down deep into his pockets, ignoring the fishermen sitting on a bench outside the Dolau Inn, smoking their pipes and kicking their boots together, before coming out on to the quay where a few boys were crabbing with bacon rind tied on the end of string. A group of men in Army uniform were wolf whistling at passing girls and there were a lot of people out on the sand either snoozing in deck chairs or digging holes with their children.

He threaded his way through the crowds and went to sit on the end of the quay, gazing out over the sun-glazed water and wondering whether life would always be this miserable. Verney's boat came chugging into view and he was faintly amused to see that, even on such a hot day, the old scoundrel was still wearing all his overcoats while his First Mate, Caitlin Thomas, was busy sorting fish on the aft deck. After he had dropped anchor and got down into his row boat Caitlin lowered the flapping boxes down to him and they both rowed to the beach where three men walked out into the water to meet them and help them with their catch. But not any three men, Gareth realised with a start; the three Norwegians from Norway who had stepped over him on the cliff top when he had been playing with himself. They were laughing among themselves like old friends and he knew exactly what they were saying about him too.

Do you know we were out having a walk this morning along the cliff by Llanina and we came across young Gareth Morgan having a wank in the grass.

Oh that boy is famous for wanking all over Cardigan. In fact it's all got so out of hand the Rev Enoch has started denouncing him in the pulpit every Sunday.

Never to God.

It's a fact. The Rev Enoch has been saying that young Gareth Morgan, the third son of Rachel Morgan and a pacifist nationalist, has got to give up wanking or he'll be going blind any day now. They're even passing around a collection plate for him in the chapel to raise money for a Labrador and white stick on the great day.

Never to God.

It's a fact. His Mam is even threatening to make him wear boxing gloves unless he stops galloping his maggot like that.

Well, well . . . if all that's true then I'd better ring up the Cambrian News and get them to run a story on their front page about it. Then I'll get in touch with the BBC and ask Arthur Askey to mention it on ITMA on Monday nights. Perhaps he'll stop that filthy habit then.

They were all laughing together like drains and Caitlin slipped her arm into one of the Norwegians as they all walked up the sand in the direction of the pub. Gareth could never remember being so down and out. Arthur Askey surely wouldn't start shouting out details of his filthy habits on *ITMA* would he? Everyone around here listened to *ITMA* and all he needed now was for Dylan Thomas to write a poem about his stained sheets and he'd be in the doghouse for all eternity.

LATER THAT afternoon he returned to the lane outside Cliff House where he hid behind the hedge again and watched for any movements. He wondered if he might dare risk getting any closer in case the kitchen curtains were still drawn but they weren't and, ten minutes later, the pacifist and his slut came out the house pushing a pram, evidently going for a walk.

It was difficult following them in broad daylight but they stuck to the main path on the cliff before lowering the pram down into one of the coves. He didn't risk following them down to the shingle but did discover that, if he crawled right up to the edge of the cliff, he could look directly down on them. Oh no! Not that! The dirty beasts were at it again. What was the matter with them? Didn't they ever stop?

There the pacifist was going up and down into her as her long legs waved around as if she was on some invisible, upside-down bicycle with The Boy lying asleep in the pram next to them. What did they think they were doing? Gareth put his hand over his mouth fearing he was going to throw up. The Boy could wake up at any second and see what they were doing. What was going to happen to him then? All this was having a bad enough effect on Gareth and he was a grown-up but The Boy was only a baby and the sight of all this would surely damage him for life. They were still going at it like a couple of billy goats and it was something you just didn't want to look at. Hot and flustered, he crawled away from the cliff edge and then crawled back again. He couldn't breathe properly, feeling a bit like Danny Price when he was having one of his asthma attacks.

He decided there was nothing else for it but to finish off his earlier, aborted wank so he crossed back over the path, jumped over a barbed wire fence and a few grazing sheep moved away from him sharply as he went down into a concealing gully, crouching down like a Red Indian listening out for the sounds of cavalry and putting his hand down inside his shorts again but losing interest when he spotted the bare skeleton of a sheep nearby which was swarming with flies and had been picked clean by foxes.

You simply could not have a wank looking at that mess so, with his hands waving, he ran back to the spot where he had been watching the pacifist and his slut doing it on the shingle. Well at least they weren't wriggling together anymore but laughing and sharing a cigarette. It was really disgusting when you thought about it. There they were laughing together and after all they'd done in front of The Boy. Didn't they have any shame at all?

Well, if they didn't, he most certainly did so, finally, he got to his feet and walked back to the farm feeling rotten to the core, unable to eat any of his tea of ham and chips – which fat Dic ate for him – and going to bed early, just lying there, keeping his arms stiff by his sides and his hands bunched tight, absolutely determined his wanking days were over forever.

But then even his dreams turned against him since he found himself sitting on the front pew in a packed congregation as the Rev Enoch, in his pulpit, addressed them about all the stains on Gareth Morgan's sheets.

'My text this morning, dearly beloved brothers and sisters, concerns the parable of young Gareth Morgan's stinking sheets. Now Gareth has been giving much thought to the fleshy bits of Miss Dolly James of Cliff House of late and, in consequence, not only is he coming close to wanking himself straight into the Blind Institute, but his white sheets are turning brown and even dancing around in his bedroom on their own. If, perchance, you do not believe me, then look at what I am about to show you.'

The congregation gasped when the Rev Enoch began unrolling one of Gareth's sheets over the front of his pulpit. 'Young Gareth Morgan says he is a pacifist who wants to become an intellectual and a politician but, my dearly beloved, I *beseech* you to just *regard* the size of this stain. And note this one here. Look at all these brown and yellow dribbles. And that one which looks like a relief map of the African continent. So, in the sight of God and with my hand on this holy Bible, I am going to call on you all now. I am going to call on you all and ask you one simple question. Do these *look* like the stains of someone who is going to be a pacifist politician?'

'Can't help it,' Gareth cried out into the disgusted darkness. 'Something's happening to me and my body and I can't help it.'

But he could, of course. He knew that as well as anyone. He knew he could stop all these dirty thoughts *if he tried*; if he made a bit of an effort; if he bucked up his ideas and pulled himself together.

Chapter Fourteen

DOLLY'S FACE was a mask of pain and confusion as her
bloodshot eyes, puddled with tears, kept glancing around her in
the tribunal trying to work out what was going on.

Something *was* going on, that much was for certain but she
couldn't be sure *what* as she looked up at the forbidding figure
of Judge Artemus Jones on the bench and at the scrubbed,
carbolicky men in pin-stripes sitting at their tables fiddling with
documents tied up in red ribbons and at her beloved Dafydd, all
done up in his one and only suit with not a trace of a smile on
his normally smiling features. The Rev Enoch was sitting next to
her and trying to console her by patting her hands or offering
her his outsize handkerchief which she used to blow her nose or
dab her eyes before giving it back to him.

The odd thing about her gusting turmoil was that Judge
Artemus Jones had not yet even delivered his verdict but she
knew it was going to be bad, if only because he was famous for
his bad verdicts throughout Wales, and she knew that, given her
luck with men, Dafydd would be bound to be taken away from
her, particularly now that he had been making every fibre of her
sing and dance and she wanted a lot more of it – and him – a lot,
lot more.

Another pin-stripe came to whisper something into the Rev
Enoch's ear and she looked up, worried that something might
be being hatched behind her back, when the pin-stripe left and
began whispering into the stenographer's ear, now moving
away out of sight altogether.

Under her expert tuition and with his enthusiasm for learning all the tricks, she had turned Dafydd into a brilliant lover – far better than she had ever experienced or even imagined – forever taking her on the stairs or on the kitchen table or even, on one memorable afternoon, right in the middle of the potato patch. She couldn't even remember the last time they had sweated over that awful Welsh primer although they had sweated over almost everything else. He was absolutely and joyously inexhaustible, didn't even seem to want a half an hour rest when he was sniffing around her again, looking to start up that incredible marching band all over again.

Also Dafydd had not made a particularly impressive statement to the tribunal and she had noticed that Judge Artemus Jones had rolled his eyes ceilingwards a few times when Dafydd was arguing that this was a capitalist war, almost certainly sponsored by European Jewry, which had nothing to do with Wales. 'I am a nationalist and a pacifist who, in all conscience, could not pick up arms to fight and especially for a country I have no faith or belief in. I only believe in Wales and only for her would I fight and die.'

Yet more pin-stripes were moving around in front of her when Judge Artemus Jones indicated he was ready to make his decision and she chewed on her lip and looked at Dafydd again who appeared almost angelic as be stood directly in a shaft of sunlight which sliced straight through the smoke-burnished gloom all around.

'Young men have a duty to defend their country although, this being a free country, we do allow them to make their views known,' Judge Artemus Jones began, and she knew immediately that it was going to be far worse than she had expected. Perhaps he was about to have Dafydd shot at dawn or something.

'But, having heard this young man's arguments, I see no particular attraction in them. Wales is simply not an independent country with its own culture and history as he

150

claims. Wales is firmly a part of the United Kingdom which is squarely facing the common enemy of a Nazi Germany. The Welsh nationalists have been earning an unfortunate reputation for being anti-Semitic and here, with this man, we have heard it all again. I see no merit at all in these disagreeable statements and, as an earnest of my rejection of them, I am not allowing him the soft option of becoming an agricultural worker or driving an ambulance, but am hereby ordering that he be detained in the camp in Weston-Super-Mare for the duration of the war.'

. . . detained in a camp in Weston-Super-Mare for the duration of the war? Whaaaat . . . Uuuurgh . . . hereby ordering . . . She jumped to her feet to protest and Dafydd glanced at her nervously but the Rev Enoch put his arm around he shoulders and made her sit down again. *Just what was the point of locking up a peace-loving follower of Tolstoy like that? Only yesterday Mr Churchill was telling the House of Commons that God always defended the right. Where was the right in all this?*

'Where's the right in all this?' she called out to Judge Artemus Jones who merely frowned at her and adjourned the hearing. 'God always defends the right so where's the right in all this?'

LATER SHE was sitting on a bench in the foyer of Cardigan Town Hall, still weeping into the Rev Enoch's capacious handkerchief when the minister began fiddling in his pockets, took out a small silver hip flask and offered it to her. She screwed up her nose questioningly and he explained: 'Brandy. I always keep some on me purely for medicinal reasons. Not for me, you know, but it does calm people down.'

She took one swig on the hip flask and enjoyed it so much she took another, actually feeling slightly better as the warm brandy began trampolining deep inside her. Then a tall shadow loomed over her which, she took some time to work out, contained a policeman.

'You are allowed ten minutes to say your farewell to Mr ap Iestyn. I must also advise you this farewell should be done in a proper and dignified manner and that it will be ten minutes and ten minutes only.'

She nodded and followed the policeman down a long corridor, which smelled of disinfectant, with the Rev Enoch, hands clasped prayerfully around his medicinal hip flask, bringing up the rear. They were ushered into a room and her heart shattered when she saw him sitting there at a table looking up at her like a little boy lost in Woolworth's. She took hold of his handcuffed wrists with tears waterfalling down her face. A whole gale of sorrow was blowing through her heart with so much of her shaking she had the distinct feeling she might be about to fall apart any moment now.

'Just take very good care of yourself . . . ' was about all Dafydd managed to say when Dolly hitched up her dress and began climbing up on to the table to hold him in her arms for one last time. With one knee on the table she had nearly got hold of him too and Dafydd was leaning back on his chair, trying to evade her grasp when the policeman grabbed her by her right shoulder and tried to haul her back. The Rev Enoch also caught her by he left arm and they both seemed to be winning when, with a great wail and an even greater wriggle, she broke free from their grips and began pulling her dress up over her head. The policeman was too flabbergasted to do anything about this sudden striptease and the Rev Enoch was so shocked he turned his back on her and lowered his head waving his hands around uselessly.

'Now, now we'll not be having any of that nonsense in here,' the policeman said when he'd recovered his composure except that Dolly had actually whipped off her dress and, still weeping like a running tap, was trying to pull her cami-knickers down over her gartered stockings.

'And we are *definitely* not having any of that in here,' the policeman said rather more firmly as he reached down to try and pull up her cami-knickers, resulting in a strange tug-of-war at the whereabouts of Dolly's knees with the Rev Enoch hovering over them and imploring everyone to calm down and talk about this while Dafydd continued sitting at the table with his head lowered as if the mêlée had nothing at all to do with him.

'All right, all right,' Dolly said, still half-naked and holding up her arms as if in surrender. 'All right, let's just calm down and talk about this,' she added and, when the two men stood back, she leaped onto the table and dived at Dafydd again only to be caught, almost in mid-flight, by the policeman and the Rev Enoch and another policeman, who had joined the struggling scrumdown with the ball nowhere in sight.

'Dolly, just stop being so childish and get dressed will you?' Dafydd finally broken his silence with a parade ground roar. 'Just put your clothes back on.'

Dolly picked up her dress meekly and put it back on as the policemen and minister looked at one another in wonder. She tidied her hair with hands and had even stopped crying. 'Take this Dafydd darling,' she said, as calm as if she was merely trying to decide what to buy in the General Stores and almost a different person to the earlier hysterical harridan. 'Here's a garter to remember me by when you're locked up in Weston-Super-Mare. It's a horrible place too. Went there on a paddle steamer once. Worst beach you've ever seen – all rocks, mud and seaweed. I'm sorry about all this minister. Strange things always happen to me if I so much as smell alcohol, especially brandy. The roof goes off and all the rain comes in. Perhaps you'd better see me home if you don't mind.'

DYLAN SAT at his writing table with innumerable balls of crumpled-up paper around his feet as the smoke from his cigarette occasionally caught in his eyes and made him squint but, even so, his concentration was total as he kept chipping away at his poetry with his 'tower of wood and lead' on unyielding sheet after unyielding sheet; the simple tools of his dramatically complex craft and art.

Beads of sweat speckled his furrowed brow which he sometimes let drip or wiped away with his shirt sleeve. He coughed and cigarette ash fell on his poem in progress, covering some of the words and spoiling their earlier resonance so he scrunched up the paper and started on the poem all over again, hacking at words and phrases again, trying to get them to reveal an unexpected inner beauty, rolling them around like a master baker or metal worker looking for that one perfect shape.

The summer sun had turned Majoda into a sauna and, even with all the windows open, there never seemed to be enough air within those asbestos walls. A wasp flew in through the window and he watched it warily as it flew out of another. He could hear the very house groaning and aching under the weight of all this fierce sunlight; groaning for the sun to go away again and leave its parched timbers in peace.

'The sleeping haystack,' he boomed suddenly, rolling the phrase around his mouth and mind, 'the haystack deep in its morning sleep . . . the haystack caught in the hands of the morning . . .'

He muttered such phrases in soft love whispers and in Big Ben booms, trying them for depth, passion, sonority but also always on the look-out for pretentiousness because pretentiousness always destroyed all art and particularly his kind of art. Even the most beautiful phrase should look as if it had been turned over easily and quickly in a conversation in a pub and he always knew when he had hit the target; always knew precisely what clumps of words would firmly and finally destroy the reader's resistance to his poetic charms.

A watching stranger could sometimes pick up his vibrating intensity while at work by the way his blood might suddenly drain out of his face or the way his hands started shaking wildly before his pencil began picking at the paper again. This was a dedicated craftsman working with the raw materials of his poetic intelligence and deep feelings; using all his intuitive skills to try and get close to the very secrets of life itself.

But he wasn't getting anywhere; the thing just wouldn't come together for him and unfold in a spirit of ordered wildness so he started doodling and writing out lists of words – *rabbit, ruffian, tranche, trenchant, googly* – filling up several sides of paper with them, poking them, prodding them, sniffing them for signs of life. Doodles of Christmas trees and dead dogs were dotted around these lists and, somewhere beneath all these random drawings and words, another poem might be lurking just below the surface – the fat, elusive pike waiting to be hooked and hauled up, wriggling brilliantly, into the applauding daylight.

He had really fished well in his time in Majoda so far, grinding out a dozen or so major poems here, including *Fern Hill*. His new collection, *Deaths and Entrances*, only needed a few more pike and that would be ready to take to the market too.

CAITLIN LAY lay naked in the bedroom as he worked, her hair still wet and matted after taking an afternoon swim in the sea. She always enjoyed the release of a hard swim in the sea, even if only because it relieved her of some of her bursting Celtic intensity. She was still getting some release from such intensity with that oaf Dic Morgan on the floor of the beer cellar of the Black Lion. He was sweetly amusing and amusingly rough but she had long stopped looking forward to these couplings which were so cold, mechanical and *unromantic*. Her romanticism still clung to her hard; it was still, she knew, her major disease and, in that respect, and perhaps in that respect alone she had something in common with Dylan. They both failed to see life clearly, always took the romantic angle and that may well have been at the root of their common despair.

She smoothered her awful hands up and down her long, lovely limbs as she listened to her old man work.

Despite all her melodramatic dreams and endless self-pity

she was often capable of such savage insights into her real being. She knew as well as anyone that life was hard and should only ever be tackled on its own terms; she knew as well as anyone that there was always a high price to pay for being outlaws; that they had both actually chosen to live on the edge and would always therefore be treated as such. Rebels never won anything; they were always beaten down mercilessly in the end.

Not that she usually levelled the gun at herself like this: mostly it was everyone else who was to blame for levelling the guns at her except that, this warm afternoon, she was looking closely at herself and seeing that she too had played a major role in the way their lives were falling apart all around them.

'The angel of the morning. A morning angel. The angels riding the morning . . .'

Words, yes. She had allowed her better judgement to be seduced by his empty, beautiful words which really meant nothing at all and was the reason why they were both buried, yes *buried*, in abject poverty. All his words had disguised the real nature of reality in their eyes: they had blinded them to the truth of life, making them unable to see things as they are which was why they had ended up in this state. Words were only ever words. Deeds were what mattered: what you did with your life rather than what you said about it.

But there was no going back now. Once you set off down a certain path you burn your bridges and there is no return. There would never be any security or stability in her life. She had built on the shifting sands of his words and, in so doing, embraced the margins where she would live and die.

DYLAN COULD feel a headache taking up lodgings in his brain so he put down his pencil, looked in on Caitlin who was dozing on the bed and decided to take a walk in the nearby Aeronwy Valley, shoving his hands down into his pockets and shuffling along as he soaked up the endless balmy delights of a Welsh summer.

It was shaping up into a real summer too, strutting through West Wales gaudily like a coronation procession, scorching the black earth into brown dust and putting all the farms under the hot hammer. Little grows on brown dust and, even with all the new fertilisers introduced by the County War Ags, the farmers were complaining that this year's hay had thin stalks and fat seed heads. Green aphids were already sucking the life out of the corn and the cows were bellowing loudly because they never seemed to have enough water and, when they didn't have enough water, they never produced enough milk.

Dylan continued past the pink cottage on the outskirts of the town when he heard some scuffling noises behind, turning to see a young boy who was hurrying after him, shouting his name and waving his hands around. It was young Gareth Morgan from the farm and Dylan waited for him to catch up before walking on again.

'I thought it was you, Mr Thomas, and I'm glad I've bumped into you because there's always been something I've wanted to ask you.'

Dylan looked down at him and lifted his chin slightly in query.

'I just wanted to ask you how to write a poem.'

'I don't know.'

'You haven't even got any tips then?'

'No. None. You can't explain how to write a poem any more than you can teach someone how to breathe. You can either do it or you can't. All you do is grab hold of some words, keep bashing them about and hoping for the best.'

'And that's all?'

'Pretty much. But come on, walk with me for a while. Tell me about what you've been trying to write.'

As they walked together the poet found that the lad knew a lot of things and he enjoyed talking to him, identifying immediately with his young uncertainties. Grown-ups always put the wind up Dylan but he always responded to the multiple fears and uncertainties of youth since, in them, he always saw himself.

'Well it's certainly a day to make a Baptist preacher smile,' said Dylan, 'and this is such a beautiful valley, perhaps the most beautiful in the whole of Wales.'

'The Welsh names on the farms are interesting too,' Gareth pointed out. 'They're really lovely names and they've all got the word milk in them. So you've got Milk House, Milk Aspect, Milk Wood and Under the Wood. Then there's the river here, the Aeron. Aeron means fruit or harvest. So we have the river of the harvest – the river of fruit – all under the farm of Milk Wood. I would have thought there might even be a poem in all that somewhere for you.'

'Yes, there might indeed, there might indeed. Do you smoke do you?'

'No, but I'll take one for my friend. He smokes like a chimney.'

They walked on for a while saying nothing and enjoying the summer burbling in the hedgerows when Dylan spotted a figure walking towards them being followed by a bantam cock.

'Don't stop and talk,' said Gareth. 'She'll keep you here all afternoon. Just nod and walk on.'

The approaching figure was like no one Dylan had ever seen since she had a face as dark and wrinkled as an old prune and was wearing a trilby held in place by a red scarf tied under her chin. Then there were her clogs and an old lace shawl tied around her shoulders and waist. She was also puffing on an old Churchwarden clay pipe although the truly odd thing about her was the chicken plodding along in her wake like a devoted puppy.

She stopped as the two passed her, blowing a small gale of foul-smelling smoke over them. 'Nice day for a sunrise, gentlemen,' she cackled. 'But the question is when will it set? It may set in the night although, there again, if it knows what's good for it, it will do exactly as I tell it.'

Gareth smiled wanly and kept touching Dylan's hand, trying to keep him walking. 'Good to see you, Shani,' the boy said. 'The chicken's looking nice today.'

'He's cleaned his teeth he has, as all good chickens should. And I tell him – you clean your teeth like a good boy and I'll take you for a nice walk.'

The pair walked on leaving the woman talking to herself.

'*What* was that?' Dylan asked.

'Shani Bob Mam, they call her. Lives on Cei Bach beach in an old wooden hut together with about twenty chickens.'

'Amazing. You couldn't make someone like that up.'

'She gets by on three shillings a week parish relief and makes some extra money by selling her eggs which she dyes brown with cold tea. They're very good eggs too, some with double yolks and she never has any trouble selling them.'

'You seem to know a lot about the people around here.'

'Well, I don't miss much, you know. My brother Dic always swears I'm some sort of Peeping Tom because I'm always looking in on things. And the people around here *are* strange too. I met a waterfall tuner the other week.'

'Never. What does he do? I mean, how do you tune a waterfall?'

'It's all to do with the height of the fall, the arrangement of the rocks and the kind of tune you want the waterfall to make.'

'Never. Do you want another cigarette for your friend?'

THEY STOPPED on the corner of the road to Talsarn when Gareth pointed at a long black cloud settling ominously on the rim of the distant horizon. 'I thought it was going to rain,' he told Dylan, 'because the sun had been getting behind the butt of the wind. That should get to us around five o'clock but it'll only be a small summer storm. It won't be doing the land any good but be sure to cover all mirrors and open all doors when it starts so your house doesn't go trapping any thunderbolts.'

'A house can trap thunderbolts can it?'

'Oh yes, most certainly.'

'Gareth, you should become a writer. You know things I never knew at your age.'

'Oh this is just farming stuff I'm telling you. You get to know these things when you grow up on a farm. Actually don't tell anyone but I'm hoping to become a politician. A nationalist with Plaid. And a pacifist. That's what I really want to be.'

'Forget about all that nonsense, boy. Become a writer and clothe all that knowledge of yours with beautiful words. There's no money in it and the arse of your pants will always be hanging out but you'll get more fanny than Errol Flynn.'

DYLAN'S HEAD was still buzzing with all the things Gareth had told him as he lay on the sofa in Majoda later that afternoon, staring into space when, at five o'clock sharp, a massive summer storm began building up over the Bay beginning with faint hisses of lightning and muted rolls of thunder.

He jumped up to open the front door and was covering the mirror above the mantelpiece with a towel when Caitlin walked in. 'Dylan, just *what* are you up to now?'

'Letting out thunderbolts, Cat.'

She glanced around the room, as if expecting to find a thunderbolt curled up in front of the firegrate or sitting in the deckchair. 'Just say it's me, if you like, but I don't see any thunderbolts.'

'They're not here yet but they'll be getting here soon and that farm boy Gareth Morgan told me to keep the doors open and the mirrors covered so they don't get in and get trapped.'

'Why you always listen to those oafs always beats me. But explain one thing to me now: if the doors are closed and they stay closed how the fuck is this thunderbolt going to get in in the first place?'

'That's a good question.'

'And, if it does get in, how the fucking hell – and I do mean how the fucking hell – how the fucking hell is it going to just stand there and just admire itself in front of the fucking mirror?'

'It's what I was told, Cat. We're city people but these people know about the countryside and I don't want to take any chances. I can't just sit here writing poetry with thunderbolts chasing one another around the room.'

But despite her cynicism Caitlin made no attempt to close the door or cover up the mirror as the storm began building up with power and fury. Indeed she even sat with Dylan and gave him a bit of a *cwtch* in her arms on the sofa, nursing him like her other baby as his body jumped and twitched along with the many bangs and crashes of the storm. Pink stammerings of sheet lightning flashed through the furious rain and thin streams of asbestos dribbled from the shaken eaves.

Another vibrant thunderhead made Dylan hold her ever tighter, whimpering softly and burying his face into the soft folds of her belly. She liked it when he became as needy as this, smiling down on him and smoothing his hair before beginning to sing a soft Irish lullaby. Then she slipped a nipple from under her jumper and let him chomp on it for a while, actually feeling the fear and tensions drain out of him until he even began gurgling with small tremors of happiness and finally fell fast asleep.

Chapter Fifteen

THE STORM had not given the briefest respite to the parched land and, the next morning, Dylan was standing in the doorway of Majoda looking out on his garden where the sea breezes were whipping the dust around in spinning tops and two giant moths were tumbling in the heat hazes on the crest of the road.

He could feel a touch of bronchitis lying warmly on his chest so he lit a cigarette to loosen it up a bit, taking in the smoke and holding it down for a while before exhaling hissily and getting the mucus chattering and slipping around more easily. He always liked to feel a good rattle deep in his chest when he coughed which was why he smoked so much, he said; to stop the mucus settling down and doing some real damage to his health.

'Dylan, I'm going down to the sea for a quick swim,' Caitlin's voice called out to him from within the house. 'I don't suppose I'll be more than half an hour.'

'Well, put a costume on will you?'

'Why?'

'The dirty old men in the Black Lion are always talking about your bobbling boobies that's why.'

'I don't mind anyone seeing my bobbling boobies even if you do. And anyway they don't bobble that much. You've always said I've got nice boobies.'

'Nudity and the Welsh don't go together, you should know that by now. All babies are born in their best clothes in Wales and people even wear bathing costumes in their baths in case they might see something that would hurt their eyes. They even fuck by telepathy, you know, dirty thoughts sent over the airwaves.'

'Bah. They are what they are and I am what I am. I do *not* like wearing a costume in the sea.'

'It's me who's got to face them in the Black Lion every night. That old sea captain is the worst. He's always watching you through that telescope of his when you go to the sea with your bobbling boobies.'

'Well I just hope the old bugger enjoys it. That's all I hope.'

AS IT turned out the very thought of Captain Port Talbot getting his jollies off while he watched her swimming added to her delicious sense of freedom as she dropped her dressing gown on the shingle and waded through the cool waves before diving straight in.

Swimming in the nuddy was one of her few serious pleasures and she loved gambolling around in the insistent currents, feeling the small fish nipping her legs and enjoying the way the cold water enveloped her so completely. There was a liberating rapture about swimming like this and she wouldn't even have much minded if the whole town had come out on to the beach to watch her. That would have been real fun, especially as it would also get right up the trumpet of her daft, puritanical husband. He had frequently railed against D.H. Lawrence and his ungodly worship of sex and sun but she had always quite approved of all that: the more sex and sun the better.

Her swimming was swift and strong as she went out about a hundred yards, stopping to tread water and wave back at Dylan, standing in the garden of Majoda and staring down at her.

He had his moments but he really was such an ass at heart, his natural warmth and exuberance constantly being chilled by the cold shadow of the chapel. Sometimes he could be the best and funniest

163

Bohemian on the planet but then, for no reason, he would start worrying about the watchful aloofness of God again and he became a different person, cold and judgemental, sitting on the set fawr in his deacon's clothes and admonishing her for actually being what he had frequently said he had fallen in love with. Perhaps you always want to change what you fall in love with: maybe because you never trusted that love in the first place. But it was right not to trust the nature of love; it was always a deeply unreliable and basically pissy emotion.

She was about to strike back to the shore when she spotted Dolly James walking along the beach alone. The talk was that she had become a sad, stricken figure since her pacifist teacher had gone and got himself locked away in Weston-Super-Mare and she'd turned into a modern Miss Havisham in her Satis House, going progressively more loopy now her love had been taken away from her, shying away from the questions of strangers like a nervous colt and just dying of breaking heart before their eyes.

Watched both by Dylan in the garden and Caitlin treading water out in the sea, Dolly continued walking along the beach, with the gabbling gulls gliding and swooping all around her, when she raised the back of her wrist to her forehead and fell sideways on to the sand like a sack of cement.

Caitlin screamed out Dylan's name but all he did was take the cigarette out of his mouth and put it back again so she struck out with a powerful over-arm before hurrying up the beach and kneeling down next to her. She had seen enough people pass out in her time but that was usually because of excessive drunkenness so she wasn't at all sure what to do now except pat her on the cheek hopefully when Dolly came around with a start and her eyes fluttered in alarm when they saw a wet, naked woman looming over her. 'Oh please get dressed mummy,' she muttered before fading away again. 'Do put some knickers on before all those nasty schoolboys see you.'

'Just relax now Dolly. Take some deep breaths and you'll be fine.'

'I always liked wearing my knickers over my arm myself. They always seemed to fit better there.'

'Just be calm Dolly. Let's get you up and you'll be fine.'

Caitlin helped Dolly to her feet and she soon recovered her balance, brushing a few stones out of her corkscrew curls with her hand before shaking her head and trying to get some sense back into her brain. 'It's happened a few times now, you know. The sun goes dark and . . . well . . . '

Caitlin glanced up at Majoda where her useless bastard of a husband was still standing in the same spot smoking that same cigarette. *You might have thought he'd come down and lend a hand or something. But not him. He was as useless as a damp fart in a monsoon. No, even more useless than that . . .*

'I'll walk you back up to Cliff House.'

'No, really, I'll be fine.'

'I'll walk you back just the same. Wait here for a second while I get my dressing gown.'

Dolly was already walking back along the beach by the time Caitlin had donned her dressing gown and caught up with her again but she seemed well enough now. Caitlin insisted on staying with her, talking brightly as they walked together and suggesting they might both go over to see Dr Pugsley for a quick check-up.

But Dolly wasn't having anything to do with that idea *or him*. 'I wouldn't go to him if I was on my very last breath.'

'Why not?'

'They always tell nasty, horrid tales about Dr Pugsley and what he's always trying to do to his poor wife.'

'What kind of tales?'

'It's not for me to say but you'll find out soon enough.'

WHEN CAITLIN did finally return to Majoda she found Dylan sitting in the kitchen and unable to look her in the eye. *What* had he been up to now? 'I would have thought you would have come down to the beach and at least *tried* to help that poor woman.'

'Cat, you know I'm no good in those situations. Never know what to do. And it's all woman stuff isn't it?'

'What do you mean woman stuff?'

'You know, stuff that women are good at sorting out together. We men can sort out men stuff and women can do all the women stuff. I mean to say it stands to reason doesn't? You took her home did you?'

She glared at him but decided there was no point in trying to argue with his species of imbecility. 'I did. But she never invited me in or anything and you know what? I'm pretty sure she's pregnant. There's a good bump down there and I'd say that she was five or six months gone. That teacher of hers must have had a good time before they locked him up.'

Had she looked closely at her husband's face she would have noticed his flabby muscles stiffening in a rictus of fear which was usually, but not always, a prelude to a nasty outbreak of red blotches. Had she actually been able to see into his mind she would have seen the dark image of a lonely lifeboat station standing in the middle of it, together with a flurry of bare, drunken limbs locked in a lurid sexual encounter which was going well until it went straight to the dogs. She would also have seen, threaded through this deeply unfortunate encounter, some hasty calculations as to how many months it had been since New Year's Eve.

But perhaps luckily for the continuing good health of everyone in that kitchen she did not look at his face and neither could she read the sexual antics and mathematical anxieties in his mind so she merely shrugged her shoulders, walked over to the stove and lifted the lid of a simmering pan of stew. 'Do you want some of this?' she asked him. 'Or are you on one of your hunger strikes again?'

THE FOLLOWING Thursday Gareth was messing about among the cows in the milking shed when he was surprised to see Dolly's silhouette framed in the light of the doorway.

166

'I haven't seen you for a long time, Gareth. I was hoping you might come over and baby-sit for me tonight while I go to the pictures.'

'I've been busy I have. There's been lots to do around the farm here.'

'But I don't just want you for baby-sitting you know. I want you as a friend too. I miss having you around and talking like we used to. I *need* a friend, Gareth. Everyone needs a friend.'

'What's the matter with the pacifist then?' He couldn't quite manage to take the sneer out of the question.

'Well, he's locked away isn't he? He's still a friend but I need a friend I can talk to. Someone I can be with.'

She walked down into the milking shed and Gareth was surprised to see the gaunt illness in her face; her drawn cheeks and the darkness all around her eyes which seemed to have lost all their sparkle.

'Gareth, I am really, really desperate. Please start calling over at Cliff House again. I know these are difficult times for you but I could help you if only you'd be my friend again.'

'Difficult times?'

'You know what I mean. I've got two younger brothers and I know what boys of your age have to go through. Just start coming to see me again the way you used to. I don't want to lose your friendship. I really don't and I could be a good friend to you if only you'd let me. Let's try it again shall we?'

He blushed deeply not because of the intimacy of her request so much as the image of those bare, long legs of hers went bicycling through his mind. She must have had hundreds of men at her beck and call but, there again, maybe he could take over after the pacifist had got locked up; he wasn't proud and maybe he'd get a turn himself in between those bare, long legs. 'Yes, I'll come over tonight,' he said, 'maybe around seven after tea.'

HE WENT around the farm whistling a lot after she left and

even decided to have a bath before going over to Cliff House *just in case* but, sitting there in the zinc bath, his eternally fragile happiness shattered again after he began pulling his peter from side to side to see if there were any signs it might be about to fall off after he'd been pulling it around so much. It seemed to be pretty well stuck on to him when he noticed that there were exactly eight hairs growing around it. They weren't all that thick or long but they were *there* all right and he got sick with worry again. This was all getting out of control and these *were* difficult times for sure. *Just what was going to happen to him next?*

Chapter Sixteen

A STRAY leaf bounced on the back of a slow breeze blowing across the farmyard and Mrs Rachel Morgan paused to watch its fluttering path while wondering why it had fallen so early in the summer. Autumn wasn't about to start was it? It was too early for autumn but maybe the trees were suffering along with everyone else in all this ferocious heat. The leaf landed near a baking cowpat swarming with flies before the breeze lifted it up again and carried it on down towards the well.

She had been carrying a full milk-pail from the cowshed to the farmhouse when she had stopped to watch the leaf although she was surprised at how heavy her pail had suddenly become and looked down into it to see if the milk had somehow turned into shale or cement.

Dic was carrying an armful of loose staves, on his way to fix a broken fence, when he looked at his mother curiously, perhaps wondering why she was just standing there motionless as if in a trance. She stared back at Dic with a severe and even puritan hardness, as if he was some sort of malingerer she was about to sack, before her eyes settled on Ernst who was following Dic holding a hammer and a bag of nails in his hands.

She had always liked but had never quite accepted this Norwegian who had just turned up one day on the farm and just stayed. He worked hard enough – never trying to avoid the heavy tasks and was clearly as sharp as a ferret's teeth – but she had never quite accepted him because he never told her much about himself. She couldn't work him out at all and had always prided herself on being able to work people out, particularly men.

There was a distance and correctness about him which her friendly Welsh nature could never quite come to terms with. Those two Norwegian friends of his also worried the life out of her, never actually coming on to the farm but waiting for him at the gate when they would go off together and do whatever it was that Norwegians did in their spare time.

Trefor emerged from the kitchen door holding a bloodied knife with which had been gutting a rabbit. 'Mam they're coming next week. I just heard it on the wireless.'

'*Who* are coming next week?' Her eldest son's imprecision had always exasperated her.

'The refugee kids. They're saying that anything up to two hundred might be coming to New Quay next week.'

Something hard and cold began growing inside her and she studied Trefor's face carefully as Dic and Ernst stopped still, perhaps wondering why she was continuing to just stand there holding that milk-pail. You'd think she'd put the bucket down or something but she didn't seem to want to move anywhere. She had never quite worked out where Trefor had got his slightly daft innocence; her other sons were as bright as stars in the night sky but almost everything about Trefor was slightly daft, from his big owly eyes to his bushy eyebrows and large mouth which took an age to form words. *The whitewash on the side of the pig sty was still bubbling and flaking. She had told them a dozen times that the sty had to be painted. Pigs like to be in nice surroundings too.*

'Did you hear me Mam? The evacuee kids should be here within a week.'

That hardness and coldness seemed to be growing and gathering all down her left hand side and, with a slightly fearful sniff, she put down her pail and began wiping her hands slowly in her blackened pinafore. This was the small, almost hourly ritual of all Welsh housewives before they embark on yet another domestic task but, this time, she seemed intent on doing it with a special care, as if her next task was going to be very important indeed. When she had finished wiping her hands she turned them over and back again, inspecting the red-raw palms and fingers to make sure they were properly clean before looking back at Trefor again.

The hardness and coldness thickened right across her chest and, as she stood there, quietly and even desperately hanging on to her composure, she could feel herself becoming short of breath and oddly, in the circumstances, she picked up her milk-pail again as all her strength seemed to be draining out of her legs like oil out of an emptying sump. She patted the side of her silvery hair with her free hand to make sure it was tidy and her eyes rolled upwards at a blue sky full of screaming gulls. 'I'm sure I asked one of you to whitewash that pig sty at the beginning of the summer,' she said but no sounds came out of her mouth, just an empty necklace of soundless vowels and consonants.

Her eyes glanced around her again and caught the rolling, green fields of her farm; the rolling, green fields of her *much-loved* farm and she thought of Gareth and her throat filled up a little as she recalled his terror-filled helplessness and the way he had always needed her to protect him from the casual cruelties of his brothers. He would become a very fine man, she knew, but he had a long way to go yet. But she did so wish he was at her side now, if only to help her with this heavy milk-pail. The boy had always been her body and blood but she had never thought of Trefor in that way; Trefor had always been so slow and, well, daft.

Ernst caught her stare next and she noticed that his cold blue eyes were studying her closely and carefully. He never missed a thing did Ernst and she would have liked to have known more about him and would have particularly liked to have known something about his mother since, had she known the mother, she might have been able to work out more about the mysterious son. But no answers came even to her most innocuous questions and he had an extremely irritating habit of tapping the side of his nose and claiming all kinds of trivial things were 'Top secret'.

All her body was now seizing up, with every muscle and bone failing to respond to her wishes, and she knew something awful was about to befall her – you always knew about these things – and she would really have preferred it if it hadn't all been quite so public; that, at least, she could have been indoors or in her bed or somewhere *private* when what was about to happen did happen.

'You'd better come in and sit down Mam. We'd better have a chat about all these evacuees. Maybe we can have a few of them on the farm. Will they be bringing their own gas masks do you think?'

'The pigs need to have their sty whitewashed properly,' she said but again, even though her lips were moving, no words came out. Her voice might have belonged to a woman on the next farm or even the next county and her body still didn't seem to want to have anything to do with her either when her voice strangely rediscovered itself in her mouth. 'Trefor, you'd better get that sty whitewashed proper. I've always told you pigs don't like to be in mucky houses. It's just us who think they always like to be in muck.'

'I'll do it tomorrow Mam.'

'No, do it *today*.'

What she really could not understand – what was really amazing when you came to think about it – was how, with her whole body frozen and almost without any strength, she was still managing to stand erect holding a full pail of milk.

The short, workman-like figure of Tada hove into view carrying an ailing lamb and her eyes filled with tears: Tada, the man who, for close on forty years, had been her very eyes. She had never understood why she had married him, to be honest, and there had been other offers, but he had never once let her

172

down, always worked hard and finally won her with his sheer, dogged devotion.

Now, she noted with some alarm, the eyes of *all* her men were firmly fastened on her, none of them moving or saying a word, almost as if they had all gathered in that yard waiting for her to make an important announcement.

At that moment all her growing hardness and coldness seized hold of that slippery fist of muscle and blood which was her heart and, with a relentless squeeze, brought it to a halt. For a brief moment she actually saw her very being hitching up her skirts and fleeing across the farmyard to another place and another time. Then she died as she stood.

All four men dashed towards her with hands outstretched, as if in some forlorn attempt to catch her before she hit the ground, but none of them were fast enough and her body landed face-down and spread-eagled over the hard, fly-blown ground while the milk pail clanged like an ironic death knell and the milk spilled all around in white rivulets in the fine, golden light of a Welsh chapel morning.

A PORTLY and grave Dr Pugsley arrived at the farm within the hour, just about managing to squeeze his fat belly from out behind the steering wheel of his Morris Minor before being shown up to the main bedroom by Dic where he found Mrs Rachel Morgan stretched out on the bed, her body stiff, her eyes open and her fingers stretching out as if eager to get on with some work as usual. Her stockinged feet had holes in them and the milk had stained her serge clothes.

Tada and Trefor stood up from their chairs and looked at the doctor as he stood there sighing, their faces still ashen with shock but their eyes full of a gambler's hope that the doctor might do something; that he might, by some Lazarus-like miracle, raise her from her farmyard collapse and put her right again. But all the doctor did was check the time on his fob watch before sighing again and walking over to Mrs Morgan and closing her eyelids with his fingertips. After a brief examination of the side of her neck and an even briefer examination of her chest he checked his watch again before announcing that he was deeply sorry but she had passed on and there was nothing that could be done.

'I'll send a district nurse who'll lay her out and put on her best clothes. The vicar will need to be told immediately so he start thinking about the funeral and you'll need to get Adams and Black to bring in a coffin.'

'It's all over then doctor?'

'Yes, it is. But it was a good death if there can ever be such a thing. Distress of the heart, I'll be writing on the death certificate. Quick and no pain. One of the very best ways to go.'

THE QUICKSILVER shapes of dolphins gambolled out in the flat, sun-burnished Bay as Ernst walked along Llanina Point, despatched to 'sort out' the minister because everyone else was too upset to think about anything at all. It was a task he accepted readily because he felt a duty of care to hold everyone together while they were falling apart; in a sense it was his job and he had always taken his job seriously.

He stopped outside Cliff House, where Gareth had been spending a lot of time lately with Miss Dolly, hoping to be able to tell him he had better get back to the farm, but there was no one around so perhaps they had gone out for the day. He had never actually spoken to Miss Dolly, although there had been a few curious looks, but, like a lot of other men, he had long been one of her admirers from afar.

He continued through the town where the grapevine had already been electrified by Mrs Rachel Morgan's dramatic demise in her own farmyard; the news sweeping pretty much everywhere, rung through to the General Stores, tongued all along the terraces, jumped over garden fences, swept through astonished parlours and even sent scurrying back to the General Stores where, disappointingly, the group of shoppers in there had heard it already.

Ernst finally knocked on the old oak door of the manse high on the hill, looking up and around him at this huge gloomy place. It was the house of a philosopher who had long abandoned philosophy, he thought; a once holy place which had gone and lost its way in the fog of another world war. *Any self-respecting God needed to make sense and there was never any sense to be had anywhere at a time of war. Only the bare facts were sufficient unto themselves and all metaphysical speculation was particularly nonsensical at a time of war. The only truths were mathematical depending on no outside conditions. Where there are no a priori truths – or empirical facts – everything is nonsense.*

'I have been asked to come here by the Morgan family in Llanina,' Ernst said when the Rev Enoch answered the knock eating a sandwich. 'Mrs Rachel Morgan died this afternoon on the farm. It was a condition of the heart and arrangements have to be made for the funeral.'

The Rev Enoch's jaws stopped chewing as he absorbed this news and he waved Ernst inside with the remainder of his sandwich. 'I am very sorry to hear this. Mrs Rachel Morgan was a grand woman with a fine, Christian heart. Take a seat in here for a moment would you?'

Ernst was ushered into a library full of old and mildewed books which, he quickly saw, were mostly theological and hence of no interest to him. The Rev Enoch motioned him to sit in a leather armchair while he sat behind his own desk piled high with opened books and untidy stacks of papers.

'So will you please explain to me again why you have come here, my son. I am getting very old now and can't remember a thing.'

The old man even seemed to have forgotten what he had been told on his own doorstep but he listened carefully and finished his sandwich as Ernst went through it all again, in more detail this time, explaining how Mrs Rachel Morgan had died of a heart condition in the farm at about three o'clock that afternoon and, after the doctor had been called, he had been sent here to inform the minister about the sad news so that suitable arrangements could be made for the funeral.

'This is terrible, terrible news and I am very upset,' said the Rev Enoch lifting up his blotter and peering under it as if looking for something important. 'I have known Mrs Rachel Morgan almost all my life and, in a way, we have shadowed one another down all our days. So another light has gone out and this also tells me my time will also be up soon. But I *am* ready for it. I *am* going to be more than glad to finally find my out of this labyrinth of tears. Our young people are welcome to it.'

Ernst sat there politely as the Rev Enoch continued working his way through his labyrinth of tears, pretending to listen but also absorbing the details of the room: the rumbling Act of Parliament clock, the huge empty fire grate and the heavy tapestry curtains open wide enough to reveal a marvellous view of Cardigan Bay. The minister began shuffling his papers on his desk again when a skull with uneven smiling teeth emerged in the mess.

That skull had to be the one that Dylan Thomas was always moaning about in the Black Lion; the one which the minister had stolen off him after it had been trawled up out of the Bay by the fisherman Matthews. He had long been curious about that skull and there it was, all round and bald and smiling as if enjoying some kind of graveyard joke.

'You're not from around here are you, my son?'

'No. I am from Norway and we have been stationed here for a while. That skull is very interesting, I think.'

'Yes, it is. I keep meaning to give it some kind of proper burial but haven't got around to it yet. I know Norway slightly. Which part are you from?'

'You can bury a skull can you? You could give a skull a proper Christian burial?'

'Well yes and no. Maybe not a full one as we'll be having for Mrs Rachel Morgan. But a smaller one with a blessing. Much smaller with a big blessing. I haven't quite decided yet.'

'So I will be able to tell the family you will come over as soon as possible will I?'

The Rev Enoch hesitated for a while until the penny dropped. 'Oh yes. Oh most certainly. Oh yes, I'll be coming over to the farm just as soon as I've finished my tea.'

THERE WERE but six regulars in the Black Lion early that night, four standing some way from one another at the bar and Dylan, his first pint still untouched, engrossed in a game of dominoes at the far table with Dai Fred. The clack of each domino was curiously amplified by the emptiness of the bar and even the conversation of the four men didn't seem to want to challenge the pervading silence with their sentences sometimes falling away from them, hesitant and uncompleted, onto the cold flagstones.

'Helped a lot of people in her time,' said Joshua the Bluebell. 'The original Welsh Mam she was – never drank, never smoked, never said a bad word about anyone.'

'I was sure she'd be getting a telegram from the King on her hundredth.'

'That farm is never going to be the same without her. I somehow can't see Pop Morgan carrying on with the, you know . . .'

'I'll tell you one thing. Rachel Morgan had secrets even her family didn't know about. Someone, somewhere, is in for an awful lot of money and all I know for sure is it's not me.'

'Rachel Morgan had money did she?'

'She did. Bloody tons of it.'

Silence colonised the bar again as the men pondered on Mrs Rachel Morgan's tons of money while Dylan and Dai continued with their clacking dominoes. The Black Widow came in to claim her usual seat where she stared sorrowfully into space as Percy Hoskins took over her pint of cider and placed it in front of her when, without a word or taking her eyes off that spot in space, she paid him with coins counted out of her purse.

A further five silent minutes later Dic Morgan walked into the bar, his beefy features set in a deep melancholia, as the regulars all moved away from him slightly, as if to give him more space than he actually needed, and Percy pulled him a pint of Buckley's Best.

Dic grabbed the pint with both shaking hands and more or less managed to put it down in one go, now wiping his mouth with his shirt sleeve, belching and nodding at Percy to pull him another as the others continued to watch him silently.

'It is perhaps unnecessary to say we're all upset by the death of your mother,' Dylan said after leaving his game of dominoes and taking Dic by the elbow. 'Death always brings us down with a nasty, sharp bump. The Christians say we should welcome death but it's so unnecessary really and so painful for all us poor buggers left behind.'

'She was just standing there, you know, as right as ninepence and, pop, she's dead. I *still* can't believe I've seen what I've seen. Just standing there looking at us, as if she was about to give us all a good bollocking or something.' He shook his head in exasperated disbelief and tears flew out of his eyes. 'No warning. Nothing. Just standing there looking at us.'

He reached for his second pint but Dylan put his hand firmly on Dic's arm, indicating he should not pick it up. 'No Dic. Not this way. There are times to be drunk and this is *not* one of them. Your mother has just died Dic and today you should stay sober. For her.'

All eyes looked at Dylan with slightly raised eyebrows but no one made any comment, particularly the obvious one.

'Dic, you have today lost the greatest thing that you have ever had in your life. You have lost the love of your own mother, the only love that gives and gives without any thought of a return. Your mother's love is the green fuse which gave you your life and, today, the day of her death, is *not* the time to get drunk.'

'What am I supposed to do then?'

'Go back to the farm, Dic, and be with her while she's still there. Grieve for her properly like the others. Face up to the pain and start working your way through it. Getting drunk now will just dishonour your mother and all that she has ever stood for *and given you.*'

Dic looked at his pint and at Dylan and at the others in the bar who murmured some sort of agreement even if they really didn't have a clue what the mad poet was talking about. Even The Black Widow seemed uncharacteristically interested in the conversation.

'Come on, I'll walk back to the farm with you,' Dylan offered, tapping Dic on the hand. 'We'll all drink lots another day but, today, we'll just go home and be with your mother while she's still there.'

IT WAS dark and moonlight shivered on the sea expensively when Dolly and Gareth came pushing the pram down to Cliff House after a long day shopping in Abersytwyth. Gareth helped her unload the bags on to the kitchen table and she invited him to stay for some tea but he said it was late and he had better get back to the farm and ran home, warm with her friendship and affection and pausing only for a few moments to watch the small, silvery waves washing the feet of the night and listen to the owl in the oak tree crying plaintively about his loneliness.

He started running again and came to the top gate of the farm where he stopped and stared hard at three unfamiliar cars parked in the farmyard. A few people were getting out of one of the cars and he had to step out of the way sharply when he heard another strange car coming up the shale path behind him, its engine growling softly and its headlamps taped up and hooded. He did not recognise the dark silhouette at the steering wheel as the car passed and, by now, all his radar was on full alert as he gazed down at the lights of the farm again and the dark shadows of people moving around ominously in the rooms inside.

His very body seemed to be stiffening with fear as he proceeded along the grass verge of the shale path, crouching like a Red Indian working out how best to attack the circled wagons. His mouth had gone dry and his chest kept tightening until he found he could barely move forward at all, his whole body gradually becoming more and more immobilised by a cold, creeping illness. He practically had to whip his body to get it to move on down behind the cow shed, where the cows were lowering mutinously, as if they hadn't been milked, and, careful to keep well back in the concealing darkness, he looked in through the kitchen window where five men were sitting around the table chatting and drinking tea by the light of the puttering gas lamps around which several moths fluttered darkly.

The bald man facing him was his rheumaticky Uncle Will, whom he had not seen for several years; there was his brother Dic and that wild shock of silvery hair could only belong to the Rev Enoch. Then there was that strange Norwegian with blue eyes, who always seemed to be hanging around and who Gareth avoided like the pox, and, next to him, the puddingy face of Dylan Thomas, the only one smoking a cigarette. *What were they all doing here? Hadn't they any homes to go home to?*

Tada walked into the kitchen and said a few words to the gathered throng but, try as he might, Gareth could not pick up a word. A woman walked into the kitchen but he could not work out who she was because she was crying into a handkerchief. The Rev Enoch stood up to console her and Dic offered her his chair as Dylan stood up and walked out of the room. Gareth could hear the engine of another car start and slid away deeper into the darkness lest the intrusive headlamp might pinion him and his deepening bewilderment and anxieties against the milk shed wall.

He made his way towards the hay shed where he picked up yet more voices and, from afar, saw that the other two other Norwegians were sitting around a trestle table in the hay barn drinking cider in the syrupy yellow light of a hurricane lamp. He had seen them around with Ernst often enough but this was the first time they ventured on to the farm and actually settled down as if they owned the place. Gareth had the strong feeling his world was both changing and falling apart before his very eyes.

The nightmarish quality of this warm, sweating night then deepened when he heard a low, purring engine and turned to see another set of taped and hooded headlamps coming down the main path except that this was no ordinary car but a hearse which braked outside the front door. Two men jumped out and proceeded to unload a coffin which they carried into the farmhouse.

A loose chicken, clucking softly to itself, went walking past Gareth as he continued to stand there with acid bile rising and falling in his throat like mercury in a barometer on a day of wildly changing weather. His watering eyes looked up at a few ragged clouds drifting across the face of the grapefruit moon and he even started dribbling before wiping the dribbles off his chin with his fingertips.

Still carefully keeping to the shelter of shadows he crossed over to the other side of the farmyard to see if he could get a better view from there except that he was beginning to feel really ill by now, his whole body going hot and cold at the same time. What he really needed was a good, long drink of water and perhaps he should run back to Cliff House to get it.

He was now almost too terrified to move and even the farm detritus seemed to be menacing him – the old machinery and broken gates, the zinc bath lying on its side, the piles of mouldy sacks and that empty banana box – all standing around him with unexpected menace; all telling him to stay exactly where he was or he'd be in for the high jump.

But, while his body was frozen with fear, his mind was working overtime: there had been a big skirmish in the war in France lately, Dolly had told him, so it had to be something to

181

do with that; some distant member of the family had gone and got himself shot over there and had been brought back to be buried in New Quay, probably in Llanina churchyard, which was well-known for having wonderful views of the sea and was certainly a favourite of sea captains who, it was also said, could, on some nights, all be heard singing together out deep in the Bay.

And, if that was indeed the case, then all this was none of his business. Whatever that coffin was for was nothing at all to do with him. Nothing at all.

He would have to tell Dylan Thomas the story of that drowned chorus of sea captains, come to think of it, because the poet was always interested in strange stories like that and usually gave him a cigarette if it was a particularly good one. Dylan had even given him *two* cigarettes the other day when he had told him about the strange Lord who had just moved into Sea View with a vast collection of clocks which were chiming so much and so loudly they were driving all his neighbours mad.

But, if that coffin was meant for some distant member of the family, who had gone and got himself shot in France, why had it been brought back here? Everyone had a home of their own so why hadn't it been taken there? It didn't make any sense.

Thoroughly perplexed but slightly more at ease he returned to the other side of the farmyard and sat on the new tractor, pulling the steering wheel one way and another. Tada had occasionally let him drive this tractor out on the fields and he loved the way the gulls came swooping down in his wake and gorging themselves on the fat worms he kept turning over. One of the Norwegians came out of the hay barn to urinate in the darkness and Gareth waited until he had finished before coughing slightly hoping to attract the man's attention. Perhaps *he* might be able to tell him what was going on but, if the Norwegian heard his cough, he didn't show it, giving himself a vigorous shake before buttoning himself up and returning to his friend inside the barn.

Just then a sound broke out into the warm night air which was so unexpected and shattering it made Gareth jump off the tractor and start running around the farmyard like a headless chicken, not even worrying about the cover of darkness any more, just running around and around as fast as he could go.

About a dozen people were singing *Abide With Me* in the front parlour and the slow heartbreak of the hymn was acting like acid in his ears, almost blasting them open until, gulping for air and nearly fainting, he kept running around with his hands clamped to his ears just hoping, no praying, that this whole hymn-singing nightmare would come to a quick end.

Finally, too exhausted to run any more, he burst in through the kitchen door, hoping to make it to the stairs and the safety of his own bed, except that a man was sitting on his Mam's rocker and spotted him as he tried to slip past.

'Gareth, boy, everyone's been looking for you. Where've you been?'

The lad seemed to be rooted to the spot, trying to catch his breath and with his eyes gazing longingly at the foot of the stairs where, with a few bounds, he might even be able to get straight to bed. Another blood-curdling stanza of the hymn was being sung with a rugby stadium fervour.

'You've grown so much since I last saw you. Come here and let me look at you. You do remember me don't you? It's your Uncle Will. It's been a bad day for all of us.'

He remembered his Uncle Will all right – the same man had once stood on one of his little chicks when he was a child – and, while it might be a bad day for him and all the others this was nothing at all to do with Gareth because *all this was none of his business*. He still had not taken his eyes off the foot of those stairs when the kitchen door opened whose sound, for Gareth, was like that of a gun at the start of a hundred yard dash since he bolted and took the stairs three at a time, slamming his bedroom door behind him and flinging the bolt before, squealing mutely like a hunted animal, undressing quickly and jumping into bed, pulling the bed clothes over his head and wriggling deep down into the comforting darkness.

He knew of no enemies in the world which could infiltrate the dark security of his bed clothes; here he was safe from everything and he understood it completely when Dylan Thomas had once told him that, whenever his wife attacked him, he always made for the safety of his bed since she never hit him once he'd got in there, no matter how enraged she might be.

Someone tried to open his bedroom door and, after a puzzled silence, there were three knocks on it. 'Gareth, Gareth.' It sounded like Tada but, when he stayed put and closed his eyes inside the bed clothes the knocking and the voice finally went away.

It took him an age to get to sleep with voices continually erupting up through the floorboards in a house which was always silent and fast asleep at this hour and he kept trying not to think of anything and particularly about what might or might not be going on downstairs.

But it all got so worrying in the end that he did what he often did when he really was in trouble and actually got out of bed and went down on his knees to ask God if he could have a good night's sleep and would God also make everything all right again in the farm house by the time he got up and would God also please, please remove all those awful hymn-singing strangers with their terrible cars and coffins so everything would be normal again and he could have his breakfast in peace like he always did.

That's all. Thanks. In your own time, of course, and if you're not too busy with other things. Thanks again. Gareth Morgan, here in Llanina.

God actually did seem to answer Gareth Morgan of Llanina's prayer since he really did have the deep, dreamless sleep of the dead that night and he woke up feeling wonderfully refreshed and lying back on his pillow, with his hands behind his head, as was his wont and staring at the roof beams, when he frowned and a cold dread caught his heart since he began hearing all those strange voices and unfamiliar sounds again and he knew, without a shadow of doubt, that everything was far from normal; that some terrible tragedy had engulfed the farm which was also going to have dire consequences for him.

He dressed and stood at the top of the stairs where he listened for a while to a dreadful, doleful music which seemed to be seeping out of every corner of the house; a desolate song of pain which was so unbearable he could not stay in the place any longer and he made his way down the stairs, careful not to bump into anyone, and ran straight through the kitchen and out into the outlying fields, not pausing for breath or to look back, just running away and determined that he was not going to return to that farm or listen to that dreadful music ever again. *Not ever*.

Chapter Seventeen

ON THE morning of the funeral Dic Morgan woke up in bed in his little whitewashed house on the end of Mulberry Close belching and farting like one of the cows suffering from too much gas and his wife, Peggy, beat a hasty retreat from the potentially lethal gas chamber of their bedroom.

As soon as he got up he clumped down the stairs in his long johns and staggered out into the back garden where he not only continued to belch and fart but also began throwing up all he'd drunk the night before; a squirting symphony of farts, belches and honks which rarely followed one another in any kind of musical order but often actually tried to break out of his suffering body at the same time until, at one eye-watering moment, there was something or other escaping from every orifice and he was pretty sure he was going to do himself some real damage.

This was *not* the state anyone should be in on the morning of their mother's funeral, was about the only coherent thought he had in between his various seizures. He really should have kept himself tidy for this one morning of all mornings and he was not remotely tidy. *Ooooooooh –eeeeeeergh- sssssssssss – splot – ooooooooh – aaaaargh – fillupit – splot . . .*

Shaving was an even bigger disaster since his hands were shaking so much he must have cut himself in a dozen places with his razor, and he had to staunch the various wounds with bits of newspaper until it looked as if his face was being attacked by a swarm of blood-sucking moths. *Ooooaaah – er –*

fugging – aaaaargh – shit – ssssssss . . .

But if all that had been difficult it had been as nothing as when he tried to get his stud into his rogue starched collar, which kept springing out into shapes he did not want, until he did manage to more or less get it around his neck when he knew he was going to be sick again and just managed to make it to the outside lavvy where, during the second heave, the stud popped out of his collar and plopped straight down the hole. *Ooooh – sheeee- it . . . sss . . .* He didn't have another stud so he managed to coax Peggy into doing the best she could with a safety pin.

He was feeling half human when they both walked out of Mulberry Close, he looking like some old union leader about to confront the coal barons and she done up like a scarecrow in black weeds about to go on a haunting, when he stopped at the top of the hill and felt sick all over again since not only was it starting to pick with rain but he could see huge crowds milling around outside the chapel with many more coming down the hill. Somehow he was going to have to face this lot stone cold sober and he would have given anything for a pint or three to set him up for his appointed task which was to act as a main usher in the vestry, greeting all these black-clad bastards and putting them all in their pews and keeping in mind that the front ones *were reserved for immediate family.*

Peggy went on inside and Dic nearly started a fight there and then when Mabel Johnson, the hairdresser, whom his Mam had always hated for good reason, together with her even more hateful husband, Harry, claimed that they were immediate family but, if they were, that was the first Dic had heard about it and he managed to jam both of them in a corner pew behind a big pillar where, with any luck, Harry wouldn't be able to see a thing and Mabel's out-of-tune screeching voice would be drowned out in the hymns.

Cars began drawing up outside the chapel, disgorging yet more black-clad dummies and Dic saw that they were mostly the Lewises and Davieses from his Mam's side of the family in

Llangollen, an ageing, stuffy bunch, who all looked as if they had been freshly dug up from old graves for the occasion, and you could tell they still had lots of money what with their fancy cars and fur collars and huge hats the size of coracles. Oh aye, *all* the Lewises and Davieses had indoor lavvies in Llangollen; you would never have to take the wooden seat indoors and warm it by the fire in Llangollen. Oh no. They all had money coming out of their ears in Llangollen and they wouldn't ever think of giving it to the bloody Welsh nationalists either.

This was still a very sore point with Dic was this and he still could not believe what had happened to the family money and could not even think about it without feeling a severe shortage of breath. Not one of them in the Morgan family had known about this sick turn of events until a man had called on the farm a few days after their Mam's death and announced his name was Goronwy Powell and he was the local treasurer of the Welsh Nationalist Party.

'I have been sent by the party to convey our deepest condolences. Mr Saunders Lewis and Mr Dewi Bebb have both asked me to inform you that they will both be attending the funeral together with any other members of the party who can see their way to being there. We have all been most upset to lose such a great benefactor.'

'A great benefactor?' Tada did not understand and he looked at Dic who didn't understand either until this little Welsh prick, with a scraggy throat which Dic kept wanting to grab and squeeze hard, explained that, unknown to everyone except the nationalists, their beloved Mam had gone and left the lot to them, Plaid Cymru, except for a small provision for the education of young Gareth.

Most of Tada's side of the family – the Morgans and the Steads – began arriving and all, unlike the Llangollen mob, looking as broke and rough as usual. Dic greeted each of them warmly by grabbing their calloused hands, hoping there might even be a good fight afterwards in the reception at the Black

188

Lion since it was well-known that all sections of this sprawling family hated one another heartily and there was nothing quite like a wedding or a funeral, fuelled by lots of free drink, for bringing all these tribal hatreds bubbling up to the surface.

His Aunty Elinor would not go anywhere near a member of the Lewis family, for example, since she was convinced one of them had poisoned her beloved cat twenty three years ago when she had gone on a Whitsun Treat to St David's. She still brooded about that savage and cruel murder and it only took one sniff of sherry before all the pain come storming back again and she began shouting lots of things about the Lewises most of which she regretted almost immediately they took that bottle of sherry off her.

Then there was his bald Uncle Will who couldn't stand the sight of any of the Davieses because Beth Evans had gone and got herself knocked up by one of the Davies boys when she had long promised to marry Will and even to this day – forty two years after that ill-advised pregnancy with a boy who went on to become a fashionable undertaker in Cardiff – Will still went all funny if he found himself anywhere near Beth. He had never recovered from the shock of her betrayal, they said: still suffered the loss of her, particularly on the anniversary of the birth of that bastard undertaker when for around eight days, on both sides of the anniversary, he went into a black mood and wouldn't say a word to anyone except to tell them to bugger off.

And this old bag here, coming up the chapel steps with imitation flowers in her hat and talking to herself, was his Aunty Lil, the original Missing Link, with more money than King Midas and who lived in a big house outside Oswestry along with about fifty cats and another lifelong resentment against the opposite sex after her husband Harold had gone off to fight in the Boer War and liked Africa so much he had deserted the British Army and settled down in a mud hut with some beefy African tart.

The story of this Transvaal defection was so funny that Dic

all but cracked up with laughter every time he clapped eyes on his mad old Aunty Lil and he found it all so much the more pleasing when he pictured his Uncle Harold sitting in lion skins and eating boiled cabbage in that mud hut in the middle of the savannah while also going on to his beefy African tart about how unutterably wonderful life had become now that he had escaped from his loopy wife and all her bloody cats in that big, damp house outside Oswestry.

Dic had also never believed there were so many suits in Wales since they were all turning up burnished and best-suited, even Ernst from Norway who, now that he had settled down here, wasn't showing the slightest inclination to return to Norway nor indeed anywhere else. *Everyone* seemed to like Ernst since he seemed to be getting more and more Welsh by the day, picking up the local sayings, working hard and willingly on the farm and even becoming good company in the pub, never flinching when it was his turn to buy a round, unlike most all of the others who always got *rigor mortis* in every muscle when they were in the chair.

'Is there a pew in there near the bar, Dic?' It was Dylan, ever the joker, who was also wearing a formal black suit which no one knew he owned together with Caitlin also in black and carrying a small bunch of black violets. 'You know I never like walking far to the bar.'

'You'll get the bar later, Dylan boy. Just get in there and you won't get crushed by the family but, if you do manage to find a bar under the altar somewhere slip one out for me.'

Dic had come to like Dylan a lot; the poet often came over as a clown but he had an uncanny ability to absorb people's sadnesses and almost make them his own. Dic would always be grateful for the way Dylan had looked after him on the day his Mam had died; how he had kept him straight and sober and made him face up to that death and, in so doing, start dealing with it. There was a deep seriousness beneath all that drunken comedy and he would have to read some of Dylan's poetry at some time since people told him they were as serious as sobriety.

What Dic wasn't too pleased with himself about was the way he was occasionally giving that Caitlin one. He couldn't work her out at all, couldn't even start to understand the complexity of emotions which she aroused in him. Indeed there were days when he loathed her heartily but she appeared to see that and didn't even appear to mind. Yet after a few drinks she always seemed to know when he might be available, always managed to give him a sign when they were off to the beer cellar again or down to the darkness of the beach and wham, bam, it was all over in a matter of minutes.

He couldn't even start to guess what she got out of it all and she certainly wasn't about to tell him since she never said so much as one word after it was over and hurried away. It might all have been some sort of revenge against Dylan, of course, but revenge for what? Dylan was sweet and innocent enough in his stumbling, drunken way but there again maybe everything Caitlin did was an act of revenge against Dylan for being more popular than her, being more talented than her and, perhaps more than anything else, more famous than her.

Yes, Caitlin was one screaming screaball of revenge and here she was at his mother's funeral, even looking at him coldly and openly in the eye. That was Dic's other problem with her. She never seemed to know the meaning of guilt or how to deal with it while Dylan always seemed to be in constant danger of drowning in the stuff.

THE CHAPEL was packed, with the warm, sorrowing air coming out of it in waves, when Dolly turned up with Gareth who was still looking evil with a sour face and black, grieving eyes. Dic had gone quite mad when the boy had run to Cliff House for comfort after their mother's death – *and then stayed there!* – even if he soon accepted that the boy wasn't going to get much comfort back home on desolation farm where even the cows had given up producing much milk. But it was the way that Dolly seemed to have become Gareth's mother figure that was continuing to get on everyone's nerves although they knew there was nothing they could do about it and it might even do the boy some good to come under a woman's care. We get our comforts where we can find them, Dic had to grant, and anyway *he* wouldn't have minded being comforted in Dolly's arms if only he could find a way of worming into them. But he did hope she wasn't doing *that* with him although, rather predictably, the boy was now saying he was going to be a poet like Dylan Thomas and, even more worryingly, Dylan was actually encouraging him in this doomed venture too.

He put Dolly and Gareth next to Dylan and Caitlin and his wonderful morning was made complete when Saunders Lewis, the Welsh nationalist chairman, stepped out of a car before looking around at the gathered crowd of onlookers. A reporter from *The Cardigan Times* asked him if the party had changed its attitude to the war.

'This is no time to discuss that. We are here to remember Rachel Morgan, a great friend and benefactor to Plaid. Excuse me, I must go inside now.'

A great friend and benefactor to Plaid! Jesus wept! The Morgans had worked and slaved on that farm for year after year and his own mother had gone and given away a huge pile of money, which they didn't even know she had, to those nationalist barnacles who wouldn't even fight for king or country. But Dic did manage to extract a small revenge on the little Welsh nationalist shit by stuffing him behind the big pillar next to Mabel Johnson where he wouldn't see much and her singing would drive *him* crackers.

Aye, aye it was one big bastard of a funeral all right and he was so busy throwing people out and jamming others in he hadn't even had time to think about that woman in that coffin, whose day this was, until the funeral cortege arrived. *Oh Mam! You may have given away all our money but you didn't deserve to get into an elm suit so soon; you were the mother of mothers you were and you did not deserve to end up like that.*

FORTUNATELY, AS main usher, Dic didn't have to sit inside the packed chapel for the funeral service so he pretended he had to sit outside to keep law 'n' order in the vestry. It wasn't that he didn't feel anything about the death of his mother, because he felt a lot of real pain, so much as he didn't feel anything about the ways of the chapel and particularly the Rev Enoch who never seemed to know when to shut up.

The Rev Enoch had once asked Dic what *he* thought his sermons should be about and Dic had replied, 'About five minutes.'

Dic was having a quiet cigarette when his blood froze as he heard the squeaking of a handcart in the street outside. The custom was that the body could be brought to a funeral in a motorised hearse, but it then had to be taken to the cemetery in this handcart – something to do with going out as broke as you came in – and the two eldest boys would have to do the job. Trefor would be all right because he was strong and didn't drink, but Dic's already unsettled belly began rumbling biliously when he saw that bloody handcart just sitting there outside the chapel door like a lop-sided and wheeled curse.

It wouldn't have been so bad if they had ever put some oil in that squeaking axle but they never did. Cause maximum discomfort for everyone: that's the way the chapel liked to work. Nothing was worthwhile unless it came with a lot of balls-aching effort. Get anything easy and you might as well throw it into the gutter and stamp on it. Anything easy was as worthless as it was pointless. *Make life difficult for every poor bastard in sight and, for those who weren't in sight, somehow try and pull them in and make them suffer too.*

He could have murdered a few pints in the Black Lion but didn't have time since the Rev Enoch had finished roaming the vast oceans of God's tears and they were all on the final hymn with gusts of warm body smells practically singeing his cheeks and eyebrows. The coffin came out first and the throng around them was thick as Dic and Trefor took hold of the handles of the handcart when, with a push and a heave, they were off up the first hill, followed by the line of mourners, and, every time the iron-clad wheels hit a cobble, they seemed to shake Dic's teeth that bit looser. 'I tell you what, Trefor. There's no poor bugger going to push me in this thing when I die. I've left strict instructions I want to be burned and my ashes scattered in the bar of the Black Lion.'

The bar of the Black Lion was never far from Dic's mind and, when they both laboured past that sacred shrine, a few words seemed to just jump out of his mouth of their own accord. 'I don't suppose we could drop in for a quick one, could we?'

'What do you mean a quick one?' Trefor muttered.

'A quick pint,' Dic replied out of the side of his mouth, deciding he might as well push his luck because he really did need one even more than the air he was breathing. 'Wouldn't do any harm, would it? Then *everyone* could have a quick one too.'

'What? And leave Mam propped up against the bar you mean?'

The handcart veered across the road as they continued their argument, almost as if deciding to go into the Black Lion under its own steam while the mourners followed these changes of direction uncertainly.

'That's not what I mean at all,' Dic blustered. 'But we could leave her out in the garden for ten minutes, couldn't we? There's no one going to steal her is there?'

'I can *not* believe my ears,' Trefor grunted, giving the handcart a huge, exasperated shove and sending it veering away from the pub door. 'I do not believe I am hearing this. Tell me there's something wrong with my ears, will you?'

'There's nothing wrong with your ears, Trefor. It's me there's something wrong with and a quick pint would put it right.'

Dic didn't get his quick pint and, by the time they got to the cemetery at Llanina, he was so knackered and gasping for a drink they might as well have thrown him into the hole as well and got two for the price of one.

'The days of the woman are but grass,' the Rev Enoch was saying. 'For she flourisheth as a flower of the field.'

Bodies pressed forward and hands picked up clumps of earth and dropped them on the coffin while Captain Port Talbot nearly lost his footing and fell in on top of her.

Dic had really had enough by now and decided to come back and pay his respects after the circus had left so he took off back to the Black Lion letting the Rev Enoch push back that bastard handcart on his own, if need be. He was first into the reception room and, after ripping off his starched collar, could never remember anything tasting sweeter than his first pint of Buckley's except, perhaps, the second.

DYLAN HAD only downed two pints and was moving sunnily through the funeral reception, giving an old woman a wink here and a young girl a beery kiss there, now telling a bald uncle a joke, which he did not understand, but mostly harvesting the gossip of the hour.

Gossip had long been Dylan's food and drink, particularly when accompanied by a lot of alcohol, and he loved gathering it in and giving it away. What people chatted about helped him to understand the human condition, especially the Welsh human condition although, given that this was a funeral and everyone was suffering from severe intimations of mortality, much of the talk was, predictably, about their health.

Mabel Morgan from Llandysul, he learned, was still having a lot of trouble with her rickets and young Stephen had gone deaf after being caught in some nasty shelling in Sicily. They had made Uncle Arthur's new surgical boot all wrong so he now walked everywhere with an emphatic starboard list and Uncle Brian had finally gone and left his wife to live with his fancy woman in Aberaeron where he had stayed for all of two weeks but then had gone and left her because he could not stand her desire to keep everything about him so polished and tidy. *Duw*, poor old Brian was as bald as a snooker ball and she even tried to do something about that, rubbing the whites of eggs and parsley into his dome to make the hair grow again.

But Brian was quite fond of his baldness and finally, in despair, he ran home to his relieved wife who had always been quite fond of his baldness too.

Dylan turned and caught Dolly looking at him strangely. Her eyes jerked away from his and he kept staring at her when she looked back at him. Was she lusting after his body again? He couldn't quite read the look but, if Dolly had gone and got herself in an interesting condition – as the chapel might have put it – there might well be another little Dylan Thomas on the way soon and the only real question was if she was actually going to finger him and that New Year's Eve party with a paternity order? And how would Caitlin take it? Well, pretty fucking badly that's how; pretty fucking badly indeed.

He probably wouldn't even be able to deny it very convincingly when the brat did fall out particularly if it turned out to look like him. Llewelyn, their eldest and still with Caitlin's mother in Blashford, and little Aeronwy, more or less permanently parked with the neighbours, both had his distinctive pop eyes and frog-like chin so, if Dolly's new baby came out with those sad, quirky features, while also, perhaps, calling out for a pint of bitter, his precarious marriage to the Cat woman was bound to eventually come to an end, if not in tears, then in a murderous rain of right and left hooks.

He lost sight of Dolly and moved over to the bar for another pint. Banks of cigarette smoke hung over the gathered crowd and, with the drink taking over, the volume of the chatter began getting louder. He sipped his pint and stared down at the saw-dusted floorboards nursing a sentimental moment. The real problem was he still loved his wife in his young, unwise and nicotine-stained way; loved her vivacity and passionate Irish heart; loved her sexy Bohemian dresses and those long legs which went all the way up to her ears.

But, if he *did* lose Caitlin, how bad would it be if he then ended up with Dolly? She had a fine house on the cliff and an even finer figure. He quite liked the idea of himself as the father earth figure on the cliff-top, sitting on the rocking chair, with a pot-belly and sagging breasts and cracking out babbling poems with all her stray children gathered around him and clamouring to be read one of them. Then later in bed he would make her body sing with sexual rapture in a steamy midnight clinches.

Apart from Caitlin who, for some reason, was always rather rude, if not downright satirical, about his prowess between the sheets, he had always made his women sing with sexual rapture. He was the Errol Flynn of Majoda, the big bug with the outsize organ, who made all his women sob with trembling gratitude when he'd finished with them *and* they never forgot – or recovered – after he'd taken them for a slow waltz around all the sexual circles of heaven. Dynamite on two legs he was *and* he was now on his fourth pint.

It would probably also be possible for him to write some fine work in Cliff House and the characters in the town were already lining themselves up to take part in long prose poem, many beginning to occupy certain key places in the long, shadowy corridors of his imagination, sometimes just standing there coughing loudly at night or else calling out to him in his dreams and suggesting a new position in the corridor with some of them even writing little speeches for themselves.

They all might become bit players in some long, Homeric poem about a town that had gone mad and he would certainly have plenty of material what with the Rev Enoch who specialised in stealing skulls off poor poets; Shani Bob Mam who dyed her eggs with tea; that deeply mysterious Norwegian with unreal blue eyes, who just seemed to have popped up out of the sea one day, and, of course, pneumatic old Dolly James herself who seemed to keep finding and losing her men in the most suspicious circumstances. The undoubted power of her fanny seemed to do in every man she came near and it might even be that he was now in for the big chop too.

Yes, they were all here in Milk Wood all right and not forgetting any number of retired sea captains, mad, obsessive housewives and peripatetic waterfall tuners ... all he really needed was a pencil and a long stretch of silence and they would all release themselves, screaming and squirming into the daylight.

'It's time the family had a wedding,' an old woman, with a dead fox draped around her neck and smelling of camphor, screeched quietly at Dylan. 'Me, I long to see flowers and funny hats in the springtime again. Not all this glooming. Families grow strong at weddings but always lose their way at funerals.'

The black-clad crowd parted and Dylan spotted his young friend Gareth sitting next to Dolly and staring down blankly between his knees. Dylan's heart went out to his new young friend because he knew how boys like him had an infinite capacity for suffering. He knew this because he saw Gareth in himself and, when he saw the boy running around Llanina, he also saw himself, at the same age and in much the same state, running around Cwmdonkin Park in Swansea. Yes, they were both brothers in fear and darkness and, if Gareth persisted in his ideas of becoming a writer or poet, he would help him for sure.

'I'll tell you one thing for nothing. There's going to be a lot more funerals in Wales before Mr Hitler has finished with us.' The old crone with the dead fox and smelling of camphor was back. 'They all think Hitler thinks Wales is something that swims in the sea but, after he's flattened London, he's going to start on us here in Wales.'

Dylan got another pint and spotted the Norwegian from Norway on the far side of the bar and was making towards him when he was confronted by a man slightly smaller than him. 'Mr Thomas? Mr Dylan Thomas? I've heard a lot about you and have even read some of your work. My name is Lewis. Saunders

Lewis, chairman of the Welsh nationalist party.'

He had the lifeless handshake of a dead cod and Dylan gave the cod a few desultory shakes before taking an immediate dislike to the chairman of the Welsh nationalist party. 'Ah yes, Saunders of the River. I've heard a lot about you also. Tell me now. Are you here for the drink or in the hope of shagging a loose woman?'

Lewis either ignored the question or didn't understand it. 'Rachel Morgan was a most assiduous supporter of our party and I've just come to pay my respects along with everyone else and, anyway, I always attend funerals if I can. It's the last thing you ever do for anyone after all. You knew her, did you, Mr Thomas?'

'Vaguely. Friends of friends you know. But tell me, Saunders of the River, is your party still trying to do a deal with the Nazis?'

Lewis blinked a lot but held his ground as many curious faces moved into position around them.

'We never really *tried* to do a deal. Hitler made an offer. An offer in which we were most interested. We never took it much further than that. But, now I've got you here, Mr Thomas, explain to me something I've always found very puzzling about your work. What's *your* stand on this war?'

It was a big question to which Dylan had no big answer and he glanced behind him as if Saunders was talking to someone else. He had never tried to understand the big political issues and often said he hated all politicians from their corns to their dandruff. He was a socialist only insofar as he hoped that the state would one day nationalise all his debts. He lit a Woodbine and blew a few thoughtful puffs straight into the little Nazi's face hoping he might be rescued soon before he started asking any more big questions. 'Well, if you pressed me on that, if you really pressed me I would have to say that I think a squirrel stumbling in a Welsh lane is more important than the German invasion of Europe.'

'A squirrel stumbling in a Welsh lane?' The bemused look on Lewis' face showed that he understood this position about as well as Dylan. 'Just *what* are you talking about Mr Thomas?'

'Well at least I'm not trying to do a deal with the fucking Nazis,' Dylan boomed, unwilling to have his mystical credentials challenged. 'At least I'm not trying to kiss Adolph Hitler's fat arse like you fucking nationalists.'

'All right, all right, Mr Thomas. Calm down now. Calm down. Why don't we try this another way. I've read quite a few of your poems and I want to ask you where you'd say *Wales* is in your work.'

First he'd challenged the poet's mystical credentials and now he was sniping at his patriotism. 'Wales is in every word I write, you useless piece of Nazi shit. It's there in every syllable and every line. But *you* tell me one thing now. Where would *you* say Wales is when you wrote your love letters to Adolph Hitler? Where does Wales stand in *your work*?'

DIC'S EYEBROWS rose a point in quivering delight when he heard the unmistakeable sound of angry, raised voices since they told him that a good family fight was about to break out any moment now and, not wanting to miss a single blow, he waded through the crowd to find Dylan Thomas facing Saunders Lewis and, oh boy oh boy, about to stick one on him at any moment.

Dylan was almost incandescent with rage, spitting out his words furiously while trying to tower over little Lewis when, rather disappointingly, the poet seemed to lose interest in the confrontation and walked away.

'It would have made an interesting conversation,' Lewis said to no one in particular. 'We are from opposite sides of the spectrum, I know, but I do wish we could at least have kept it going and found out if we have *anything* in common.'

Dic went over to Dylan, who was being consoled by Ernst and another pint, the ship of his sobriety already sinking fast.

'Lewis is telling everyone you're a snivelling coward,' Dic told Dylan. 'He's saying you're a squirrel in a Welsh country lane and that you fight like one too.'

'Bastard, bastard, bastard.'

'We should talk about this before it all gets out of control,' said Ernst. 'Let's just sit here quietly for a moment and talk about it.'

'Well, I wouldn't let him call me a fucking squirrel in a Welsh country lane,' Dic persisted. 'He'd get a real belt in the bollocks from me if he tried that.'

'Bastard, bastard, bastard.'

Dylan finished his pint and handed his empty glass to Ernst before striding back to Lewis and, before anyone knew what was going on, launched himself off both feet and landed a soft punch in the neighbourhood of the nationalist chairman's right eye. 'That's one for Hitler. Just stand right there and I'll give you another one for Mussolini.'

'And here's one for my Mam,' an overjoyed Dic shouted as he threw a punch over a dead fox on a woman's shoulder, hitting Lewis in the neighbourhood of his left eye.

Everything then degenerated into a little swirl of cartoon violence with the women screaming and more and more men entering the fray to try and sort it out but, in time-honoured manner, making it worse until the whole reception seemed to have got involved in it, with punches going in here and head butts going in there, with Dylan and Lewis somehow locked in the middle of it all.

In fact the fight worked out way beyond Dic's wildest dreams and he even managed to work a few punches into the hated Davieses of Llangollen, who were also trying to break up the fight, while Dylan, completely carried away by drink and exuberance, was busy whacking everything in whacking distance. Ernst tried to drag Dylan away on several occasions but the poet was enjoying himself too much, wriggling out of the Norwegian's grasp and fighting his way back into the frolicking fray.

But then the fight seemed to break up as suddenly as it had started, as if some invisible referee had blown a soundless whistle for full-time, with everyone losing interest in the scuffle and all the men trooped back to distant chairs and positions, flicking their cuffs and brushing themselves with quiet indignation before the women attended their cuts and bruises with sympathy and handkerchiefs.

Saunders Lewis had a fine black eye and a bloody nose which, particularly for Dic, had made all the huffing and puffing worthwhile. The disenfranchised Morgan family had been avenged and, now that the bad blood had been let, they could all settle down and get good and drunk.

But Dylan, who had only picked up a small red bump in the middle of his forehead in the scrap, was already good and drunk, it soon became clear, because he had already fully and finally parted company with his common sense and was sitting with Aunty Lil from Oswestry and making the imitation fruit in her hat bounce up and down as he gave her the benefit of one of his prize-winning, late-night, seven-pint rants about whatever might have wandered into his head in the last second or so: 'Do you know that all you can get in the General Stores these days is peanut butter and Gardenia Vanishing Cream. I've never known what Gardenia Vanishing Cream does – what does it vanish precisely? – but I do know that I absolutely hate that peanut butter which tastes and looks like rat shit. It's like eating the puke you've just thrown up – horrible stuff whose taste stays in your mouth long after you've eaten it. I had it once, oh yes, but I won't be having it again, not ever . . . '

He paused from his rant when he noticed that the Rev Enoch was hovering over him and, as was his wont, the poet sobered up immediately.

'I hear you've made another spectacle of yourself on this solemn occasion.'

'It was just a bit of pushing and shoving, vicar, nothing to get worked up about.'

'Alcohol is going to ruin you, my son, just as it has ruined just about every other Welshman with any talent who has ever lived.'

Dylan sprang to his feet and, for one appalled second, everyone thought the poet might be about to take a swing at the Rev Enoch but he didn't and started talking to the minister with words which he was picking with slow and exaggerated care. 'Vicar, it was just a bit of shoving, nothing to get worked up about. Just a few drunken meteors in a sky full of sober stars. Nothing more. But, while you're here and I'm here, there is something you can do for me.'

'And what would that be?'

'You can give me my fucking skull back. I've heard from my Norwegian friend over there you haven't buried it at all and you're keeping it on your desk and I want it back because it's mine, given to me by the Ancient Mariner, otherwise known as that smelly little fucker Verney Matthews.'

'He doesn't mean it vicar, he's just drunk and stupid.' Caitlin had emerged from somewhere and joined the discussion. 'He always gets stupid when he's drunk and just doesn't have a clue what he's talking about.'

'Oh yes he does,' Dylan snorted. 'He wants his fucking skull back and he wants it back because it's his, given to him by the Ancient Mariner.'

Chapter Eighteen

ERNST STOOD across the road from the Welfare Hall watching the buses turning up and dropping off the evacuee children, all looking as cold and fed up as Hottentots on an ice floe, as they were shepherded into the hall, each with a label on their coat, a small bag of belongings in one hand and a cardboard box in the other in which they carried their gas masks.

They looked around at their new home anxiously and fearfully; some of the girls snivelling but most too tired and miserable for even that. Ernst had often seen this in his men: the way things got so bad they couldn't even work up an emotional response to it; that time when you simply didn't care any more and would even calmly embrace death if it was offered.

He walked over to the door of the Welfare Hall where he could see them standing or sprawling over the bare floorboards as the WRVS boiled up tea in silver urns and handed out huge ham sandwiches which the children seemed uninterested in. Their sounds carried in tinny eddies around the huge hall but, unlike the full-bodied roar of a playground, they were timid, uncertain sounds, the sounds of mice skittering in the darkness. An ARP warden was moving among the children and checking their names on a clipboard and Ernst noted that many of them had nervous tics or were scratching their heads, as if they had vermin, or else there were rashes on their necks which told of poor diets.

They were all just little slum rats and he wondered what kind of world it had become when it was declaring war on children like this, rooting them up out of their homes and wresting them from their families and dumping them in faraway places like New Quay. And he could be sure that the plight of the children in the Fatherland would be a lot worse; yes, it would be a lot, lot worse.

Memories began unspooling inside him and he re-entered the dark days of Hitler Youth in Munich in the Thirties, a time when the children had been terrorised too except that they were Jew children, slapped in the street and hunted by gangs through the parks. One had spun out of a lane on the Ludwig Strasse and grabbed Ernst by the leg, crying out as a gang pounced on him. It was a horrifying moment which still haunted his memory as he kicked out at the young attackers who were snarling and baying around him like ravenous wolves. His aggressive defence of the boy finally made them retreat, shouting 'Jew-lover' or 'Commie dog' as the boy continued to wail and cling to his leg.

Yet those young wolves had been children too but the whole nation had been poisoned by party rallies in Nuremberg and street fighting with the Bolsheviks and by constant seepage through a contaminated media about the so-called global Jewish conspiracy. This poison had plunged the country into *Nacht und Nebel*; they had become a nation in the grip of fantasy, red in tooth and claw, thinking with the blood and rising up to cleanse the world of Jewry and Bolshevism for ever. But it was nonsense all of it; mad, dangerous nonsense and, now he had found a quiet Welsh womb, he had no intention of ever returning to the Fatherland ruled over by that demented Nietszche in his concrete bunker raving on to the music of Wagner.

Yes, he wanted to remain enfolded in this small Welsh womb for ever and quite enjoyed living with Christian in the crumbling two-up, two-down cottage belonging to the Fisherman Matthews. Helmut had not been able to settle down and had left two weeks earlier, having acquired some 'papers' from somewhere and announcing he was going to take his chance on British railways, perhaps going to a port in Scotland and trying to get a friendly berth from there back to Germany.

But Christian was as enthusiastic about the place as Ernst – which might be something to do with a fetching young girl he was seeing in the next village – so they had both fully resolved to sit out the war here where absolutely no one had ever asked to see their papers and all the locals ever seemed to worry about was where the next pint of beer was coming from.

Yet there was one very big Nazi fly in the Welsh ointment and that was the U-boat. There was no possibility they could get rid of that from its cave and, should it be discovered, they would simply have to make a run for it and so two haversacks were tucked away under the stairs of the cottage, each containing a change of clothing, compasses, condensed milk, bars of chocolate and ersatz coffee. They had even picked out the motor bicycle they were going to steal in the event of such an emergency and had also worked out a route which would take them into the relative safety of the mountains of North Wales where they would think about matters again.

PEOPLE KEPT coming into the hall, some nodding at Ernst still standing in the doorway, before going over to the evacuee children and scrutinising them with searching looks and the odd question before deciding which ones to take home.

The single, strong boys were the first to go – the farmers found them a useful and cheap pair of hands – and next were the pretty, young girls since women can never get enough of pretty, young girls, especially if they had none of their own. Quite soon only about thirty children remained, mainly large families of brothers and sisters who did not want to be split up under any circumstances with some clinging to one another and protesting loudly at the prospect. One young boy looked particularly tough, standing in front of his five brothers and sisters, with his arms folded and jaw stuck out like some Berlin SS bully boy, almost offering to fight anyone who might have the temerity to try and break up his filthy tribe.

Ernst continued to watch the proceedings with a quiet interest when he became aware of a mass of golden curls next to him and saw it was the *fraulein* from Cliff House accompanied by young Gareth Morgan from the farm. He knew Gareth was always uneasy in his presence and he had sometimes exchanged a small wave or greeting with Miss Dolly and although they had never actually spoken to one another.

And still they didn't speak to one another, the three of them just standing there, a little like three grizzled old farmers in a Cardigan cattle auction, saying nothing but waiting carefully for the right moment to make a profitable bid.

A stray sheep wandered into the hall and the evacuee children looked on in absolute disgust as it let out a short bleat, wagged its tail vigorously and evacuated its hairy bowels with a steaming pile of oval pellets all over the floorboards. 'Urgh!' they exclaimed. 'Argh!' they groaned. 'Oh blimey,' they sighed before Gareth chased the sheep back out again and a WRVS woman arrived with a dustpan and brush. 'Perfect for the old man's tomatoes,' she said cheerfully. 'Just stick this around them and stand well back.'

'We have to take some children home with us,' Miss Dolly told Ernst. 'We have a large house and could take two or three. Have you any suggestions?'

'Take that boy with the large family over there.'

'Really? He looks very fierce.'

'Yes, but he will be a father to them and large families have ways of looking after themselves. If you can control him you will control the whole family. It will not be easy, but it will be worthwhile. Single children will give you all the problems under the sun.'

'But there are six of them. I couldn't afford to look after six.'

'Afford! You will *make* money with a family like that. You will receive ten shillings and six pence for the first child and then eight and six each for the rest. With other allowances you might get five or six pounds a week. You could easily feed a big family with money like that.'

'You seem to know a lot. You're not some sort of official are you?'

'No, no. Just an interested observer. I am from Norway and we are staying here for a while until we are called back to fight for our country. I have been doing some casual work on the Morgan farm and I learn lots of things from the radio. Gareth knows me well enough. But go and talk to the boy and decide for yourself.'

'Oh dear, I'm not sure about any of this. What do you think Gareth?'

Gareth coughed and swallowed but did not take his eyes off the family in question. 'I think they'd be a lot of trouble,' he said after a while.

'Well, you seem to know a lot,' she said, turning back to Ernst. 'I wonder if perhaps you would go and talk to the boy for me.'

He nodded and walked across to them, a few still lying on the floor, bickering over a few sandwiches, but all the other eyes settling on him. There was a real defiance in the lot of them and not one of them was snivelling like so many others in the hall. He decided to concentrate on the eldest, a rather flabby but strong lad who returned his look unflinchingly. 'Tell me your name,' Ernst said.

The boy moved his weight from one foot to the other but made no reply.

'Please. I must know your name.'

'George. George Shepherd an' these are me brothers an' sisters. We wanna go 'ome.'

'Very well, George. You will all go home in time but meanwhile we need to find you a home here.' Ernst deliberately stood over him; he *loomed* over him and brought his face close. Everything about him smelled of the slums but he knew all about boys like George Shepherd; the Kreigsmarine was riddled with hardened slum rats like George Shepherd. 'I want you to tell your brothers and sisters we have found the best house in Wales for them. Please tell them you will all be well fed and well looked after until it is time to go home.'

'I tole you. We wanna go 'ome. *Our* 'ome. This place is just full of sheep shitting everywhere. It's bleedin' disgusting if you ask me. Sheep shitting everywhere like that.'

'You will go home, George. You will. But you have to be clear in your mind about certain things. All you need to do is stay with us for a while and work for your brothers and sisters. In this way we will keep you together and make you strong. When you are strong enough you can either return home or have your own independence.'

The open defiance in George's face was replaced by uncertainty; he did not know what to think or what, exactly, was being offered. Another difficulty was that the boy had a criminal mind and would cause problems for the *fraulein*. Ernst had always been able to smell criminality in a dog but couldn't back down now. 'In this home you will be free to come and go as you wish. It is a splendid house overlooking the sea and you will be looked after and you will be able to stay together as a family.'

George turned to the others and jerked his thumb. 'C'mon you lot. We've got somewhere to stay for a few days an' I do 'ope there'll be no sheep shitting the kitchen or anyfing like that.'

'No, no. No sheep shitting in the kitchen.'

They all began picking up their things immediately and Ernst was impressed. The boy would have made a fine commander.

He returned to Dolly. 'They are the Shepherd family and they will come with you now. The boy's name is George and remember he is the key to everything. Do anything you can to get him under your thumb. Once you have him, you will have all the others.' There was amusement in her eyes as he spoke and a certain flirtatiousness too. 'But do watch him closely.

George must always be watched. It is nothing serious but he might become a little – how you say? – difficult at times.'

She looked at Gareth worriedly and back at Ernst. 'Are you sure this will be all right? I wasn't planning on taking so many.'

'I will not say it is right. That is for you to decide. But do not expect it to work quickly. They will give you hell for a while but they will settle down in time as long as they are distracted. George is intelligent and intelligent boys need to be distracted. Give him work which demands something of him and promise him a reward. You always have to reward boys like George or else they lose interest. Boys like George always respond to a little money.'

He could see she was impressed and, even as he spoke, he took a few steps away from her, as if needing to put a little distance between them. Gareth was still looking at him suspiciously and Ernst would simply have to put that right at some time.

'Do you intend staying here long?' she asked.

'We are waiting on orders from the Norwegian resistance. Maybe we leave soon. But the truth is we do not know.'

'My name is Dolly James. You know where I live. Call on us soon, will you? It would be a great help if you would. If they really are going to give me hell, a man might be useful to have around. I . . . er . . . do have a man but he's away fighting in the war.'

She went over to speak to George who issued a few more orders to his family and they left the hall together. She looked at Ernst again as she passed him but, this time, he could not quite work out what it was she was saying, if anything, in that look. He followed them into the street and watched them walking off, raggle taggle, down the hill looking like a defeated army in a Moscow winter.

Yes, it had been a long, long time. *Ja.*

DOLLY WAS woken by a huge bang (as in bomb) followed by a

long shrill scream (as in very young girl being tortured) and a bright, musical smash (as in something extremely valuable being broken.)

The whole of her body quivered with tension and she buried her head under the pillow when, if anything, the noises of riot seemed to get louder and even more destructive. Yet another day as Old Mother Hubbard – as Dylan was now calling her – had begun in the outsize shoe of Cliff House with a fight between Phyllis and Mabel and, with both of them still wailing, Dolly did not even attempt to get up and sort it out since they always seemed determined to continue their fight whether she was around or not. 'This is family, Dolly, it don't 'ave anyfing to do wiv you.'

She had Ernst to thank for this mess and almost her very first thought – well before getting out of bed or thinking about tea or washing her face – was to curse him and all Norwegians everywhere. She just could not believe she had been so stupid as to listen when he'd said that a large family would be less trouble than one child *and* he hadn't got the size of the allowances for them right either. He had clearly never heard of the Shepherd family from London's Hackney, a travelling circus in their own right who, when they were not fighting amongst themselves, were out in the town or causing trouble or thieving from the General Stores where, whatever they took, they were spotted and the incredible bulk of Mrs Thomas was soon on the doorstep of Cliff House demanding the immediate return of said goods. More often than not Mrs Thomas was on the doorstep *before* the thieves had got home and Dolly asked why she hadn't nabbed them in the stores. 'I wouldn't lay a hand on them. You never know what you might catch if you caught hold of one of them.'

Dolly put on her dressing gown and crossed the landing to the bathroom where she locked the door carefully before standing in front of the full-length mirror and pulling parts of her face around with her fingertips, wondering if it was really possible to age several years in the same number of weeks. This was not the face of someone who had won the Miss Pears competition way back in 1927; this was the drawn and haggard face of some old bag who had not had a good night's sleep for ages; the face of a worried and fagged-out woman who could not see where, if anywhere, her life was going except straight down the toilet.

She let her dressing gown fall away and smoothed her hands over her bump which was swelling well particularly with all the trampolining that was going on inside it. It wasn't just a trampoline he had set up in there so much as a whole gymnasium and, when he had finished jumping up and down on the trampoline, he only needed a short break before he was working out on the bars or swinging around on the ropes.

Jesus wept! There she was surrounded by children, including one of her own, and now there was another on the way who was clearly going to be a world champion gymnast. She had tried to simply ignore him for a while but, after collapsing on the beach and being found by Caitlin Thomas, she had gone to Dr Pugsley who had examined her thoroughly – rather too thoroughly she thought – and announced that she was up the duff. *Up the duff!* What a terrible way to describe it and then he'd had the cheek to charge her half a crown for this most unwelcome piece of news. 'Any discount for a good feel then?' she had been tempted to ask but didn't.

It wouldn't have been quite so bad if the father had been around this time, except he had gone and got himself incarcerated in Weston-Super-Mare, and she had never known the father of The Boy since she had been far too drunk at the time of that conception *and* half-hanging out of a bedroom window at a Wapping party at the time. Her only concern had been to hang on to the window frame or she would have fallen three flights to her certain death, she remembered as The Scarlet Pimpernel was banging her and, when she did finally manage to haul herself back into the room – because the bastard had just left her hanging there – he had vanished straight back into the party and, although she did seek him here and seek him there, she couldn't find him anywhere and soon ended up with a bump the size of a tractor wheel and an irate father who immediately exiled her to Wales.

So where was he going to exile her next when he found out what had happened in his beloved Wales?

After dressing and poking her head in to check on The Boy – who was about the only child in the house who seemed to need any sleep – she passed little Albert, who was busy carving his initials on the stairway, and went down to the kitchen where she found Phyllis lying on the table and Violet quarrelling over a magazine which was about to be ripped apart at any moment.

Wearily she offered them porridge but, no matter what time of day it was, all they ever wanted was 'bread and butty' or, if they were feeling really hungry, a chip sandwich. They seemed to live on 'bread and butty' or chip sandwiches and nothing ever got close to persuading them to take any of the cod liver oil or orange juice which The Ministry of Food had decreed was so good for them. When she wasn't trying to keep the peace she spent most of her waking hours peeling potatoes and her hands had become as rough and white as pumice. The children often wet the bed too and her arms had developed pronounced muscles from stirring all the bed sheets in the copper then putting them through the creaking old mangle and not forgetting pegging them all out on the line.

Her so-called friend Gareth called by at nine as usual, the one she had always enjoyed talking to more than most, except he no longer seemed interested in her and, after cadging a cup of tea, went straight out into the garden to be with George. She was slightly intrigued by the flickering flames of jealousy this relationship had provoked in her even if she had long seen that Gareth was always hungry for new friendships which he only ever seemed to be able to handle one at a time.

Yesterday it was her and the day before that it was Dylan or

213

Dafydd and now it was George and she did so wish she knew what it was that they managed to talk about all day long but, even when she tried to eavesdrop on them, they always spotted her and moved away, unwilling to let her in on their shared secrets. It was probably something to do with the prolonged torture of adolescence, she decided; something to do with sex, more than likely, or else the absence of it.

But the Norwegian had been right when he said that George was the key to the Shepherd family since the children shut up when George told them to shut up – but not before – and for most of the day, as long as he permitted it, they whirled around his sun like brawling planets. He was their mother and father, their protector and mentor and Dolly tried all she knew – from offerings of farthing everlastings to old fashioned flattery and even a little money – to get George on her side. But it was no use. George was the only one in charge of the Shepherd family, unwilling to divest or dilute his authority in any way. They didn't even mind being hit by him, almost seemed grateful for the attention.

Dolly always liked to have her own way with men but never got close to having it with George. There was, of course, one way of handling him and getting him to share her view of things but doing *that* with an evacuee child in her care – no matter how big he might be or how worthy the motive – was almost certainly against some law or other and punishable by a huge fine, if not a heavy prison sentence.

BUT, AS if sensing that Dolly needed a rest from all his quarrelling siblings, George did take a break from his interminable and secret discussions with Gareth and got up to order them out to play. 'There's sunshine an' bleedin' green fields out there. Look at it. Real bleedin' sunshine. Go an' 'ave some fun in 'em for Chrissake.'

It was pathetic really, Dolly thought, as she watched Gareth kick them up the garden path and order them to go out and have some fun in the bleeding sunshine. Not one of them wanted to go anywhere, particularly when George made it clear that he had no intention of going with them and they kept turning around and staring at him mutinously before he came after them again with his fists bunched and told them to get going.

Other foster parents of the evacuee children in the area had reported that these city kids were hopeless in the countryside and simply did not know what to do with themselves in it. Those green fields filled them with uncontrollable terror as did those huge, menacing trees or nasty, big cows who were going to run amok at any moment and gore them to death. Any eggs found in hedgerow nests were smashed on the spot and, if a pig did manage to get near, he would not only bite you but leave all his teeth in your poor arm after he'd finished. Fresh vegetables were to be avoided at all costs because they were full of dirt and slugs although they might be tempted by something which they had seen come straight out of a tin. The sea also had to be given a miss because they could not swim and would certainly drown if they so much as paddled in it or else get sucked under by a giant octopus which they had once seen in a film during the Saturday morning tanner rush in the Hackney Empire.

And even as Dolly was standing there looking out through her window and noticing the way this gorgeous summer was unrolling like a giant red carpet for someone very important, the Shepherd family had already returned from wherever it was that George had told them to go and were massing at the end of the path, anxiously checking on George's whereabouts before rushing back into the safety and security of Cliff House and soon happily fighting with one another again and filling up the place with endless bangs and screams until she made them another pile of chip sandwiches which, along with a mug of sweet tea, *might* keep them quiet for all of five minutes.

She still missed Dafydd achingly but was honest enough with herself and her basic nature to know that what she really missed was a regular tenant to inhabit the increasingly derelict chapel between her legs. That's what she needed to relieve all this tension; one strong and lusty man who would get her shouting out some verses from the Bible in Welsh again.

Dylan was calling over from time to time but he had proved himself useless at it next to the lifeboat station on New Year's Eve *and* she had no intention of making an enemy of Caitlin. There was always the Norwegian from Norway, of course, who occasionally brought her a bag of potatoes from the farm, but he seemed so cold and enigmatic she couldn't even think of how she might invite him to partake of a spot of quiet worship in her chapel.

There was also another factor which was not remotely going to help her on the sex front and that was that, in a sense, her chapel already had a sitting tenant in the form of that gymnast bastard who kept bouncing around inside her womb all the time. Even sozzled with alcohol she couldn't quite see herself getting to grips with any man at all in this state and, no matter how she looked at it all, she could only conclude that she was well and truly on the shelf and likely to stay there for a long time yet.

THE REV ENOCH, never a man for much sleep or rest, was out prowling the night, cleaning up the streets with his flash prayers as a crescent moon burnished the slate roofs of the terraces and the bright notes of Sandy McPherson's organ went bouncing down the cobbled slopes.

The wandering minister stopped to talk with Thomas Trefor, the ARP man, busy looking for tell-tale chinks of light and pushing his bike up the hill. 'We've been told to crack down on the wrong-doers,' Trefor told the Rev Enoch. 'Only this morning *The Cardigan Times* ran a story that the lighting in West Wales after sunset was so great as to constitute a grave danger to public security.'

'Well you get after those wrong-doers and give them what

for,' the Rev Enoch smiled encouragingly. 'We don't want any bombs here in New Quay do we Trefor?'

'No, minister. We most certainly do not.'

Yet everyone did seem to be taking the black-out seriously, the Rev Enoch thought as he continued his rounds. All the blinds were in place on the windows with heavy sateen tacked up on the doorways. His wayward flock could get up to all kinds of funny business behind cover like that: only God alone knew all about their grubby little adulteries now.

He fired off another flash prayer outside the Black Lion, where he could hear the sounds of Dylan Thomas and his cronies carousing in the bar, before continuing on to the kissing gate at the Butcher's Field and taking the path to the top of the hill where he would, as was his nightly practice, read aloud The Prayer at the Time of War.

But he had barely spoken the first few words of the prayer when he stiffened as he spotted some red mist swirling around him, a portent which told him that something dreadful was almost certainly coming down the track. He kept reading the words of the prayer slowly and hesitantly but guessed that the dragon might be about to visit him again and, while he accepted that the dragon was a mystical messenger from God, that did not mean he liked or welcomed the beast whose roaring pain actually menaced his mental well-being.

Yet he refused to take on a mantle of fear in the unruly, threatening circumstances and was even preparing himself to start bleeding from his hands again when the ground began rumbling strangely as if warming up for an earthquake. The air had become unusually hot too when he realised that he was surrounded by crackling flames and he was actually standing inside a volcano.

This was not his usual dragon vision and neither was this his usual dragon music; this was an entirely new creation in the imagination of God and his resolve not to be afraid was falling away into the predatory flames as he dropped his Prayer Book and raised his hands crying out to God to deliver him from this new prison of volcanic fire.

But these walls of volcanic fire kept revolving around him, searing his very marrow with their heat and talking to him in fiery tongues of magma. Yellow glass eyes stared at him and mouths guttered with spasmodic bursts of black smoke. He turned and turned again looking for a way of escape but there wasn't one and he stepped up against another high wall of fire, full of long, distended faces which kept changing shape. They could have been the faces of the people of his hometown – his very own parishioners – but he couldn't be sure since, every time he faintly recognised one, it changed shape again.

He cried out so loudly he thought the roof of his skull might burst and the main thrust of his cry was that the Lord might be merciful to his people because the Rev Enoch thought – no, he was *convinced* – they didn't deserve all these terrible, swift judgements of ice and fire.

The night became even hotter with steam geysers erupting out of the earth when the Rev Enoch spotted a man dressed in flaming sheepskins actually stamping through all these rolling revelations of fire. He might even have been a person like him – *a sinner just like him!* – and he called out to the stranger to take cover except he took no notice as he stamped on, now walking up a small hill and stretching out his arms as hands – *shadowy, vengeful hands* – grabbed him and nailed him up on a singing cross of fire. *A singing cross of fire!*

He could not take much more of this and hoped he had come to the end of his vision, *prayed* that he might have come to the end of it, when a giant pair of wings passed overhead and cold water came waterfalling down on to this fiery nightscape, making everything explode with so much hissing steam he could barely see his own trembling hands in front of his sweating face. Indeed he was sweating so much he could even have been crying with hot, scalding, salty tears.

And then there was nothing.

He may have stood in the dying embers of his visionary fire for minutes or hours but he had lost all consciousness of himself as an individual when he felt a hand on his shoulder and a voice saying: 'Minister, are you all right are you?'

It wasn't the voice of God but that of Police Constable Ianto Jones out on his nightly patrol and ready to deal with the crime wave that never actually seemed to break. 'You're all right are you, minister? Let's get you home for a nice hot drink.'

'I've got something in here somewhere,' the Rev Enoch replied, fumbling in his pockets for the hip flask of brandy which he always carried with him in case of emergencies.

Chapter Nineteen

DYLAN WOKE deep in the depths of six hangovers and immediately began coughing his guts up, his purple and yellow tongue forking out along each cough like a bronchial snake's, his fluttering hand reaching out from beneath the bedclothes and banging around on the chair next to the bed, searching for the Woodbines without which he could not face another day and just about managing to light one, with his head still lying on the pillow, when he began coughing again, his blubbery lips spluttering with foetid whiffs of smoke and tiny sprays of spit, the tears streaming from his bulging, bloodshot eyes.

He finally flung one trousered leg out of bed and sat on its side, alternately coughing and taking long drags on his reviving fag before cocking his leg up and farting with monstrous violence; a long floaty sound like an endlessly ripping inner tube. He was fully clothed in his old green shirt and baggy check trousers and even his polka dot dickey bow was still intact, albeit badly wilting at the ends, like a plant in the middle of a long drought, but he had managed to take off his shoes before passing out, revealing holed and mismatching socks.

He stood up shakily, took one step forward and then another, then, with a sudden heave, he began throwing up, some of the vomit splashing inside a chipped chamber pot but a lot more over the ragged lace curtains. After a few more heaves he pulled himself erect again, holding out his cigarette and tapping the ash into the pot as he examined, with morbid curiosity, what he had been drinking and eating the night before: a few shreds of cabbage, a couple of strings of meat and bits of tomato although the main feature of this early morning stew was a lot of discoloured beer and gobbets of silvery gastritis. Well at least there weren't any lumps of blood in it, which happened from time to time and scared him shitless.

When he had finished throwing up he unbuttoned his flies and pissed into the pot, actually enjoying the first glad surge when Megan Evans' cockerel, doubtless late getting up this morning, began its unlovely serenade.

Cockaloodaloo

            Cockaloodaloo

                        Cockaloodaloo

Dylan always stood with one foot in the grave and the other on a slippery bar of wet soap and the shock of that hated sound caused the bar of soap to slither straight across the bedroom.

Cockaloodaloo

            Cockaloodaloo

Another cataract of vomit came gushing up out his mouth, drowning his cigarette and joining up with his faltering urine to turn into an erratic, steamy waterfall which, speckled with shreds of cabbage and strings of meat and bits of tomato, now covered most of the front of his check trousers.

He kept retching and trying to suck on his wet fag – but there was nothing left to throw up; his insides were empty and sore, and he said a little prayer of thanks for his final delivery from all this early morning torture before dropping his fag into the pot, drying his hands in his shirt tails, tucking his dick back in and climbing back into bed, feeling as if he had already done a hard day's work.

'FINISHED THROWING up now have we?' Caitlin asked,

putting down a bowl of warm milk next to this bed with lumps of bread in it. 'I heard every heave out in the garden. They can probably hear it all over New Quay. Between you and that fucking cockerel it's a close run thing.'

'Do you think, Catey,' he said after a while, stringing his words together in a soft, flat whine. 'Do you think you could fix that cockerel for me once and for all? Could you go in there and lassoo its larynx or slit its throat or even dig out its voice?'

'I don't know. I'm not a bloody chicken doctor. But, if it upsets you so much, why don't *you* try sorting it out? Try complaining to Megan Evans for a start.'

'I can't speak to women in this state. I can't speak to anyone when I'm in this state. *Everyone* scares me when I'm like this.'

'Like *what* exactly?'

'Oh, you know, like this. You wouldn't believe what I've been throwing up into that piss pot.'

'I'd believe it all right. I'd believe it but you wouldn't catch me looking at it. Dylan, you've simply got to knock the booze on the head for good or it's going to knock you on the head for good. You were on the whisky again last night weren't you? You always get like that when you've been on the whisky. Why don't you just stick to the beer?'

'It's not *me*, Catey. It is simply not me. It's all those pisshead bastards in the Black Lion. *Have some of this, Dylan. Try a drop of that, Dylan. I've put one over the bar for you, Dylan.* It goes on all the bloody time. Why can't I just have a quiet game of dominoes and be left alone with a few quiet pints?'

'Perhaps I'm stupid but I must say I never thought they had been trained by the Gestapo in the Black Lion and they all tied you down on the floor and stuck a funnel in your mouth and *forced* you to drink the stuff.'

'You know what I mean, Cat. I drink with them because I don't like to give offence. They know I've got gout and fits and keep coughing up pools of blood but still they keep forcing whisky on me and I don't like to give offence by saying no.'

'We've got to leave this hole, Dylan. You are sick enough as it is but you are simply not going to stay alive if you stay here any longer.'

'But I can't. I just can't leave them.'

'*What* are you talking about?'

'*Them.* All them in the pub. They crowd my dreams and inhabit my fantasies. They're in here all the time, square dancing, and I'm the fiddler who keeps them going.'

'Rubbish! Even by your rubbishy standards that's complete rubbish. You're not married to them are you? You're married to me in case you hadn't noticed. '

'I am, Cat. That's exactly what I am. I've become married to them and I cannot think how I'm going to get away from them either. They're all such characters. Yarning sea captains, mad housewives, the doctor who's always copping a quick feel off his female patients. Even the Norwegian from Norway is like no other Norwegian from Norway I've ever met. He knows everything about philosophy and I had a game of cards with him the other night and I lost my skull.'

'You lost your *what*?'

'Yorick. I had three tens and he had three threes. The best possible hand in brag and I lost Yorick. He wanted it very badly. You'd think it belonged to someone he knew.'

'Oh, I've heard everything now. You got that skull back from that fucking minister after shouting at him for fucking stealing it off you. Now you've lost it at fucking brag. We have *got* to leave and soon.'

'What about Dolly?'

'What about Dolly?'

'She's going to have a baby. She needs looking after and I thought you were her friend.'

'She's got the fucking Norwegian from Norway in case you hadn't heard. He's walking her out now and he knows about her baby but doesn't seem to care. That's a real man for you.'

'Yes, but I don't think he's going to stay around for long.

Sometimes he says things which tell me he's going to vanish fast one day. How's Dolly going to cope then?'

'Tell me one thing, Dylan. Do you fancy Dolly? Is that what all this is about? I've seen the way you look at her and I'm pretty sure you fancy her. Well, do you?'

Dylan's nose sank beneath the bedclothes when, fortunately, Megan Evans' cockerel broke the blushing silence.

Cockaloodaloo

'Do you know, Cat, I am always going to eat chicken in every restaurant I patronise in the future,' Dylan said from beneath his sheet. 'Every time I lift my knife and fork, I am going to pray that I am eating that bastard cockerel.'

Caitlin left her old man still suffering and talking to himself under the bedclothes and walked out into the garden looking out at the glittering sea sitting under a clear blue sky. Such sunny, innocent mornings often filled her with an unreal hope but now an immense sadness was decanting inside her since she knew that drink was going to do for both of them in the end. She was as tough as a dumper truck and no amount of alcohol seemed to affect her the next morning – or even give her a hangover – but her frail little tadpole was far from healthy as it stood and was definitely going to end up in an early grave. All his multiple sicknesses had almost certainly been brought on by the drink and she saw them all coming together one black hour seeing him off for good. Then she, the really unlucky one, would be left alone.

She even began crying into the listening morning as such insights came thick and fast. Drink took everything and gave almost nothing back in return, she knew. In no time at all it reduced you to the rags on your back and pretty soon reached out and even took them. Drink had scarred almost every part of both their lives, had made them feckless and stupid and poor and she saw it all too clearly in herself; in the way she often hit strangers because she believed, on no evidence, that they disliked her; the way she resented how he could always make people laugh and the way she lay down on the floor with oafs like Dic Morgan when she got practically nothing out of it.

Yet in that respect she was a man: no female doubts or sensitive insecurities for her. When she wanted sex she just took it even if it was only ever done in drink and it was inconceivable that she would ever try it sober. What she would never have stood for, of course, was for Dylan to take a lover too and, in that respect, she again showed herself to be a man. Another selfish, hypocritical, plundering man, may God rot all their faithless souls.

She had never been one for the chapel but she was sure the pulpit was right on one issue: drink was the very brew of the devil. Drink brought out all that was nasty and evil in people and she hated it with a real intensity and passion. The Thomases hadn't set out to be nasty and evil: it was just the way they had become when drunk. Drink had blighted both their lives and whole sections of them had gone missing in consequence. She didn't even know – nor could she even guess at – the identity of the man who had burgled her virginity. He was a dark thief who had just appeared in an empty darkness and made off with it.

She would have given up the drink completely but she just didn't know how; couldn't even start to think how they might both then fill the great spaces which would quickly emerge. So she drank some more and it made her feel better for a while. That was the real insidiousness of drink wasn't it? The way it killed you while making you feel better at the same time, a real trick of the devil if ever there was one.

So here she was looking at a clear blue sky with tears raining down her cheeks, feeling full of sorrow at the way they were both being destroyed and unable to do absolutely fuck all about it.

WHEN DYLAN did finally get out of bed he was still feeling quite venomous and farty as he walked along the cliff path towards the town in the hope of an early hair of the dog in the Black Lion.

But he was also feeling really tired and decided to call in at Cliff House to see Dolly, as had become an irregular habit, letting himself in through the kitchen door without knocking and finding her at the sink peeling her daily mountain of potatoes. The rest of the house was echoing to the sounds of anarchy; that ragged music of youth misbehaving and he knew he wouldn't be sitting here for very long listening to that racket.

'Just checking on Mother Hubbard and all her children,' he said, sitting down at the table. 'My Cat woman worries a lot about you, you know: she's always saying how we should both keep an eye on you.'

'Oh, I can look after myself, Dylan. I've had plenty of practice after all.'

Even within the tensions of his still-present hangover he could still feel a hormonal surge and longed to hold her and rest his head on her mighty bosom and tell her that he would look after her and their baby forever but all that came out was: 'You know, Dolly, I had some cabbage soup yesterday and I just can't stop farting.'

'Really? How interesting.'

'Everyone's getting a blast and sometimes they're big too and I've got to go and stand somewhere on my own with all these whirlwinds in my bum.'

She laughed and looked at him carefully before picking up another potato and starting to peel it.

'Caitlin tells me you're going out with the Norwegian from Norway.'

'Not going out, Dylan. He's just helping me with all these kids *and* he's taking me to the pictures next Wednesday. But we're not going out as such.'

'Not that kind of friend then?'

'What kind of friend would that be Dylan?' she smiled mischievously showing she knew exactly what he was talking about.

'Oh, you know . . . '

'No, I don't know. You're the word man Dylan. Explain to me what you're talking about. In words.'

'I think I'd better be going now. Need a drink to steady myself up. Hit it all a bit hard last night.'

'Rather early for the Black Lion isn't it? Are they open already?'

'They're always open if you know the right knock. I don't suppose you fancy one do you?'

'At this time in the morning! You must be joking.'

He slipped back out and made his way to the pub, hands in pockets and whirlwinds still in his bum, as he made his way, dejected and unloved, along the road.

AS BEFITS a budding poet and a lapsed nationalist young Gareth Morgan's education developed significantly under the tutorship of George Shepherd, even if these developments were not the kind you might expect to develop in any normal classroom. George seemed to know everything you weren't supposed to know and Gareth was an avid learner from the word go; swallowing the knowledge of the Hackney streets which opened up whole new vistas for him to worry and wank over.

He was still suffering spasmodically from the loss of his mother, when he allowed himself to think about it, but the first indication that there were larger mysteries, even beyond the death of your own mother, came when he was sitting out on a sunny headland overlooking the sea one afternoon with George, both sharing a Craven A cigarette.

George took a few deep pulls on the cigarette before handing it to Gareth who coughed and spluttered over his first drag before giving it back. 'You know 'ow I was saying we might get a good blimp of Hairy Mary's twat if we played our cards right? An' you know I was saying 'ow it had to be a bigger bush than a bleedin' lavatory cleaner? Well I was thinking. 'Ow many 'airs 'ave you got down there then Gareth me old mate?'

'Enough. I've got enough.'

''Ow many's that then? 'Ow many's enough?'

'I haven't counted them if that's what you're asking.'

'Guess then. Give us a rough idea.'

'Oh, I don't know. Six or seven.'

'Six or seven! Six or seven? Six or seven *what*?'

'Well maybe there's more. I haven't counted them, Maybe there's twenty or even twenty five.'

''Ere. Take a butcher's at this lot.' After a great deal of elbow flapping, rather like a magician about to perform a particularly good trick, George unbuttoned his flies and carefully parted his soiled underpants. ''Ow many do you think I've got down 'ere then?'

Gareth's astonished eyebrows danced all over his face as he looked down at the big, brambled bush between George's legs. The boy had never seen anything like it and had never imagined such a vast tangle even existed; he might have had six or seven *thousand* hairs down there. 'How come you've got all them?' he squeaked as George buttoned himself up again.

'Ointment,' George replied tersely.

'Ointment? What kind of ointment?'

'Any kind. Zambuk. Vaseline. Linseed oil.'

'Linseed oil? I thought that was for rugby boots.'

'Doesn't matter what you bleedin' use. What matters is you keep a tin of it in your pocket and rub it in reg'lar.'

'What ointment do *you* use?'

'Well I don't any more, do I? Got enough bleedin' hairs I 'ave. Why would I want any more when I've got all these?'

Why indeed? Gareth looked at the sea but didn't focus on anything. Life was getting more and more difficult by the hour and, while he had long suspected it, he was now absolutely convinced there was something seriously wrong with him and he would have to go and have a good chat with Dr Pugsley soon.

And then came that equally fateful afternoon when the pair of them were sitting on a wooden box, gas masks at their feet, in a deserted lane around the back of the shellfish factory. To one side of them was a large mound of shells which stank foully every time the wind turned; on the other, the fresh, empty sea.

George said he had fixed up some business which was going to be a bit of a laugh but no amount of prompting would get him to say what it was but, knowing George, it was undoubtedly something filthy and Gareth felt he was going to throw up as he sat on the box racked with equal measures of excitement and guilt.

His worst fears were confirmed when he saw two girls walking slowly down the lane towards them: one was the butcher's daughter, Margaret Williams, a dull, hatchet-faced tearaway who was surely going to end up in prison, they said in the gossip, and the other was Mary Braddock – otherwise known to all as Hairy Mary – a fifteen-year-old evacuee from Liverpool who they all reckoned modelled herself on The Wild Woman of Borneo on account of her brawny build and masses of curly, black hair. There was nothing remotely pretty about Hairy Mary what with her snub nose – which might once have been badly broken in a fight – those brick-sized hands and a squint so bad no one could ever quite work out exactly what she was looking at.

They came to a halt about ten feet away and Hairy Mary folded her arms as George got up and began a round of muttered negotiations with Margaret, finally handing some money over to her before returning to his seat on the wooden box next to Gareth.

"'Ang on to yer 'at, Gareth boy. Yer about to get a blimp of everything there is. You're going to be beating yer bleedin' buffalo for 'ours after seeing this.'

Margaret went over to Hairy Mary and whispered something to her but Hairy Mary merely glowered, stamped her foot twice and shook her thick mop of black curls when, after a

229

lot more fevered whispering, Margaret returned to the boys and announced: 'Mary says she won't do it in front of Gareth Morgan. She says she thought it was just for you but, if it's going to be a stage show, she wants more money.'

With a theatrical groan George rummaged in his pockets before telling her he didn't have any more money, but she was welcome to a couple of toffees and a frog clicker. 'Tell 'er that's all we've got.'

'What about him?' Margaret nodded at Gareth. 'What's he got?'

Gareth went through his own pockets before coming up with a length of string, a penknife, some bits of plasticine and a half a sheet of transfers. He held each object up to Margaret and she picked out his penknife.

'That's my penknife,' Gareth pointed out.

'Not any more it isn't.'

'Oh give 'er the bloody knife,' George butted in as Gareth held out his hand for the return of his knife. 'I'll get you another.'

Margaret returned to Hairy Mary who was still doubtful, giving the tin frog a few trial clicks before putting it into her blouse pocket along with the penknife. After a bit more whispering Margaret returned for another round of negotiations. 'She's still worried about Gareth Morgan but says it'll be all right if he puts on his gas mask.'

'I'm not wearing any gas mask,' Gareth shouted, jumping to his feet only for George to grab him by the shoulder and force him to sit down again.

'That's fine, Margaret,' George said. 'Tell Mary that's fine.' Then, turning to Gareth: ' Put yer gas mask on and shut yer face. We've come too far to back down now.'

'But how can I see anything if I've got a gas mask on? The mask fogs up if I get excited.'

'Just shut yer hole an' put it on.' He put his lips close to Gareth's ears and whispered. 'When you can see 'er twat, just take it off.'

Gareth found it all too stupid for words but he put on the gas mask anyway, feeling his constricted breath fill up his ears and hoping the visor wouldn't fog over completely before he glimpsed Hairy Mary's twat.

As it turned out, he barely caught a glimpse of anything at all since Hairy Mary lifted her skirt, displayed her baggy calico knickers and lowered her skirt again. And that's your lot, she seemed to be saying when George stood up and started loudly demanding his money, sweets *and* frog clicker back.

'Don't forget my knife,' Gareth chipped in after pulling off his gas mask. 'Don't forget about that.'

'Look, shurrup an' put that mask back on. We 'aven't finished yet.'

A few further negotiations seemed to resolve the impasse and Hairy Mary took a careful look around before pulling her calico knickers down around her ankles and lifting her skirt high above her waist. Gareth all but drowned inside his gas mask – partly from pure excitement but mostly from suffocation. The visor was getting fogged up but his bulging eyes could just about make out the mulberry bush between her legs which merely seemed a smaller and better-cut version of her tangled head of hair. But that was some bush and no messing about. He wondered what kind of ointment *she* had used.

His shaking fingers were struggling with his fogged-up gas mask when he looked around and saw the appalled face of Police Constable Ianto Jones appear in the fog of his visor. Police Constable Ianto Jones! How much had he paid to get into this?

'You are both committing a disgusting and serious offence,' Police Constable Ianto Jones shouted as the two girls scarpered off the way they had come and, with all the excitement and a severe shortage of air, Gareth fell off his feet and fainted clean away.

WHEN ERNST called at Cliff House that night a sense of

delighted wonder spread through his normal calm composure as he looked at Dolly who gave him a quick twirl in a short black sequin dress with nylon stockings and high heels which perfectly set off her long legs.

Her normally wild hair had also tied up in a floppy black velvet bow, revealing her strong, almost African neck, although it was her make-up which added the final flourish with bold eyeliner, some smudges of rouge on her cheeks and a bright, red lipstick which told him that here were a pair of lips which were ready, willing and able to be kissed in any way he chose even if they had not yet quite got around to holding hands.

'You like the look of it all then Mr Ernst?'

'Oh yes, I do. You look unbelievably handsome,' he replied, unable to take his eyes off her and moving his weight from one foot to the next. He would have been proud to have escorted her to the Opera House in Berlin – let alone to The Ritz here in New Quay – and what a pair they would have looked: he in his full U-boat kapitanleutnant's uniform with Iron Cross and strolling with her through the Tiergarten on their way to the opera.

'Me and the girls have been experimenting with make-up all day. You can make lipstick by boiling beetroot you know but I won't tell you what these nylons are made of. A girl has got to have some secrets.'

She took him by the arm as they walked along the cliff path and he felt wonderfully correct as they promenaded into the town, amused at how stiffly he was holding himself as she chattered on about what a wonderful day she'd had with the kids experimenting with all kinds of things from beetroot to blacklead to get the seams of the stockings. This was a woman unusual in women because she seemed incapable of any kind of subterfuge or deceit; if it was on her mind it was on her tongue and he was delighted with this straightforwardness which had never been a quality that he had ever noticed in German women.

The long queue waiting to buy tickets outside the Ritz fell

silent and stared at them as they walked to the back of it, this impossibly glamorous couple who might even have stepped out of a Hollywood film themselves. They paused only to chat to Caitlin Thomas with Dylan sulking distantly behind her. 'The fat frog here hates going to the pictures but I threaten to turn off his beer supply unless he takes me at least once a week. You can usually get him to do anything if you threaten to cut off his beer supply.'

Ernst noticed Dylan looking at Dolly in an almost moonstruck way and, beautiful as she was looking tonight, he couldn't help but conclude that Dylan was a little in love with her; that there was something more than ordinary admiration in that look, certainly in the way he seemed to want to look at her long and hard but couldn't quite manage it.

They took their place at the end of the queue and Ernst caught himself walking up the vast steps of the Berlin Opera House again, the men in their dress suits and women in the glittering gowns as they both entered the golden, chandeliered vastness of the reception area. *We have time to have a small aperitif before the curtain goes up.*

As it was reality took over again when he caught himself looking up at the sagging, corrugated roof of The Ritz and shuffling up to the glass-walled booth where Gwyneth Lewis muttered sums to herself as she tore the tickets off a big roll and worked out the change before they walked into the hall itself which smelled of body odour and disinfectant with a steady thundering coming from The Gallery where the boys were already charging around madly trying to impress the girls in a way that would have got the lot of them shot at dawn had they tried it in the Berlin Opera House.

In fact this was something more like Berlin Zoo, he thought as the usherette put them down in the back row along with the other courting couples, particularly with everyone eating all around them, either crunching into apples or nibbling at pigs' trotters or rustling bags of crisps while a steady rain of objects was continuing to pour down from The Gallery.

Dylan and Caitlin, who had never been treated as a courting couple by anyone, were placed somewhere in the middle although Ernst did notice that Dylan was quite agitated and kept getting up and looking around at Dolly and then, on catching Ernst's quizzical stare, turning his eyes away sharply and pretending to look at something else altogether.

It had never crossed Ernst's mind that Dylan had ever harboured any sort of emotional desire for Dolly although, there again, any man only had to take one look at her on a night such as this and he would surely be smitten for a long, long time. She was a real woman, full of warmth and sexuality, who you could lie down with and quite happily never want to get up again. He had never thought about any woman like this before and, in fact, had to pull his hand away when she put hers on his because he didn't want her to know how much it was shaking or give any indication of the wildness of the feelings she was whipping up inside him.

The house lights dimmed and there was a further clatter of hurled, falling objects when the programme began with a bugling cockerel and Pathe News. The first item was about the Wehrmacht who had been raiding Egypt except that 'our brave boys were busy fighting back' and 'victory over the Nazi bully boys would soon be ours'.

This news, delivered with the usual English hectoring bluster, reminded Ernst that the war was actually still on and, in a real world, he should still be fighting in it. But he had long escaped the real world and all these words and images could even have been about the Boer War for all he knew or cared. He was well out of it and even the news that Roosevelt and his American troops would soon be joining the fight in Europe meant nothing to him.

What he was more concerned about was the war flaring between his Bavarian thighs and how he might contain this conflict in a gentlemanly manner because, if he didn't, he was surely soon going to cross the no-man's land between their seats and engage in a little hand-to-hand fighting. He should not even have allowed himself out in this growling, wretched state although, if Dolly knew what was going on inside him, she didn't show it and, anyway, his tension was soon released when they both began laughing at a Laurel and Hardy short and when the main film came on, a Buster Keaton comedy, almost all the audience was laughing riotously right from the first frame.

There are some films which might have been perfect for some hand-holding and a little light romancing but this was not one of them and he did not even attempt to put his arm around her as Buster Keaton hung off the end of whirling ladders or dangled off high buildings or kept narrowly missing being run over by a speeding train. Certainly Dolly was enjoying it a lot and she might even have groaned the loudest when, with the whey-faced and hapless Buster about to be cremated in a bonfire, the projector broke down in a screaming rattle of jamming celluloid and the cinema was plunged into a foot-stomping darkness.

As the house lights came on Ernst took a small bottle of schnapps out of his inside pocket, along with two tiny glasses, which he stuck between his legs, pouring one for her and one for him. She seemed delighted by the gesture and they chinked a toast, causing others to look around, before throwing down their drinks in one. He so enjoyed the warm rumblings of the schnapps deep inside him he poured out two more and they sank them both in one too.

The house lights went down again, with the film re-starting, and he knew his luck was changing in a big way, after he had pocketed the bottle and glasses, and she lifted his right arm and put it around her shoulders before snuggling down warmly on his chest and occasionally brushing her schnapps-flavoured lips around his chin. He wasn't quite sure how to handle all this – didn't even trust himself to do anything at all in fact – and *tried* to concentrate on the continuing antics of Buster Keaton, who had somehow escaped being roasted alive on that bonfire and was now hanging off the end of a fire engine ladder again which was whirling him around and around in the air.

And that wasn't all that was whirling either since Dolly was getting even more adventurous, almost climbing over the arm-rest between them and trying to get into his seat, when she appeared to change her mind and flopped back into her own, putting her face back on his shoulder again and giving his heavily flushed neck some light tonguing as the fingers of her right hand started moving around over his nether regions when, unless he was very much mistaken, she began trying to undo his fly buttons.

A lot of difficulty was attached to this simple operation as he was wearing one of the Fisherman Mathews' spare long johns but, as her nimble fingers worked through the various layers of difficulty, all he could do was sit upright, along with his dick, which was also sitting more than upright, and *try* to concentrate on Buster Keaton, still hanging off his ladder and being chased by several police cars. He wasn't clear why all these policemen were so determined to catch Herr Keaton and became even more confused when Dolly managed to raise his erect dick to periscope level and, with shivers of electricity darting up and down his whole body, she bent between his legs and took it into her mouth.

Ooooooooooaaaaaah! Aaaaaaaaaaawhoaaaaaah! Eeeeeeeeerrrruiuuuuugh! He was gargling and choking with pleasure, soon floating about three inches above his seat, his jacket strategically placed over her head as the whole cinema roared with laughter when the police, having caught Buster, unceremoniously flung him into a prison cell. *There could only have been about two inches left in that schnapps bottle at the most and he would have to get a whole lot more from somewhere fast. Perhaps there was some hidden away in the U-boat where he'd be first thing in the morning. He had never thought he would see the day when he held schnapps in such high esteem.*

He was now about five inches up out of his seat as she still busily sucked on his lollipop and he had to hold on to the seat in front of him with both hands in case he floated up and away towards The Gallery like one of those infernal barrage balloons. *Eeeeeeeeeuuuuuurgh!*

His eyes widened, even focused on the faces in the side wings of the Gallery and he could not be certain in all this flickering, laughing darkness but that surely was Dylan's face, cigarette in mouth, looking down at him, glaring at him, despising him for what the woman he loved was doing to him. How had he got all the way up there and what had happened to Caitlin?

Not that there was anything he could do about it now – nor *wanted* to do about it now – since he was as close to heaven as he was ever likely to get when he noticed a huge woman carrying two shopping bags standing right next to him and asking to get past. *Oh where the hell had she come from?*

But Dolly was not deterred in the least – even if she had noticed – her lips continuing to bring him to the boil as he glared up at the fat shadow hoping she could not see what he was feeling. He opened his mouth to say something but nothing came out. He folded his body and arms over Dolly's jerking head. 'Go the other way,' he gasped finally. 'I cannot move. I have a wooden leg.'

The woman did not move at first, clearly not believing this story about his wooden leg, but relented in the end, disturbing another courting couple instead.

Miraculously, in the circumstances, Dolly was still sucking and blowing away and he sat back up again to watch the film as his whole being began swaying one way and another like a submarine trying to make a fast, evasive run for it. Buster Keaton was hanging off the hour hand of a clock – *What had happened to the fire engine? How had he got out of prison?* – and Ernst was unsure if he was sinking or sailing, being imprisoned or released as the depth charges exploded all around him and the whole of his innards went fountaining up into her mouth. It was a rumbling sensation of profound and impeccable delight, his every anxiety released like a crowd of runners at the start of a marathon.

Dolly sat back in her seat swallowing and gulping for air as he packed his old boy away. 'Sorry about that,' she whispered into his ear. ' I got a bit carried away. Something to do with that drink I would guess. But feeling all right are you?'

'Never better,' he replied, fishing out the *schnapps* bottle. 'I think we still have a little more of this.'

'Not just yet darling. I haven't told you what an awful effect alcohol has on me have I?'

'It seems a very good effect to me.'

'It gets a lot worse, I'm afraid. One sniff of drink and it always gets an awful lot worse.'

Chapter Twenty

DOLLY WAS never a woman to suffer from too many illusions when it came to the old mating game and she knew, almost as soon as she got her Mr Ernst back to Cliff House that night and into the darkness and privacy of her bed, that this was going to be a warm, full relationship, founded on plenty of warm, full sex.

He had a taut, fine body and, most unusually in men, seemed to know exactly what to do with it, calming down after the early, nervous moves and then working on her quietly with his tongue inch by inch until he gradually brought her up to kick-off time again – her second that night – and she clung to him grimly and gratefully as he led her home until, with everything weeping and failing inside her, he was done and he played with her hair for a while and kissed her on the lips softly.

Perhaps it was simply a case of being away from his woman back in Norway for so long, since no man could possibly perform like this unless he was very experienced at it, but she wanted to just roll over and fall asleep and may even have nodded off a few times for a few minutes when he was at it again, working his tongue around the inside of he legs and right up into her when, rather amazingly, she was wide awake and up for the cup again and he was taking her all the way back to Wembley and she practically cried out in joy to the gathered crowds as he deftly set her up for her hat-trick.

Rather strangely the little gymnast bastard inside her belly wasn't going through any of his usual routines while all this was going on and she could just see him in there, frowning and looking around in appalled disgust as this thing kept coming in there and whitewashing the sides of his bedroom. It would have to be appalled disgust because that's how the Welsh always reacted to carnal joy and, as his father's son, he would be Welsh through and through.

Her Mr Ernst almost certainly knew about her pregnancy and perhaps it made him even hornier but he didn't say anything about it – didn't even seem to care – just snoozing for a while after he'd done when, oh no, he was putting on his football jersey again and leading her out on to the Wembley turf again. She couldn't take any more of this – didn't *want* any more of this – there were enough silver cups on the top of the china cabinet after all, but here she was going for broke again, her whole body crying out with fatigue and gratitude and a million other emotions besides as he hoisted her up into the air to head in her fourth goal.

Yet even with whole rivers running down between her legs and half-dead as she was and still hanging grimly on to this relentless roller-coaster, she caught herself smiling – smiling that, for one night and maybe one night only, all her misery and anxiety had been taken away from her and dumped in the dustbin outside; smiling that she had been made a woman full of loving possibilities again and smiling in the knowledge that, even here in chapel-bound rural Wales, it didn't need to be just guilt-ridden suffering followed by a prolonged and painful death.

DOLLY HAD always believed in the redemptive powers of sex and, if it did wonders for her, it was nothing to what it seemed to do for her Norwegian who, without arrangement or even any particular discussion, not only seemed to take hold of her but began controlling her large, wild family too.

He seemed to have an almost miraculous way with them from the start, never bullying them or even raising his voice, but having the ability to *interest* them in almost everything he did, even coming back to Cliff House one morning and saying that, if anyone was interested and wanted to watch, Daisy the sow was about to start dropping piglets on the Morgan farm.

Even George accompanied them for this strange exhibition and they all stood around open-mouthed as Daisy just lay there with a squirming piglet popping out of her every five minutes or so and then scrambling around with the others trying to get straight on to the mother's teats. But their wonder turned to pure horror when Ernst picked up each of the piglets and snipped its teeth in a loud snap with a pair of pliers, causing the piglet to scream furiously at this outrage and the gathered children to protest at this cruelty even more.

'They would destroy the mother's teats if we did not cut them. She will probably have ten or twelve babies who will rip her teats to shreds unless we cut them and the longer we leave it the bigger the teeth will become.'

Dolly smiled as her new man explained the necessities of piglet dentistry, seeing he must have grown up on a farm in Norway although she had never asked him about his background. She sensed he didn't really want to talk about it so she never persisted, just happy to have this extraordinary man in her arms, even if it was for a while. Love was always a shy thing which only ever hung around for a while, she believed.

BUT HE wasn't acting as though he was going anywhere at all and, if anything, seemed to be getting more and more Welsh and tribalised by the day, even joining in the annual rat hunt lead by Dic Morgan.

This rat hunt, Dolly knew full well, was merely another excuse for them all to get as drunk as wheels and what happened was that about twenty men, mostly farmers, visited the local farms where they fumigated the houses, barns and outbuildings before letting loose the dogs. The men then stood around with shotguns and shovels and those rats which managed to escape the snapping jaws of the dogs, which weren't many, were either blown to smithereens by the guns or pancaked flat by the shovels.

The farmers put out large, earthenware jugs of rough cider for the hunters to drink after they had finished on each farm with the men putting it down so fast and eagerly it wasn't too long before half of them were singing Welsh hymns and the others were having grave difficulty standing up let alone pancaking a fleeing rat with the back of a shovel. Rats escaped in all directions as the hunters spun around like whipped tops or simply fell over, barely able to see anything at all with their bloodshot eyes as they brained one another with their shovels or shot aimlessly into the air.

Certainly Dolly had never seen anyone in such a state as Ernst when she went to pick him up in the Black Lion later that afternoon. It was the first time he had ever been carried *into* a pub, he was later to recall – although he didn't actually recall anything else about that afternoon – and Dolly had to take him back to Cliff House in the wheelbarrow, normally reserved for the safe return of Dylan Thomas, and in which Ernst only kept repeating that he was never, ever, going to drink any of that rough cider ever again.

BUT THEN a wild storm blew up one night and blew their brief Indian summer of love apart.

This storm began, as most really wild storms do, on a blisteringly hot afternoon when the sea was flat and still and the very walls of the houses seemed to be sucking in the heat and holding it tight to themselves.

The pocket beach in New Quay was jam-packed with splashing children, knitting mothers in deckchairs and men with sunburned bald heads while, over on the quay itself, Dai Thomas was selling his watery ice cream and a small crowd gathered to watch Verney and Caitlin unloading their morning's catch.

The rippling gorgeousness of the afternoon spread right across the arching shoreline, with yapping dogs romping in the tiny wavelets as they retrieved their owners' sticks and right down to the graveyard in the church at Llanina where a sweating man, stripped to the waist, was digging a grave, his muscles rippling as his pick struck down into the unyielding and inhospitable earth. We don't want your bodies, the earth seemed to be telling him: go and bury them somewhere else.

But then the lazing rapture of the hour was subverted by a distant cracking which was so sharp and even precise it could even have been the sounds of some distant, invisible giants moving furniture around. The people on the beach looked at one another sharply and knew they would have to make a quick move because the blue sky was already turning a deep mauve and then a greasy, threatening black. Now those invisible giants began losing their patience and started flinging their furniture around angrily and there was a long ominous crackle, as in thousands of volts of electricity in search of someone to fry, and people were clutching their belongings and hurrying like war refugees to the steps leading up from the beach when the first of the rains hit them, not a light drizzle to get warmed up either, but a sudden torrential downpour which came so quickly and thickly the swarming refugees became wet through immediately and knew there was now no point in hurrying anywhere since they couldn't possibly get any wetter than they already were.

It rained down on the police station and the Manchester Cloth Hall; rained, in equal measures, on the Black Lion and The Dolau Inn; rained on the General Stores and the Lifeboat Station; rained on the chip shop and the shellfish factory . . . it rained on everything and nothing, anywhere, escaped this impeccably democratic downpour of rain – even the man digging that grave in Llanina.

The meteorological mechanics of what happened next were not clear but the boys in the bar theorised that there were, in fact, two storms within all this gusting ferocity, one controlled by thunder and the other by lightning, and these two storms went head to head with one another, fighting and feeding one another, cuffing one another around the head with blasts of cold winds and flashes of lightning and then calling up high waves which began hurling driftwood and clumps of seaweed right up around the low-lying streets of the town, even as far up as the Dolau Inn.

No one could ever remember waves quite so high and they were now engulfing the Lifeboat Station and practically erasing the quay in hissing roars of wild water. A railway sleeper was washed straight through the front window of the chip shop and the sewers didn't know how to deal with all this water either, gargling and spilling and spitting out torrents down the cobbled streets where litter rode them like brave, lone coracles.

As evening approached and the storm looked as if it might be about to blow itself out, it got worse, the thunder cracking and the lightning flashing as that brawl in the clouds seemed to get that much more violent with thunderheads cannoning from rooftop to rooftop over the town, bursting in the odd window and shaking yet more slates loose as the whinnying waves kept rising up ever higher as if determined to sweep the whole town away and start again from scratch with a clean headland.

Down in Llanina churchyard the half-dug grave was already full of water, with the raindrops hitting the brown surface in small javelins, and Dylan was standing in the church porch, looking out at the brawling storms and listening out for the drowned voices of all the sea captains who had been buried here. Young Gareth Morgan had told him this story on one of their long walks together a long time ago; of how the voices of those captains buried in Llanina could be heard here, particularly at night and during a storm. He'd heard them dozens of times, Gareth had claimed and, sure enough, Dylan was sure he could hear them too. Well, what exactly? A chorus of disconnected words in the driving rain perhaps or else the

244

odd distinctive voice being carried on a hard gust of wind. You could almost be tuning a wireless, Dylan decided, as his ears picked up another disjointed saying or a clamorous shriek of buried madness from beyond the grave.

YET IT all came as something of a surprise, particularly to those who had been kept awake all night worrying their roof was about to be blown off, to find that the storm had completely cleared by first light, the sky a ravishing, rinsed blue, the whole town cradled in bright, still sunshine and the dolphins leaping exuberantly out in the glittering waters of Cardigan Bay.

But there was one notable difference to the idyllic summer scene the day before because the harbour master had spotted a huge, black shape floating in the sea about two hundred yards from the end of the quay. It could almost have been a dead whale although, after studying it for a while through his binoculars, the harbour master decided it must be some sort of upturned ship, capsized in that storm perhaps and so he set off a distress rocket which exploded deep within every ear drum, jerking people out of their morning dreams and making the gulls fly up into the air and cry out in alarm. Then he let off another, upsetting the gulls even more and already the children, many of whom were half-dressed, were running down the hill as was their practise particularly when the distress rockets went off since they always meant some sort of entertainment. A few adults drifted down too, some wondering if, after being left alone for so long, the war might even have finally arrived in New Quay and they were about to get their share of the action too.

Soon the bleary-eyed and hungover lifeboat crew were making an appearance and a few returning fishing boats were circling the hulk even if they clearly hadn't a clue what they were supposed to do about it. Brian Shrimps flung a bucket at it although what he hoped to achieve by this action only Brian Shrimps knew and the fishing boats continued to circle warily until the lifeboat got there and they managed to winch Stephen Stephens on to the hull who began tapping it with his torch and waiting for a reply which never came.

More crowds were gathering on the quay when Verney Matthews appeared briefly, took a quick look at what was going on, gulped hard and disappeared fast.

'We're going to need divers to get in here,' Stephen Stephens shouted back at the lifeboat. 'There's no way of getting in up here.'

'Let's lump some hooks into her and we'll tow her in with ropes as far as we can. Tie them on the propellor shaft and see where that gets us.'

The hulk was surprisingly responsive to the lifeboat's first tug, creaking a little but as seemingly anxious to get back to dry land as everyone else and following the lifeboat obediently until it got to about thirty yards out where it just seemed to get stuck and the lifeboat's engine kept revving smokily but failed to budge it a further inch.

They tried again and again but gave up when the rope snapped and, with everyone wondering what to do next, the hulk, as if by some underwater trick, began turning slowly upright, revealing a conning tower draped with dripping seaweed, metallic gills which kept hissing with gouts of angry water and – oh fuck me bilious – a large gun mounted on the deck and the legend U-258 which had been roughly covered by black paint.

'It's not one of ours Fred. That's a fucking Nazi U-boat that is. There could be thirty or forty dead bodies in there. Better get on to the War Office.'

There might have been hundreds on the quay and beach now, all silently watching this resurrection from the deep and you just knew that all the children, in particular, were thinking about was what all those drowned German bodies were going to look like when they were pulled out.

NEWS OF the U-boat which had taken a wrong turn on the way home to Germany and ended up on the beach at New Quay ripped through the town faster than hundred yard sprinters, even knocking on the door of Majoda and prompting Dylan to abandon his work to go and take a look for himself even if he only got as far as the Beer Garden of the Black Lion where, pint in hand, he could see everything he wanted to see at a safe distance.

Two Army lorries had clattered up to the Lifeboat Station with dozens of squaddies carrying rifles jumping out and taking up positions along the beach and quay. The police were also there in force as were St John's Ambulance and the Rev Enoch. Even a stray donkey came wandering over the sand, adding a nice surrealist touch to the proceedings and it was all turning out to be some kind of chapel Whitsun treat.

Most of the activity was going on around the conning tower with the hard, dancing flashings of oxy-acetalyne indicating they were trying to open the hatch from the outside. It was a long job, which ended when they realised the hatch hadn't been locked in the first place, and several squaddies had their rifles at the ready as one leaned over the hole and shone his torch down into the U-boat's interior. But there was no fear or particular apprehension in the men since there'd been no response to their morse tappings on the deck and the general assumption seemed to be that, whoever were down there, were all as dead as dogs.

So the killer whale had gone and got itself killed, Dylan thought. Not blown up by depth charges but just died beneath the waves as if by some mysterious heart failure. Yet it was the way of war, he guessed: nothing ever seemed to go the way it was planned at a time of war, possibly because the enemy was always coming up with plans of his own, damn his black heart.

More men were now climbing down into the submarine and the whole world seemed strangely silent, as if holding its breath and waiting for what was going to happen next, when an Army lorry pulled up outside the Beer Garden and the driver, a sergeant with a shorn head and angry black eyes, shouted at Dylan: 'We're looking for Cliff House. Where's Cliff House?'

'Who are you looking for?'

'We've had a tip the U-boat men are living there.'

'There's no U-boat men living in Cliff House.'

'We 'aven't come here to argue with you mate. Just tell us where bloody Cliff House is will you?'

Dylan was having a lot of trouble working all this out, didn't like the sound of this at all and couldn't even think why the Army should be interested in Dolly although they could well be interested in the Norwegian from Norway, of course.

'Do you know where Cliff House is or doncha?'

'Over on the cliff,' Dylan said, waggling his empty glass in the direction of Llanina. 'Turn around here and follow that road over there.'

'Which road where?'

'I'll jump on and show you. Turn round here.'

Well, at least he had finally seen some kind of front-line action, the poet thought as he mounted the running board and the Army sergeant ground through the gears doing a ten-point turn. He finally had something to tell his children about what daddy did in the war and it somehow seemed right he was directing operations with an empty pint glass.

They pulled up outside Cliff House within two minutes and Dylan did hope someone had seen him leaping off the lorry like Douglas Fairbanks and pointing his pint glass at the front door. A dozen soldiers leaped out of the back of the lorry in a sharp clatter of cleated boots and Dylan was already regretful he had become involved when, rifles at the ready, they charged up the front path and, without so much as a knock or a warning shout, kicked the front door clean off its hinges.

The men rushed through the house and it was full of children's screams as doors were slammed open and rifles were pointed into the bedrooms. Dylan followed the sergeant into the kitchen where two men had surrounded Dolly who was sitting, her eyes swollen and red, at the table.

'Where is 'e?' the sergeant demanded.

'I don't know. I really don't know. Oh, Dylan please tell them to leave me alone?'

'It'll be all right, Dolly,' Dylan said, putting his glass down on the table and placing his fat little hands on her shoulders comfortingly. 'I think they must be after Ernst, so you'd better tell them where he is.'

'He's gone. Gone. The other one came here on a motor bike and they left almost immediately.'

'Did he say anything before he left?' the sergeant asked, his angry, black eyes becoming angrier and blacker. 'Anything about where 'e might be going?'

'No, nothing. He just gave me a kiss and said goodbye. What's all this about? What's he done? *Who is he anyway?*'

Chapter Twenty-one

CHRISTIAN GAVE the motor bike throttle full gun as they sped up the coast road towards Aberystwyth, the air rushing all around him, beating against his goggles and surging right up his nostrils.

Ernst sat well back on the pillion without holding on to his colleague, staring up into the emptiness of a day which he already knew was going to be his darkest and most painful. Nothing was going to be the same ever again and he saw her face in every field and tree; felt the loss of her with every breaking wave on the rocky shoreline and called out to her with every passer-by.

The motor-bike engine kept firing erratically, often losing power and slowing before picking up speed again; this was an engine which should have been serviced regularly and, in the old days, he would have made sure that this was done, but the old days had gone and he was not even especially concerned that the engine might break down altogether. He would at least get a good meal and a nice cup of Welsh tea if the Tommies captured them *and* there might be a possibility that he would see her again.

Yet the motor-bike was bringing them into contact with the countryside in an interesting and vital way, he thought, unlike life in a submarine which only brought you into contact with your darkness, and, despite what had happened, he was surprised at the freshness of the countryside and sea all around them: the gusting, ozone smells of the waves, the roses staging climbing competitions in the cottage gardens and the whole lines of gaudy hollyhocks standing guard next to willows weeping over village ponds.

They turned inland before reaching Aberystwyth and raced past a pub, where a group of drinkers were sitting outside drinking beer on a trestle table, when, just past the next corner in the road, Christian was forced to slow down behind a cattle wagon with the big, brown eyes of the cows staring out at them between the slats. One of the cows lowered dolefully as if he knew she was on the way to the slaughterhouse; as if the beast had also been stricken by an unbearable sense of pain and loss.

They were not absolutely certain they were going in the right direction since all road signs had been taken down in the war but they were following the line of the sun like the mariners they were and hoping to reach the relative safety of the mountains of Snowdonia before dark. The road kept unwinding beneath them as they went under a water viaduct, passed a high waterfall and stormed down a long canopy of overhanging oak trees – it felt like they were speeding down the aisle of a huge cathedral with the sun occasionally bursting through the stained glass windows above in evanescent showers of diamonds.

He was actually beginning to enjoy the ride when an Army lorry, full of armed soldiers, roared past them in the opposite direction and he noticed that Christian was glancing around a lot and even panicking a little, not holding a steady speed and either going too fast or slow. This was a certain way of attracting unwelcome attention to themselves and perhaps it was time he took over the handlebars when they passed a large Celtic stone cross on the side of the road and it was Ernst's turn to panic, except he was not sure why. They were doing something wrong and, for a moment or two, he couldn't work it out when he shouted into Christian's ear that they were going down the wrong side of the road.

The warning was barely out of his mouth when they

smashed straight into an oncoming Wolseley 12, bundling Ernst sideways into the darkness of a ditch and throwing Christian up into the air before he belly-flopped straight down on to the roof of the car. Even in all the rapid split seconds of this fast and furious accident Ernst's eyes caught a surprising amount of detail . . . the way Christian's head hit the top of the car, his goggles breaking away from his head, the almost instantaneous gush of blood from his mouth, the bright snap of a breaking bone, possibly an arm, the car continuing to move forwards grotesquely, shoving the motor bike out of its path, and the shocked faces of the elderly couple inside.

He managed to find his feet in the ditch but his legs were shaking so much he fell over again, just lying there for a minute or so listening only to some car wheels turning when it was as if Dolly had come to his help since her hands helped him up and even steadied him when he feared he was going to fall over again.

When he scrambled out of the ditch he could see that Christian's arms and legs had probably suffered multiple fractures while his face had been badly smashed up and his eyes were staring blankly up at him. He took a step backwards as if waiting for the eyes to wink and say it was a joke all along but they didn't because those dark eyes, set in a bloody death mask, had already turned to stone.

'*Auf wiedersehn, Kamerad*. You and me, we had a fine war.'

He was clearly in a big fix here and, as the situation got hotter he got colder, looking back at the old couple, who had recovered from their own shock a little and got out of the car to stand next to him, the woman wailing uselessly and the man muttering 'No, no, no' repeatedly.

Ernst held up a hand, telling them to calm down, then going down on one knee and taking hold of Christian's hand, surprised to feel it was already turning cold and kissing it lingeringly and passionately. *So we fought together and you finally lost my kamerad. Perhaps we'll meet again in some distant place where there is no war. Our souls will survive beyond our deaths, of that I am now sure. All this couldn't have been for nothing.*

He made sure his body was shielding the movements of his hands from the eyes of the couple and removed Christian's papers from the pocket inside his leather jacket and replaced them with his own. He was not sure why he did this, merely guessing that it might give him some sort of future advantage if a report got out that he was dead.

'You must now stop with this man while I go to get an ambulance,' he told the couple abruptly, holding out his hand and becoming the kapitanleutnant again. 'Where are your car keys?'

'They're still in the car.'

'Keep a close eye on this man in case he moves and, if he does, give him water.'

He picked his travelling bag off the pillion of the wrecked motor bike, strode to the car and flung it into the rear seat before switching on the ignition, listening to the engine fluttering nervously before revving it up hard and then, crunching through the gears and stamping on the accelerator, roaring off in the direction he had come.

The windscreen was so splintered he could barely see the road at all; the engine's tappets were also missing worryingly and the petrol gauge told him there was almost no petrol left in the tank. He even banged the gauge with the side of his fist but it was still registering empty and he knew he wasn't going to get far in this English heap of junk.

He took a right at the next crossroads and could feel the power failing again so, more in desperation than anything else, he swung off the road up a farm track and just managed to get to the top of a hill when the engine failed completely although, utilising the weight of the car and the force of gravity, he got it to trundle down across a sloping field and crashed it softly into the undergrowth of a wood, causing an alarmed fox to jump out of clump of brambles and hightail it over the slope as fast as he could go. *You and me both, Reynard. You and me both.*

Just along the right hand side of the valley was a farmhouse with a smoking chimney but he didn't dare go near that and struck out directly through the wood which brought him down to the edge of a small lake where trout jumped and moorhens paddled. He circled the lake and came to a railway line which he followed until it brought him to a disused mine and, a mile or so further on, a gate marked *Hendre* but he decided to stay with the cover of the countryside, passing some standing stones in a field and then striking out over brown and purple moorland.

A scattering cloud of midges buzzed above his head and a few woodpeckers went roller-coasting past as he sat on a stone and carefully opened a tin of corned beef. He didn't know where he was and he didn't like that at all, particularly as it would soon become dark and it would be extremely hazardous trying to survive a night on this open moorland.

He packed his rubbish away into his travelling bag and pressed on, finding an old gravel track which took him to another farmhouse, also clearly occupied, so he crossed another field and found a stream where he washed his face and drank before standing up and spotting a derelict country mansion sitting in the next valley in an orb of thin, late afternoon sunshine.

DAWN CAME flooding down the mountain and sweeping away thick mists as he trudged up the twisting path slowly, as if weighed down not just by his travelling bag but also by the burden of too much grief. The grassy slopes all around him were dotted with grazing sheep and pellets of sheep dung. Even the barbed wire fences hung with hanks of sheep wool which flapped in the breeze like miniaturised washing day lines.

He paused occasionally to look at nothing in particular when he experienced some strange and almost religious feelings, perhaps inspired by the weeks of his long, lonely trek through this ancient kingdom of the Celts. The sun was now climbing directly above him, rising directly from behind the distant peak, tossing around the morning clouds and causing the whole mountain to shiver and dance as if it was on fire. The sky surrounding the mountain's crown was a hard, bright blue and he knew that, had he been so inclined, this might even be a fine moment for prayer.

Not for the first time in these lost days his body seemed to be detaching itself from his spirit as he continued his climb and he might even not have been there at all; just a questing spirit, in the mood for prayer and journeying to the very heart of God Himself.

The brown and grey slopes were quite empty of everything but sheep who often stopped munching just to look at him before jerking away sharply to forage elsewhere. Directly behind him and across the valley were the symmetrical lines of a slate quarry, all looking like the architectural blueprint of a great new cathedral which would soon rise up out of the mountain and maybe even replace it. Just below the slate quarry were lakes where islands moved around within glittering frames of sunshine and, as he watched them, he felt human no more; just a wandering wraith out looking around his bailiwick.

The sun became stronger and so too did the song of the mountain; a rich, soft series of notes rising in perfect pitch out of the sound of the breezes chattering in the dying bracken, the steady munching of the sheep and the occasional throaty calls of the crotchety crows.

His prayerful, detached spirit pressed on, much appreciating the song of the mountain, when, right in the middle of nowhere and with not even any visible tracks leading to it, he stumbled across a broken-backed chapel with a collapsed roof, rotten floorboards and one wall missing completely. The mountain song became louder as he examined the ruined remnants of the vestry and the decayed pews where the faithful had once sat. Bleached sheep skulls and bones dotted the ground thickly around the altar where once, he guessed, they had sheltered from the storms. He looked out through the wall-less walls which framed immense and passionate views of the mountains outside.

He walked back to the porchway and stood looking down the slopes, hearing a century of Welsh hymn and prayer, seeing the faithful struggling up these slopes for the Sunday morning service and even managing to smell the polish on the pews. The stormy voices of great preachers rose and fell too, one minute beseeching their flocks softly and the next castigating them savagely. He knew all about those preachers of old; his own Bavarian childhood had been full of them.

But then something bolder and more tragic seemed to gather itself together in that broken chapel's air; nothing less than the savage, crumbling music of the breaking heart of God; a sweeping Wagnerian music which was so full of pain he actually ran out of the chapel shaking his head and holding his ears until the music halted and he went back into the chapel for his bag before continuing his climb towards the summit again.

A black cloud came sweeping in from his right and he knew that his strange morning of music and mist was about to change dramatically when it began spluttering with cold rain. Far away there was a flash and an explosion so loud he dropped his travelling bag and covered his head with his arms.

That savage, strange music struck up again except that, this time, there was no Wagnerian sweep to it, only Stravinsky discord, telling everyone with ears to hear of nightmares and heartache without end. The very mountain seemed to be amplifying this nightmare music and he couldn't be at all sure what he was now, bereaved human or wandering wraith, and probably nothing at all really, just something beyond death and yet still feeling the cold rain on his face and seeing a developing procession of black clouds, full of thunder and yet more rain, all driving towards the peak and gathering around it in a huge, deeply ominous crown.

Now these clouds were being shunted in from behind him too, all travelling towards the peak like late trains desperately trying to catch up with their timetables, all crashing together in a dark maelstrom around the summit when something brilliantly red and slimily alien began stirring inside this black, crashing mess, making Ernst drop his bag and cry out.

The very mountain rumbled and shook as the head of a huge beast rose up out of the crown of black cloud, its mouth snorting and running with fantastic streams of white and orange fire. The black clouds then covered the fiery head almost immediately but then, in another gap in the cloud, Ernst saw a huge, scaly belly expanding and contracting as yet more streams of fire exploded into the skies above. A huge tail lashed out and sent boulders tumbling down the slopes all around Ernst in loud, primordial cracks and he could feel everything inside him contract with terror once again when the central focus of his dragon vision moved and the beast seemed to hover directly over him, its dragon fire scorching through the crisp coldness of the morning and almost turning him to toast.

But, even all this hallucinating confusion, he realised he was not being physically threatened in any way and that the dragon was somehow just trying to tell him the truth about his own distress. This was an ancient beast suffering from an ancient pain but, as he held out his hand in sympathy, the dragon's eye shattered and dissolved into black cloud and the fiery spectre disappeared as suddenly and mysteriously as it had come.

Chapter Twenty-two

IT WAS such a gorgeous harvest festival afternoon Dolly was more than content to let the horse find his own pace to Henllan although she occasionally flicked the whip on the horse's sweating fly-blown rump if only to remind him that she and Caitlin were still there.

The horse's pace was seldom much faster than very slow and sometimes wasn't even that, particularly if he spotted some cow parsley in the hedgerow for which he had a special fondness and then Dolly had to really wallop him to get a move on.

'I swear there's something alcoholic in that cow parsley since he definitely seems to try going sideways after he's been munching it.'

But the slow pace was welcome for another reason too since she did not want to hit any big bumps at speed as she was now in the final weeks of yet another eternal pregnancy and had a big bump of her own to worry about. Her belly was an enormous barrage balloon and the little gymnast in there was doing hand-stands, cartwheels and God knows what else almost all the time. She shouldn't be out at all, particularly driving a horse and cart but she had to have a break from all her kids now and then; time to just look at the countryside and be with her friend.

Caitlin liked to indulge in a little daydreaming too, enjoying the way the autumn sun settled on the thrumming land in this strange, dreamy season running up to the harvest when you could pick up the rifle shots in the apples falling in the orchards where they were then drilled hollow by the slugs and wasps. It was a time of earwigs in the dahlias too, tomato plants ripening on the withering vines and daddy long legs sunning themselves in warm doorways. Everything kept changing before your very eyes in the run-up to harvest.

'I had a letter from Dylan in London this morning,' Caitlin said, breaking the silence. 'He says his drinking has been most moderate but, if you believe that, you'll believe anything. He's too lonely to drink, he says, and I don't believe that either. He says he plans to come back on Wednesday and hopes Aeronwy is fine. When did he ever care about her?'

'How long's he been away?'

'Ten days? He says he's got some film script work from Donald Taylor and just wants to get back here and get on with it. I worry about his mystical attachment to New Quay, you know. But mostly I worry that we're never going to get away from here. He says there's a play about to stage a break-out from his brain but he won't tell me anything about it. You know how secretive writers get when they're starting something new.'

'New Quay's not a bad place to live or write in. Particularly with this war on. I don't expect to leave here now. The Morgan boys want me to take over the farm for good. The idea is they work and I wash and cook. Men are useless without a woman around. But I don't mind. Running the farm for them would give my life some sort of meaning and it would give the kids a better place to grow up in.'

'Yes, and Dylan's just a kid at heart, of course. They don't get any more juvenile than our Dylan. A professional child, I've always called him. He'd get me to wipe his arse for him if he could.'

'Tell me one thing. If Dylan wants to keep living here why does he *need* to go to London? Can't he just write to his contacts?'

'You know what he's like. He calls going to London "Capital Punishment". But I know him. He'll do the rounds of his bed and breakfast tarts, have some sex with whoever happens to live near his favourite pubs and, when he's run out of energy, he'll come home again.'

'You don't mind?'

'Why should I mind? I used to think I'd mind a lot but I now accept there's nothing at all I can do about it. When I do challenge him about it he says he only does it to keep warm. Typical. All that matters is that he comes home when's he's finished doing whatever he's been doing and he then gets on with his work again. And no, I don't mind him having fun with his tarts. You could never expect a man like Dylan to stay faithful. You know you'll never have someone like him all to yourself. I always thought he'd had an affair with you, to be honest. He gets quite funny when you're around. His voice goes a bit strange and I've never been quite able to work out why.'

There was a short pause, which could have meant anything, when Dolly said: 'You feel you've got to stay broad-minded with him then? Is that what you're saying?'

'Yes and no. The real problem is that I'm like him. Both of us keep changing all the time. It's not easy to say what our relationship is about. Most days like today I can honestly say I don't feel jealousy; then, a few drinks, and he can turn me into a screaming virago who wants to hit him all the time. His one real talent is for arousing emotions in me that I never knew I had.'

'Do you love him then would you say?'

'Oh love. What would that be? Yes, he did fill me with foolishness and hope when we first met but now he mostly just fills me with pure exasperation and I want to bounce his head on the floor. Most of the time I just tolerate him and just hope that he lives long enough to realise his enormous talent with words. But he's dying you know. He's so unhealthy and the drink is killing him – and his talent – slowly but surely. I do what I can, which is not much, but there's not enough love in the heart of any woman to keep a man like that alive. He's born to suffer is Dylan. He's our very own man of the cross.'

Dolly flicked her whip. 'For what it's worth, I really *do* hope you both stay in New Quay. You've been a real prop to me since Ernst's death and I don't know how I would have managed without you. Really. Losing one man this year might have been carelessness but losing two looks like fate.'

'You're still writing to the one in Weston are you?'

'Oh yes. Dafydd writes often enough. I've told him he's about to become a father. Not sure how he's going to take it but that's what I've done. Someone's got to be the father but I can't tell you how much I miss Ernst. We were only together a short time but I'm still crying in my sleep over him. Still waking up in puddles of tears. Ernst made love like a stallion and one night we didn't get any sleep at all.'

'Ah yes,' Caitlin smiled wryly recalling a few distant stallion moments of her own with Dic Morgan on the floor of the beer cellar of the Black Lion. She never told anyone about it, not even Dolly, assuming it was still a secret although, apart from Dylan, only a few sheep in the county might *not* know about it. 'We're always talking so much about what we want or what makes us happy but, if the truth be known, I'd even be happy in a dump like New Quay if I had a man who made love like a stallion. '

'You mean Dylan isn't a stallion in bed?'

'A stallion in bed? Dylan Thomas? When he tries to make love it's like being tickled between the legs by a very small frog.'

They both roared with so much loud laughter the horse must have believed they were having a go at him since he actually broke into an involuntary trot for a minute or two before returning to his normal pace. They passed the mashed-up body of a dead cat and, a few miles further on, a man was selling coracles outside a chapel set in a large graveyard with lots of lop-sided headstones.

DOLLY PULLED up the horse outside Henllan camp which didn't remotely look like a place where they locked up Italian

261

prisoners of war since there were no guards on the gate and
single strand of rusty barbed wire wound its way around th
compound that might have been put there more to keep an
wandering sheep out than prisoners in.

'I hope we can find a few better workers than the last lo
Dolly said. 'None of my children has been working properl
since Ernst left us and we're going to need all the hands we ca
get for the harvest. It's impossible to get road men anywher
And these Italians are cheap.'

'How cheap is cheap?'

'Well they're officially called Co-operators and th
arrangement is they get ten shillings a week, half in real mone
to send back to their families in non-occupied Italy, and th
other half in tokens which they can use to buy beer or fags.'

'That's cheap. Dylan wouldn't last five minutes on five bob
week.'

'The snag is they don't like to work. They're not bad if th
sun is out but, if it rains, they get lazy and morose and go o
about the Geneva Convention whatever that is. The onl
English they seem to know is "Go home now?" or "Time t
eat?" and some of them run like mad if they see a rat. That
why the camp commander told me to come and pick out a fe
for myself after I complained about the last lot.'

There wasn't any sign of life around the Nissen huts so Doll
drove the trap into the parade ground, halting the horse next t
a flagpole with no flag and a washing line. A freshly marked-ou
football pitch was on the other side of the Nissen huts and wa
up on top of a slope was a larger Nissen hut, painted white witl
blue window frames. Caitlin spotted the backs of many me
crowded into the Assembly Hall at the far end of the footbal
pitch.

They sat there for five minutes or so, with the horse grazin
contentedly, before an Army corporal walked over to them. 'Yo
two ladies might have come to see the camp commander?' h
said briskly. 'He warned me you might be coming but, just fo

262

the moment, he's got the men in the Hall where he's giving them a good wigging. If you go over to the side you'll be able to hear what's being said. The commander is always keen for the public to understand his problems.'

There were about three hundred men in the Assembly Hall with the commander standing on a dais and addressing them in English, pausing for an Italian major to translate his words. The commander wasn't impressed by those in his charge, that much was clear.

As they listened to his righteous wrath Dolly and Caitlin turned to one another and giggled like schoolgirls. What was vexing the commander was that, despite repeated warnings, the men had been going out into the local villages and importuning any woman between eight and eighty to join them in a bout of 'jiggy-jig'.

The translation of this bit provoked a huge uproar of Latin jeers and, when they had subsided, the commander continued: 'Furthermore you keep touching these women up, brushing up against them unnecessarily in shops and bus queues. You are also causing a lot of alarm by picking babies out of prams and kissing them. There has been complaint after complaint and all this must stop, repeat, *stop.*'

He glared at them hard as the translation followed. 'Well you have been warned often enough before but now, to show you how seriously these complaints are being taken, I am hereby ordering that all prisoners be put on bread and water for two weeks. All straw palliasses will be confiscated for the same period. Every one of you will also sign a document declaring this most unfortunate practice will cease immediately.'

The roars of disapproval all but took the roof off but, by the time the full import of his message had been translated, the commander had marched off the dais and away to the white Nissen hut with blue window frames – clearly his HQ. The corporal ushered Dolly and Caitlin along behind, the two women finding it extremely difficult to contain their mirth.

'Sit down, sit down,' he said pouring himself a large gin with a tiny splash of tonic. A stack-pipe stove stood in the middle of the room and a portrait of the king hung next to a Union Jack behind his desk. 'I'm sorry you had to listen to all that nonsense but these men are oily, garlic-smelling organ grinders. I'd have the lot of them whipped daily if I could.' He not so much drank his gin as swallowed it whole, choking on it in his anxiety to get it down him as fast as he could and causing small storms of gin and tonic to swirl around his lips. When he had choked his first glass down he poured himself another and pointedly didn' offer anything to his guests.

'Oh I don't know,' said Dolly. 'I guess British prisoners of war are doing much the same to the women in Germany. Being locked up in a foreign land must do funny things to men.'

The commander was about to put his next drink to his lips but was so appalled at what he'd just heard he had to put it down on his desk. 'The British wouldn't get away with any of this in Nazi Germany. Do *that* in Nazi Germany? Even if they were allowed to wander around the countryside – which they are not – they wouldn't be allowed to touch up German women in the grocery shop. They'd be shot if they tried putting their hand up some young *fraulein*'s skirt. It's a pity we can't shoot a few of these macaronis. That'd put a stop to it. Ah, if only . . these men are all sex-mad, foul-smelling cowards who'd sell their granny's knickers for a penny.' He stood up, sat down again, drank and dribbled some more. 'All they do is complain and moan and then complain and moan again. All they think of is sex. If you tried to cut open their skulls when they died all you'd find is a large ball of pubic hair.'

Caitlin gave Dolly an anxious look since the man had a clear drink problem and that nose of his was close to unravelling into an explosion of bloody veins.

'I don't know why you've come here, quite frankly. There's not an hour's hard work in the whole bloody lot of them. *Not one!* They're just not made that way.'

264

'You must have three who can do a decent day's work?'

'No. There's not one here who I would trust to dig up a single turnip. But that's why you've come here, isn't it? To look around for yourself. Well, you may know what you're looking for, but I don't.'

The three of them toured the compound, but the men's mood was sullen and it was almost as if the commander had brought in two attractive women in to make sure they had received his message. No lascivious leers. No offers of a bit of 'jiggy-jig', and, somewhat disappointingly, not even a suggestion of a quick grope since, even despite Dolly's bump, these two women had a real bedtime air about them.

Dolly always said she could judge a man in a single glance but she wasn't having much luck here. Many of them were graceless peasant boys with no English or, if they had, not owning up to it. One was so fed up he turned his back on them so, with so little to go on, she finally picked two men who managed a sort of smile when she spoke to them; one had grown up on a farm in Tuscany and she chose the other because she liked the glinting devilry in his dark eyes.

There were no obvious candidates for third choice so she decided to leave it at that and they were walking back to the trap when they heard a fine tenor voice singing in the showers. The voice had real quality, full of olives and Mediterranean sunshine, and unafraid of the high notes.

'Who is that?' Caitlin asked.

'Mario Marinnelli,' the commander replied. 'He's also not exactly averse to a bit of work, come to think of it. When he's not singing his empty head off. But his problem is he never stops talking and you can seldom understand what he's talking about.'

'Can we speak to him?'

'If you must.'

The commander went into the showers yelling at the singer to make himself decent because there were some women here who wanted to know if he was interested in work on their farm. He was already talking before he emerged from the shower.

'You womans want me work on your farm? I work on your farm, okay. Mario Marinnelli from Pisa. Si. I come work on your farm good. Have heart like lion. Work like ten mens.'

He had a towel tied around his blubbery waist and Dolly was half expecting some form of accident when he took both her hands and fixed her with a comically courteous, black-eyed stare before kissing them with his soapy, moustachioed lips.

'We're from the Morgan farm in New Quay,' she explained. 'We need some good workers for the harvest.'

'Ah yes, Mama, I know of you and your Morgan farm. My friend Guiseppe work on your farm and you return him back in post because Guiseppe is multo lazy. But Mario Marinnelli from Pisa no lazy. Okay? *And* he no afraid of rats. Guiseppe shit himself when he see rat. Mario Marinnelli kill plenty rats. Mario beat Mussolini for killing rats. Work like ten mens. Have heart like a lion. But you must let me sing, Mama. Without song Mario Marinelli from Pisa he cannot work. Mario sing for Pope once. Si.'

'Of course you can sing.'

'I come. I come work for you. Okay? Work like ten dogs. Have heart like lion. You womans wait. You see. Those rats packing their bags, okay. Every day you give thanks to Pope for what I do. Every day.'

Chapter Twenty-three

UP HERE, high in the mountains, ice gathered in smooth, round fists on dark rocks and icicles hung off hostile ledges as buzzards rode the cold thermals and every molehill was frozen and cracked. As the rising sun worked on the ice the rocks became wet and glistening and frozen streams began working themselves loose and, deep within the ice on the dark rocks, fat drops of water were wriggling down inside them like huge, dark tadpoles struggling to find a way out. A lone walker began articulating himself as a small dot on a distant path, disappearing into a brilliant pool of sun on rock only to appear briefly on the next rock and then disappear again.

Otherwise nothing moved in this high, frozen kingdom – not even the sheep which had all clearly emigrated looking for somewhere warm – and even their hanks on the barbed wire had frozen stiff and would actually snap when touched.

A slate mine sat on the next valley wall, a derelict geometry of drams and sheds with piles of grey slate rubble spilling out of it and down the icy, grey slopes, coming to settle in a grey frozen avalanche near an abandoned railway line.

A cave gaped on the next high escarpment and, inside it, just beyond where the sunshine actually reached, a huge shaggy creature stirred in the semi-darkness, its body twitching several times and audibly groaning as a wall of high water fell about five feet away, its rushing fury mocking the icy stillness of the dawn outside.

Chicken bones and empty tins lay scattered around him,

together with the smouldering remnants of a newly dead fire and, just above, was a shelf with a row of items on it: a door key, a cigarette lighter, an open travelling bag, a crumpled photograph, a lady's garter and a human skull.

These were his possessions and sometimes he just sat there, in his cave, staring at them and wondering what they could mean and how they might unlock the mystery of his identity except, shattered by the blinding intensity of his visions, there was no order in his thoughts and certainly nothing by way of a reasoning faculty and all that ever happened was that such thoughts as he had rose up like angry waves before collapsing back into the shingle and darkness.

There was nothing to help him in his isolation; nothing that gave him clues to anything important, just a line of items on a ledge, a line of anonymous objects which sometimes taunted him briefly before going silent again.

He had donned sheepskins over his clothes to give him some warmth in his autumnal mountain exile and what with the odd bits of food which matted his straggly beard and his dirty and torn hands and long unkempt hair he might even have been a Stone-Age man wintering in this hissing cave. Only his eyes had retained their pristine blueness, staring out of his filthy bedragglement with a fierce purity.

His hand picked up a shard of slate off the cave floor and he examined it with an absorbed interest before putting it down in exactly the same spot he had picked it up from. He began massaging both his legs which were sore with the cold. What he really needed was more wood for the fire . . . shingle and darkness again . . . wood for the fire . . . shingle . . . darkness . . .

BUT HE didn't in any way skulk in his cave like a fugitive, coming out of the dripping darkness and into the sunny brilliance of the mountain morning when he was ready, as bold and defiant as The Baptist in the wilderness, an emblem of Biblical confidence and strength as he strode across the brow of the escarpment until he came down to a slate footpath which took him down into the valley with the slate mine which, in its turn, took him to the town.

His feet crunched on the slate chippings as he walked and a flutter of alarmed wings made him look around carefully for any possible hostility but, otherwise, his movements were bold as he stepped into the town streets where, sitting on the bench in the square, people occasionally brought him tea and food while children gathered at a safe distance to watch him eat and drink.

Perhaps predictably the townsfolk christened him John the Baptist but even though no one knew where he had come from – and he wasn't telling because he didn't know himself – they quickly accepted him in their midst and watched out for him too, careful he wasn't attacked or taunted by those who were always ready to attack or taunt what they didn't understand.

The only time he really seemed to lose his confidence was if he caught the image of himself in one of the shop windows when he slowed and stared hard at this creeping wild thing imitating his movements, coming up out of the darkness and the shingle and pretending to be him. This imposter visibly upset him and he made a quick return to his mountain fastness again, watched by many curious eyes in the town until he disappeared from view, back into the darkness of his cave where there were no shop windows to upset him and he could sit and be safe with his mysterious possessions.

Sometimes he stared hard at the photograph of that woman for hours on end by the light of his fire but she meant nothing to him really; just another shadow, albeit a pleasant one, in a world of shadows. And shingle . . . and darkness . . .

This cold autumnal day, when the sun had sunk behind the massive black peaks of the mountain range, sending up cloudy orange bars veined with red, he stood in the mouth of his cave, watching the end of the day, and, silhouetted by the fire behind him, he might even have been the wild Baptist come again in the land, trailing clouds of glory, urging people to repent and preparing the way for a new Messiah.

THE REV Enoch also picked up on a sort of visionary magic infusing the night air as he did his pastoral rounds in New Quay and, despite the chilliness of the night, he kept feeling himself strangely warmed as he climbed the slopes to the kissing gate and the path which would take him to the point near the oak tree where he gave his daily blessing to the town.

Here the night became even warmer and this warmth broke over the rooftops in slowly breaking waves and, just at the point where the sun had earlier sunk into a red-veined orange sea, oddly coloured lights were speckling the sky and he was most disconcerted to hear an alien sound in the shape of a strange pinging and the drone of something like that of a queen bee, only fatter and deeper: a *mechanical* drone.

Worried he might be about to be engulfed in another vision he took out his Prayer Book and began reading out the words, when that sound got harder and throbbier and he looked up at the oddly coloured lights, seeing them drift apart and come together again as they patched themselves around a giant silhouette of a man standing on a mountain, surrounded by dancing revelations of fire.

But this was no ordinary man standing there in the fire; the primeval savagery of his dress suggested an avatar come out of the wilderness, come to save men. But then there was that droning again and the Rev Enoch knew that he was joining with something, somewhere; but not on any formal level, just a communication of shared intuitions where he and another man in some distant place were offering one another mystical structures and wondering if there might be any common connection, asking one another if, when all the leaves had been stripped away, there might be a hard truth which they both might share and hold.

CAITLIN AND Dolly had gone to the pictures that night leaving an unhappy and strung-out Dylan to baby-sit in Majoda.

He had been smoking and working on a poem which just would not yield to his pencil's constant probings when his ears picked up on a strange droning in the warm night air and, with his concentration broken, he first checked that Aeronwy was fast asleep in her truckle bed before going to the window where he took an anxious pull on his cigarette as he looked out into the moonless night and across the placid waters of the Bay at the spiked and square lumps of the barely visible town on the opposing headland.

He had begun sweating and could have murdered a pint, unable to understand why the night was so warm and what that droning sound was all about when he noticed that the silhouette of the town was gradually becoming more visible beneath a strange speckling of light and there were odd pinging sounds too when, all at once, his imagination seemed to strip away all this engulfing darkness and he saw a complete and penetrating vision of the town at sleep.

He saw, in his mind's eye, all the townsfolk sleeping in their beds, either smiling or muttering in their bad dreams; he saw the dew falling on them and the cats napping on the garden sheds and the fishing boats bobbing on the sea; he saw the birds and horses all fast asleep and snoring; he saw all the chintzy front parlours of the houses and he saw mad people in night gowns, some holding candles, making their way down past the chapel, the bakery and the pub, and sailing over all this was Captain Port Talbot, high in his crow's nest, looking out over the Seven Seas and seeing everything for miles even though he was as blind as a bat.

As Dylan beheld his people at sleep, lost and wandering inside their own dreams, he felt and even heard words falling out of his mind – one by one and two by two – fine, descriptive words which kept knocking him about the head like light, teasing punches until he was forced to sit back down at his desk and catch the words with his pencil, alternately smiling and weeping at the complex majesty of his vision of the night, his pencil quickly sketching the Bible-black darkness and the harbour and the boats and the rising terraces in which his people lived and dreamed and, as he continued writing, he kept on smiling and weeping because he knew that he had finally found the opening pages of that play for voices set in this small seatown which he had long known was locked inside all those rooftops, just waiting for him to find the right key to open that rusty lock deep in his mind so that the play could finally escape.

THE FOREST was a dark and sweating tangle of muted voices and Ernst lay awake on a bed of thick moss; a stricken insomniac behemoth, trying to make sense of all these voices except they didn't seem to be making any sense, just meaningless sounds which kept repeating again and again.

Even in the incoherence of his madness he retained an extraordinary sensitivity to everything around him, not only hearing the muted voices but every tiny movement around him from the hurrying dormice to the sudden clatter of bird wings in the leafless branches overhead.

He had been on the move for five days, travelling from somewhere to somewhere else, walking endless country lanes carrying his travelling bag and relying on the hospitality of strangers until he had arrived here, this sweating forest in the middle of nowhere which overlooked a huge, moon-varnished lake with high stone dams strung out between church-like turrets.

The chatter of the voices was now being dominated by a soft and even sinister pinging; dull pings which had no music in them but told of danger. Dull sonar pings. Sonar? What is *sonar*? He sat up and trembled as the pings began being overlaid by a thickening drone, a *mechanical* drone. This droning began getting louder and *nearer* and he jumped to his feet with every part of him alert as he stared down at the glowering lake and up at the chattering branches, trying to stay quite still as his senses tried to work out where the droning was coming from.

'A flying machine,' he shouted, somewhat surprised to find words in his mouth as he went crashing around the undergrowth in erratic circles looking for some deep cover. 'A flying machine,' he shouted again.

He then spotted a large bomber dropping down out of the moonlight like a huge angel of death and its noise had become almost deafening as he continued to stumble around in a complete panic when he tripped over a tree root and went spinning down a steep slope like a runaway wheel only stopping as he crashed into the trunk of a felled tree.

Warm blood washed his face and trickled down into his beard as he hauled himself up on to the trunk by his arms and watched, goggle-eyed, as the bomber flew past him, black on silver, very low on the lake's surface. A huge revolving cylinder dropped out of the belly of the bomber and bounced along the surface of the lake in the aeroplane's wake so furiously it was as if it was actually trying to catch it up but the aeroplane just about managed to stay ahead of its manic leaps.

Just.

Ernst looked ahead of the bomber and saw that the revolving cylinder was going to hit one of those turreted dam walls, maybe even destroy it, but the cylinder bounced maybe four or five times along the lake before leaping right over the dam and disappearing out of sight with a faint sigh. He stood up waiting for an explosion which never came as the throttle of the bomber's engine opened up and the flying machine set its controls for the incandescent eye of the watching moon.

THE REV Enoch was standing at his bedroom window in his night-gown and staring out at over the sleeping town and at the still sea when he noticed a black speck gradually growing in the moon.

His Act of Parliament clock was chiming midnight within

the manse as a night wind moaned in the chimney breast and he rubbed his eyes with the hams of hands so that he could get a better look at this menacing speck. What he really needed was his spectacles but there wasn't enough time to retrieve them since the speck was already getting closer and even taking on a new shape with wide wings clearly visible on its sides and he was already picking up on that droning sound which had been haunting him of late.

But this was no aeroplane. This winged monster was so unearthly it might even have been Lucifer himself bearing down on him and his flock; Lucifer, once the most beautiful angel of the morning, who walked proud on the mountain until he tried to stage a rebellion against God and ended up chained with all the other dark angels and flung into a pit of fire for a million years. So now he was back among us all, having broken his chains and escaped the pit of fire, bearing down on his parish doubtless with dire consequences for everyone, particularly those who had turned their back on God and would not receive God's protection.

The Rev Enoch threw up his old, big hands, with his long fingers fluttering wildly as he tried to erect a defensive bunker of prayer against this new attack but he knew it was useless and there would be no escape for anyone when he spotted a huge revolving cylinder drop out of Lucifer's belly and come bouncing towards them over the moon-stained waters of the Bay . . . one time, two times, three times . . .

THEN IT was Dylan's turn to be again imprisoned within one of his boiling dreams and he kept muttering to himself as a huge spinning object swooshed over his head and he ran for his very life past the trees and over the corporation lawns of Cwmdonkin Park.

He was always running for his life through Cwmdonkin Park, largely because the parkie was always hot on his tail over some small misdemeanour like sailing a paper ship on the park's ornamental pond but this whirling object overhead was far more terrifying than any mere parkie and he did so wish it would go and whirl somewhere else.

His dreams often took him back to this park which shaped his childhood but they were never happy dreams, which was strange as he had had such a happy childhood, so much as doomed and tormenting dreams in which he was always being pursued and threatened with immediate hanging on the dawn gallows or being disembowelled in some dark dungeon.

If it wasn't the parkie who was about to hang him it was the hunchback who came to sit on one of the benches here each day to eat food out of a newspaper. All the children, as innocent as gooseberries, were scared stiff of the hunchback and particularly concerned he would one day be given no food in his newspaper and would, in consequence, grab one of them and eat him instead.

And if all that wasn't threatening enough for one somewhat prolonged childhood he now had whirling objects to deal with; a huge cylinder which would flatten him like a rolling pin if he didn't get a move on except that the parkie then rang his bell in a series of toneless clangs to announce closing time and he awoke shouting the truth of his torment to the uncaring darkness.

OUR NEW Baptist in sheepskins stood high above the city which stretched out beneath his feet in haphazard clusters, green swathes of rolling parkland on one side and the cranes and ships of a busy dockland on the other. The slopes on which he stood formed a kind of high amphitheatre in which the city seemed to be taking shelter and, directly below him, were the huge civic buildings and, beyond them, the sea itself, nagging the huge, curving shoreline with a continual mumble of ozone words.

Just next to him was a line of large posters in the road which advised him to WALK WHEN YOU CAN *and ease the burden war puts on transport* or to GROW YOUR OWN FOOD *and supply your own cookhouse* or LEND A HAND *by taking out some war savings.*

He walked down into the streets crowded with shoppers, drawing only the occasional inquisitive looks as he passed cafes like The Kardomah or shops such as Eddershaw's, Price's Fifty Shilling and Crouch the Jewellers. Everyone was a stranger although it was on the corner of College Street that he spotted Dylan, with a Woodbine in his mouth and a pork-pie hat on his head, hurrying through the crowds towards him, doubtless out on some mysterious but important mission.

Ernst froze and put his bag down between his feet as Dylan approached, feeling a chime of recognition of something from an earlier life perhaps, which may or may not have been a life at all, as Dylan hurried on past him down towards the centre of the town and Ernst picked up his bag and followed him until the poet went in through the front doors of a pub and Ernst stood at the doorway, watching him as he ordered a pint at the bar and sat down on his own at a table where he stared down into the white, foaming beer before picking it up and drinking greedily.

Dylan was about half-way through his pint when Ernst went into the bar too, sitting at the next table to him and attracting the odd worried looks from the punters although none of them actually made any comment on his scraggy, caveman appearance, nor did Dylan who didn't even glance at him and might not have seen him at all before finishing his pint and striding out through the pub door when, as if by some strange trick of smoke 'n' mirrors he disappeared into the milling shopping day crowds.

ERNST CONTINUED to ghost the city streets as the shoppers thinned out on departing buses and the shops were being closed and shuttered for the night.

He walked around for three or four hours, staring down into the dark alleyways or haunting the cobbled streets around

Salubrious Passage in the dockland when he tensed to that sound of droning again and there were several firework flashes all around him and a thunderous firestorm broke out in a nearby group of warehouses with such an intensity he had to shield his eyes with his bag so he could look at it.

Brilliant flashes mingled with deafening explosions as the air raid sirens screamed in a roller-coastering panic and he felt the very ground lurch beneath his feet as yet another bomb landed, causing rooftops to burst into huge blooms of light as yet more small green parachutes fell through them, erupting into yet more shattering explosions of breaking glass and flying brick. His mind was blank as he kept walking through the flaming darkness with red tracer dicing up the night and the anti-aircraft guns opening up on the bombers with their erratic shells ripping ragged and angry rosettes of fire out of the night.

More bombers came cruising in to be met by more angry rosettes and another incendiary sheeted up into a huge mushroom of stammering flame, burning deep into his vacant retinas, turning night into day and frightening hundreds of birds who fluttered up from their roosting ledges and wheeled away from all these noisy explosions.

Incendiaries followed more land mines and Dylan came dashing out of a pub to grab hold of Ernst's arm, trying to pull him back into the safety and security of the bar except that Ernst merely shook his arm loose and continued moving forwards with sparks of phosphorus skittering around his head and making tiny fires in his sheepskins.

Men and ARP wardens kept hurrying past them with ladders and blowing whistles as he came to another main street where the land mines were effortlessly taking out many of the department stores – Doctor Scholl's, Burton Tailors, Boots Cash Chemist, Leslie's Stores, Stead and Simpson – the flames bursting out of the windows in huge, lashing tongues, often meeting up with huge, lashing tongues coming out of the other side of the street, all creating a furious and violent volcano through which our Baptist, somehow or other, still walked.

A LAND MINE hit the docks at that moment, sending a high wave of light zipping straight across the sea in pullulating surges to surround the Rev Enoch who was standing in his place above the town and crying out in horror as the rooftops of New Quay were swamped with fire.

Pillars of black smoke were rising up out of this sea of fire and he could see the souls of his people rising up out of the flames and making their way to heaven's vault, in ones, twos and threes, where a door was already open and several angels were welcoming their arrival. Some of the departing souls hesitated and just hung about nervously but others marched in boldly, neither wanting help nor pausing to look around.

The Rev Enoch was fearful his vision might be about to get a lot worse, perhaps with the arrival of the angry dragon but, rather to his surprise, God seemed to have rewritten the script for this one since he then spotted a man, an ordinary man like himself, stamping through the fire towards him.

Ah yes, he had met this man before; he was that man whom he'd seen often enough nailed to that singing cross of fire. *Yes, yes and not only have I come across him, we've had conversations together; conversations like no other. We have long been serenading one another with mystical visions across a huge and unfathomable divide. But why was he now wearing those sheepskins?*

ERNST KEPT walking mechanically between high walls of flame in which faces kept appearing and changing shape as he stepped over the tangled hoses of the many fire engines fighting the blazes. A woman ran past him with the body of a child in her arms as another bomb came screaming down into the next block, shattering a roof and spilling the walls of a house over a road.

A fireman was on the roof of the burning market when it gave way and he fell silently down inside it, waving his arms around silently before he disappeared into the flames.

These flames kept eating up the huge office blocks and department stores, biting into them hard and busily stripping off the wood and brick before reducing them to the bare skeletons of black girders and roofless roofs. The Home Guard had also turned out but kept falling back complaining that the heat was even burning through their boots as more brick walls groaned and snapped and three bodies just lay on the pavement visibly shrinking in the heat.

Ernst could almost feel himself shrinking too, his skin tightening over his bones and head with a sudden viciousness when a flying brick struck him on the side of his neck causing a soft, hot ooze of blood to start seeping down his right hand side.

But still he kept staggering on through yet more blazing pools of fire, occasionally shading his eyes from the primitive savagery of all these flames when he came across a tableau right in the middle of the road whose very intensity made him reel backwards as if he had been punched straight on the nose.

Right there, directly in front of him, Dylan, fag in mouth and shirt sleeves rolled up, was hammering a man's hands into the crossbeam of a large wooden cross, pounding in the nails with a shattering and uncharacteristic cruelty until others stepped forward and pulled up the cross which was then placed into a hole in the ground. Dylan stepped back in bloody satisfaction, his whole body aglow with a translucent yellow light as he looked up at the cross and dropped his hammer before taking a draw on his cigarette.

And the Rev Enoch hung there on his singing cross of light, arms outstretched and blood running from his palms; a supreme vision on this fiery, worshipping night sprung on sweeping Welsh visions, gazing down at his tormentors with his old eyes beneath the enormous eyebrows.

Nothing moved in Ernst's mind or memory as he stepped up to the Rev Enoch and they became one on the cross of singing fire although he did say one thing before they died together.

'There might be shelter here,' he said as he reached out to embrace the Rev Enoch and took a massive explosion of brick and flame straight in the face.

Chapter Twenty-four

GEORGE SHEPHERD had long advised Gareth not to think so much; that it was 'bad for 'im to fink' and, if he wanted to do something really useful he should 'fink about 'Airy Mary's wunnerful bush' and wank more often. But Gareth couldn't really accept this Cockney wisdom since he had a brain that was born to keep churning over as he sat in the outside lavvy worrying about this or that.

His main worry these days concerned all the changes he could see around the farm and all the strange characters who were moving in and out of the place which had practically become a refugee camp in its own right. Apart from Dolly and all the Shepherd children there were also his two brothers still working the farm and three Italian prisoners of war as well as the regular visits from Dylan and Caitlin usually wanting to borrow something like milk for the baby or fresh vegetables.

Nothing was as it was and it wouldn't have been quite so bad if he could still have a good think in the outside lavvy except that he kept being thrown out of that all the time by these invaders.

The trouble was he still had a clear recollection of a farm of peace and hard work, all held together by the love of his Mam before this war had broken out. The road men came and the road men went; the sheep men came in their turn and the sheep men went. They had cows and sheep out in the fields and the harvest consisted mainly of whatever happened to grow. You used to throw spuds into furrows and hope for the best; if they didn't come up in the way you'd hoped for then tough.

These days you could do almost anything on the farm without ever actually getting up out of your seat and they also owned a reaper binder, together with three neighbouring farms, which meant the end of the road for the road men since the reaper binder could gather in all the harvest in a day or two. This reaper binder also cut the corn and out bobbed the bound sheaf but, even so, it still kept breaking down – or the twine would snap – sending corn and often bits of dead rat flying in all directions.

Their basic crops had also changed, largely thanks to that Mr William Brown of the County War Ags who was still turning up on his bicycle from time to time and sticking his nose into everything; you name it and he had his nose stuck into it.

He had banned growing any more potatoes because they were losing half of them to a particularly virulent wireworm, for which there was no known treatment, and these days they were experimenting with mangolds, sugar beet, turnips and flax. Mr Brown had also introduced a wide range of new insecticides which had all but turned the fields into gas chambers as they killed off the flea-beetles, leather-jackets, root grubs and caterpillars. You couldn't find a worm to go fishing with after he'd finished fumigating every lump of earth although Gareth had once overheard in the farmhouse kitchen that Mr Brown had made the farm efficient and it was about to turn a modest profit for the first time.

There was something going on with Dic too who was no longer his usual ebullient self and Gareth had heard that he was in some kind of serious trouble with the police after blackening his wife's eye in a drunken row outside the Black Lion. Some other woman had been involved, it seemed and Dic had an appointment soon with the beak in Cardigan Assizes. Gareth knew who that woman was too but he wasn't about to tell anyone and could barely believe it himself.

Trefor was only ever like Trefor.

But, in spite of all this bustle, there was still a huge hole in the heart of the farm after the death of his mother; a black cloud of emptiness and unrealised longing which had so affected Tada that he had all but given up, content to sit in his rocker next to the kitchen range where, often at night, he might chatter to his wife for an hour or two.

There were times when Gareth might have followed Tada's grieving lead although, surprisingly, he rarely grieved for her for long largely because he spent most of his waking hours convinced that she was still alive, often running home to the farm composing what he was going to tell her when he got there.

Dolly continued to be a sort of maternal figure to Gareth although the boy was becoming increasingly resentful at the way Mario Marinnelli was soaking up so much of her attention. Mario had become instantly popular on the farm because he only had to walk out into the fields for an hour or so when he would stand up, arms outstretched and cheeks of his arse sucked tight, and give everyone a quick burst from *The Marriage of Figaro* or something. Everyone stopped work when that happened and even the grazing cows looked up in alarm.

But when he wasn't singing or working Mario also had the distressing habit of bursting into tears, usually when Dolly was nearby and, Dolly being Dolly, she would mother him endlessly until he stopped.

'I just found him in the corn field crying like some alcoholic scarecrow,' Dolly told Gareth. 'So you just can't turn your back on something like that and I gave him a good *cwtch*.'

'What was he crying about?'

'Oh it's always the same thing. He's crying about the death of his father.'

'That's something to cry about, I suppose.'

'Gareth, his father died nine years ago and Mario has been crying about it ever since. He adored his father, he says, and it wasn't so bad when he was back home in Pisa because he could always go and lay flowers on his father's grave. That always helped but it's all got worse since the war began and Mussolini even had to stop him driving tanks because he kept on bursting into tears instead of firing at the enemy.'

'Are you telling me Mussolini personally went down to Mario's tank and told him to stop driving it because he was crying so much?'

'Something like that.'

'And you believe him?'

'Oh, I don't know. He's just another over-emotional wop isn't he? Italy must be full of them. Mario only sneezed the other day and started crying he'd got pneumonia and would certainly be dead within hours.'

CAITLIN MEANWHILE was suffering from a particularly prolonged mood of isolation and neglect and starting to moan a lot to Dylan about living in 'this blob of snot by the sea' while also getting unexpectedly desperate to return to the fleshpots of London, no matter how many bombs might be falling on that grubby capital.

'But I'm working, Cat. There's something bubbling up in my brain and I want to catch it while it's still bubbling. I'm hearing the voices, Cat. I just want to sit here quietly for a while and listen to the voices.'

'Bah. You've got more tunes than Glen Miller you have. One minute you want to leave and the next you want to fester away in this dump and listen to voices. They've all got voices in London you know.'

'Not these kind of voices they haven't. I've never heard a bunch with all these sorts of voices. These are the authentic voices of Welsh madness and I've got to catch them while they're all around me.'

'Hey, listen to this fucking voice then if you really want to listen to voices. An Irish voice. That which belongs to your fucking wife who hates it here surrounded by all these oafs and

284

in all this poverty with everyone flat broke and living on bread and scrape. Most of the kids haven't got a pair of socks between them and I went to the General Stores for rolling tobacco this morning and all they had in there were fucking mothballs and broken biscuits.'

'You're not saying there are no shortages in London are you Catey. There's shortages everywhere and at least you can get fresh milk for the baby on the farm. Dolly wouldn't ever let us go short.'

'And every wall in New Quay has got a fucking slogan on it. Watch out for the squander bug. Buy national war bonds. Dig for victory. They're all driving me around the fucking bend.'

'Well, they're sure to have them in London aren't they? They don't just put them up in New Quay to annoy you.'

'You don't notice them so much in London. They know how to *live* in London. They certainly don't wash their light bulbs once a week in London or air their bedrooms with a candle in a flower pot.'

'These are called war economies, Catey. We are all still at war in case you've forgotten and London is simply not a safe place to be. So we are all staying here until the war's over and that's fucking that.'

BUT CAITLIN didn't exactly despair at being imprisoned in this blob of snot by the sea since she knew that Dylan rarely took up the same position about anything for long and, while he might be happy to stay in this dump today, he might well be singing from another song sheet tomorrow, and indeed her opportunity to effect an escape actually came early the very next morning.

A grey, clear dawn was spreading over the Bay with the dolphins already up and gambolling exuberantly when she was awoken by the urgent call of Megan Evans' cockerel who was in particularly fine operatic form. After pulling on her dressing gown she went into the kitchen finding an unshaven Dylan sitting at the table surrounded by fag ends and crumpled-up pieces of paper on which he had probably been harvesting his voices.

He was clearly stressed by many hangovers, as usual, with his podgy hands fluttering around his ears like demented moths as Megan Evans' cockerel continued his cracked aria. 'Catey, darling,' Dylan whined slowly, deliberately and plaintively. 'Catey, my baby, if you go over there now and fix that cockerel once and for all – if you could just do that for me – I promise we'll pack up our bags and be out of this place. And that is a solemn promise.'

ALL THE chickens in Megan Evans' chicken run jumped around frantically and practically shat themselves with fear when Caitlin Thomas, a new Jack the Ripper in a tatty dressing gown, kicked in their door with a mighty crack and stepped amongst them, wild-eyed and brandishing, in her right hand, the biggest fucking carving knife in the world.

The chickens fluttered around on their perches and squawked in alarmed shrieks of exploding feathers as she slashed her way through them, her wild murderous eyes fixed on one bird and one bird only: that big, bastard of a rooster who hadn't even noticed her coming his way and was warming up for another of his death-welcoming, nerve-destroying cockaloodaloos when she grabbed him firmly by his bugling neck with her left hand and he looked up at her and her raised right hand, with terror decanting in his little eyes, since he clearly knew his cockaloodalooing days were finally numbered.

Indeed he tried to squeeze an entirely different shriek past Caitlin's grip on his throat but she wasn't letting it through and the shriek sounded more like a mere hiccup as, with a skill which suggested she had been born and bred in an abattoir, she swung her carving knife and severed his hiccuping head from trembling body in one clean slash, showering her own face with tiny feathers and flecks of blood.

'All right buster let's see you cockaloodaloo your way out of that,' she shouted as she dropped the headless rooster on to the floor. 'Let's see how many other poor poets you can disturb now.'

The headless chicken did a full circuit around the chicken run, with blood gushing out of the stump of its neck, before dashing out into the lane where it went charging off towards New Quay with a speed and urgency which suggested they were selling off new chicken heads in the General Stores that morning, bouncing off Margaret Pryce's wall at one stage before actually turning right at the crossroads and continuing down the centre of the road and past the bakery were Tony Price came out, flanked by his wife and her sister, watching this 'bleeding thing' shooting past.

Windows were shooting up and heads were poking out as the chicken careered past the houses, losing steam and staggering about as it ricocheted off the wall of the Black Lion only to finally make it to Dai Fred's doorstep and sending Mrs Dai Fred catatonic with shock when she opened her front door to look down at a headless rooster dying right there at her slippered feet while also bleeding brightly all over her new coconut matting Welcome Mat.

'THERE WAS blood and guts everywhere on the doorstep an' it was like something out of the last world war,' Dai Fred told the boys in the bar of the Black Lion that night. 'The missus even made me pick it up and take it out into the back yard although, as soon as she recovered, she was even talking of roasting it for our supper. But then Megan Evans came by 'cos she had followed the trail of blood an' she was at the door saying she wanted her chicken back.'

'And what about my new front door mat?' Mrs Dai Fred asked Megan Evans. 'I only bought it in Cardigan Market last week an' now it's covered in blood an' no one will be able to wipe their feet on it.'

'Never mind about that,' Megan Evans snapped. 'I'll wash

your mat for you but I want that chicken back because it's mine.'

DOLLY QUITE enjoyed the rich complexity of her new life on the farm during the day and being with her new extended family at night, although she didn't much enjoy lying alone in her empty bed.

It wasn't as if she hadn't tried – oh how she'd tried all right – but her love life was one big nothing and there she was lying on her tear-stained pillow with her belly full of a little Welsh conscientious objector, who wanted to be a world champion gymnast, while her heart was grieving for a German U-Boat commander who had gone and got himself knocked down and killed on a Welsh road.

As if all that wasn't enough for any woman she was also now mothering an Italian prisoner-of-war and very thankful she was full of a Welsh conscientious objector otherwise her Italian Co-operator could well get her up in the barn loft, give her a sniff of Chianti and who knows what might happen then?

There was also the extremely vexed question of the husband of her best friend, otherwise known as Dylan Thomas, who, she was reasonably sure even if he had yet to admit it, believed *he* was the father of her new baby after that unfortunate tumble on the beach on New Year's Eve. She had often caught him gazing at her bump and had noted the way his voice went all quavery when he spoke about it.

Oh yes, her situation was so stupid, if not downright mad, it didn't even bear thinking about. Certainly her poor father would have died of heart failure if he'd learned the half of it. The locals were picking up enough whiffs of her real story, of course: you can never damn the unstoppable tides of Welsh gossip and they were sure to be suitably scandalised by her international sex life which, in the gossip, probably now had it that she had screwed almost every soldier on all sides of this wretched war.

Yet there would be a strong element of truth in all this

whirling Welsh gossip, she had to grant, because she had always functioned as a woman as long as she was getting plenty of it and, oh all right, it didn't really matter what side he was on either; if he had a nice big cock and a glass of something strong in his hand his nationality was irrelevant.

She sighed and moved her bump around again, dozing off from time to time and slipping from one anxiety dream to the next, waking up and sliding into yet another threatening situation with the roof off – and the rain pouring in – when she felt a cold hand fiddling around down below her bump and between her legs which wasn't the worst thing that had happened to her all week except that, apart from being very cold, she would *quite* liked to have known whose hand it was down there, even if it was just another of her upside down dreams.

'Do you think,' she asked, 'do you think you might just warm your hand up before putting it down there because it's bloody freezing.'

'Well, it's a freezing night, *cariad*, and I thought that, as I was passing, I might just pop in here and warm up my hand.'

None of this exchange made any sense – even in the evident nonsense of her dreams – when she tensed with alarm as the cold hand began smoothing her belly and the little gymnast bastard in there was doing all kinds of excited hand stands by way of response. The warmth of the man's breath on her face was also suspiciously real too.

'Oh *cariad* I couldn't stand it any longer. I've escaped to be here with you.'

Immediately realising this wasn't another of her old missing-you dreams – or indeed any other kind of dream – she was awake in an instant. This wasn't Ernst back from the dead either but the soft, singing voice of her dreamy Dafydd ap Iestyn, late of Weston-Super-Mare and hopefully back home here in New Quay in time for the birth of his baby.

But there seemed nothing to say and so she just kissed him

fondly and wetly on his eyes, nose and lips before starting to cry like the onset of a particularly wet autumn; crying for Ernst and herself and Dafydd and the baby about to be born; crying with frustration and happiness and gratitude; crying for all the people and children on the Morgan farm and, perhaps most of all, crying with fear that Dafydd might be about to be taken from her again.

She could never remember crying so much before and the tears kept flowing and didn't look much like stopping in this life – nor indeed the next – as they lay in one another's arms and that owl in the oak tree hooted emptily and even satirically at the crescent moon suspended in drifting black clouds over Cardigan Bay.

And all this weeping caused such physical spasms that she didn't at first notice that other spasms were at work too and it was only when she lay back on her bed and stared up, red-eyed and cried-out into the darkness, that she realised that there was a tightening between her legs which kept loosening before tightening up again and, unless she was very much mistaken, that meant her contractions had begun and she was going to give birth at any moment now.

Oh thank the Lord, thank the bloody Lord. *She was going to have the baby at any moment now and, wonder of bloody wonders, she was actually going to have this baby by a man she knew and cared about and who also happened to be right here in her arms.*

DOLLY WAS running with sweat and moments of dizziness as she sat up in bed, propped up by her shaking arms and staring down at the spot between her knees practically willing the little gymnast out.

Indeed her concentration on the event was so complete she could barely make out what was going on all around her, only occasionally becoming aware of Dafydd sitting at the bedside next to her or of Caitlin hurrying back and for with towels or sending one of the Shepherd children down to the kitchen where they should boil up as much water as possible.

Another contraction was shivering right down inside her cramping loins and she knew she was very close now when there was the sound of a lorry drawing up outside Cliff House and the sharp clatter of cleated boots coming up the pathway followed by a huge crash – as in front door being kicked off its hinges – and several screams from the children as the Army streamed into the hallway and began rummaging through all the rooms.

For a moment Dafydd seemed more terrified than she was since they both knew who the Army was looking for but he made no attempt to run for it as the bedroom door was kicked in off its hinges and three squaddies burst into the room and all pointed their rifles at Dafydd's head.

''E's up 'ere sarge. This must be the chummy we've bin looking for.'

'Why don't you just open the door instead of kicking it in all the time?' Dolly shouted. 'I've only just had them fixed after your last visit.'

A sergeant walked in whom she recognised as the bruiser who had last come here several months earlier looking for Ernst. 'I don't believe this,' he said in an exaggerated tone which suggested he really didn't. 'Tell me, are you screwing every man in this war, regardless of what side he's on?'

Dolly let out an unearthly scream and fell backwards as she felt her bum being washed in a warm and deepening puddle. *Yaaaaaaah!* she yelled, still clutching Dafydd's hand as her other kept opening and closing as if looking for something to hold on to before finally grabbing hold of the sergeant's somewhat unwilling hand. *Yaaaaaaaah!* she yelled again, feeling all kinds of bumps and pains banging together between her legs.

Caitlin tried to get her legs into a more suitable birthing position as Dolly's whole body shivered with another lance of torment while more Army men, attracted by the screams, were filing into the bedroom until there were maybe seven or eight of them in there now, all standing around her bed and looking down at her, slack-jawed and fascinated as they prepared to watch their first ever birth. *Yaaaaaaaaaah!*

In normal circumstances Dolly would almost certainly have objected to her birth becoming such a public spectacle but circumstances were hardly normal and, as her mind battled with her roasting loins, and she would quite happily have died rather than dealing with any more of this pain, she actually felt some perverse pleasure that all these men were here; that they would all finally witness what poor women went through when they kept putting their big dicks into them; that this Welsh nationalist in particular would understand what it was like when women gave birth to little Welsh nationalists. *Yaaaaaaaaaah!*

She stiffened with yet more explosions of pain and almost felt like a human hammock, strung out between Dafydd on one hand and the oddly attentive sergeant on the other; both sweating themselves now and urging her on as she kept trying to suck down big gulps of air.

'It's coming Dolly,' Caitlin squealed in excitement. 'I'm just seeing its head. Now have a small rest and then we'll have a nice big push.'

Yaaaaaaaaaah! she went, looking up at all the faces looking down at her as if she was some victim of a traffic accident and wanting to tell them not to just stand there but do something but, with every new spasm, her mind went blank again and all she could yell was *Yaaaaaaaaaah!*

The small, frightened faces of the Shepherd children appeared and disappeared and she was dimly aware that even more people had turned up and that she would have had marginally more privacy had she decided to give birth in the middle of the bar in the Black Lion.

'And into the darkness of the final hour of the final day a voice was talking of a new beginning in light. This voice came singing of fresh births in the midnight dark. It told of the first

292

yell of life in the kingdom of the dark.'

Oh fuck me, Dylan had joined the watching throng too, speaking his gibberish in a loud organ voice, two fags in one hand, glass of whisky in the other and eyes brimming with tears.

'Dylan, who the hell let you in here?'

'Stay with me love because I am sick of flagons,' Dylan cried on. 'Stay with me now and be my rock because the beer has gone against us and we are left . . . '

'That man is pissed out of his mind. Someone get him out of here.'

'Stay with me love because I am sick of flagons . . . '

'Come on now, sir, we'll take you downstairs and give you a mug of something hot.'

'He never turned up for the birth of his own fucking children you know. The first sight that anything was happening he took off for a fucking fortnight.'

Dolly's eyes opened, closed and opened again since the fat face of William Brown was now down between her legs and she just couldn't believe it. How had *he* got down there and, more to the point, what did he know about delivering babies? He was an expert in such things as lambing and she wasn't a bloody ewe was she? She wasn't part of the agricultural war effort.

William Brown continued to peer and fiddle between her legs with all the others moving around for a better look at her exploding fanny, including Mario Marinnelli and young Gareth. This was all too much. *Yaaaaaaaaaaaaah!*

Next thing a squaddy fainted clean away but no one attempted to clear him up any more than anyone had tried to escort an extremely drunken Dylan out of the room because no one wanted to miss one second of this great and bloody event.

But by now Dolly was finding the presence of all these people oddly reassuring and was anyway more concerned by a severe shortage of breath when, with the next heave, she began feeling the whole physical mass of her baby opening up between her legs with all the immense and fantastic glory of one of the first flowers of spring. *Yaaaaaaaaaaah!*

THE JOY was unconfined and the applause prolonged after William Brown cut the umbilical cord with what looked suspiciously like a pair of sheep shears and held up the bloodied, gelatinous lump for all to see and marvel at as she – for it was a girl – let rip with an outraged scream.

Mario sang an operatic line of welcome. Dylan punched the air and missed.

Dolly merely sat there smiling and crying as Caitlin took the baby off Mr Brown, wrapped her in a sheet and put her on Dolly's bosom where she continued to scream as this jostling, motley crowd of soldier, deserter, adolescent, opera singer and War Ag official all continued to look down at her in sheer marvel at what she had done.

She nodded at them all in turn, as if thanking each of them for all their own hard work which they had so unstintingly put into making this event the great success it had been.

Dafydd hadn't stopped crying since the baby's head had first appeared and Dylan, who seemed to have found a new source of whisky from somewhere, was well up the road too, proclaiming that the baby would 'always have the sun of a great poet's words, carrying the legacy of word-spinning with him until he reaches his own dark grave' when Caitlin asked if the Army would remove that 'silly bastard' who just happened to be her husband and lock him up somewhere secure for a long time.

Their mood had quickly changed again to one of jubilation and self-congratulation with everyone shaking one another's hands as if they really did believe they had all made a significant and even important contribution to the birth.

There was clearly a party coming together and when it was announced that the Black Lion was still open – and would remain open for anyone who wanted to wet the baby's head –

the sergeant announced that the Army would be pleased to buy everyone a beer before Dafydd was taken back to the jug.

THE ARMY lorry would take Dolly and the new baby for a quick check-up in Aberaeron hospital, it was decided; Dylan should be put to bed somewhere dark to sleep it off and, while the lorry was away, everyone would avail themselves of a drink or three in the Black Lion before Dafydd was taken back to face the music in Shrewsbury.

It soon became quite a party too with Dafydd looking extremely thoughtful as he stood at the bar in handcuffs and the gathering throng took it in turns to slap him on the back in congratulation before picking up one of the many pints that Percy Hoskins had put on the bar, all paid for by the Army.

Word of free beer courtesy of the Army spread quickly through the town with yet more coming in almost every minute, including a few of the ARP wardens who had been out on late patrol. Even The Black Widow turned up wondering if the Army might stretch to a pint of cider.

Within half an hour the pub was crowded with mounting jubilation when all this merriment was cut dead by a terrible screaming coming from outside and all heads swivelled around when Caitlin burst in, her eyes blazing and her face white with anguish.

'Dylan has fallen off the cliff. Please help me will you? Dylan has gone and fallen off the fucking cliff.'

Fallen off the fucking cliff? How can someone even as daft as Dylan manage to fall off a fucking cliff? And everyone thought he had been put to bed in somewhere dark.

'You're the Army so please go and find him will you?' Caitlin shrilled on. 'He's only got chicken bones and he's probably broken every single one of them.'

'Where'd 'e go down then?' the sergeant asked.

'I'm not too sure. He seemed to have sobered up, as he does, and was walking well ahead of me when I heard the cry he always gives when he's frightened. He could be almost anywhere along the beach.'

'Well, we'd better find 'im then,' the sergeant said decisively. 'We've found one deserter tonight so it won't take long to pick up a drunk poet too. We'll get down to the lifeboat station an' take it from there. Everyone back in 'alf an 'our if we don't find him.'

Dafydd was left at the bar and looking even more thoughtful when he caught Caitlin's eyes and one gave him a broad wink.

SMALL WAVES collapsed on the shingle with long, heavy hisses as the squaddies searched the darkness with their rolling flashlight beams, calling out to one another as they combed the beach, disturbing a few lovers who jumped up and scuttled away, but otherwise finding nothing particularly by way of a Welsh wordsmith lying around with all his chicken bones broken.

As it happened the said Welsh wordsmith had all his chicken bones intact and was sitting alone deep in the darkness at the far end of the beer garden of the Black Lion where Percy Hoskins, out picking up empty glasses, found him nursing almost *a pint* of whisky.

'Dylan, boy, what the hell are you doing out here? There's a whole bloody Army out on the beach looking for you. Mrs Thomas said you'd fallen off the cliff.'

'Well, I'm by here. And I am by here because I was told to sit by here. Don't go up there, said the Cat woman. And, whatever you do, don't go down there. Just sit by here in the dark and you will be fed with lots of whisky. So here I am, by here, behaving myself and drinking lots of whisky.'

'WHAT A fucking shower of shit you all are,' the apoplectic sergeant screamed after his men all drifted back when word had gone out that Dylan had been found, alive if drunk as a monkey, in the beer garden. 'The fucking beer garden was the where you brainless twots should have looked fucking first.'

But his anger was as nothing when he learned that not only had the poet been found in the beer garden but that Dafydd had taken advantage of the general confusion and disappeared into the night along with a brand new pair of Army handcuffs.

'Get out there and find that pacifist bastard you fucking morons an' don't come back 'ere 'til you do. Every fucking one of you is going to be on a fucking fizzer if you don't find 'im. An' where's that Caitlin fucking Thomas? I wanna 'ave a word with 'er too.'

But Caitlin Thomas had made a strategic retreat back to Majoda, taking Dylan with her in a wheelbarrow, perhaps scared she was going to end up on a fucking fizzer herself.

AND SO the British Army's finest began another search through New Quay, turning up this lane and searching down that, peering into dustbins and scouring backyards, poking their bayonets into compost heaps and rootling around in the back of pig sties.

They did become briefly excited when they spotted a lone figure walking high on a hill only to discover the figure was merely the Rev Enoch out on one of his midnight prayer rambles. Later still there was another flurry of booted activity down near the shellfish factory when another wandering figure was spotted and briefly surrounded until they found that it was again the Rev Enoch still out doing his rounds.

The Rev Enoch was now so fed up with having torchlights and rifles waved in front of him he decided he would be far better off if he just went home to his house.

Chapter Twenty-five

THE WIND blew ragged clouds of yellow and brown leaves from the small woodland behind the crescent of Cei Bach beach, sending them dancing around the two crude wooden huts on the pebbles and out onto the sea itself where they rode around on the swelling waves like the scattered and defeated armada of the Royal Navy of Lilliput.

The two ramshackle huts gave the beach a secretive, almost tropical air which was further heightened by the occupants of the huts themselves: Shani Bob Mam now standing outside her hut boiling water on a fire, pipe clamped in her mouth and wearing a trilby, surrounded by her chickens, and a reclusive figure in sheepskins in the other hut, about thirty yards away from Shani's, who spent most of the daylight hours hidden away in there.

Ernst had just fetched up there one day and Shani had let him sleep in her empty goat shed, which, even three weeks and many rain storms later, he was showing no inclination to leave. Occasionally he bathed in a river just behind the small woodland but mostly he just smelled and remained filthy and Shani gave him some food, when she thought about it, although all he ever really seemed to do was just sit in his hut looking out at the rain or, as today, the sunlight scattering diamonds of light around the dead leaves on the sea.

The very act of watching the almost incessant movement of these waves made him feel safe and secure and his only real insight into the all-encompassing murk of his existence was that he had once emerged out of the sea; that somehow he had got shipwrecked here after coming out from beneath the waves.

A few chickens came clockworking into his hut, pecking around at his feet looking for something to eat but he took no notice of them – nor they of him – although they did sometimes get lucky with a discarded piece of bread or bit of mouldy rind over which they fought noisily.

No one ever visited the strange couple of Cei Bach although the local children did sometimes come to gawp, often hiding themselves in the woodland where they waited for something to happen which never did so they soon got bored and went away again.

Not one of these visiting children had ever actually dared to set foot on the pebbled beach, still less actually peer into the goat shed and the real problem was that Ernst's face was a complete mess after he had survived the bombing of Swansea and, apart from the wild, matted shagginess of his hair and beard, even his eyes were out of alignment while the tannic acid they had used to treat his burns had almost completely destroyed his complexion which was now red veined and mottled like the side of a decaying salmon. His eyelids had been discoloured with gentian violet and his hands were black and torn although his eyeballs themselves had retained their pristine, fierce blueness.

He had managed to hang on to a few possessions, however, which were set out on a tea chest next to his makeshift bed: a lighter, a photograph of a woman, a torn railway timetable, a skull and a garter.

Dusk was thickening on the water and Shani, followed by a few of her chickens, brought him some tea with a few slices of bread and a big hank of cheese, not looking at him nor saying anything at all as she put them down on his tea chest next to his skull rather like a manservant waiting on a king before retiring back to her own hut, again pursued by her faithful chickens, where she relit her pipe with a glowing stick from her fire.

Not once in all the weeks he had been there had they bothered one another with the trivialities of words or ideas and, in some ways, they really were the perfect couple, bonded by their oddity and just getting on with the eccentric courses of their singular lives.

AFTER HE had eaten his food and drunk his tea Ernst came out on to the beach itself, sitting on some railway sleepers and watching the sun go down in a massive storm of pale yellow fire.

A nearly full moon was already showing in the sunset, with a small but perfect bite out of its side, and he didn't even bother to light a fire and never seemed to feel the cold of the chilly autumnal breezes, just sitting there as motionless as the black shapes of the gulls who had come to land on the water in front of him, all settling down in readiness for the long snooze until dawn.

When the night had settled in over the headland he followed the lane over to New Quay, ghosting past the slumbering houses and occasionally standing back in the concealing shadows to watch out for movements. Already he had become familiar with many of the nocturnal habits in the town and, just being there, was curiously warming particularly in the later part of his strolls when he would stand high on the hill and look down on the town and the bold curve of the Bay.

After wandering through so many different parts of Wales Ernst had firmly and finally settled here in this strange town of singing crosses, warming love and dragon music.

THE TOWN already had its own resident midnight rambler, of course, in the shape of the Rev Enoch, now stepping up the steeply rising cobbles past The Dolau Inn with a sprightliness which, in itself, gave a glowing reference to a long life of lots of prayer and no alcohol.

The old minister particularly enjoyed his walks when there

was a nearly full moon since he could at least see where he was going in the haphazardly enforced blackout. 'Well at least the wardens can't tell us to put a blind over God's moon,' he liked to chortle at a time when even the lines running down the middle of the roads had been painted out.

The usual mindless chatter was coming out of the bar of the Black Lion and the Rev Enoch recognised Dylan's rich, barrel-organ voice in the middle of it, telling some disgusting story about how he had woken up that morning from a dream in which he had been running around as a boil. 'It could be a bit of a disaster being a boil, you know, but I was actually a rather beautiful sort of boil with all the women running around after me trying to squeeze me or wanting to kiss me on my big yellow pimple.'

The minister shook his head and walked on; he had always liked Dylan well enough, a man of words like himself, but he was positively alarmed by his fondness for alcohol; by the way that this talented young poet was going to throw his life away because of it. They all thought that the Rev Enoch knew nothing about alcohol but he knew everything there was to know about the demon brew.

He had also heard that the Battling Thomases were soon to leave New Quay, largely because Mrs Thomas couldn't settle down here, and he was very sorry about that because Dylan had some very good qualities even if he often went to excessive lengths to cover them up. The Thomases were going to have a farewell party in Majoda soon to which almost everyone, including the Rev Enoch, had been invited but he would never go to anything like that; he had heard about those parties in Majoda and would probably end up being unfrocked in an instant if he ever went near one.

He continued his patrol across the main square and past the General Stores, following the shale path to the kissing gate which he climbed to carry on to the top of the hill when he stopped still. He had been told about this John the Baptist figure in sheepskins, who had been caught in the bombing at Swansea and had now come to live in a shed on the beach in Cei Bach, but this was the first time he had ever actually seen him in the flesh and there he was, a wild Biblical figure straight out of the Old Testament, standing up there on the top of the hill, directly on the Rev Enoch's own prayer point, and looking out over the moonlit Bay.

The minister began moving towards The Baptist slowly, rather like an experienced sheepdog slowly bearing down on a rogue sheep, not making any sudden or aggressive movement lest he should panic his quarry and make him run for it. Indeed he might have got within ten yards of Ernst when Ernst clearly picked up the sounds of the Rev Enoch's shoes on the shale path and looked around at him, seemingly unsure what he should do next. They eyed one another silently for maybe twenty seconds as if waiting for the other to lose their nerve and break away from the confrontation and it was the clergyman who finally broke the deadlock by raising a trembling hand in what he hoped was a sign of peace. He just wanted to talk to this man, to show him some Welsh hospitality and kindness and tell him that, although he was yet another orphan of the war, the church and God cared about him too.

But the Baptist didn't want to speak, taking a few slow steps backwards before limping away hurriedly down through the field on the other side of the hill and quickly vanishing into yet another breaking wave of moonlight.

ON A cool, calm night on the headland leading out to Llanina, with the land warmed up by yet another long Indian summer day, which had even dried out the slimy fallen leaves, Dylan stood at his garden gate sucking on a Woodbine and guarding a zinc bath full of fruit punch which seemed to be steaming with its own potency.

A jazz band was warming up at the other end of the garden and, in total defiance every black-out regulation, all the rooms in Majoda were lit up like a cruise liner at night as Caitlin and Dolly, both in the their best floral party frocks, were preparing small hillocks of sandwiches in the kitchen in readiness for the arrival of all the starving locusts who were due to land after the pubs had shut.

Such moments were always quiet, if a little tense, but so too is the eye of a storm as everyone wonders if anyone is going to turn up and Dylan, still a shade uncomfortable in a new worsted suit which, like the party, had been funded by a good advance for his new collection of poems, started on his second glass of punch and was already beginning to feel a little glassy-eyed himself when he spotted the first of a long line of revellers coming along the cliff path, accompanied by the chink of many bottles and lead by Captain Port Talbot arm in arm with Rosie Rees and both singing.

Dylan was extremely pleased to see the flame-haired Rosie Rees and gave her a special welcoming wave with his Woodbine because, apart from having the biggest pair of jugs in the county, which she usually didn't mind showing any man who might be interested or desperate enough to want to fondle, she was also a must for any party that you hoped might go wrong and even get well out of control which was always Dylan's underlying ambition for any party he ever threw.

Rosie took a glass of punch off Dylan and set the tone of her intended behaviour that night by confiding in him that she had put on her best red knickers for this party and he knew they wouldn't be staying on for very long although she had only ever publicly owned up to one indiscretion: the whole of the New Quay rugby team except the scrum half who she said was queer although he had insisted he was merely fussy.

More guests arrived along the chinking cliff path including Mr and Mrs Dai Fred, Stephen Stephens, the Ancient Mariner in all his overcoats and that strange boy behind the General Stores who liked to go around the place barking like a dog. Dylan gave each of them a glass of punch when they arrived and, if they

303

had brought a bottle of anything strong, he just poured it straight into the bath regardless of what it was.

Then, rather to his surprise, The Black Widow turned up on the arm of a man who she introduced as Terry Godwin, her husband – *her husband!* – who had just returned from fighting with partisans in the war in Greece. Dylan shook his hand uneasily and didn't like the look of him at all; a little *twp* after losing his brains in the war, he decided as the man stared around angrily, clearly battier than his batty wife. 'Have a glass of this Mr Godwin.'

'What's in it?'

'Oh, you know, a bit of this and a bit of that.'

'No, thank you.'

More party-goers materialised out of the darkness, including all three Morgan brothers, with Trefor looking extremely stiff in a high, starched collar which was chafing his fat neck and Dic already looking fairly well ratted by the look of his bloodshot eyes which, even from a distance, seemed to have fastened onto Rosie Rees' prize-winning figure. Gareth told Dylan he had been working on some new poems but Dylan was off poetry that day and advised him, if had any sense, to burn them. 'Poetry is not the way, boy. Become a land agent or car salesman or something useful.'

The Icon Jazz Band, hired for the night from Aberaeron, began in good Dixieland form, immediately getting everyone on their feet with their chugging exuberance and flirtatious clarinet.

It was that punch which made it such a madly riotous party, everyone was to decide later. God only knew what Dylan had thrown into that bath – it could even be meths or Jeyes Fluid – and Mrs Dai Fred was to later claim that she only took one sniff of hers and it practically straightened out her new perm. Even The Black Widow began to jig around after a glass of that punch and no one could recall her ever smiling, let along dancing, while Stephen Stephens had already made a bee-line for Rosie Rees and the betting was heavy among the Black Lion boys that, the way they were now jitterbugging, her knickers were going to be flying into the air at any moment.

Many of the lifeboat crew were also pretty legless when they arrived and, as a small matter of historical fact, Norman Lewis disappeared at some stage in the evening and perhaps fell off the cliff and drowned in the Bay – or maybe he had finally seized the opportunity to escape the tyrannical and cleanliness-obsessed Mrs Lewis, who even dusted the canary and his bald head – but no one ever clapped eyes on him again.

Not ever.

The garden was soon almost full to bursting and Dylan moved among them, determined not to get too drunk too soon, as was his wont, and being gently amusing with his guests, who often laughed at his words but mostly didn't have a clue what the hell he was going on about.

'I like to look at the sea from time to time to see if it's still there,' he told Captain Port Talbot, who merely pulled a funny face, and then he asked Mrs Probert about another of his long-standing problems: 'What does Gardenia Vanishing Cream actually vanish, Mrs Probert?' A little later he dug himself deep into a discussion with Percy Hoskins about how long a man could drink and still stay on his feet. About five hours, Percy Hoskins reckoned but Dylan believed a real drinker could manage three days and, what is more, he had done it – or at least *thought* he had.

He continued to circulate around the dancing throng, pausing for a moment to take a sip of his punch and watch his beloved Caitlin dancing on her own; she always leaped about like a whirling Celtic dervish when she heard music, which was why she always preferred to dance on her own, her whole face lighting up as if she had been just given a personal lease on the sun as those thunderclap thighs and long greyhound legs kicked ever higher.

He was the brains and she was the body, they had agreed

when they first met; he was going to be the greatest lyric poet in the world and she was going to become its greatest dancer.

Oh how thrillingly she moved too even if, unfortunately, Dylan never danced himself since his increasingly flabby frame was pretty much free of anything resembling a working muscle and anyway he needed to conserve all his available energy to light cigarettes, fill in betting slips and lift heavy pints of beer.

But, in a life generally bereft of any kind of certainty, he was certain of one thing and that was that he was still very much in love with his darling Cat woman. Oh sure he was often unfaithful to her, particularly when he was out on the town in London on his own, but those grubby little adulteries had never meant anything to him and he could not even remember the names of most of them or indeed any of them, and could not even bear the thought of anyone ever laying their hands on his jewel an' darlin' Caitlin as he had laid his hands on so many others. Hypocritical jealousy lived inside him as eagerly and insistently as his fondness for drink.

The jazz band lifted everyone higher as happy, drunken spirits raced through the party like flaming streams of petrol with Captain Port Talbot doing a really strange dance with Betty Penderyn, possibly some sort of samba he had picked up in a brothel in Rio, Dylan thought. The baker was dancing with his wife and her sister and even the Ancient Mariner was up there and dancing with his overcoats and that blob of snot forever dangling off the end of his nose.

Dylan's belly lurched when the dancers parted again and he spotted Dolly dancing and laughing with the Italian Co-operator, Mario Marinnelli; he might still be in love with his Caitlin but there was still something deeply sexual about Dolly which always gave him a good old twinkle deep in his scrotum whenever he looked at her, particularly tonight when she was as beautiful as the froth on a fresh pint of beer, with her green crepe party frock resting lightly and revealingly on her scenic curves, which had quickly recovered after the birth of her baby, and her thrupenny curls pinned up on top of her head showing that full African neck of hers.

Yes, she was sex on wheels was Dolly and Dylan had long noted the way men studied her intently if they thought their wives weren't looking and the way those wives also always broke out into moralising spots and sniffed desertion and betrayal whenever Dolly was around. But Dolly was being very well-behaved these days, she wanted it known by all, having fully and finally given up on all men and sticking to the orange squash which meant she could at least keep a decent control of herself and her wilder appetites.

Indeed Dylan had braced himself for the worst after the birth of baby Lowri, convinced that, if she didn't actually finger him as the father, she would surely demand that he maintain the little bastard. Maintenance from him! The poet with the sun always shining through the arse of his trousers! Caitlin would almost certainly have had a lot to say about it too and, for a while, his every intestine was sick and twisted with worry, unable even to sleep, except that Dolly not only showed no sign of fingering him for paternity but there were also no signs of his own frog face or pop eyes in the baby herself who he had studied closely and often.

In fact Dolly had even then claimed that the pacifist bastard, Dafydd ap Iestyn, was the father, probably to save him from Caitlin's wrath, and she even knew where the baby had been conceived, she had then added cruelly, which was nowhere near the slipway of the lifeboat station but closer to the big rock of the shellfish factory where Dafydd had taken her after she'd drunk half a dozen gin and oranges in The Dolau Inn one night late in February.

Dylan had dealt with this bit of news with a mixture of disappointment and relief even if he still retained a strong suspicion that some of his dynamic, if drunken, hormones had helped in the making of baby Lowri somehow; that a crucial one had managed to infiltrate his way in there somehow even if he was the first to admit that he really didn't have the remotest clue as to how babies were actually conceived.

Of Dafydd himself there had only been gossip and rumour since the night of his disappearance from the Black Lion with one story having it that he had gone into hiding with a gang of runaway pacifists in the densely wooded hills of mid-Wales. These Welsh dissidents were even thinking of taking some direct action against the English government, according to one report, perhaps by even lighting lines of fires on the mountains to direct the Luftwaffe to key cities in England.

The Army had been very keen to get Dafydd safely back into one of their glass houses and a patrol regularly pitched up at Cliff House on the off chance they might catch him there – although they had stopped kicking in the front door and now knocked it like everyone else.

As for Ernst he was an even bigger mystery in the town and they continued discussing him knowledgeably in the bars even though they didn't have a single fact to go on. He had just been with them for a short time, coming from God knows where, possibly on that washed-up U-Boat, and then he had gone and got himself killed in a car accident on a road near Lampeter. Apart from a brief affair with Dolly that's all any of them knew about him although Caitlin had often hinted that she knew a lot more about him but, if she did, she wasn't letting on, not even to her own husband.

And now another colourful figure had stepped into their midst, Mario Marinnelli, an opera singer who was a grave disappointment to Mussolini and a failed tank driver from Pisa. Dylan lit another cigarette and stared angrily at Mario as he continued to dance with Dolly; he didn't like the look of this Mario Marinnelli with his ardent moustache and Puccini belly may God bayonet the warbling wop. More specifically he didn't like the way Dolly was always laughing when he was around and the way he seemed to be taking advantage of her good nature by crying a lot and getting her to calm him down with motherly cuddles.

But what he was most worried about, if he were to be honest, was that Mario would now start giving her a good seeing to, particularly now that her body must have recovered after having her baby; that she would continue to invite a sort of United Nations of men to the party which she had been holding more or less continuously between her legs almost all that year, beginning with him. It was absolutely disgusting, when he came to think about it, that he, the greatest lyric poet in the world, had shared a fox-hole with a Welsh nationalist, a U-Boat commander and now, possibly, a bloody Italian Co-operator. And they were always making jokes about Rosie Rees!

AFTER FEELING unrelentingly miserable almost for ever Dolly couldn't ever remember enjoying herself so much when she broke away from Mario and reeled out of the dancing throng to catch a breath of fresh air. She liked dancing almost as much as Caitlin and had always especially loved the bouncing thump of traditional jazz, not even needing drink to oil the joints and loosen her inhibitions when a good band was playing.

You don't need a drink to enjoy yourself, she had to keep telling herself in a chapel sort of way; drink always undoes you in the end, just as it had undone her so often in the past.

She stood at the edge of the party looking out into the semi-darkness and feeling the sweat drying on her face when she spotted a shaggy figure in sheepskins standing on the other side of the hedgerow just over the road and watching the party.

Indeed he seemed so intent in watching what was going on he didn't seem to have noticed her at all and she didn't attract attention to herself either, shrinking back into her own patch of concealing darkness and wondering whether, in a life full of strange men, she had ever seen anyone quite as strange as this. He was like the Abominable Snowman, just standing there, resplendent in ragged mystery, as if he had just strolled down from the foothills of the Himalayas. His battered, bearded face looked as if it had been poured from a mould made by aliens although, in the bright burbling of the partying night, there was a huge sadness about him which seemed to envelope him like a small cloud.

She wanted to hold him and take him into the party and introduce him to everyone except that, at that moment, Mario came out of the party and called out to her; 'Mama, I've been looking for you always. Come back in. Mario is missing you.

'I'll come now, Mario,' she all but whispered, looking around at the Italian and waving her hand at him wanting him to be quiet except that, when she looked back at the Abominable Snowman, she was most disappointed to find that he had gone, disappeared back into the darkness of those Himalayan foothills.

Mario took her by the hand and back into the party where the band kicked into *My Bucket's Got A Hole In It* and that boy who liked to bark like a dog asked her for a dance except that gave him a pat on the head and told him perhaps later. She couldn't quite get rid of the image of that sheep-skinned stranger out of her mind and found that she was becoming quite disturbed and even distressed by it; this immensely sad figure standing out there and watching them all party happily.

By now the party had almost completely collapsed, with many in stumbling disarray, probably under the influence of Dylan's punch, and she noticed that the poet himself was actually down on all fours with his head up some woman's skirt, as if he had lost something up there, while she just kept blithely chattering away to another man, as if people lost things up her skirt all the time.

But Dolly herself had lost her earlier happy mood – perhaps the Baptist's lonely sadness had affected her too – and, without thinking about it, or indeed the consequences, she looked around and spotted some drinks, left by the dancers on a small table near the kitchen door, and walked over to them, picking up nearly half a pint of that punch and downing it in more or less three long gulps.

Well she *should* have thought about it quite hard, was about her only coherent thought as all that alcohol went racing into her bloodstream like the start of the Grand National horse race, singing songs and staging parties of their own and chasing one another around boisterously and she could also actually feel herself becoming as horny as a bag of adders, virtually the whole of her vagina turning inside out and about to scream out for some male lodgers.

Indeed she became so convinced it really was going to scream out she had to turn away and put her hand over it, just to shut it up, or else there was no telling what sort of embarrassment her big mouth was going to cause her. Just *what* had Dylan put in that punch?

Well whatever it was it worked well enough since, without any further ado, she turned to Mario, grabbed him and said: 'Right, Mario Marinnelli of Pisa, let's see if there's anything leaning about *your* tower.'

'Mama,' he said as she lead him into Majoda. 'Mama, whassgoing on?' he added as she took him into the bedroom and closed the door. 'Mama?' he went again nervously as she lay back on the bed, wriggled out of her knickers and spread her legs.

'Come on, Mario. Don't just stand there. Let's see if there's anything leaning about *your* tower.'

Even as his extremely well-endowed Bologna sausage entered her she wrapped her arms around his neck and began crying although not through any particular rapture or even faint pleasure so much as an absolute disgust with herself and the way that she would only sniff the booze once and she would let almost anyone at all up her passage.

DYLAN WAS not quite done for – but well on the way – when he decided that he had finished examining what was going in the suffocating darkness under Mrs Stephen Stephens' dress and came back out again, standing up and realising that Dolly had disappeared from the party and, more ominously, so had The Warbling Wop.

This was extremely annoying and he began threading through the remaining dancers trying to find her, just wanting to know where she was so that he could then relax and enjoy his own party. But he couldn't find her anywhere and he was beginning to get very angry indeed, going out into the road and then circling the party again with Caitlin eyeing him curiously.

When he had done another complete circle of the house he accelerated back into the party surprised, even in his drunkenness, at how his whole being had suddenly become envenomed by hot jealousy which may or may not have been inflamed by that punch which he had also clearly drunk too much of.

There were quite a few packed inside the small house and he opened his bedroom door, ears cocked and picking up, above the sounds of jazz and party chatter, some strange sounds coming from the direction of his bed. What he didn't realised was that he was listening to verses from the Bible being declaimed in Welsh all intermingled with triumphant Latin whoops and he still wasn't sure what was going when he struck a match and went over to the bed where his darkest fears were confirmed when he found Mario Marinnelli's big, pasta buttocks butterflying up and down between Dolly's long, lovely legs and it all came as such a shock to Dylan he sobered up in a shocked and horrified instant.

'Oh, Dolly, Dolly, what have you gone and done now?' Dylan inquired by match-light, a little primly, particularly for him.

Dolly opened her eyes and the rolling and mysterious cadences of *The Book of Revelation* froze in her mouth as she looked up at Dylan's face framed by the sulphurous flare of his match.

'You simply can't keep shagging every man in the world,' Dylan went on. 'There are limits, Dolly, *limits*, and you seem determined to find them and cross every one of them.'

'It was that punch, Dylan, I was all right 'til I drank that punch. But this tower doesn't lean at all, you know. That's a pretty good tower he's got down there by any standards. What did you put in that punch anyway?'

The end of the match burned Dylan's fingers and he paused while he lit another. Mario must have been well into that punch too since his buttocks were still butterflying up and down and his voice was still letting out the odd Latin whoop, apparently completely unaware of the conversation that was going on over his hunched, heaving shoulders.

'*Everyone* has been drinking that punch, Dolly, but, fortunately, that doesn't mean that everyone goes around shagging anything that moves.'

'It's only shagging, Dylan. It doesn't mean anything.'

'What do you mean *it doesn't mean anything*? Are you saying it's just press-ups are you?'

'Yes. Yes, I am. It's just something that happens when I drink but it doesn't really mean anything. I just want to get warm and make everyone else warm while I'm at it. It's just a happiness thing. A drink thing and it just doesn't mean anything at all.'

Dylan lit another match and frowned as he thought about this bit when they both realised that something was going on with Mario who had stopped whooping and was now wailing like some dog which had been locked out in the rain.

'I think he's about to come,' Dolly said, pulling a face. 'Just hold on a bit, Dylan, and he'll be there any moment now. He hasn't had it since he left Pisa, he's told me, so there might be quite a lot of it, if you know what I mean.'

So they both waited for Mario to come by match-light when, from behind them, they heard not so much a cry of Italian orgasmic surrender as a strange metallic sound which everyone in the party, who had heard it, would remember for the rest of their lives. It was the ominous snap of a safety catch being taken off a sten gun and then the war finally arrived in New Quay in a rattling, deafening hail of real bullets.

Rat-at-tat-tat, *rat-at-tat-tat*, went the gun, bright yellow flames spurting out of the barrel. *Rat-at-tat-tat*, it went again as Terry Godwin, the *twp* husband of the *twp* Black Widow, proceeded to fill the roof of Majoda with more holes than a tea strainer. *Rat-at-tat-tat*.

The jazz outside spluttered to a halt as women screamed and others dived for cover. Even the normally chopsy Caitlin was silenced as thin rivulets of asbestos came spiralling down on top of everyone in the living room, making them looking the ghosts of miners going in search of their pit.

'If you'd wanted another drink, Terry, you only had to ask,' said Caitlin, trying to defuse a dangerous situation.

'I don't want a drink. I want my wife. The one you all call The Black Widow.'

'We haven't got your wife, Terry.' Dylan had appeared as sober as a hangover with Dolly and Mario standing wide-eyed with fear behind him. 'She was here earlier but she must have gone home. Has anyone seen the . . . er . . . anyone here seen Mrs . . . you know . . . Mrs Terry?'

Caitlin walked towards Godwin, holding out her hand. 'Your wife's not here and you're going to get into a lot of trouble with that thing.' She lifted the machine-gun strap over his head and let it dangle in her hand. 'What if you'd killed someone? That wouldn't have looked bright on your record would it? Coming back from all that fighting in Greece and then getting locked up for the rest of your life.'

The party had collapsed completely by now with the band loading up their instruments and not even waiting to be paid as the other revellers made their sober ways back to the town.

'I told you they're all raving mad in New Quay,' the banjo player told the drummer. 'There's not a sane one amongst them.'

Chapter Twenty-six

'CATEY, I thought we had a plan, a *proper* plan to go to London, and now you're telling me it's all changed and we've got to go back to Laugharne.'

Dylan was sitting in Barry Island's deckchair with the baby sleeping in one arm and holding a cigarette with his free hand, a half-empty bottle of beer standing on the floor between his bare feet and his right eye completely black which he was *reasonably* certain had been the handiwork of his wife the night before but not *absolutely* sure. What he was sure of, however, was that he was not about to ask her about it in case he might end up with another one to make a match.

'Plans change, Dylan. We have no fucking money, Dylan. You blew all you had on that fucking stupid party and we can't go back to London without any money. But we *can* go back to Laugharne.'

'Laugharne's a dump and, if you really want to know, I'd far prefer to stay in this dump than go back to Laugharne. I could finish off my play if we stayed here and then we'd get *oodles* of money.'

'And how are we going to live – how are we going to eat – while we are waiting for all these oodles of money to land? Look, Dylan, do I have to tattoo it on your thick skull? The Thomas Flotation Fund has fully and finally sunk. *We – have – no – fucking – money.* Everyone wants money off us and they can't have it.'

'Everyone? Who's everyone?'

'Well the fucking owner of this very house for a start. We haven't paid any rent here for at least six months and now he's belly-aching about all the fucking bullet holes in the roof.'

'They're nothing to do with us. We didn't put those bullet holes in it. That mad bastard Terry Godwin did that and he should pay.'

'That's not the way the owner sees it. As tenants we're responsible, he says, and wants us to pay for fixing it. The General Stores are also after a fiver by next Tuesday – or no more tick there – and even Megan Evans is now saying she wants a quid for that fucking cockerel.'

'A quid! That cockerel was never worth a quid. All the people around here should have given you a quid for cutting its rabble-rousing head off.'

'And there's the Black Lion of course. They're saying you've passed over so many IOUs in there they're all wiping their arses in them.'

Dylan took a deep, distressed drag on his cigarette and blew a cloud of smoke over the baby who didn't wake up but began coughing in her sleep.

'Don't blow smoke over Aeronwy like that. I've told you often enough haven't I?'

'So what are we going to do? I've become poor Percy Bysshe Shelley again have I, doing yet another moonlight flit?'

'You have. I've been on the phone to Ben Rees in Swansea and he says he's prepared to bring the furniture van up here tomorrow night and take us to Laugharne. But he's not prepared to come over here to Majoda because he says it's fucking dangerous.'

'Dangerous?'

'That's what he says. There won't be a moon tomorrow night, which will be good for us, but, together with the blackout, he doesn't want to risk his van getting too near the cliff. But he is prepared to park in the square outside the Black Lion like he did when he first brought us here and we've somehow got to get all our stuff over there.'

'Caitlin, you're not suggesting I carry it all, I hope. My back's not what it was and neither are any of my muscles come to that. The lungs too.' His right hand banged his chest for effect. 'Worse than ever they are.'

'I'll get Dolly to get the Morgan boys to help.'

'The horse and cart! What about the horse and cart?'

'That horse died a few weeks ago. They just noticed he stopped moving one day: just standing in the field and dying on his feet. Didn't even bother to fall over.'

'Well fancy that. But I can't go lifting anything Cat. I'm sure to end up like that horse. I might be able to manage the baby here. But that's it and even she's getting a real lump these days.'

'I've told you Dylan. How many fucking times do I have to tell you anything? I'll get the Morgan boys from the farm to help but, given everything, you must not tell anyone about our departure, particularly all those oafs in the Black Lion. You got that?' Lots of tapping the side of her nose with her forefinger. 'We have just got to vanish into the night like fucking ghosts. This moonlight flit of ours has all got to be top fucking secret.'

ERNST WAS out on his hill late the next night, well-concealed by the moonless darkness even if he could just about make out the humped shapes of the boats in the harbour tricked out by a little thin starlight which kept disappearing into cloud.

Even on such dark nights he still enjoyed the music of the town and still liked to look in through the windows and at the small household dramas of bed-time; the night caps, the teeth being put into the glasses next to the bed, the cup of cocoa and the final readings from the Bible in the antimacassar'd front parlours.

The routine normality of the place replenished him even if this night was far from normal since he kept picking up on the sounds of distant explosions which kept erupting in huge, creamy mushrooms of light on the horizon before collapsing back into themselves. His ears kept on picking up on distant and invisible bombers too, as yet more silent, creamy mushrooms rose up sending faint luminescent glows across the countryside and the slumbering houses of New Quay.

These flashes also brought his own appearance into a sharp and angry focus; this stranger in sheepskins standing there and brooding over his lost and wandering flock; this new Baptist who had come into their midst as if he was about to start warning them to prepare for the Return of the Son of Man. There were more stammering mushrooms and the faint crump of distant explosions when his sharp blue eyes picked up alien movements on the distant shoreline. He became immediately attentive when he noticed about eight people, some carrying torches, all carrying bits and pieces of furniture rather like a line of ants, all busy making a midnight move to another hill.

What they were up to – if they were up to anything at all – meant nothing to him but, when they disappeared into the all-consuming darkness again, he stepped slowly down the shale path to take a closer look at this sudden nocturnal movement in his hometown.

GARETH WAS carrying a pitcher and a bowl as he walked with Dylan who was holding the baby as they trudged along the cliff path and around the curve of the sea. The boy had been telling Dylan that he had finally found himself a girlfriend, Mona Jones from 4A, and they had been enjoying a few feels together behind the bike shed but Dylan, who normally liked this kind of talk, didn't seem remotely interested, worrying, instead, that they had possibly picked the wrong night to make a run for it, particularly as the Luftwaffe had also clearly chosen the same night to start bombing Wales.

'I'm sure they're getting closer and closer,' Dylan fretted out loud. 'You don't think they've lost their way in the dark do you and decided to get us instead?'

'Well, I don't think they're supposed to take their bombs home with them,' Gareth replied. 'I was reading in the paper that the Nazis don't like it when they go back with a full load so they've got to drop them somewhere.'

'Even New Quay? There's nothing to bomb in New Quay.'

'New Quay's somewhere. If you have to drop them somewhere – or get the big chop from Hitler – New Quay's as good as anywhere. But they look a long way away – perhaps even beyond Aberystwyth.'

'Ah, now. Aberystwyth's a good place to bomb. If I were a German bomber I'd head straight for Aberystwyth and let them have the lot.'

The distant Luftwaffe crumpings also seemed to be waking the town and, as Mario and Dic reached the top of the road, both carrying boxes of books, a window went up and the shadow of Billy Jenkins in a night-cap began shouting at them for making too much noise and waking the bloody baby.

'It's not us,' Caitlin screamed back. 'It's those German planes after Liverpool again. We're just moving some furniture.'

'Well, what bloody time is this to be moving bloody furniture? Furniture should be moved in the bloody daylight not in the middle of the bloody night. That bloody poet is in the middle of this, I'll bet a pound. Only a poet as bloody mad as him would move furniture in the middle of the night.'

'If Dylan Thomas is moving furniture,' another voice shouted from a dark distance, 'that means he's on his way out at last. I've had nothing but the shingles since he moved in here with us.'

'You can't go blaming him for your shingles you daft booby,' Caitlin shouted back, moving up next to Dolly who was carrying a bed with Trefor. 'My husband gets the blame for everything that goes wrong around here and, whatever else he's done, he didn't give you the fucking shingles.'

'Language, woman,' yet another voice chimed in. 'I've got children in here and they're not supposed to hear that kind of language.'

'I've had the shingles all over my back since the day you

moved in. You get the shingles through worry and you Thomases have worried the life out of me from day one. You can come and look at my back if you like.'

'Who are you going to blame for everything when we've gone, that's what I'd like to know? Who are you going to blame for spreading fucking shingles then? That's going to be hard isn't it?'

Dylan shuffled through this alleyway of insults, keeping his head down over the baby and vaguely hoping that no one would notice him. All this shouting was giving him a headache and he was far more concerned about the possibility of finding a pint of something soothingly alcoholic. Caitlin had insisted that he stay stone-cold sober for their top-secret moonlight flit but he'd have given anything for a pint or three at the moment, even little Aeronwy here although he couldn't think of anyone who might want her.

More stammering mushrooms of distant bombs framed the high roof of the Black Lion and the furniture van waiting outside in the square and Dylan wondered if he might even manage to rouse Percy Hoskins to give everyone a pint all round.

The shouts, cat-calls and Nazi distant bombs had now woken others and yet more windows were going up with yet more heads looking down at this shady caravan of passing furniture which was already being loaded into the back of Ben Rees's van. But there was still a lot to do. Even with six hands on the pump they were going to gave to make three or four journeys back to Majoda although Dylan knew he was fagged out enough already and wouldn't be making any more journeys himself, just wishing he could find somewhere to park this extremely heavy baby of his.

What really got right up his trumpet was why Caitlin always tried to involve him in any sort of emergency; he was no good in an emergency and there had never been an emergency which hadn't got worse when he tried to do something about it.

Anyone caught in an emergency when he was around might as well have just died and be done with it; emergencies just got amazingly more emergent in his useless hands.

'Normal people don't go moving furniture in the middle of the night Dylan Thomas. Why aren't you like normal people? What's so special about you?'

'He always goes around the place as if he's got a leek up his arse and she was never the same after she got her bust cooked.'

'I'm going to call the police I am. You ought to be locked up the lot of you. I'm under the doctor for having too much wax in my ears and you're *still* keeping me awake.'

Dylan was close to tears as he sat on the wall outside the Black Lion and the three Morgan brothers went back to get some more of their furniture and several more people came wandering down into the square. He didn't know why they had bothered with all this really; they had nothing which was worth much more than a tanner and he had only ever cared about his books, his Rousseau print and Barry Island deckchair but it was his Cat woman who always got sentimental about the rest of their rubbish.

Yet one thing was absolutely certain and that was that there was nothing top-secret about this operation; they might as well have put an advertisement in *The Cardigan Times* inviting the whole county to come along and join in their move.

'Dylan, boy, what are you doing out here?' It was Percy Hoskins, come to sit next to him on the wall. 'You can't just sit out here with the baby. I'll open the bar for you, if you like.'

'Just listen to all these loonies shouting out Percy. I don't know how you can live with it. All these voices and there's not a single brain between the lot. But these voices are going to come together and make a marvellous play for me one day. I've written a lot of it in my mind already and I can just see the curtain going up on all of them now: dozens of mad voices in a town driven mad by the war. The background music could be the sound of continual bombing.'

321

'Come and have a pint.'

'I can bring the baby in with me can I?'

'Well, you can't leave it out here can you?'

'It's a she, Percy. Aeronwy.'

'Must be a good baby, sleeping through all this racket.'

AT THAT moment, directly on the other side of the town, on the Cardigan Road, Dafydd ap Iestyn was stumbling past Mr Robin Probert's white-washed cottage, the first on the outskirts of New Quay, as a fiery Jack Russell dog barked at him and flung himself furiously up against the slats of Mr Probert's garden fence.

The dog always got wild-eyed and slavering when anyone walked past his territory but, at this time of night and already worked up by the bombs, he was in an especially hysterical mood made all the worse by Dafydd's bloodied, dishevelled appearance.

Much of Dafydd's torn white shirt was red with blood and he was finding it very difficult to breathe as he kept stumbling forward, wrapping his arms tightly about himself as his consciousness kept lighting up and darkening along with the flares of those distant bombs. Indeed he wasn't even aware that those mushrooming lights were bombs, suspecting, perhaps, they were merely another aspect of the hallucinations which had been besieging him after the Army had put a few bullets into him in a field outside Llandysul.

He had scrambled over some fields and somehow managed to escape their search in the moonless darkness which was particularly fortunate that night since even the Army wouldn't have had much trouble following his trail of blood which he had been splashing generously all over the Llandysul road while it also kept seeping warmly and stickily down his shaking, leaden legs.

More houses loomed over him and he dimly recognised a few of them as he somehow made his legs keep propelling him forward before his consciousness began flipping over again like some bizarre, slow-motion ride in a funfair. Images of the recent chase kept bobbing up in his mind along with the incandescence of the faraway bombs, the blinding flashlights and the clattering bootfalls, the sharp darts of pain in his side from that bullet which had ripped straight through his hip-bone.

He passed the bus shelter and stopped still in the middle of the road, almost as if he had become a petrified statue with blood dripping out of his feet and pooling all around him. He coughed and his eyes rolled around without focusing on anything and he was certainly unaware that his every sigh and stumble had been monitored closely from the nearby darkness by Ernst whose eyes had been locked on to Dafydd's progress almost from the time he had roused the fury of Mr Robin Probert's Jack Russell.

But Ernst had made no attempt to help him in his plight – or even get particularly close to him – when Dafydd jerked forward again, now making his slow way past the General Stores when his consciousness started to roll over again but seemed to change its mind and roll back before he found himself on the edge of the main square next to the Black Lion with torch beams swirling around and over one another and people moving around a furniture van whose open doors beckoned him invitingly.

Unsure what to do he put his arms around a lamp-post and held on to it tightly, putting his hot, flushing cheek up against the bevelled coldness of the iron-work and closing his eyes. Soon he was as still as the lamp post he was holding and the only sign that he was still alive came when he occasionally let out a low and pitiful groan.

DOLLY WAS carrying a bedstead along the cliff path with Mario and wondering who but Dylan and Caitlin would manage to get her out in the middle of the night to carry furniture into the town.

She was certainly going to miss The Battling Thomases particularly the way they always seemed to attract strange people to them who were always then prepared to do anything they wanted – even outlandish acts such as this. It wasn't as if Dylan was especially forceful either; he had the courage of a rabbit and suffered from terminal shyness when he was sober but still they gathered around him, even prepared to look after him when he got falling-down drunk and had to be taken home in a wheelbarrow.

Had it not been for Caitlin she probably wouldn't have struck up with Mario either; The Warbling Wop, as Dylan had so charmingly christened him, whose Bologna sausage was at least keeping her physical clamourings quiet even if he never actually did anything for her emotional needs, still all over the place after the defections of Dafydd and Ernst. She couldn't even talk to Mario and get any sense out of him, content to let him paddle along in her wake while humming or bursting into an aria or three. It was like having a singing dog around the place.

'Why don't you lot out there hire a bloody marching band or something?' another angry head in a window wanted to know. 'You've already woken the bloody baby and now the bloody wife is up too.'

It would certainly be difficult to imagine anyone other than Dylan managing to turn the town into such an uproar as it was in now – *and at around three in the morning* – with people standing around the furniture van in chattering groups, some even helping to load it up with Ben Rees directing the operation and Mrs Will Rogers holding an aspidistra plant and offering it to Caitlin.

'Please, Mrs Thomas, have it as a sort of farewell present. Will has been so happy since Dylan came here and he's always had something to talk about after coming home from the pub. I don't know what any of them are going to find to talk about now. This is just my way of thanking you both for bringing some laughter to New Quay.'

Perhaps predictably Dylan, the centre of all this activity, was nowhere to be seen although it didn't take Dolly too long to work out that he was in the bar of the Black Lion, baby on the counter and pint in hand as he tried to auction a few of his first editions to a dozen or so of the locals, probably to try and settle a few of his debts before he left.

'This collection is by W H Auden – Wystan's Whimsy – but it's a first edition and signed by the great man so it's got to be good for twenty pounds at least. There's a bookshop in Swansea that would rip you hand off if you offered them something like this.'

Dolly watched this auction for a while, admiring Dylan's silvery tongue – which suggested he had managed three pints but hadn't yet got onto four – as he actually got the crowd waving banknotes in the air, all begging to buy one of these extremely rare, signed first editions. But her smile soon vanished when she went back outside into the thrumming square, about to walk back to Majoda, when an Army truck pulled up and armed squaddies began clattering out of its rear. Oh no, they were surely out looking for Dafydd again and almost certainly about to return to Cliff House and upset the children.

'Ah, it's Miss Dolly James,' her favourite sergeant said, shining a torch in her face. 'Well, no prizes for guessing who we're looking for again tonight, Miss James. 'E's on the run again an' is bound to be around 'ere somewhere. We're pretty sure we may 'ave injured 'im too. You seen any blood around your 'ouse by any chance?'

'Haven't seen him for months sergeant and, if I had, you'd be the very last to know,' she replied, more than a little relieved that Mario had already taken off back to Majoda because she wouldn't have wanted to answer any awkward, sarcastic questions about her relationship with the fat Italian Co-Operator.

SEEING THAT the bar of the Black Lion was open and, indeed, strangely full for the time of night, the sergeant told his men to take a break and have a quick pint, if they wanted, while he remained standing outside the bar door, unable to make much sense what was going on all around. Apart from all the townsfolk standing around in gossiping groups, with hands in pockets, like unemployed sailors standing on a port corner waiting to hear news of a berth, he couldn't quite see why a few people kept drifting out of the distant darkness to load furniture into a van. Well he could see that someone was moving house but why at this time of night and why wasn't the furniture van actually parked outside the house? These West Walians were strange people, no doubt, although who could be stranger than that poet in the bar who was now busy auctioning some of his books?

'Just a few more bits and pieces, Dylan and we're going to be ready to go,' Caitlin shouted in at him. 'Wrap it up now will you and don't forget to bring the baby either.'

The sergeant had never trusted Bohemia; never trusted anything that you couldn't spit on and polish and he frowned with yet more puzzlement when one of his men put a pint into his hand and he watched Dylan pay out some money and then pocket some more before asking one of the regulars to take the rest of his books out into the van, picking up the baby and going to sit in the front of the cab with his wife.

The sergeant had always revelled in the routine of the Army, knowing when you were supposed to get up and go to bed, knowing when you were going to eat and what and at exactly what time. But not one of this Thomas family seemed to know what they were going to do next *and then went out and did it*.

BEN REES closed the back of the van and getting on for a hundred locals, with a sprinkling of squaddies, gathered around to take their last look as The Battling Thomases, together with their baby Aeronwy, set out on their latest escape from the gathering hordes of men in bowler hats.

Indeed there were even several attempts to sing 'For He's A Jolly Good Fellow' but few joined in that maudlin anthem because they didn't want to go that far but the gloom on their faces was real enough as the van reversed up across the square to make a circular turn when Dolly emerged out of the darkness waving Dylan's much-loved Barry Island deckchair.

'It's not locked in the back,' Ben Rees, sticking his head out of the driving window, shouted at her. 'Just open it up and fling it in.'

At that moment another round of bombs began falling on Aberystwyth, flashing over the land like beacons and, as Dolly opened the back doors of the van, another few stammering flashes revealed a figure, in extreme distress, clinging to lamp-post right next to her. And this wasn't any old figure either, she knew immediately, but her very own Dafydd who was certainly going to be picked up by the Army and taken back to one of their glass houses, almost certainly to be shot properly, if they spotted him there.

Acting on instinct rather than fast thinking she unfolded the deckchair and managed to find enough room to get it to sit up in the back of the van before taking hold of Dafydd and, with a miraculous surge of sudden strength, picking him up and dumping him straight down into the deckchair where he let his head fall forward between his legs, gurgled and began bleeding freshly again all over the deckchair and the floor of the van.

But there was no time for messing about here so she just slammed the doors shut and banged the side of the van twice indicating that Ben could finally drive away.

Dolly's eyes brimmed with tears and she had no time to whisper any messages about their sacred cargo as the van accelerated off into the night and, flanked by Mario, she kept on waving even long after she knew they could no longer see her as they set off on the long journey to Laugharne.

More bombs flared again and the three in the front seat all

uttered a sort of 'Who the fuck is . . . ' when one of the flashes picked out Ernst, the Baptist in sheepskins, standing by the side of the road like some shaggy animal transfixed in their headlights but Ben Rees merely stuck his foot down and accelerated away.

Directly behind them – and closer than any of them could have imagined – another of Dolly's former lovers was busy bleeding like a stuck animal and groaning softly as he bounced around on Barry Island's deckchair. Mostly he was slumped forwards but every time the van picked up speed he slowly rose upright with both his arms hanging straight down from his shoulders like a boxer who had just been slugged senseless.

'Well, that was all a fucking good bit of fun for a change,' said Caitlin, surprised how relieved she was to see the back of New Quay. 'You don't normally associate that dump with having any fun.'

'And I made a nice few pounds in that auction too,' said Dylan who was also feeling unusually cheerful even after being pulled out of a pub while the bar was still open. 'Perhaps I should give up writing books and start trying to sell them for a change?'

'You a fucking business man,' Caitlin snorted. 'I don't think so. I really don't think so. Talking of books do you think it'll be too long before you get out your play?'

'A few weeks maybe, my darling love. A piece of piss really. If I don't get too many interruptions I could get it out in a few weeks. Absolute piece of piss. It'll write itself really. I'll just pick up a pencil and let that lot back in New Quay write it for me. They won't even need me. All I'll have to do is turn up at a desk and let them get on with it.'